The Melting Pot

Martin Cororan (Koh-roar-ran) was born in Stafford, 1976.
He lives in a tiny house with a large collection of musical instruments.
'The Melting Pot' is his first novel.

Hey stranger

Thanks for the purchase.

Keep in touch ...

Mark
~x—

P.S. This isn't a very fluffy novel !

First published in 2007 by the author
www.martincororan.com

This is a work of fiction.

A CIP catalogue record for this book is available from the British Library

978-0-9555517-0-3

Typeset by Folios Print Solutions, Hornchurch, Essex

Printed in England by Cox & Wyman, Reading, Berkshire

For Bost
Back from the dead.

Special thanks to:
Matt, Kay, Simon, Tim, Kristian and Nicky

Contents

Excerpt from 'Thirty-eight' (unpublished)

I am sending you this manuscript so that you may, in time, come to regard me in a more favourable light. It has been left anonymous for three reasons. Firstly, in order to inject some much-needed suspense into the proceedings, secondly, so that by the time realization dawns you might have become sufficiently enraptured with my account so as not to torch it, but thirdly and most importantly, because I am anonymous. I am a non-person, deconstructed and scattered. I no longer know what I was, let alone what I've become.

I hope these words find you both well. As for me, I have the sensation that I might be on the cusp of my defining moment. Then again, I may be on the brink of extinction.

Chapter 1

Last Day

As he penned the final word a building opposite exploded. Kelly looked up from his thoughts. Across the plaza objects of stone and flesh had broken apart and were flying in all directions. It was 10.14 a.m. and the world had no more room for horror, and yet still it came, marauding in wave after relentless wave.

A burly man passed his table and pulled down corrugated shutters, sealing out the city.

It crossed his mind to feel angry at the way in which events had transpired, that he should end up the lynchpin when countless others seemed infinitely more worthy. Kelly had made an art form of burying his aggression down deep, but could now feel it ascending and narrowing into a fine pinpoint of rage.

He stirred his coffee. The dark liquid formed serene, swan-like motions in the tiny cup as the spoon disturbed its stillness.

Doubt enveloped him. He wrestled with his demons. Between them they threw up the image of a woman. He closed his eyes and saw visions that caused him to shake. With the recollection of feminine features came a compassion that sat uncomfortably alongside the ferocity like vapour over water.

He took a sip from the tiny cup and winced.

'Got any sugar?'

'Eh?'

'*Azucar?*'

'Ah . . . *si*.'

The burly man signalled to the café's one and only waiter, a dishevelled-looking young man in canvas trousers and an open-collared shirt.

You could leave now, alone. Take what you have amassed and leave the city.

His legs seemed unwilling to respond. He removed a beanie hat, and ran dirty hands through hair that had not been washed in days.

I didn't ask for this.

The scrawny waiter approached his table with a bag of sugar. Kelly stared at him blankly. The man flinched with sudden recognition. His eyes begged the question: *what are your intentions?*

Kelly took some time before opening his mouth, careful to transfer more in his phrasing than the two words alone should allow.

'Speak English?'

The waiter looked confused. 'A little.'

'What's your name?'

Now he understood. Some of the tension left his shoulders.

'Ernesto?'

'Strange name for a waiter?' Kelly commented.

Ernesto grinned, revealing an impressive array of white teeth amid his straggly black beard.

'Is good enough for Che Guevara, is good enough for me.'

Kelly took the sugar and shook his hand. 'Quite right. My apologies.'

Their conversation was interrupted by a shower of hailstones that rose in volume from a gentle patter to deafening booms as debris started raining down on the outside walls and roof. There was the sound of breaking glass, a car alarm going off and disorientated shouting. A large slab of plaster fell from the ceiling, sending swirling stalactites of dust pirouetting to the ground. Kelly placed a weathered hand over the espresso to guard it from contamination.

'Is Arty here?'

'Eh?'

'*Arty? Esta aquí?*'

'Ah *sí*.'

Ernesto disappeared into a back room, leaving the burly man drying dishes with a greasy looking cloth.

Kelly's mind swung unexpectedly towards self-preservation and he found himself rising from his seat, taking the dark liquid to the back of his throat, absorbing the hit that flowed down through his exhausted body and making his way across the room. Fingers closed around the door handle.

He stopped.

Indecision is out of character. What are you playing at?

The handle began to turn.

Your life is no longer your own. It was bought at a price.

Kelly's head came to rest on the doorframe and his hand fell limply by his side. There seemed no point to anything that had gone before and no hope in anything ahead.

Esperanza, what would you do in my shoes?

A tempest swelled in his heart, violently suppressing the urge to leave. Kelly turned around and met the gaze of the burly man who quickly looked to the ground with a shudder. It seemed inconceivable that life had come down to this, that he could be lured out into the open, only to be cheated by a fate crueller than his own nature. A cursory glance around the café revealed any number of potential weapons. Veins were standing out on his arms. He became aware that he had stopped breathing.

Kelly exhaled loudly and the menace left him as suddenly as it had arrived. A long-forgotten conscience stirred.

You have to be cleverer than this.

'*Uno mas espresso*,' he shouted. The burly man nodded subserviently and reached for the coffee beans.

His composure restored, he walked slowly back to the table and sat down.

Despite the wealth of its owner, the café had been allowed to fall into disrepute. Over the years the wallpaper had succumbed to tobacco-stained yellow and brown streaks. Formica covered every surface – chipped, scratched and in desperate need of repair. Angles were slightly off, shelves slightly warped.

I will be glad to see the back of this place.

'*Mister* Kelly!' a deep voice bellowed with vindictive relish. 'I'd say the chances of you living through the day are pretty *slim*, wouldn't you say?'

From the corner of his eye Kelly saw a shapeless mass enter the room. He didn't look up.

'Opinions vary.'

Arty sat down with a graceless thud that made the chair creak painfully beneath his bulk. Kelly felt greedy eyes scanning his body for potential gain, noting the various bulging pockets with anticipation of imminent rewards.

'What are you doing out in the open?'

Kelly shrugged. 'Who'd harbour me after this morning?'

'True.'

'Besides, who's gonna find me here? You never have any customers.'

'Now Mister Kelly,' the café owner chided, pretending to take offence, 'you know it hurts me when you say things like that.'

'Tell someone who cares.'

Only now did Kelly turn to face the man. Arty was wearing his trademark pinstripe trousers, held up around his monstrous belly by thin red braces. A shirt, unbuttoned to the waist, revealed a thick mat of curly grey chest hair and shoulders that merged with his head. Tumbles of flesh hid any remnants of a neck.

'With remarks like that a struggling businessman might be inclined to bolster his modest financial position with the reward posted for news on your whereabouts!'

Kelly ignored the comment and gestured towards the front door. 'That'll be the department of sanitation then?'

Arty nodded and did his best to portray melancholy regret. 'It was only a matter of time – worth more as rubble.'

Ernesto returned with the second espresso. Kelly reached into his pocket for payment, but Arty grabbed his wrist.

'Money's no good here, except maybe for keeping the fire going.'

Kelly shook off the grasp and withdrew his hand. 'What then?'

'What else you got?' the café owner replied with a hawkish glare that swept once more across Kelly's clothing.

'Nothing you could afford.'

'Come on,' Arty teased, 'what about the liquor?'

From his inside coat pocket Kelly produced a small bottle of single-malt whisky. He appeared to mull over the proposition for a moment; a necessary part of the bargaining.

'The *whole* bottle? For that I'd expect free drinks for life.'

'Done.'

'And a favour.'

Arty's eyes narrowed as his fat fingers sort to prize the object from Kelly's hand. 'Depends.'

Kelly relinquished the bottle without protest. 'Good, then we have a deal?'

'I said it *depends*.'

'Come with me.'

Before the café owner had time to react Kelly jumped up from his chair, crossed the room at pace and opened the front door. The room was immediately filled with clouds of billowing black smoke and ash, rolling in across the floor and up along the walls, snuffing out any remaining light and making the darkness complete. Behind him he heard a tremendous crashing of chairs as Arty fell backwards in response to the shadowy arms that reached for him.

'You son of a bitch!' he shrieked.

'Stop whining and follow me.'

'And how am I supposed to do that you miserable thief? I can't see!'

At the far side of the room Ernesto felt someone press a scrap of paper into his palm. He later found it to be a napkin; the words *Meet me behind the café at 12.00* scrawled on its surface.

Outside the sky was like an eclipse. As ridiculous and unnerving as the phenomenon was, it seemed almost fitting; a life compromised beyond repair.

Kelly closed his eyes and stood silent in the street, feeling the tiny shards of glass and brick-dust strike his face, coating his skin and outer clothing in a layer of grey and terracotta. The stillness was intoxicating. The staggering hurt and losses of the past weeks, months and years felt at bay, held aloft for a brief moment.

For those fleeting, fragile seconds he believed himself to be someone else, a person of principles – ethical, upstanding, free from damnation, a believer of some description, light-headed and unbothered by guilt.

'Is anyone there? Can anyone hear me?'

A stranger's voice sucked him back from his delusion. He was *not* a good man but an opportunist – a liar, a swindler and a usurper, spiritually broken and corrupt.

'*Hello?* Knock if you can hear me?'

There were footsteps over loose-moving ground, searching hands brushing against unseen obstacles. It hadn't occurred to Kelly to look for survivors. He shrunk back towards the café door, frightened and intimidated by the selfless deeds of others.

Shielding his opening eyes from the debris he could now see shades in the dark, the corners of buildings, a path beneath his feet, edges of the road.

The far left-hand corner of the plaza d'armas has vanished; lost in the choking murk rising up from a crater. The blast had rippled out across the adjoining streets and broken their many paving slabs into unintentional mosaics.

Arty was by Kelly's side, squinting into the aftermath.

'*Man*, you'd think those clowns would've worked out how much explosive to use by now!'

'Show some respect, for crying out loud. There are a lot of bodies lying out there.'

'Since when did you care?'

'I don't.'

The years of slow-burning tension had painted central Corderro with a pale, gaunt, yellowish skin. Whole suburbs had fallen into disrepute; a transformation from proud districts to bowed and burdened slums. Even the most ancient parts of the city were blotted with foul eyesores, smouldering trenches, burnt-out vehicles, dogs hanging from lampposts and vacant vessels lying in the road.

The relentless barrage of cruelty had always washed over Kelly, but now he felt its weight bearing down on him, crushing the air from his lungs.

There was a man across the plaza, scrambling frantically in the rubble, tears pouring down his face. Kelly felt the absurd notion to join him in his search.

'El Rey must be getting pretty short on funds to stoop this low,' Arty commented.

'With you everything always comes down to money.'

Arty scoffed. 'Pot – kettle – black.'

As the dust cleared Kelly felt the eyes of the city upon him, telling him he was no longer welcome, that he had taken much without giving anything back in return. He was used to inconspicuous movement, and the wide-open building-less plaza left him suddenly exposed.

Arty was relishing the spectacle with a look of unrestrained awe.

'Come on,' Kelly whispered, 'I want to show you—'

Something caught his eye.

Behind the café owner, barely visible beneath the soot and ash, he made out a large 'A' spray-painted onto the shutters. The letter was framed within a circle with its tail punching through the circumference:

The sight of it momentarily lifted his spirits. 'Why *Arty!* It seems you've joined the revolution!'

Arty was not amused. 'Ernesto!' he screamed. 'Clean this obscenity from my café. *Puta!* I hope they string that delusional do-gooder up by his thumbs, defacing my property.'

'Hardly the worst of his crimes.'

'I'd like to wring El Ambiente's neck.'

'Never happen.'

'They'll find him.'

'*No, they won't.*'

'What makes you so sure?'

'Trust me, they won't.'

Arty composed himself and peered into the miasma. 'So, what am I looking at?'

'It's nearby. We need to walk a short distance.'

'Forget it. You know my policy on exercise!'

Kelly took Arty's arm; a gesture of intimacy that embarrassed both men. 'It's really important that you see this. An awful lot rides on it . . . *please*?'

He hid his true intent. The café owner took the plea for a compliment.

'This had better be good!'

'It is.'

He led Arty from the plaza d'armas, along the remnants of downtown and into the market district. The raw destruction of moments ago was replaced with a more subdued and anaesthetized carnage. They passed into a labyrinth of dark alleyways and bohemian courtyards; small pockets of colonial beauty that did their best to mask the rack and ruin beneath colourful drapes, music and movement. Down they continued, squeezing through nooks and crannies, bars and bargaining dens, a metropolis that had been Kelly's dwelling place for the past four years; never his home.

The road rose steeply to a plateau overlooking the ocean. Arty began to snort and rasp. Kelly watched with mild amusement as he stumbled every few steps hiking up his enormous trousers.

'Is it much farther?'

'No.'

'You're a liar!'

'This is not news to either of us.'

They came at last to the Hotel El Sacramento. Large oak doors opened out into a central atrium that reached up into rafters without either ceiling or roof. On each of its many dishevelled floors precarious wooden balconies branched off into unseen bedrooms. The black and white chequered foyer tiles were awash with rainwater, twigs and leaves. Upturned chairs had not been righted, but instead left to soak up the moisture.

'Why on earth would you bring me here?' Arty whined.

'As I said, I need your help.'

'This place is beyond help.'

Kelly ignored the comment and walked into the hotel.

The reception desk stood as an elaborate centrepiece. Its black marble counter was flanked by immense wooden horses rearing up on their hind legs. Behind the desk stood an equally elaborate-looking man – short and bald, sporting a gargantuan Zapata moustache and dressed in a three-piece lilac suit, lime shirt and bright-orange silk cravat. Upon seeing the two men he reached below the worn surface, one hand rising with a set of keys, the other with a shotgun.

'Wasn't sure if you'd come back,' he said.

Kelly smiled coldly. 'Neither was I.'

The man led them into the hotel. A series of twists and turns brought them to a corridor where the carpets ran thread bare, and the walls swelled. At the end of the passageway a stairwell led down into a series of small sub-rooms, and finally to an underground garage. The man left without a word.

The only source of light came from a tiny window. The room was vast, but most of its features were hidden. In the far right-hand corner Arty distinguished the outline of a vehicle.

'My patience is wearing thin, Kelly.'

'Almost there,' Kelly replied. 'Tread carefully.'

The vehicle was a blue van. Even in the poor visibility it was evident that there had been a collision of some sorts. Attempts had been made to hammer the bodywork back into shape, but its original white colour was still visible beneath the lumpy panels of a clumsy, haphazard respray.

'You think you can walk a few more feet?'

'Drop dead!'

The two men made their way through the fog-like haze, the loose ground moving and tumbling beneath each step. Kelly tapped lightly on the side panel, inserted the key in the lock and flung the back door wide open. He didn't look inside, but instead watched the expression change on the café owner's face.

'Here is the favour I seek.'

Arty stared at its contents for some time, first in disbelief, then in confusion, finally bellowing with raucous laughter.

'*Mi Dios!* How the mighty have fallen. Did Katrina put you up to this?'

'Let's just say that she redeemed my shitty life.'

'And what the hell does that mean?'

'*I don't know.*'

Arty pulled at his jowls and shook his head from side to side. 'You want my advice? Leave this van, leave the keys in the ignition and walk away, find somewhere quiet and lie low for a couple of days.'

Arty spoke with such vigour that he almost sounded sincere, but Kelly knew of his ulterior motives.

'What are you, an *idiot?* Take a look around – the city is falling. This is just the tip of the iceberg. There are too many people disappearing. It's become too unsafe.'

Arty smiled. The many folds of his flabby face parted in deep satisfaction. 'I know their patterns, who they're looking for.'

'They're not always targeting, you *know* that. Sometimes it's just random.'

'There are ways and means of becoming immune, Mr Kelly. You'd do well to take a leaf out of ole Arty's book and check your allegiances.'

Kelly regarded the man with intense scrutiny, as if taking him in for the first time. In his mind he reached into the man and ripped the tar-infested lungs from his chest.

'You're remarkably well informed for a café owner.'

'I thrive on the trafficking of information, not the skin trade.'

'It's not like that, and you know it.'

Arty waved his arms in mock protest. 'Fine, my mistake, you're a *saint*, and the last four years have all been a charade.'

The trap was set, the bait hanging ripe and succulent. Kelly lowered his defences.

'Tell me something, Arty. What on earth does life amount to, I mean really?'

True to form the café owner jumped on the uncharacteristic honesty, smelling what he thought was weakness. 'Bit late to be searching for a sense of purpose, wouldn't you say?'

Kelly switched back, his abrupt actions implying regret. 'I'll need travel documents.'

'By when?'

'Midday.'

'You're joking?'

'If I was joking I'd say, "Why did the fat man cross the road?"'

15

'It'll cost you.'

'Fine.'

'Five hundred – dollars or gold – no petras.'

'I *said* fine.'

Arty chuckled to himself, enjoying the good fortune that had fallen into his lap. 'Ah, the blessings that war bestows.'

Even by Arty's standards the comment was mercilessly poor, but ever the pragmatist Kelly took what he could from it.

Thank you. Now my path is set.

'I'll call you in a few hours.'

'Make it three, a guy's gotta eat!'

'OK, three then, but be ready.'

'Of course – give me a lift back.'

'I'm staying here. Why don't you flag down one of your black sedan friends, seeing as you're so close?'

'You ungrateful little—'

'I'll express my gratitude in money.'

Kelly extended his hand. When the café owner begrudgingly shook it Kelly gripped tight and locked eyes.

'I'm trusting you, Arty.'

'Sure thing, Slim.'

Arty walked back through the rolling, churning debris, cursing under his breath. Only now did Kelly look into the van. Something within flickered in the darkness. He closed the door.

Back in the hotel someone shouted, '*Lo siento, mas gordo.*' ('I'm sorry, too fat.')

Moments later Arty replied with, '*Hijo de puta.*' ('Son of a whore.')

Kelly got into the driver's seat and let his head fall back.

It's a strange sensation to realize that your life amounts to nothing.

In an even stranger way Kelly felt some measure of gratitude for the misfortune that had befallen him, stripped of everything he'd once held dear, but standing none the less.

'There may yet be time.'

His owns words failed to bring comfort.

Time for what?

The revelation wouldn't come. Kelly shook the thought from his head, put the van into gear and cautiously pulled away.

Chapter 2
The Port of Green Waves

Six weeks earlier

1.

Nowhere was the economic chaos felt more acutely than in El Puerto de Las Ondas Verdes. It was situated to the east of the city and got its name from the high algae content that turned the water a brilliant shade of emerald as it neared the coast.

The port formed the commercial hub of Corderro. Despite international laws preventing tourists from visiting its shores the principality still traded freely with the outside world. Boats arrived on an average of five an hour. Most were empty, hoping to bleed the city dry and leave the next day heavily laden with cheap goods.

In recent months the emperor, El Rey, had appointed a new Chancellor of the Exchequer, Tito Majagranzas. Within days of his employment the national currency, La Petra, went into freefall, and had now disintegrated to a point where it was virtually worthless. The Chancellor's efforts to rectify the situation created hyperinflation on an unprecedented scale. Prices rose into the echelons and a barter culture effectively replaced the currency. Vague notions of value were chalked up on huge blackboards in relation to US dollars, euros, petras and gold, to give some indication of relative worth, but these values changed dramatically from minute to minute, the boards were constantly out of date and fights were frequently breaking out with traders accusing one another of loading the figures in their favour.

The Chancellor's latest attempt to restore equilibrium was to introduce a whole raft of measures – taxes, levies, extortion, arson and creative accountancy – none of which had proved successful.

Corderro's financial instability was equalled only by its civil unrest. Law and order had long since been abandoned as a mythical, unobtainable concept. The significant military presence at the port was largely corrupt, and generally turned a blind eye to the unorthodox and mostly illegal activities that took place in favour of supplementing their meagre salaries. El Rey's spies were rife in the trading area, but were fairly easy to spot due to their general ineptitude in buying and selling. Even so, it was considered wise to avoid them, or at the very least show ignorance as to their true disposition.

The levies and taxes had been steep even before Tito came to office. Now, with the rates rising almost daily, the only way to make any serious money was not to declare anything. As a result smuggling had become second nature, and a large number of individuals were attempting to steal pretty much everything that arrived in El Puerto de Las Ondas Verdes.

The most successful of these were three men – Paolo, Raoul and Kelly.

Paolo and Raoul worked together. Both men were tall and scruffy with unkempt shaggy brown hair. They dabbled in all goods that arrived, but their preferences were for food and clothing.

Kelly worked alone – a dark, brooding, selfish man. His single-minded but modest approach had honed his skill to the point where he was both the most successful and the least noticed tradesman in the port. Under his watchful eye sizable quantities of every conceivable commodity went astray from under their masters' noses day after day, reappearing in a variety of black market warehouses and bartering dens.

All three men had worked in the port for four years.

The average life expectancy of a smuggler was two.

2.

Katrina met Paolo and Raoul at the quayside. She tipped the taxi driver twenty petras – a handsome sum a week ago, now nothing. The man snorted his disgust and pulled away. Seeing the two men, particularly Paolo, always made her feel anxious. She was stretched and misshapen from living perpetually at the end of herself, and yet for all her sacrifice Katrina was merely treading water in a sea her friends had been immersed in their entire lives.

The pathway was littered with haggard-looking fishermen hunched hopefully over their lines. She drew glances as she passed by. With her shock of red hair and pale complexion she always stood out amongst the mix of Hispanic and Indian features.

Paolo's smile was so warm and genuine that Katrina felt as if she would fall to her knees and weep. Its presence on his face defied the immense misfortune he and his family had endured.

'Esperanza,' he greeted, 'this is a mistake.'

Overlaying the smile Katrina saw deep tracts of angst. Raoul's head angled down toward the wooden jetty.

'I have to agree, señorita, this is foolish. *He* will not join us. There is much to lose, and little to gain.'

Katrina had learnt from bitter experience to hold their words in the utmost regard, but she was stubborn, and desperately wanted to prove herself.

'Is he as good as you say he is?'

'Better.'

'Then I must try.'

Her usual obstinacy had been expected. 'OK,' Paolo conceded reluctantly, 'but watch what you say and don't expect a warm reception.'

They led her down a series of gangplanks to the outer circle. Here those who were either too poor or else too notorious to venture beyond the tollgates gathered to sell smaller items, mostly scraps and oddities stolen from anyone who entered without their wits about them. It was commonplace for traders to work in tandem, one selling an item and the other stealing it back before the buyer had even left the stall.

Gambling was also widespread in the outer areas. It was the one vice that could be afforded no matter how low a social standing. The unspoken rule was that a person could never bet what they didn't have. To be found short when debts were being settled was worse than murder in the eyes of El Puerto de Las Ondas Verdes. Loan sharking of any description was abhorred and anyone found in contravention was lynched there and then, or else excommunicated and banned from trading forever.

Katrina was overcome by an unwelcome clash of smells – thick enveloping cigar smoke, sweaty blood-soaked cockerels fighting in cages, gutted fish, rotting fruit and beer-drenched folding tables with card games in full swing; various foreign currencies soaking up the froth in heaped piles. Raoul took her hand and pulled her through groups of overenthusiastic men thrusting a variety of objects in her face – sharks' teeth, coral necklaces, squid, lobster and bottles of intoxicating liquid.

Through the din of smoke and demanding voices Katrina was dragged into a clearing where the masses petered out. Two heavily armed but lethargic-looking men stood guarding the rusty iron gates to the inner port.

Raoul and Paolo presented IDs that named themselves as Federico and Julian. Paolo's was accompanied by a roll of notes.

'My sister,' he indicated towards Katrina. 'She doesn't have an ID, but isn't here to trade. Am I OK to bring her in as an observer?'

The lie was ridiculous. Paolo had clay-coloured skin and was at least twenty years older then her. Katrina felt herself being looked up and down. The guard slipped the notes into his pocket and handed back the IDs. 'Of course she is.'

The gate was opened without another word.

Once inside, the stalls and tarpaulins were replaced with huge steel containers the size of double-decker buses. It was like the eye of the hurricane. The hectic people sounds fell away into a background hush. Here the select few worked their subtle arts, free from the distractions of vice.

They passed under a watchtower. Katrina was mesmerized by the rifles that aimed down into the trading pits, looming over them with the ever-present threat of a sudden, unforgiving eruption.

'There he is.'

The man Raoul pointed out was stooped over a mug of coffee. He was dressed in a crumpled leather jacket, brown cords, heavy-duty boots and a beanie hat.

Katrina found herself wondering why she had not singled him out beforehand, given his piercing eyes and sharp features. He appeared preoccupied and introspective. Like so many before her Katrina was lulled into a false sense of security. She approached far more boldly than was wise.

'Kelly? Can we have a word?' Paolo asked.

The man looked up from his coffee and calmly panned across from left to right before glancing away dismissively.

'Why?'

'It'll only take a minute.'

He shrugged. 'OK, but make it quick.'

'This is Katrina Esperanza.'

'Please to meet you,' she greeted him, stretching out her hand. Kelly did not shake it.

'I'm sure.'

'My colleagues have told me a lot about you.'

'What do you want?'

She looked to Paolo for clarity. He rolled his forefingers around one another as if to say 'Get to the point.'

'I work for an organization . . . called Satellite. We're a humanitarian organization.'

'We?'

'Yes . . . us,' she indicated the men on either side of her, 'and many others throughout the city. It's–' she noticed Paolo and Raoul exchange glances of annoyance '–growing all the time.'

'Congratulations.'

'We'd like to enlist your help.'

'With what?'

'Well, it's a little sensitive.'

'My time is precious, lady. You don't have the liberty of being sensitive.'

Katrina was clearly riled by the smuggler's rudeness. Paolo held his breath and prayed that she would keep her temper in check.

'OK,' she replied slowly and started again. 'Well, there's a greater need for supplies than ever before amongst the poor and homeless . . . food, medical sup—'

'Satellite, you say?' Kelly interrupted.

'Yes.'

'Well, well–' his mouth slid into a sinister smile revealing tiny teeth '–that explains a lot.'

An elaboration wasn't forthcoming. 'Well, as I was saying,' Katrina continued, 'there is an urgent nee—'

'Ever hear of Rodriguez Santiago, Miss Esperanza?' Kelly interrupted once more.

'No . . . can't say that I have.'

This time she waited.

'Ask your man here,' Kelly said, pointing towards Paolo. 'No one's quite sure what he did, but the port guards, they strung him up just over there, ropes around his arms and legs, a modern-day crucifixion, you might say – sun beating down, nose and ears blistering, breathing getting laboured. Anyway, round about noon on the *fourth* day the guards start asking him questions – his name, how old he is, where he was born, where he is now. He's too far gone by then, doesn't know the answers. All he keeps saying over and over is Satellite . . . Satellite . . . Satellite.'

Kelly took his eyes off her for a moment and examined his shoes before surreptitiously looking over his shoulder at an incoming ship.

'I wonder . . . how is it a person could be a member of an organization, and not know something like that?'

'I—' Katrina felt impotent anger.

Kelly stood and turned on his heels; body language that blocked her from further conversation.

'Paulo, did you see the crows pecking out his eyes, Rodriguez still alive, trying to fend them off, his arms bound, no resolve left, not even for a whimper?' His voice was more upbeat now, mocking in its tone.

'Yes, of course I saw, Kelly, we all did.'

'You think I want to hang up there with the crows pecking at my eyes? You think they'll look kindly on this *monkey* just 'cos she's a *girl*?'

'*Hey*!' Katrina began to protest.

'Come on, she didn't mean you any offence,' Raoul interjected. 'She's just trying to do the right thing.'

'Well, that's the thing about smuggling, isn't it? It's essentially a selfish venture for selfish people. You take what doesn't belong to you. You get good at it by not being noticed. Now if I hook up with your Samaritan over here, blundering around with her big boots and her red beacon hair announcing to the world 'Here come the clowns', how successful and inconspicuous do you suppose I'll be then?'

'She made a mistake, Slim, that's all. Sorry to disturb you.'

'Let's not speak again. In fact, don't let me see either of you amateurs here in future, and that goes especially for Coco.'

'*Hey*!'

'Like my friend said,' Paolo reinforced, 'we're sorry, but don't presume to threaten us. We'll be down here tomorrow as we are every day.'

Kelly didn't miss a stride. 'Four years you work with a pair of guys, happy as Larry, and all the while they're playing Russian roulette! This is a cessation of all business dealings.'

'That is unfortunate,' Paolo replied coldly.

'Not unfortunate, *necessary,* given your stupidity, and begging your pardon, but I'll threaten whomsoever I like, and here's another for your troubles. If I *ever* see your lady friend on the docks again I'll be gift-wrapping her and sending her to Eleanor Blake.'

'*Hey*!'

'There's no need to—'

'Personally I have no problem seeing her strung up and blinded by beaks, but I *do* have a problem with her pointing me out first.'

'*Hey!*' Katrina finally broke through. 'Don't talk as if I'm not here.'

Having shown her strength and indignation she expected to be rewarded with a guarded apology, but instead her outburst caused Kelly to turn on her with such ferocity that she stepped back and gasped. It wasn't so much in what his aggression possessed, but in what it lacked, for while his words were growled with a tumultuous fury, Katrina realized now that in all that time his voice had never risen above a whisper.

'Do you understand the concept of being black-sedaned?'

Katrina held his gaze. 'Of course.'

'Then why are you here? The innocent disappear every day as a direct result of people like yours involvement. Where's your bleeding heart for them? If just one person on this dock thinks our meeting looks suspicious we're already marked – *all of us*. Doesn't that arouse the slightest sense of shame in your do-gooder's heart?'

Katrina took a further step back under the weight of his accusation. 'It's worth the risk.'

'Not to me it's not, you arrogant bitch. I take great offence when someone takes it upon themselves to sign my life away on a whim.'

'All right, Slim, all right. She's only trying to help. There's no need to upset her.'

'Upset her? I'll ring her neck if she doesn't take her idealistic, misguided notions out of my face, and that goes for you too, Santa Paolo.'

3.

As soon as they were clear of the port Katrina's lips began to quiver. Paolo grabbed the flesh of her upper arm and squeezed.

'Do not cry, Esperanza, or we shall abandon you.'

'Do not draw attention to yourself,' Raoul added.

'You are relatively new here. You are not accustomed to being spoken to in such ways. It will become commonplace. Get used to it.'

'But do not get used to being our spokesperson,' Paolo continued. 'Your vanity has cost us dearly.'

'*What?*' Katrina remonstrated as she was dragged along against her will. 'I was trying to—'

'You were trying to bag the lion with a water pistol,' Raoul finished. 'I told you he would not join us, *we both did*, but your arrogance told you that you could convince anyone.'

'You gave over far more than you realize, Esperanza—'

'You exposed us—'

'After four years of anonymity—'

'Just as Kelly said you had.'

Katrina bowed her head under the verbal barrage. It had all happened so fast. One minute she was confidently taking on the world, and the next she was under attack from all sides, unsure of what her response should be, hopelessly out of her depth.

'I'm sorry,' was all she could muster, channeling all of her energy into fending off tears.

'I know,' Paolo replied reassuringly and released her arm.

'Can't be helped now,' Raoul surmised. 'Let's go get a drink.'

They walked the rest of the journey in silence. The two men shed all signs of tension and assumed an air of indifference. Katrina by comparison marched rigid and intense, unable to shake off the horror of her humiliation.

The plaza d'armas existed as an oasis of serenity at the centre of an otherwise anarchic city. Giant yucca plants flanked its four corners – green leathery leaves hanging above beds of royal blue delphinium. In the absence of care the flora had grown beyond its boundaries, reaching over the unkempt lawns and grasping at the roadside. Water had not flowed through its fountain centrepiece in many months. The stone harp-playing cherubim stood patiently on one leg, his mouth and throat bone dry.

The ornate structures that surrounded the plaza had stood tall and proud since colonial times, the most grandiose and beautiful of which was El Edificio Exquisito ('the exquisite building'). Filled with high-ceilinged, chandelier-laden banqueting rooms, it had once been the home of visiting diplomats who would wave to the hopeful crowds from one of its many verandas and balconies. Somewhat ironically it had now become the temporary home of the Department of Sanitation.

El Edificio Exquisito had stood as a testament to Spanish ingenuity and craftsmanship for over 350 years – it would only stand for another forty-one days, torn apart by a blast that would interrupt Kelly's coffee and extinguish over 200 lives in a single instance of financial madness.

They took a table at El Café Empressario. Its owner, Arty Bey, a Greek Cypriot and known informer, strode larger than life into the sunshine and greeted them with his usual sniping sarcasm.

'Ah, a frowning contest! I would partake but I fear you have already beaten me hands down.'

24

Having fallen under the Emperor's grace, Arty was the only café owner for miles around with regular access to half-descent coffee beans, which afforded him the liberty of doing away with such unnecessary trifles as manners and service. He knew that he had his customers over a barrel and was not proud when it came to exploiting that position.

'For you, my friends, I have a fresh treat – Jamaican blue, dark roast, very hard to come by. The only question is – what do *you* have for *me*?'

'Wow,' Raoul replied with equal sarcasm. 'Times are tough when you have to brag about your beans!'

'Yeah, three cups of Blue will be perfectly adequate,' Paolo added. 'Now, run along, *camerero,*' ('waiter').

The good humour left Arty's face.

'I said what do *you* have for *me*?'

'Dollars, US, now that will be all.'

As soon as they were alone once more Katrina made an attempt at reconciliation.

'OK, what could I have done differently?'

'How many people were watching us at the port?' Paolo replied.

'Besides Kelly?'

'Yes.'

'No one.'

'Wrong, everyone was watching us, and we–' Paolo pointed to Raoul then himself, purposefully missing out Katrina '–were watching everyone. This is what you are missing, Esperanza. You are blissfully unaware of the subterfuge. A guy like Kelly, he walks around in broad daylight and *no one* sees what he does! You don't approach him cap in hand or he will strip the shirt from your back, and you certainly don't try and appeal to his better nature!'

'Then why on earth did you let me?' Katrina's face burnt red with childlike rage.

'Because you wouldn't take no for an answer and because sometimes it is better to pick someone up after they have fallen on their face than it is to prevent them from falling in the first place – a greater lesson is learnt.'

'Your passion is your greatest strength, Katrina,' Raoul elaborated, 'but it will also be your greatest weakness unless it is tempered with caution and instinct. Two qualities you do not currently possess.'

Katrina sat back in the chair and threw up her arms. 'Anything else you'd like to point out, just to make the character assassination complete?'

Paolo and Raoul looked at one another as if telepathically comparing notes. 'No . . . no, I think that's it for now,' the former replied without a hint of irony.

The real waiter arrived with coffee that smelt just as rich and earthy as Arty had claimed. Paolo stretched out a hand.

'Ernesto! *Mucho gusto*.' ('Pleased to meet you.')

'*Y tu tambien*.' ('And you also.')

'Ernesto here's a freedom fighter, just like his namesake – a leader of lattés, a campinero of cappuccinos.'

'Hey, don't blow my cover,' Ernesto retorted, placing the cups on a wicker table. 'Enjoy!'

Katrina brooded over her beverage as if it were an infant to protect from the wolves. As she dissected the morning's disastrous meeting a question came to mind. 'Slim?'

'What?'

'Back at the docks you called him Slim?'

'Oh, a nickname – it's short for Seriously Lacking In Moral-Fibre.'

Chapter 3
The Key with No Door

The day after the sanctions were lifted a boat arrived carrying the first passengers from the outside world in over a decade. Amongst the vagabonds, exiles, orphans and miscreants returning to a long-forgotten homeland was a young woman called Isabella Derecha.

Isabella had fled Corderro hurriedly one night almost fifteen years before. She had been a child at the time and her recollections of the city were sketchy at best. Mostly she remembered people – running, ducking for cover, shielding one another, dipping when passing windowsills. She also remembered being passed around like a baton, changing ownership as one by one her protectors disappeared. The chaotic site of El Puerto de Las Ondas Verdes did little to stir any further sense of memory. Even so, the excitement and expectation that she felt were unbearable.

Isabella was Latin American by birth, but had spent most of her life in England and spoke only pigeon Spanish. The conversations around her all seemed to be of the same theme – a lost father here, a separated daughter there. The specifics weren't clear, but she felt a connection with them nonetheless – the hope, the blind faith.

The boat was tied to cleats on the jetty and a makeshift gangway hastily hoisted into position.

The port was a sea of worldly weary faces struggling to make a living. Crates of every conceivable commodity were stacked precariously, forming a maze of markets where men and women shrugged and pleaded in the throws of bartering rituals.

It was wonderful to behold.

Less welcome was the sight of soldiers and officials, bringing order where none was needed. Checkpoints and guard towers surrounded the port.

Why now of all times?

Fear begets fear begets fear.

Smoke was rising all around. Many fires were raging uncontrollably in the city.

People poured out of their quarters and onto the deck, jostling for position, squeezing up against the railings, glancing at one another anxiously and tugging at clothes. It was as if secrets that had waited an entire generation could not wait a moment longer.

A gateway was opened, and the masses formed into a spearhead. Isabella was dragged forward in a surge of bodies. She held tight to her tiny suitcase to prevent it being ripped from her hands.

A man at the front of the queue turned around and looked directly at her. Like Isabella he was young, mid to late twenties, with scruffy brown hair and a confident expression that oozed boyish charm. Seeing that he had her attention he mouthed '*Buonos dias,*' with lips that broke into an enormous smile. He winked and was gone, skipping nimbly down the gangplank and into the crowd.

A good omen?

She saw that her boat was just one of many, a river joining an ocean, or a ventricle joining an artery. The crowds were literally charging across the concourse to a gate, at least twenty people deep, clambering over one another and rocking the flimsy fence that kept them penned in.

I'll be torn limb from limb!

Holding the suitcase out in front of her like a shield Isabella plunged into a myriad of arms and aggression. Disgruntled faces loomed up and faded past. Shoulders closed in, vying for space. Vehicles cut across the masses, honking horns and being swarmed over.

A woman a few feet ahead stumbled and fell. The ripple passed over and subsumed her. Isabella tried to stop and offer assistance, but was pulled out of reach. She was eventually spat out over a dining-room table that passed for an immigration desk.

The official's blank, timid, wide-eyed face said it all. He was completely overawed with the impossible situation in which he found himself. Hopelessly unable to control the influx of people, he'd resorted to checking through the limited number he was able to collar. Huge swathes circumvented him on either side without incident. Isabella was one of the unfortunates.

'*Que pais?*' he asked.

'I'm English.'

'*Como?*'

'*Inglesa?*'

'What-is-the-purpose-of-your-visit? Business-or-pleasure?'

'Neither.'

'I do not understand.'

'Business, I'm in the finding business.'

The official pointed at her stomach and uttered something that was lost in the din.

'*What? Que?*' she screamed to be heard.

'Is that your only luggage?'

'Yes.'

'Open it please.'

Isabella looked up at the endless flow of people passing through the checkpoints without so much as a stamp in their passports. The table rocked violently under their assault. 'Come on? My possessions won't be safe if I open my bag here.'

'I do not understand. Open it please.'

'How about a bit of privacy, you know, basic human rights?'

'Open it please,' the official repeated mechanically.

'Uh,' she scoffed showing her obvious disgust at the man's pettiness. 'You're a robot, you know that word, *robusteza*, eh?'

The official did not smile, nor did he look offended. 'Open it please.'

Isabella put up her hands in defeat. '*You* open it.'

She checked herself.

Are you really going to let your temper get you barred from the country after fighting so hard to get here?

Isabella tried to find a little grace and restraint as she watched the official haphazardly pull items of clothing from her suitcase. Carefully folded blouses were heaped in creases, underwear was paraded for lecherous eyes and then came the journal. Isabelle flinched.

Leave that alone.

The official casually leafed through its leather-bound pages, found nothing but English and discarded it on the desk. Recalling one of the journal's entries Isabella breathed a sigh of relief and smiled.

Dear Jonathan,

You wouldn't believe what a feisty little madam I am! Or maybe you would?

I did what you asked. I made something of my life. I am quivering with anticipation at the possibility that I might soon be able to show you all that you have given me.

Come and see . . .

I am ready . . .

'Everything appears to be in order. Sorry to have troubled you.' The official's eyes passed across her body before moving on to the next person. Isabella swept her possessions from the table, crammed them into the suitcase and fled.

Beggars tugged at her clothes and tradesmen fought to gain her attention with shouting and waving. She forced her way through the trading pits and up into the outer perimeter. From here the enormity of her task hit home. Through the port gates she could see high up into the hills. Miles and miles of elaborate architecture filled the landscape before her, a fallen glory laid bare like an autopsy. Shanty huts filled the spaces like sand, and, despite the years of war, El Rey's palace stood unblemished above it all. The street teemed with activity. It was like a beehive, or a colony of ants, people orbiting around one another, busy learning how to live again.

So much in one moment, so much more in fifteen years.

How will I ever find you?

Unseen music lifted her spirits. She followed it to an enclosed courtyard where a Corolli band were playing and dancing within a gazebo. Isabella counted twelve musicians dressed in cream-coloured suits with dark-brown cravats – a large double bass flanked by percussionists, a guitarist and mandolin player at either side, and numerous horn players. At their centre stood an elderly woman in a ball gown, pouring every ounce of her gravelly voice into a microphone. She remained immaculately still, careful not to dislodge the fantastical hairpiece balanced on her head. After a few minutes of jumping around and swapping positions the men fell in behind their leader, and together they began to sing the same phrase over and over.

> *'El Oh mi Dios, que soy an extasis*
> *Realmente encuentra el reconciliation?'*

The small crowd present applauded and wolf-whistled. Movement was staccato and limbs were stiff. It was as if they had forgotten how to express themselves.

'*Hola, mi chica bella!*'

The winking man from the port stood by her side. His grin was infectious. Isabella tried to remain aloof. 'Are you following me?'

'Not at all,' the man answered, reverting to English. He held an open palm to his heart as if mortally offended. Isabella frowned to show that she didn't believe him and turned back to the musicians.

'What are they singing about?'

'They are saying, "*Oh my God, I am in raptures. Can we really find reconciliation?*"'

'Do you think they can?'

'I think–' the man brought his hand up in order to suppress a smirk '–I think all things are possible. Pleased to meet you. My name is Charles Neblin. You can call me Carlos Neblina.'

'As in *mist*?'

'The very same.' He gave a little bow. 'Your Espanol is good.'

'It gets me by.'

'And yours?'

'Isabella.'

'Ah, I thought so!' Carlos gave a knowledgeable nod. Isabella got the distinct impression that he was deliberately trying to annoy her.

'How could you think so?' There was a sense of familiarity. 'Have we met before?'

'Did you arrive today?'

'Yes.'

'Then how could we have met before? This port has been closed for fifteen years.'

'Have you ever been to England?'

'Señorita, I have been to many places.'

The band struck up another number. Their liveliness made Isabella feel tired. She needed to find her hotel, get a hot meal and some respite from the chaos around her. Carlos's presence further heightened her sense of unease. His good nature appeared genuine, but there was something calculating in his approach. Isabella felt as if she was being manipulated.

'So, what brings you to this fair city?' Carlos inquired.

'I'm looking for someone.'

'What's his name?'

'I didn't say it was a man.'

'A presumption on my part . . . so, what is his name?'

'Why so many questions?' Isabella's body language became closed and hostile. Carlos's remained loose and open.

'Because I am flirting with you, *mi chica bella*. Please don't raise your voice to me. It only seeks to convince me further that you are in need of cheering up. Once I get that kind of idea into my head I am unbearable.'

'What makes you think you're not unbearable now?'

Carlos laughed. 'Uh, such rudeness in one so attractive. What's his name?'

'If I tell you, will you leave me in peace?'

'Absolutely.'

'OK, his name is Jonathan Pemburton.'

Carlos knew the name instantly, and was filled with a mixture of joy and sadness. 'How long is it since you've seen this man?'

'What happened to leaving me in peace?'

'Humour me. I am a curious soul.'

Isabella decided that there was no harm in telling him. 'Many years.'

'And what do you want with him?'

'To give him this.' She reached down into her satchel and produced a leather-bound journal.

'What is it?'

'The story of my life.'

'Ah, a woman of mystery and intrigue. How exciting!'

'Something like that,' she replied softly.

'Right then–' Carlos stood up straight and saluted '–well, in that case I have no choice but to help you find this man.'

Isabella laughed at his eccentric behaviour. 'Why ever would you do that?'

'For the honour of helping a beautiful woman in distress.'

'I'm not in distress.'

'Ah, but you admit to being beautiful? Well, you may not be in distress now, but just think how distressed you'll be if you let an opportunity like this pass you by.'

'Oh God, you're infuriating!'

'You look tired. We should discuss your quest over a coffee.'

'Ah, now we get to the grift.'

'I do not know this word – "grift"?'

'As in "scam".'

'Oh certainly not, I am a prince amongst men. Come on, I know a great place just round the corner.'

'You've not been here in fifteen years. How could you possibly know a good place?'

'My dear, this place is so good it would survive fifty years of war. El Rey would not dare bomb it for fear of an uprising. Its beverages practically support the economy, no word of a lie.'

Isabella turned her head so that Carlos would not see her smile.

He's grinding you down. Get a grip of yourself, woman!

'You're a very charming man, Mr Neblina, but I must tell you that I already have a boyfriend back home.'

'You have a high opinion of yourself, which is well deserved, but alas for both of us I am a married man.' Carlos flashed his left hand in front of Isabella's eyes revealing a wedding band.

'You could have got that tin ring anywhere!'

'An outrage,' he shouted flamboyantly and slapped his chest. 'This is platinum. My wife bought it for me in Russia.'

'You don't look Russian?'

'As I said, my suspicious one, I have been to many places. Let us make a deal. If the café is not there I will leave you in peace. If it *is* you will have a drink with me – deal?'

'What's this café called?'

'It is called "Sal de la Tierra" – "Salt of the Earth".'

'OK, Mr Mist, let's go and call your bluff.'

'*Estupendo!*'

Café Sal de la Tierra was around the corner, just as Carlos said it would be. A fresh lick of latte-coloured paint had brought out the building's decrepitude. They found a nice spot on a terrace filled with mismatched furniture. Despite the crowded port they were the only customers. Even before they were seated another band rushed onto a makeshift stage and began hastily setting up.

Carlos applauded before the first note was played. '*Hermanos*, I salute you. Such opportunism would make a vulture blush!'

They launched into a folk song that slowly rose in tempo to a rapidly paced reprise:

> '*Miro. Veo. El rey no tiene ninguna ropa.*
> *Envuelva para arriba caliente en su capa mágica.*'

Once again Isabella asked for a translation.

'They are saying "*I look – I see – The king has no clothes– Wrap up warm in your magical coat.*"'

33

'Dangerous lyrics!'

'Perhaps. The people have no means of protest and so they sing.'

'OK,' Isabella said, 'so you've got me here for a drink. What's next?'

'Next?'

'In your plan.'

'Plan? There is no plan, only the thrill of discovery.'

A waitress approached and furnished them with menus. 'Can I get you anything to drink?' she asked.

'Just an orange juice for me,' Isabella replied.

'Very good, and for you, sir?'

Carlos scrunched up his features in an exaggerated show of deep thought. 'I'm not sure. What do you recommend, Teresita?'

The waitress took a step back and made a face that was half frown, half amusement. 'Do I know you?'

'No, no I don't think so.'

'Then how do you know my name?'

Carlos tapped the bridge of his nose. 'I'm a wizard.'

Teresita laughed. 'I guess stranger things have happened in the last few weeks!'

'Absolutely,' Carlos agreed. 'Impressed?'

'Very.'

'Just a coffee, thank you.'

'My pleasure.'

'Ohhh no señorita, *my* pleasure.'

Teresita walked away with a noticeable skip in her step.

Isabella folded her arms and shook her head. 'Your wife must be long suffering.'

'My wife is a saint, and I thank God for her. *Bendecido sea Dios.*' Carlos made the sign of the cross. 'Life is for living, *mi querida!*'

Carlos asked no further questions. Over the course of his coffee he told Isabella several stories of the city, recollections of his childhood and snippets picked up over the years abroad. He talked less of himself and more of everything else; became less animated and more engaging. Isabella's suspicions abated and were replaced by gratitude. As Carlos drained the last of his drink Isabella didn't want their time together to end. She considered asking him to stay for another, but then thought better of it. She decided instead to wait and see how long their conversation played out. Carlos in turn neither offered another nor excused himself.

He seems attuned to my concerns.

Perhaps he can help me find Jonathan?

Now that's an evolutionary leap in thinking!

Why would anyone want to help a complete stranger? There has to be an ulterior motive.

The suspicions crept back in.

'Would you excuse me a moment? I have to use the ladies.'

'Of course.'

Isabella walked into the café. Teresita was behind the counter making a latte.

'*El baño*?'

'Straight to the back, then right. You can't miss it.'

'*Gracias*. Nice place you've got here.'

'Thank you señorita – we try.'

'Out of interest – how long have you been open?'

'Couple of months now. Business is booming.'

Carlos lied to me. Why?

'That's good to hear.'

You left your bag under the chair.

'Excuse me,' Isabella exclaimed, suddenly flustered, and made her way towards the exit.

Of all the stupid schemes to fall for!

The terrace came into view. Carlos was not there.

The bag?

Beneath the chair where she had left it. On the table she found a note, hastily scrawled on a napkin and held down by Carlos's coffee cup:

Lo siento, mi chica bella,

It is not usually in my nature to abandon princesses to the hungry eyes of other men, but alas something came up – a matter of life and death you might say. My sincerest apologies. Enjoy the OJ. I will look you up in due course. I hope you find what you are looking for.

Much love,

> *Carlos*

How's he going to find me? He doesn't know where I'm staying.

Isabella shook her head and laughed at the absurdity of the encounter.

Strange guy – like a Lothario who hasn't quite mastered moving in for the kill.

The music came to an end. The lead singer asked if she would like to hear another song.

'*Por favor,*' she nodded. This time the tune was slow and waltz-like, skipping every few bars into syncopated salsa. The melody was illusive, skipping around unexpectedly. She was in the grip of a journey, an adventure.

I will find you Jonathan.

The song concluded. Isabella finished her orange juice, placed some coins in a bowl by the congas, bowed to the musicians with an appreciative smile and left the courtyard in search of her hotel.

Chapter 4

Tito Manages to Single-handedly Bankrupt an Entire Nation

1.

The Chancellor sat back from his books and ran both hands through a rapidly receding hairline. The accounts set before him could not have been any more fraudulent if he'd tried (and he *had* tried!). No matter how he looked at them – sitting down, standing up, face pressed against the numbers, walking around the office or reading out loud – he couldn't see where the original mistake had been.

Where was all the money going?

Try as he might there was no way of hiding the spectacular failure of his macro-economic policy. It was referred to by the inhabitants of Corderro as La Broma ('The Joke'). Tito himself was more commonly known as El Comedin ('The Joker').

Extreme taxation had crippled the country's spending power, and, with less and less revenue, businesses were folding left right and centre. Unemployment was rife, people were in debt up to their eyeballs and social unrest had reached new depths.

Earlier that week the Chancellor had been distressed to discover that he was personally responsible for a 68 billion deficit in the country's finances. With precious little money coming into the treasury his knee-jerk response had been to cancel as many outgoings as he could think of. These included health, education, sanitation, public works, transport and environmental budgets. Defence was left well alone.

Tito's one saving grace was that his employer, El Rey, was not yet aware of these details. Locked away in his ivory tower the Emperor did not concern himself with the day-to-day affairs of his principality. His eyes were instead focused on completing his legacy to the world, a book he had entitled *The Plague of Lethargy*. It was another two months before Tito was due to publish the national figures. There were still sixty days to recoup the money, but his options looked bleak.

If he failed to rectify the situation he would die. It was that simple. Coming clean to his boss over the cataclysmic abomination that was his bookkeeping would almost certainly lead to Eleanor Blake seeking out his vital organs with her exquisitely cruel fingers. If he was lucky she would simply shoot him. On the other hand, finding that kind of money in so short a space of time was going to take seriously extreme measures, measures that could make the situation far worse before it got better.

'Oh, *mi Dios,*' he sighed, 'is there no end?'

An ever-present and increasingly loud voice told him that the deep dark hole could only get deeper and darker. Each night as he burnt the midnight oil scrawling lie after ludicrous lie he would whisper maniacally to himself, 'Stop digging . . . stop digging . . . stop digging.'

Tito's frenzied thoughts were disturbed by the entrance of his mistress, Maria. She stumbled into the room, her uncoordinated digits slipping from the brass handle and spilling generous slugs of red wine onto the burgundy carpet.

'Come back to bed, my love,' she purred, her eyes glazed.

'I cannot afford the luxury of sleep, sweetness. I would awake several million worse off.'

Tito felt the presence of large, clumsy hands – one groping his buttocks, the other massaged his scalp. He jumped up angrily from his chair. 'Maria, you know how I hate you touching my head!'

'I'm sorry, my love. You shouldn't be so paranoid. It suits you, really.'

'What suits me?'

'You know . . . your . . . nothing.'

Maria forced herself down unto Tito's lap, displacing his papers and dabbing specs of crimson onto two of the debit columns – 'Goodwill' and 'Miscellaneous Petty Cash'.

'Whoops,' she giggled.

'Please Maria,' he responded, wiping his perspiring brow. 'I'm trying to work.'

'But it's late.'

Tito found his clef chin suddenly wedged between two enormous breasts, heaving from beneath a silk camisole.

'I know it's late,' he mumbled. 'Please, stop taunting me with your bosoms. I have a weak heart and I must work.'

Maria shook her hips provocatively. 'OK, but don't be long.'

Tito watched her leave with a mixture of lust and regret. She was a stunning-looking woman, but far from his equal intellectually. That role was taken by his wife, Elizabeth, a woman who was now a virtual stranger to him. He cleared his mind of such thoughts. Tito considered there to be no point in dwelling on something that had long since passed beyond his grasp. He'd never really had the courage of his convictions to win her back. They now co-existed at opposite ends of their vast house. Tito kept an apartment in the palace where he could be assured of discretion.

The Chancellor looked down at his notes. The paper was peppered with large circles of his own making.

I am trapped.

Angrily he swept the accounts from his desk, took a fresh sheet and hastily scrawled a letter:

Señor Valere,

I am writing to complain about your company's 'Miracle cream'. The product promises to show signs of 'significant follicle rejuvenation within a month or your money back'. I have used this cream for almost half a year now with no noticeable improvement. Quite the opposite in fact – my follicles appear to be racing one another to the back of my scalp with relish. As you can imagine this causes me considerable discomfort and embarrassment.

In short, this is intolerable. If you wish to avoid being <u>black-sedan-ed</u> you will send me a more effective batch within the next forty-eight hours.

Yours disgruntled,

> *Tito Majagranzas*
> *Chancellor of the Exchequer*

Tito rang a bell. Moments later a young servant boy appeared.

'Good morning, your grace,' the boy greeted him with a bow.

Mi Dios, is it morning already?

'Good morning, Cheech,' the Chancellor replied wearily. 'Please post this letter with all speed.'

'Certainly sir.' The boy bowed once more and stepped backwards out of the room.

Frustration mixed with despair. The water had risen above his head. He couldn't bail fast enough. He was drowning.

'DAMN YOU, DIMITRI!' he shouted. 'WHAT HAVE YOU DONE WITH ALL THE MONEY?'

2.

Tito was Peruvian by birth, raised on the streets of Cuzco in the shadow of the Andes. Even in childhood his Spanish features had put him at odds with the city's proud Indian heritage. He had felt the weight of history, an ancient guilt he couldn't cleanse, an ideal he couldn't aspire to.

'Have events always been conspiring to bring me here,' he often asked himself, 'to this place of ruin?'

As a teenager he had been incapable of seeing the beauty of his home town – the wide open plaza filled with flowers, the cathedral, the twisting cobbled streets weaving and rising into the hills and the immaculate stone-cut walls. All Tito saw was displacement, beggars, open doorways inviting squalor, a dead end amidst the mountains.

He had wanted more, demanded more and envisaged the gains that awaited him elsewhere. Corderro had seemed like an amalgam of his every desire – a glittering prize, a means of escape, a new world full of opportunity, and it *had* been that, and so much more. By the time the young El Rey swept to power in a bloody coup Tito had lived in the city for over a decade. He was a millionaire, married and gloriously happy. It was as if he had the Midas touch, or was blessed with second sight. His early investments yielded tenfold profits, his first business, a barbers (which had been sold in a fit of envious rage some months earlier), opened four additional salons within the first six months – so astounding was his fortune.

During the next quarter of a century his marriage had fallen by the wayside, but the wealth had continued to accumulate beyond his wildest dreams. He ran several large and successful businesses, was well respected and felt immense satisfaction in all he did. There was no reason to think that it couldn't continue this way forever.

Tito knew of the city's history, its affiliation with vicious circles, bad luck and the melting pot, but there had been peace for so long that the stories seemed outlandish and contrived. He had known nothing but favour and prosperity. Looking back now he saw that in all that time he was simply being fattened up for the moment Corderro called him to a sacrificial altar.

He could remember that moment clearly.

Tito had been sitting on the veranda, moustache proud and upright rather than the drooping, disintegrating slug he now sported, thick head of hair, a glass of Scotch in one hand, a smoking Cohiba in the other, his trousers round his ankles and Maria naked between his legs, pleasuring him with every skill in her considerable arsenal. The sunset was casting a warm glow across the ocean and Elizabeth was away visiting friends for the week. It had been perfect.

But then, as he reached the moment of impending crisis, there had been the sound of embarrassed throat clearing and Maria had scurried off into the trees with a bundle of clothes, leaving Tito wretchedly unfulfilled.

Behind him stood one of the butlers (he'd mercifully forgotten which one), holding a silver tray supporting an equally silver telephone, its cord stretching back into the house.

'Sir, the Chancellor of the Exchequer to speak to you,' he announced in an unassuming yet immensely condescending way.

'Thank you,' Tito coughed whilst pulling up his trousers. 'Put it down on the floor. I'll get it in a minute.'

'Very good sir.'

Even before he picked up the receiver Tito had felt something change. He had always managed to conduct his affairs beneath the Emperor's radar, but now it seemed he'd been noticed.

'Hello?' he inquired timidly.

'Mr Majagranzas! This is Dimitri,' the Chancellor boomed confidently back at him. 'May I call you Tito?'

'Certainly . . . it's an honour.'

'Oh let's do away with all that nonsense,' Dimitri responded jovially. 'I'm a great admirer of entrepreneurs such as yourself.'

'Great . . . that's—' Tito was too apprehensive to know what to say.

'I can see you want me to get straight down to business. That's a good sign. It means we've made the right choice.'

Choice?

Tito felt the ground beginning to open beneath him. 'What can I do for you?' he asked reluctantly.

'Emile would like to meet with you,' came the awful answer.

Dimitri was the only person in the puppet government to refer to El Rey by his real name. Not even Eleanor in the throws of passion ever dared utter the true name of his birth.

Tito heard a popping sound. He had met the Chancellor on a previous occasion and knew the noise to come from Dimitri's grotesquely deformed lips snagging on his horrendously hooked nose when he spoke.

'What is the nature of the meeting?'

'Well–' *pop* '–I've been instructed to inform you that you've been successful in your application for the most important role in the Emperor's government–' *pop* '–that of *Chancellor*.'

Tito had not applied for the role. Such was the exacting of El Rey's will. There was no point in protesting, only in accepting and making the best of the situation.

It was good while it lasted.

'Thank you,' he replied, sounding anything but grateful. 'But where does that leave you?'

'I've been picked out for an international assignment,' Dimitri stated proudly. 'Don't know the ins and outs of it yet, but I've got a meeting scheduled with Eleanor Blake this evening to discuss it in greater depth.'

Tito's skin turned cold. He saw what Dimitri could not – that El Rey had asked the Chancellor to deliver his own death sentence.

It was the first time in his life that he'd been forced into making a truly life-changing decision. Should he speak out and tell the Chancellor of his fears, or should he remain silent and avoid incriminating himself? He chose the latter.

The embarrassment at having been caught in an adulterous act mingled with the shame of his own cowardice. The excitement in Dimitri's voice was crushing and oppressive. He spoke of his joy at the promise of finally leaving Corderro. In a way he had not been lied to. Tito imagined that shortly after their phone conversation he had indeed left Corderro, billowing up the smoke stacks in a cloud of hot ash. The official story was that he had moved to Ecuador with his family on state matters.

What did Dimitri do – or not do – to fall so magnanimously out of favour?

Tito never found out. Whatever the answer Dimitri had been completely unaware, convinced to the last that his employer had the utmost faith in him. Knowing that unassailable fact Tito was convinced that he would never sleep peacefully again.

His first meeting with El Rey took place in a basement room beneath the palace. It was a beautifully decorated chamber with figurines carved into the stone walls, but no natural light.

Like a mausoleum.

Eleanor was also in attendance, her ravishing appearance and apricot scent giving no indication as to the true horrors of her nature.

Coming face to face with the Emperor had once been described as being like meeting your maker. There was a sense that you were being weighed up in terms of worth, with the very real threat of judgement should you be deemed short of the mark. Holding a position of absolute power El Rey rarely felt the need to explain himself, or even to speak at all. He was content simply to stare and allow the silence to test those in his presence.

The space was so intimidating that it was tempting to fill it with garbled diatribe and saccharine sweet praise. Tito considered it wise to say nothing. He came through the test with flying colours and was installed in an office made entirely of gold. The trappings of office were so self-indulgent that he found it hard to breathe. El Rey would not give so much without expecting a greater sacrifice in return. Shortly afterwards huge sums of money started going astray.

The transactions were too complicated for Tito to follow. They looped round on themselves, weaving between multiple accounts, breaking into smaller amounts, branching and branching and branching until there was nothing left. Each day it got worse. Little by little he lost ground, lost his hair and lost belief in his ability to turn it around.

Tito was convinced it was Dimitri's doing, but he was unlikely to ever speak with his predecessor again, and such suspicions would not save him should he prove unable to recover the funds.

In Corderro the 'vicious circle' meant many different things to different people. To Tito is was the serrated circular edge of a coin, dropped from his grasp, rolling down a hill towards a drain. He was damned if he ran like a fool after his bounty and damned if he stood impotent and impoverished. Tito swallowed his pride and ran for all he was worth.

3.

He awoke with his face pressed against the desk. His cheek was numb and caked in saliva.

'Damn it,' he cursed under his breath, 'every night the same.'

While he'd slept the servant boy, Cheech, had brought in the day's post and placed it by his side. The curtains were open and the first hints of sunlight bathed his office in a haughty glow. Steam was rising from a piping-hot cup of coffee. The servant boy knew his habits better than he knew himself.

A sudden influx of caffeine purged him of his fatigue. He sat up straight.

And so it begins again, today as yesterday.

The morning papers were full of the usual articles – spurious, sycophantic praise for Corderro's beloved leader, speculation on the identity of El Ambiente, and mockery of Tito's economic policy. After a cursory skim he placed them all in the fire.

Next came the letters. Tito took a deep breath. It was commonplace to receive just as much abuse as he did genuine business correspondence. The first was a case in point:

To his Excellency El Comodin,

Our sincerest thanks in cancelling our contracts for the conceivable future. We can only assume that it is the latest in a series of spectacular policies that, whilst on appearance are turning our great nation into a rat-infested internationally scorned laughing stock, are in fact the workings of a great mind whose genius is unmatched in history.

As it has failed to reach your attention I should inform you that our company went into receivership six months ago.

With this in mind it has been a constant source of amusement during this troubled time that you have continued to pay us each month, and for that we thank you most gratefully and reverently.

Yours anonymously,
    Ex-employee
    Department of Sanitation (deceased)
P.S. As you seem to be unaware, 'The emperor isn't wearing any clothes. Everybody look – HE'S NAKED!!!'

Offended and enraged the Chancellor wrote to one of his clerks:

Roberto,
    Please arrange an insurance claim on the department of sanitation.
    Regards,
        T.M.

A ring of the bell summoned Cheech. The boy took the sealed memo from the Chancellor's hand and vanished from whence he came.

Tito noticed that his desk was littered with grey hairs.

Oh mi Dios, I am molting!

The Chancellor was convinced that if he could get through the financial hardships and reduce his stress levels then his hair would grow back.

Another generous slug of coffee temporarily restored equilibrium.

He placed the pile of letters to one side and opened the desk's top drawer. Taped to its surface was a crude drawing of Beelzebub, grinning with vampire's teeth and holding a three-pronged pitchfork. Written at the tips of the spikes were three words: 'Satellite – Insurance – Taxation'.

Tito had no recollection of having penned the obscure illustration. He'd awoken one morning from a particularly heavy night drowning his sorrows and found the parchment scrunched within his clenched fist. Its meaning was immediately apparent to him. It was a dark trinity, an underhand means of redemption, an inverted grace. Into its simple design the Chancellor had poured all of his hope.

As thrilled as he was to have discovered salvation Tito felt decidedly uncomfortable with the site of Satan's toothy chops and fiendishly wicked eyes gazing up at him from the tattered paper. Disturbed by its associations with the occult he hid the document within a drawer and rewrote the idea under the more respectable title 'Manifesto de Majagranzas.' But every so often he would open the drawer, listen to the rolling of ball bearings and watch in shivering awe as Lucifer's face reappeared, illuminating the road to restoration.

Each night as he dug deeper and deeper Tito told himself that it was not in a pit but a tunnel, burrowing beneath the foundations before making his way up into the light. Just lately his faith had begun to slip.

The premise of the manifesto was set out in an introductory chapter entitled 'A marriage of various economic deviances'.

4.

i. Satellites

Financial accounts can be looked upon as a high-level summation of an innumerably large number of infinitesimally small transactions. They attempt to condense so much information down to a few pages that often these figures are open to interpretation. This precipitates the accompaniment of copious notations in order to explain how the numbers are derived.

The debits, credits, assets and liabilities fluctuate and undulate, ebb and flow. They are malleable as clay to the potter's hands; moist and ripe for sculpting into deceptive shapes.

To this end the Chancellor formed Corderro Group plc – a country that was also a company. He created share options and floated them on a hastily constructed stock exchange called 'El Oportunidad Maravillosa'

('The Wondrous Opportunity').

The flotation was a mild success, but the main benefit of the exercise could be found in the formation of several discrete satellite companies. These satellites were affiliated to the Corderro group and orbited, as their name implied, unseen in the outer atmosphere. No one manned the fictitious phones and their company directors did not exist. They were vacant non-entities.

To these satellites the country's staggering deficit of payments were assigned. They were then carelessly left from the main accounts and buried within the folds of bureaucracy. To the unschooled naked eye the profit and loss looked positively booming.

The superheroes were Maria's idea.

When it came to naming the satellites Tito drew a complete blank. For all his cunning and devilry the Chancellor was sadly devoid of real imagination. Maria on the other hand read a lot of comic books and spent huge sections of her day lost in booze-fueled fantasy. She suggested 'Batman and Robin'.

Tito thought the idea ridiculous but could not think of anything with which to refute it. Batman and Robin it was! Wolverine and Cyclops Ltd soon followed suit. At the last count there were twenty-three such satellites, each harbouring a hundred million secrets.

5.

ii. Insurance

The balance sheet for Corderro Group plc showed assets in excess of 26 billion (US) dollars, most of which were locked within the bricks and mortar of the city's lavish architectural heritage, none of which was of any use to the Chancellor.

What Tito needed was cash – cold, hard, preferably foreign cash.

The buildings could not be sold as no one within the country was rich enough to buy them, and overseas investors were barred from purchasing due to mounting international sanctions.

'There has to be some way of unlocking the wealth,' he told himself over and over. Tito set his mind to the task in hand. Inspiration finally came from the most unlikely of sources – his long-suffering wife, Elizabeth.

Coming home from the opera one night the estranged couple were involved in a minor car accident. As they sat waiting at a set of traffic lights a van rolled forwards and struck them. Tito's vehicle, a Rolls Royce

Silver Ghost was his pride and joy. He was incensed to a point of rage far beyond his meagre physique.

My hair!

It was no use. He was livid. Tito punched the steering wheel and heard something heavy fall from the undercarriage. Through his wing mirror he watched the other driver emerging sheepishly.

'It's the black sedan for you my friend,' the Chancellor growled under his breath.

'TITO!' Elizabeth chided. 'Do not say such things. It's not the end of the world, and besides, we're insured.'

'THAT'S IT!' He jumped up banging his head. 'THAT'S IT!' He kissed Elizabeth, their first intimate act in years. It would also be their last.

The next morning Tito began the lengthy task of having the city's most lavish buildings revalued and insured against every conceivable and inconceivable eventuality – flood, fire, theft, arson, acts of God, acts of terrorism, anything and everything he could later claim for.

At first his ventures saddled the country with even greater debts, but once Tito concluded that he was insured to the hilt he opened the desk drawer, stared at his feeble effigy of the Prince of Darkness, and whispered, 'Now I truly make a pact with the devil.'

As if to mock him thunder echoed dramatically in the heavens.

He picked up the phone and called Eleanor Blake.

Eleanor was the head of Corderro's military. She had recently taken up residency in the palace and was rumoured to have pouted her way into the Emperor's bed.

Tito liked to look upon her as a supermodel who'd fallen prey to demonic possession – flawlessly beautiful on the outside, malevolent and wretched on the inside, mercilessly assiduous in her pursuit of others' misery, and rotten to the core. Never before had so sumptuously stunning a skin covered so hideous a frame.

When Eleanor answered in her plummy aristocratic warble the Chancellor stumbled over his words like a drunkard. Foretelling this occurrence Tito had written his pitch on a large sheet of paper to act as a prompt should his mind go inextricably blank. The premise of the fabrication was simple:

He'd received word from a trusted source that El Ambiente was hiding in a building on the outskirts of town. The land needed to be cleared for redevelopment, Tito needed an influx of funds, and El Ambiente needed to be wiped from the face of the earth. Why not rig the building with explosives and catch the terrorist off guard?

As expected Eleanor had loved the idea.

'Why Tee-toh,' she sighed, 'you are not the snivelling bean-counter I took you for.'

'Thank you,' he'd replied before realizing his folly.

'It shall be done within the hour.'

The line went dead.

The building in question had been secretly taken over by an organization which, like Tito, shared an affinity for satellites. It was used mainly as a soup kitchen for the homeless and served as a hostel during the evenings. As the people within went about the business of surviving they suddenly found themselves sealed within the walls by steel plates, driven against the doors and windows by forklift trucks and held in place by huge bolts fired into the masonry.

Finding the building inhabited by crowds of people was a bonus as far as Eleanor was concerned. With clinical delight she barked orders to her men who set charges, withdrew to a safe distance, detonated the explosives and, once the dust had settled, retrieved the steel plates.

She phoned the Chancellor to relay the mission's success, carefully omitting the human casualties from her report. In his sublime ignorance of events Tito was delighted. He immediately deplored the act in public as 'the despicable and cowardly act of a desperate man'. A sizable claim was made against a cartel of insurance companies and the money rolled in. Flush with the success of his first foray into what he called 'inverse larceny', Tito set about searching for another opportunity.

That night Maria rolled over in her sleep and slapped him hard in the face. Tito was annoyed. It was the first time in weeks that he'd slept in a bed as opposed to at his desk. The moon cast monstrous shadows across a gothic-looking candelabrum. He got up and promptly stubbed his toe against a chest of drawers.

Cursing under his breath he lit the candelabrum and took it into his study. As soon as Tito sat down the ideas began to flow thick and fast. It was as if he were channelling some restless spirit. He wrote frantically:

The secret to good accounting is knowing where to assign blame.
And to whom.
El Ambiente.
I have killed my source of income.

I need to resurrect him.

Tito got up and ran to the kitchen. Rifling through the drawers he quickly found what he was looking for – two tubes of tomato puree. He stuffed them into his dressing gown and tiptoed out into the corridor.

At the palace gates he wound down the window, saluted the jaundiced-looking guards and apologized for the inconvenience, citing urgent financial duties across town. The guards observed his attire with bemused frowns but waved him through without comment. The curfew had come into force several hours beforehand. Even with his social standing Tito was taking an immense risk being out in the open.

He drove at breakneck speed into the heart of the Corderro and to the city hall. Using the tomato puree he daubed El Ambiente's tag on the wall in a symbol six feet high:

His task complete he leapt back into the car and screeched away from the crime scene. Within the hour he was safety tucked up next to Maria waiting for the graffiti to be discovered.

He was in luck. When Cheech brought the papers the next morning he found that it had made the front page. Tito snatched up the phone and called Eleanor.

'*El Comedin*, what a *pleasant* surprise,' she greeted sarcastically.

I wish she wouldn't call me that.

Tito started confidently, but his nerve quickly failed him. 'Unfortunately, it appears that the illusive El Ambiente was not hiding in said building as . . . previously presupposed necessitating the . . . necessity of . . . er . . . further action.'

'Yesssss,' Eleanor hissed, 'so I'd heard. I understand he used some kind of tomato paste. How *unusual* of him. '

'Mmm, I agree,' Tito replied trying to sound composed. 'It's very disappointing, but on a positive note I may know where he is.'

'Are you toying with me, Chancellor?' Eleanor sneered.

'Not at all . . . an informant . . . anonymous . . . er . . . abandoned gasworks.'

'I see . . . I suppose you want me to blow it up.'

'It couldn't hurt.'

'Fine, give me the address and it will be done within the hour.'

So began their fruitful if precarious relationship. At the last count there had been forty-seven such insurance claims. El Ambiente was still very much at large.

6.

iii. Taxation

Tito considered the principles of taxation too self-explanatory to document within his manifesto. What he failed to understand was both the law of diminishing returns and the importance of securing the control and respect of his subordinates. Not only had they failed to inform him that most people no longer declared any earnings and subsequently paid no tax, they were also in the process of embezzling what little did arrive through the Treasury gates.

7.

Legal dept
To whom it may concern,

I wish to register the names 'Spiderman' and 'Hercules' as limited companies. Please progress these with all speed, and inform me once they are legal entities.
          Regards,
                    T.M

8.

The phone rang.

Oh mi Dios! Who would call at such an unsociable hour?

'Yes?'

'Go to the window El Comedin,' Eleanor commanded.

Feebly Tito obeyed. He got halfway across the room before the cord snapped tight. 'The phone will not reach.'

'Then *put it down*. You will not need it. My message will be clear.'

Tito's mind presumed the worst.

Sniper? Got to be. Right between the eyes.

I cannot go willingly to my own demise.

'What it is?' he whined.

'Just go to the window.'

How he hated being bossed around by a woman half his age.

Eleanor had timed her call to coincide with the sunrise. The city seemed to have found a moment's repose, and languished in a golden autumn hue. The site of the ocean's calm waves settled his nerves. Corderro was a truly beautiful place. Tito asked himself why he hadn't noticed this before.

High up in the hills he could see a black mass snaking its way down towards the coast – a fleet of black sedans leaving their lair for another day of abductions.

'Come back to bed,' Maria sang from the boudoir. Tito winced at the thought of Eleanor overhearing the request and using it to blackmail him.

'In a minute, dearest,' he replied, trying to sound as bored and morose as when he spoke to Elizabeth.

His eyes remained fixed on the horizon.

Come on Eleanor! I thought you said it would be clear?

At the very heart of the market district a large section of the suburb silently disappeared in a bilious, blanketing cloud. Perversely Tito's first thought was of a cash register, ringing the ill-gotten gains of another successful reclamation. A broad smile spread across his highly strung face.

Moments later the delayed din reached his ears.

It was too much to take in, too many conflicting noises. Tito clutched his forehead and tried to disseminate the sounds – rumbling, growling destruction, car alarms, creatures crying, fizzling electricity, the cracking of flames.

Silence.

And then the screaming started.

Tito realized that there were no insurance claims scheduled in the market district. His smile slowly became a warped and insane grimace.

The message could not have been any clearer.

I am not your lap dog. I cannot be tamed or used as an economic instrument. I have broken my leash and am running amuck.

From the abandoned telephone receiver Tito could hear the tinny reverberations of Eleanor's laughter.

Chapter 5

Underbelly

1.

After Katrina and the others had left the harbour Kelly returned to the cover of the tarpaulin, but found that he could not recapture his composure.

He was shaken by the encounter, far more than he would admit, even to himself. It threw up a whole host of revelations, and reminded him of things he had worked long and hard to forget.

A crane swept in overhead carrying a bundle of metal tubes. As soon as it touched down men appeared from nowhere, climbing over the gigantic metal cylinders, shouting orders at one another and loosening straps. Kelly was glad of the distraction. He took a deep breath and contemplated his coffee. 'Nothing else,' he breathed. 'Just the coffee, the circular flow of liquid, the steam rising, the aroma, the . . . '

It was no use. He couldn't shake the thoughts that preyed upon his mind.

The most immediate of which was his own staggering lack of judgement in trusting Paolo and Raoul. It made him cringe to think of all the secrets and confidences to which they had been privy.

Did you learn so little from the old world that you would repeat every foolish act in the new?

They were complicit in his crimes, of course, but Kelly took little comfort. Anything that involved reliance upon others could not be considered advantageous.

But worse than his ex-colleagues was the woman – Esperanza. She had brought something far worse than her clumsy arrogance or pitiful lack of experience. It was the awful belief that anything was possible; a sense of idealistic invincibility. Take something like that to heart and there was no telling where it might lead you. The ramifications of crushing disappointment were enough to shake the foundations of any man, or woman. Katrina had yet to learn this dark truth. Kelly knew it all too well.

A number of her traits remind me of . . .

The smuggler shot his feet.

Now she really has got under your skin.

There was nothing to be gained from dwelling on her words, but much to lose. Even now he could see blackball eyes emerging from his mind, staring at him longingly, forming faces that would never again see the light of day.

He swilled the now tepid liquid between his teeth and turned to face the outer bartering dens. There was always so much to see, so many colourful characters, rapid interchanging activities, sleight of hands, lightning-fast exchanges, squabbles, looks of invented outrage and the endless flow of money. To watch it all kept his mind constantly in motion, preventing it from stalling and forming a stagnant pool of self-pity.

The faces faded from view, replaced with hustle and vibrancy. El Puerto de Las Ondas Verdes seemed oblivious to him. He remained as always inconspicuous.

2.

Sometimes a window of opportunity arose that was so small it required a split-second decision and precise, confident execution in order to capitalize upon it. The smugglers referred to such moments as 'flickers' – a chance that arrives and vanishes in the blink of an eye.

Kelly watched as two men emerged from a van and walked towards the trading pits. From first glance it was clear they were amateurs. There was an unnecessary swagger and bravado to their movement, a conscious effort to appear intimidating. They kept glancing at one another as if they were unsure of their own relationship and had to keep re-affirming it with every step. The biggest give-away was how much they talked. Reaching the pits they entered into a river of spurious, barely distinguishable street slang. This was accompanied by dramatic arm movements, hand clapping and chin rubbing.

In Corderro the more you knew, the less you needed to say; the greater the embellishment, the greater the opportunity.

Flicker.

Kelly stood up and undid the bolts that held the crate's steel doors in place. He knew that he had to act quickly, but the encounter with Katrina had given him doubt in his own ability.

The doors swung open revealing an empty chamber. The two men were out of earshot and failed to hear the screech of hinges. Kelly moved to their van, ever so slowly, calm, measured paces. His movement blended seamlessly into peripheral vision. There was no key in the ignition but the door had been left unlocked. Kelly jumped into the cab and disengaged the handbrake. The van began to roll backwards. He turned the wheel and used the mirrors to guide the vehicle into the gaping metal mouth that waited to swallow it. The van slid smoothly into the space. Kelly re-engaged the handbrake, stepped out, closed and bolted the door. The whole operation took a matter of seconds.

'Good,' he thought; his nerves steadied.

There had been no time to check the contents. He would do so tomorrow, once the amateurs had given up their search. Even if it was empty the vehicle would fetch a good price.

Kelly made his way over to the men he had just robbed, not out of a vindictive relish, more to remind himself of the pitfalls in his chosen profession. Each day brought with it the threat of complacency. A loss of focus would spell his certain downfall. He had seen it happen many times to the undisciplined hoards that surrounded him. The same fate would befall the two men in front of him. It was a fact that neither elated nor upset him. He moved on.

The aroma of cold coffee mingled with the stench of fish packed in ice. Other scents lurked beneath, hard to define – citrus perhaps, or cinnamon? A variety of languages could be heard, Spanish and English mainly, but also smatterings of Russian, Italian and even Urdu.

Kelly watched the events unfold with apparent disinterest, no detail escaping his attention. He entered into discussions over two dozen dried cowhides. When a reasonable price was reached Kelly stopped haggling. He could have pushed much further, but it didn't pay to gain a reputation. As it stood he would make a healthy mark-up. It was important to keep the long-term game in mind at all times.

Over the next few hours he made many purchases – a case of ornate ceramic tiles, a 100cc motorbike (which he quickly resold for significant gain), fifty pineapples, a cast-iron fireplace, three cases of red wine, a tea chest full of Bibles (always popular during times of conflict), various lengths of timber, a set of brass taps and several other equally diverse choices.

None of the items were particularly high value. Kelly was careful to avoid jewellery and high-tech toys. Trading is such commodities was tantamount to drawing a target on your head. Patience was the key.

Build slowly. Let no one see what you are amassing.

Interspersed amongst the bartering Kelly also managed to pick several pockets. He only kept the paper money, throwing cards, keys, coins and wallets into the sea. By mid afternoon he had around 300 US dollars and over a thousand petras. The latter joined the wallets beneath the waves.

At four o'clock he stopped for another coffee. It was best not to appear too busy. There needed to be an element of desperation to your trading so that the guards believed you were working just to stay alive.

He hunkered down by the crate containing the stolen van and took a flask from his pocket. Annoyingly Katrina once again wormed her way into his thoughts.

She's going to expose you, either maliciously or accidentally.
What to do?

A white van drove into the trading pit. Paolo was behind the wheel. The two men locked eyes. Neither flinched as one passed slowly in front of the other. Kelly was furious. Paolo looked resolute. The van moved beyond his vision.

Another coffee break ruined!

Kelly put the flask back in his pocket unopened and returned to the trading pits. Along the way he encountered the two amateurs from earlier. They were rowing, openly accusing each other of theft. Their gestures became threatening. For Kelly there was no guilt at having been the catalyst, only mild amusement at their continued and rapid descent.

Almost immediately he was presented with another opportunity.

Flicker.
Twice in one day!

Three men engaged in minimalist discussions, their backs turned, shrink-wrapped palettes stacked above a hydraulic trolley. Kelly walked by unnoticed. As he passed the trolley his hands closed around the handle. The palettes began to move. His face projected a vision of boredom, as if he found the exercise tedious. No one questioned his actions. No one saw.

As he loaded the palettes into his own van a daily mantra echoed in his mind.

Don't be greedy.

It was his cue to stop. Enough for one day.

3.

At the port gates Kelly presented the guard on duty with his roster. The roster was the most important object in a trader's possession. It detailed what goods you brought with you when entering, and what you left with. A levy was then charged accordingly.

It was always a good idea to find something quirky to include on the list; something comical or obscure like a fancy-dress costume or a trampoline. It made a tradesman look harmless or even foolish, and reduced the threat of being searched. In the past Kelly had declared items such as karaoke machines, juggling balls, jukeboxes, clogs and jester's hats. Today he included an inflatable dinghy.

Normally he was waved through without incident, but on this occasion the guard decided to check that the contents matched the roster. Kelly wasn't worried. Despite dishonesty in every other aspect he never lied on the roster. There was simply no point – the risks were far too great. He waited in the cab whilst the checks took place. The guard would no doubt take something as a 'gift'. Standing over him would only make the moment awkward.

After a brief pause he was waved through without incident.

For the first 300 yards in every direction the streets were an extension of the port. Here the more desperate of Corderro's underbelly traded their wears – worthless trinkets, alcohol, tobacco, themselves. Most had been banned from the port and were now ripe for devouring. They arranged their goods at the centre of blankets. In the event of a black sedan's arrival the four corners could be pulled into a primitive sack which was hoisted over the shoulder as they literally ran for their lives.

Kelly hardly registered them any more. To the smuggler they were life's losers, placed there by their own inadequacy. He could think of no worse fate than relying on the charity of others. He himself had once been forced into such a position. Life had taught him that there was no excuse for wallowing in sorrow. You had to bite the hand that fed you, not timidly accept its patronizing offer.

Whilst the destination was the same each day, the route that he took always varied considerably. Nothing could ever be left to chance; complacency bred far more than contempt. Kelly followed the coastal road, briefly enjoying a period of solitude before turning right onto downtown Corderro. A thick fog had enveloped the streets leading off the sea front. The phenomenon was known as La Fantasma ('the ghost') and was an ever-present feature of the city. Common folklore stated that La Fantasma was made from the souls of those murdered in the capital since its bloody inception. As such it was believed to grow thicker by the hour.

Downtown had once been the cultural hub of Corderro, but its valuable buildings had proven too tempting for the Chancellor. It was now considered the most dangerous suburb to live in. The roads were strewn with debris and the remaining structures were perpetually bathed in beige brick dust.

Kelly weaved his way between the obstacles, making a mental note as to what had disappeared from the horizon since his last visit. Downtown merged with Cuidad Centro ('Central City'). This in turn became the Market quarter.

Kelly relaxed a little and took his foot off the accelerator. He always felt much safer once inside the bohemian bowels of the city. The Market quarter had once consisted of sixteen streets – eight horizontal and eight vertical forming a grid. Over the centuries the uniformity had been hacked up into side streets, alleyways and courtyards. Within its winding roads could be found a seductive fusion of escapism, psychedelic art, folk music, soap boxing and chemical intoxication. The people within its boundaries were not immune from abduction, but most of those who were taken were not aware of what was happening to them.

A black sedan appeared in Kelly's wing mirror – cruising, engine purring, impenetrable windows, hidden content. He took the next turning, a left into a narrow cobbled path, resisting the urge to put his foot down. Seconds later the black sedan followed him, keeping its distance, stalking.

It's random. Don't lose you head.

He let the steering flow through his finger, turning left once more.

The black sedan followed.

Kelly had envisaged this eventuality many times. Now that it was upon him he was surprised at how sedate he felt. He reached down and opened the glove box. The compartment housed a revolver.

'*Don't stop me,*' he willed. It wasn't unheard of for the black sedans to follow vehicles for many miles before veering off. Uncommon, but not unheard of.

He tried to envisage what kind of person could robotically drive around all day abducting people at random – unemotional and detached.

Perhaps the same kind that would robotically smuggle goods day in day out?
He stared at the dark window.
If you stop me I will kill you.
Despite his outwardly aggressive persona Kelly had never lifted a finger in anger against another human being, but the intent was there, stored away over a lifetime of loss, waiting for its moment to burst out and ravage the world. He eased up, allowing the sedan to move closer.
Turn away. I dare you to stop me!
Slower still, the revolver waiting to be taken up, the black sedan following.
A T-junction up ahead; the right-hand turning a dead end.
If I take another left I will have gone full circle.
Damned if you do; damned if you don't.
He swung the van to the right and parked up in a single fluid motion.
And then he waited.
The black sedan's engine stopped dead. It continued to roll forward. The silence was deafening.
They're taunting me.
Keep moving . . . keep moving.
One of its back doors opened. The vehicle was still moving. A foot appeared, a shiny leather boot with thick soles. Kelly reached for the revolver.
OK then.
Now his heart was pumping. He accepted the confrontation as inevitable and tried to summon the best course of action.
Wait until they're out in the open, reverse at speed, aim strai . . .
The leather-clad foot retreated, the door closed and the black sedan sped away.
For a long time afterwards Kelly sat staring into the wing mirror at the empty road behind him. Finally, when he was sure they were gone he released his grip on the weapon, turned on the engine and looked down into his lap. His shirt was wet. Kelly realized that he was crying.

4.

El Sacramento – the roofless, guestless hotel lay hidden in the heart of the market quarter. In more eloquent times its lavish halls and exquisitely decorated courtyards had hosted presidential banquets, but in recent decades it had fallen into disrepute and scandal when falling revenues had forced the owner to sublet it to prostitutes. The final nail was hammered in during a failed coup against El Rey when it was struck by a stray missile.

Shortly afterwards the hotel's owner was rumoured to have died of a broken heart, leaving the now worthless estate to his son Alfonso. Alfonso was an extremely camp, womanizing midget who lived in the lower floors with his long-suffering wife Elsa, seven children and various destitute family members. He was always dressed in tiny, garish, three-piece suits, and made his living by fencing stolen goods. Though the money was good he had never got round to fixing the roof.

Kelly drove into the courtyard and parked by the outdoor reception desk.

Alfonso was perched on a stool, a large tome open in one hand, a pink cocktail in the other. Today's choice of suit was a double-breasted aquamarine with bright-yellow cravat, black shirt and an orange carnation. Despite his bizarre appearance Kelly always felt strangely envious of the man. Alfonso had achieved what he could not – balance. In the midst of hardship he was happy, well-off, universally respected and revered as an astute entrepreneur. He had ascended to a position whereby he never had to lift a finger, and never missed an opportunity to boast of what he called his 'arduous routine'. After a hearty breakfast Alfonso and his wife would watch the sun rise. They would then wash, feed and dress their children before taking them to school. Alfonso drove an ice-cream van which he'd converted into a people carrier. His rationale was that a black sedan would never pull over so comical a vehicle as they would look positively ridiculous. So far he had been proved correct. Returning from the school run he would spend the early part of the day dishing out orders to his various nephews. These usually included lugging incredibly heavy, illegally obtained goods in and out of the hotel's many chambers. After lunch he would have a siesta and then commence the slow slurry march into evening. This typically entailed sitting at the reception desk soaking up great works of literature whilst his long-suffering dogsbodies brought out a continuous stream of liquid refreshment. A further siesta brought him to early evening by which time he was comfortably inebriated. It was around about then that he and Kelly normally did business. Despite the units of alcohol flowing through his veins Alfonso was as sharp as a pinhead. He claimed that the booze helped focus his mind by rendering most of his motor-neuron skills redundant, while channelling the remaining energy into his commercial acumen. After the financial transactions of the day were complete Alfonso would enjoy an evening meal so lavish it bordered on being a banquet, before donning attire even more outrageous than his day-ware, and going out on the prowl until the early hours. On the frequent occasions that he successfully ensnared a young woman he would bring her back to the hotel and hide his extramarital liaison in one of the many empty rooms. Alfonso's wife was well aware of these lapses in monogamy, but chose to turn a blind eye for the sake of the children. He always ensured that he was back by her side before she awoke, never beat her, was kind, and showered his family with every gift imaginable. In Corderro her fate could have been so much worse. She was grateful that her loss was limited to heartache.

Alfonso looked up from his reading. 'Ah, Slim,' he greeted. 'What delights do you have for me today?'

'Leather, wine, pineapples, Bibles and a twenty-five-foot rubber dinghy,' the smuggler replied.

'*Dinghy*? Does it have an outboard motor?'

'No.'

'Well what use it that?'

'I don't know. You're the fence. Maybe you could paddle your escape to Cuba?'

'Out of one frying pan!'

Alfonso rose somewhat shakily to his feet and barked slurred orders into the hotel. The courtyard was immediately filled with large men in filthy clothes. Alfonso pointed at the van. Within seconds they had checked the contents against Kelly's roster and whisked it away to various corners of the hotel.

The arrangement between the two men was simple. Alfonso took everything that Kelly offered, sold what he could (which was nearly always everything) and split the money evenly. Alfonso lagged in payment by a week at a time. The relationship had served them well for as long as either could remember.

'How's business?' Kelly inquired. His interest was purely superficial, a necessary precursor to being paid. Alfonso knew this well enough, but never missed the opportunity to stand on ceremony.

'Terrible! Oh my friend I am caught up in a torrent. My income has reached new heights, but so too have my outgoings. Every man in Corderro has his own vicious circle to contend with. For me it is my libido! *Mi Dios,* I cannot seem to keep my trousers on for more than a few hours at a time. At first I thought that I was in paradise, the land of milk and honey, sex on tap, drowning in money, but now I see that I am a fly trapped in a spider's web. I have so many mistresses my heart is bursting at the seams, and as for my genitalia, oh my! I am morphing into a single, giant, relentlessly ejaculating testicular gland.'

'Thank you. That's an image I shall take with me to the grave.'

'Seriously, I am beside myself.' Alfonso winked. 'All I can think to do by way of an antidote is to brag about it to everyone who walks through my door!' The hotelier let out a drunken chuckle.

'How does your wife feel about it?'

'I hardly think you are one to lecture me on morality!'

'Quite right. Give me my money and I shall take my pious opinions elsewhere.'

Alfonso reached into his pocket and produced a wad of US dollars. 'Money well earned, oh judgemental one.'

Kelly always killed the conversation dead whenever women were mentioned. The hotelier had yet to discover why. Alfonso handed over the money.

'You know, each day I am increasingly astounded that a man such as yourself, a free man with a British passport, *un pasaporte a la libertad,* should turn up at my door with his vagabond wares, evening after evening, all shrouded in grief and mystery, taking the risks that you do. Surely you must have amassed a fortune by now? Why do it? Why not take what you have earned and become an investor? Do what others cannot – leave?'

Alfonso made the same little speech every time they met, and every time Kelly gave a wily smile and changed the subject. 'I am thinking,' the hotelier continued, 'that you are engaged in some misguided act of attrition; a purging of the soul via penance?'

'All acts of attrition are misguided.'

'That does not answer my question.'

'No it does not. See you tomorrow.'

5.

He made two stops on his way back from Alfonso's. The first was El Café Empressario. Arty Bey greeted him with his usual self-flagellating abuse.

'Ah, I see the rats are deserting the sinking port for another day.

Ernesto! Fetch some cheese for our guest.'

Kelly sat down beside him at one of the outdoor tables and shook his head. 'You're thinking of mice. Rats eat flesh. Try to get your facts straight when insulting someone. Otherwise you look foolish.'

Arty shrugged. 'Rat, mouse, whatever. What brings you scurrying my way?'

'Where else can I be assured of such stimulating conversation?'

In truth Kelly visited the café owner out of necessity rather than desire. As a known informer Arty was a dangerous man. More people had disappeared from outside his establishment than from any other location in the city. Eleanor Blake herself often paid the café a personal visit and always left full to the brim with new knowledge. Kelly avoided being ensnared by being more valuable to the café owner than the benefits of betraying him. Even so the relationship was a precarious one.

'How many more times am I going to have to ask you to steal me some coconuts?' Arty moaned.

'They don't grow on trees, you know!' Kelly replied in kind. 'I am reliably informed that a shipment is coming in on Wednesday, as I have reminded you every day for the last week. I can't make it arrive any sooner.'

'Fine, then what are you going to provide by way of recompense?'

'I wasn't aware that I was in your debt.' Kelly looked over his shoulder. 'The service in this place is shocking. You run a loose ship, Arty. Hey Ernesto!'

The scrawny waiter appeared and greeted him with a knowing smile.

'What are the chances of getting a double espresso sometime before the curfew kicks in?'

'What have you got in return?' Arty interjected.

'You do actually *want* my custom?'

'Not necessarily.'

'What do you think I have?' Kelly replied waving a 20-dollar bill.

Ernesto refused the offer of money, pointing instead to his arm. 'How about your wristwatch?'

Kelly shrugged. 'Fair enough.'

The watch was virtually worthless anyway. Kelly was never affluent for fear of needlessly drawing attention.

'A man after my own heart,' the café owner beamed approvingly as the waiter disappeared inside.

When his drink arrived Kelly took his time to enjoy it. He endured Arty's grotesque observations and let the caffeine hit slowly revive his flagging spirit. He was bombarded with lurid stories concerning a new brothel that had opened in the industrial quarter, the implications of which did not bear dwelling on. With a final surge of hot black liquid Kelly rose to his feet. Ernesto stepped out to remove his cup.

'*Hasta la revolucion,*' Kelly whispered under his breath with a rare show of warmth.

'*Siempre,*' Ernesto whispered back.

6.

He met Miguel as he did every weekday, in an alley behind El Banco Nationale at 6.50 pm. Miguel was one of the less corrupt clerks at the bank in that his fraudulent activities only stretched as far as was required to support his family. He was short and stooping, though only in his early thirties, with a cautious methodical nature that mirrored the smuggler's.

Kelly handed over a bag containing the money from Alfonso and various other ill-gotten takings.

'Good day?' Miguel asked weighing up the bag's content.

'Good takings,' Kelly replied. 'Can't comment on the day.'

The two men had a system that had served them well for two years. Kelly couldn't shift large amounts of raw currency without evoking draconian levels of taxation, as well as revealing himself to the authorities. With the collapse of the economy Miguel no longer earned enough to eat, let alone pay the mortgage. The arrangement was simple: Kelly gave Miguel the money and Miguel in turn laundered it through a myriad of dummy companies before finally depositing it in one of several dozen accounts, for which he took a 10 per cent fee.

'Slim, you're gonna have to find yourself another bean-counter. I can't do this any more. It's not that I'm not grateful for everything you've given us. It's just getting too dangerous. I've got to get my wife and kids out.'

If Kelly was angry or disappointed it didn't show. 'I understand. This is no place to raise a family. Do you have a means of leaving?'

Miguel's stoop intensified as if he were bearing a heavy load on his back. 'Well, to tell you the truth I was kind of hoping you would be able to suggest something.'

Strangely Kelly found himself thinking of Katrina and Satellite. The thought annoyed him. Miguel had been a good business associate. He

63

would not reward him by trusting his fate to imbeciles.

'I take it you don't have a passport?'

'Confiscated.'

He considered the options for a moment. 'OK, there's a man in the port called Piedro Milagro. He exports extremely low-quality manikins to discount department stores around the world. The products are too bulky and next to worthless for smugglers to worry about. The guards only inspect one truckload in ten. Your odds would be good. Here, let me give you his address. *Don't* say that I sent you.'

Miguel's prematurely aged features lightened. 'No, no, of course not. Thank you, Slim. I can't tell you how much this means to me.'

Kelly did not like anyone feeling indebted to him. It invariably meant further communication and a passing of unwelcome gratitude back and forth.

'Don't mention it. Make sure you get a truck bound for somewhere like Nicaragua or Honduras – somewhere you can legitimately claim asylum.'

They shook hands.

'See you in the next life.'

Kelly didn't wait for a response.

7.

Across the street from El Banco Nationale an old man in dirty overalls was working feverishly to scrub a large letter '*A*' from the front of his shop. Kelly scoffed. El Ambiente may have captured the imagination of the city in recent months, but to him he was just a foolish idealist. He only had to look into his own nature to see that men were essentially selfish creatures. There could be no redemption when people did not seek to be redeemed.

It was late evening, getting close to curfew. People were streaming past him in a comical, haphazard motion. To Kelly it was as if they were being remote-controlled. Walking slowly and purposefully amidst the pandemonium he silently despised them for their docile indifference, the way in which they allowed themselves to be puppets to some unseen will.

Not one of them is master of their own destiny.

So what if I'm an opportunist fly on a rotting corpse? Better that than being herded around like cattle to the slaughter.

At a crossroads between the Market quarter and the red-light district the crowds thinned unexpectedly. In the middle of the road, lashed to a wooden rocking chair, sat a young man barely out of his teens. He was naked and both his wrists had been slashed. The cuts were jagged and heavily bruised. He had clearly thrashed violently against his restraints as life ebbed away. Hung around his neck by a scrawny piece of rope was a sign, presumably daubed in his own blood with the word *traidor* ('traitor').

Kelly didn't flinch as others did, but neither did he take his eyes off the man as he walked past. Acts of this kind were commonplace. Victims were always in rocking chairs so that they could be pushed from the back of speeding vans without falling over, and they were always young. It was as if El Rey was saying to the city, '*I will strike at what is most precious to you. I will take those who have the most to lose.*'

There were beggars outside the black metal steps that led to his apartment. Mostly they were harmless individuals, but some were known to attack in packs, stripping a person of their every possession. Kelly didn't want to take any chances. He took a handful of notes from his pocket and threw them over his head. The beggars immediately dispersed, chasing after the spoils.

'Let's not make this a habit,' he called after them as he ascended the walkway.

There was a note tacked to the steel door in front of him.

Slim,
    Your rent is due (PANG).
    It's my daughter's birthday next week. She could do with a gold necklace.
    Martine

PANG – the universal acronym for '*Petras are no good.*'

'Fair enough,' he muttered and screwed the note into a ball.

The door slammed shut with the cold abrasiveness of a prison cell, not so much sealing him in as sealing out the world. Shoulders eased and he breathed deeply, shedding the day's dishonesty.

The apartment was open plan and finely furnished with some of the more valuable spoils of his plunder. A large oak dining table formed the centrepiece, surrounded by rich burgundy coloured velvet arm chairs, shelves lined with first- addition hardbacks, no photographs. The walls were adorned with stunning swirls of abstract art, all vaguely representing the female form.

He took off his beanie hat and ran a hand through untidy salt and pepper hair before depositing his coat unceremoniously on the floor. Through a large window at the back of the apartment he could see nothing but the ocean.

He took the phone from the window sill and dialled a number.

'Hello?'

It was a woman's voice. Kelly closed his eyes and remained silent. There was a lengthy pause before the woman spoke again.

'Come home . . . time heals all wounds.'

He hung up.

Free from the constraints of Corderro's ever-watchful eye Kelly drifted into his evening ritual. One remote control activated low lighting throughout the apartment, another set 'Moonlight Sonata' in motion on the surround sound. He ran a bath and returned to grind coffee beans and open a bottle of red. The wine settled as he heated a pan, took a bloodied steak from the fridge and fixed himself another double espresso. The rich delicate touch of piano masked the sound of sizzling meat. He ate at the corner of the vast dining table, closing his eyes with every mouthful, and washed it down with a glass of wine, by which time the bath had sufficiently cooled.

His clothes fell off him like chains from a convict and he slid silently into the soothing water. By the time the music ended the curfew was in place and the city was deathly quiet. He had done well tonight. It had taken longer than usual for the thought to come creeping as it did every night.

How much longer?

The water was becoming uncomfortably cold, but not enough to deter the sleep that rushed over him.

Soon . . . soon.

Chapter 6

Memoirs

1.

High up in a bombed-out shell that used to be a cigar factory Carlos sat gazing down at the city. His body was cupped within a large glass-less circular window frame forming a crescent moon. An empty bottle of wine lay abandoned on the scorched floorboards and he was making good progress through a second.

Isabella's journal lay open in his lap.

This is wrong, hermano. It is not the way to go about your quest.

Carlos had not intended to steal the book. It had been an opportunistic act, made on the spur of the moment.

A betrayal of trust before trust has even been established! Now you will struggle where you could have soared effortlessly.

No matter, it cannot be helped now.

He looked down at the virgin words set before him.

Yes it can, you can return it unread.

She would not believe you of course, but then that hardly seems the point!

This is out of character. Shame is a means of the soul telling you that you have strayed from the path.

This is not the first important manuscript you have stolen.

But it will be the last.

You say that, but you cannot be sure. Necessity has no master.

Carlos, you are drunk and talking in riddles. You are a scoundrel, not a gentleman.

No . . . the other way around.

Reading the hopes and aspirations of another is the worst kind of intrusion. Better to burgle their home, or rob them in broad daylight.

Technically you have *robbed her in broad daylight!*

Close the book and give it back.

I can't.

Why not?

Because I need to know if she has done what Jonathan asked of her.

The same cyclical dilemma had churned around his head for several hours. With the onset of intoxication Carlos had hoped for a decision – either obstinacy, or else weak submission. Instead, he'd grown increasingly emotional and dithery.

He tried to clear his mind and concentrate on the people far below. Life continued to be a marvel, all the change taking place, the collisions and coincidences.

What is the greater good?

The greater good is to help her find Jonathan.

That's not what I meant and you know it. You can't fool me, I'm you!

Carlos took a generous slug of red wine.

How will you feel if you read Isabella's journal and find out that she's a success?

Happy but guilty.

How will you feel if you read her journal and find out that she's a failure?

Sad but guilty.

How about if you don't read it at all?

Virtuous but frustrated.

So, basically the choice comes down to guilt or frustration?

Yes, I suppose it does.

You're not going to come to a conclusion. Why don't you just toss a coin?

Good idea!

He reached into his pocket and pulled out a wallet. The worn leather pouch was bloated with loose change that spilled from his clumsy hands and rolled into various cracks and crevices. Carlos climbed out of his concrete hammock, scurried around on hands and knees and retrieved several one-petra coins.

Heads you read the journal and suffer the guilt, tails you don't and endure the frustration.

The first and second coins disappeared through the glass-less window. The third coin spun away so that he had to lunge forward in order to catch it. Carlos crashed to the ground, his nerve endings ignorant of the various bumps and abrasions incurred. He cupped the coin triumphantly and rose to his feet.

Finally an outcome.

It was tails.

Carlos frowned at the coin and grumbled something illegible.

Best of three.

He threw again.

Tails.
Best of five.
Tails.
Best of seven
Oh you idiot! You've wasted a whole afternoon when you knew from the start what the outcome would be! Stop pretending to be so righteous and just read it.

That was easier said than done. Carlos's vision was seriously hampered by the alcohol. He set the journal before him, but then had to hold it out at arms length and squint in order to see the words clearly. He chose a page at random, steadied himself, and prayed for good news.

2.

'The man who broke my heart,'

The man who broke my heart was called Peter. I met him at college when I was twenty-one. He played the guitar and harmonica. He liked dancing, watching dark comedies and thrillers, and kissing in the rain. His opening words to me were, 'If I could rearrange the alphabet I'd put U and I together.'

It was such an awful line that I had to oblige him.

We were together for two years.

The details of why we split are inconsequential, just that I loved him, and that through being privileged to meet him I have experienced some of the highest heights and lowest depths of emotions this life has to offer.

I have stepped out of mediocrity and known what it feels like to be truly alive.

None of this would have been possible if it weren't for you, Jonathan.

You'll never know the full extent of the gift you gave me.

My life.

Thank you.

Isabella, 15th Feb

3.

'Coffee'

I love coffee – the texture, the earthy aroma, infinitely more cool than tea!

I studied business and finance for three years, but when I finished all I wanted to do was open a coffeehouse.

After university I left Bristol and moved to London, and lived in a shared house on the Holloway Road with a nurse, a web-developer and a teacher. I took the attic room – musty, very private and secluded. I got a job working for a big accountancy firm in the city. I lived like a hermit for eighteen months, scraped some cash together and took out a sizable loan that my stepfather secured against his property. The next day I quit my job and stepped foolishly and ambitiously into the unknown.

I was lucky enough to be in the right place at the right time. Walking through Soho one afternoon a 'for lease' sign was being put up outside a tiny vacated restaurant. I pounced on it and hoped that the finances would add up later. Now that the venue was secured a name was required.

I wanted to find a Spanish word that sounded like Jonathan, but all I could come up with was Jornada ('Working day') and Joroba ('Hunchback!'). Neither seemed like a fitting tribute! In the end of I settled for Justamente (exactly) – El Café Justamente – close enough to Jonathan.

In the first few months I had to beg, borrow and steal even such basic items as furniture, cutlery and cups! I hired two girls – Mandy and Sarah. We dressed in black with white pinafores that resembled doilies. In time we built up a 1930s feel with oil-burning wall lamps, marble-topped tables with sculpted spruce legs, a polished brass serving counter, and a retro, state-of-the-art, espresso machine. I love being there so much that I turn up on my days off. I sit on a leather sofa at the back and watch the clientele – taking in the contented looks, bohemian clothing and all-round laid back-ness.

Our speciality is a layered latte called the 'JP'. It starts as a white froth and drops through shades of cream, parchment, pine, oak and mahogany to the peat black remnants of beans. We bill it somewhat dramatically as 'the zenith of coffee experiences'. Locals and tourists try to guess what JP stands for. The best suggestion so far has been 'Just Perfect'.

You are my best-kept secret.

As you are ultimately responsible for my every success it seemed only right that your name become synonymous with what makes me most proud.

Hopefully I will get the chance to make one for you.

Isabella, May 24th

4.

'From simple beginnings'

I think my father's name was Ash. Perhaps you knew him(?) He was a tall man with wild hair. My mother wore a headscarf. I can't remember her name, but I do recall that she played the cello.

Shortly after you saved me a French sailor found me hiding behind packing cases in a cargo hold. He held his hands up in dismay and said words that I didn't understand. I was led to the deck where several men stood around me scratching their heads and frowning. In all directions there was nothing but endless ocean.

I was given my own cabin, fed, watered and taught a few choice phrases (un, deux, trois, je m'appelle Isabella, bonjeur monsieur, etc).

I cried till there were no more tears left to shed.

At Dover I was handed over to a woman in sensible shoes.

'Cual as tu nombre?' she asked.

'Isabella,' I replied. 'De donde eres?'

She gave me a blank look. I had reached the limits of her Spanish!

I was taken to a big house full of girls dressed in their Sunday best. Every few days adults would come in convoy and we'd be lined up for inspection. Women would kneel down and swoon over us. Men would stand at the back looking uncomfortable. Occasionally a girl would be led away, never to be seen again.

No one ever explained to us what was going on. In our minds being chosen meant some unspeakable end. When the adults came we avoided eye contact, messed up our hair, sulked and scowled.

One day my time came. I remember clinging onto a wooden banister and screaming at the top of my lungs. The sensible-shoed woman tried to smile at me as she prized my fingers from the rungs, then her hair, then her clothes, anything and everything I could dig my claws into.

I found myself in the back of a car with Paul and Karen, my new parents. I was so confused. Paul was short with neat hair and Karen didn't wear a headscarf and didn't play the cello.

They drove me to a huge house with imposing black gates guarding a long gravel track. The track led to a huge sandstone house. A little girl in a blue dress stood in the open doorway.

'This is Patricia,' Karen informed me, 'your new sister.'

I stared at the girl in front of me and frowned. 'How can you be my sister? You're black and I'm white!'

Patricia ran inside sobbing.

Karen explained to me that she and her husband had been unable to conceive a child and so had adopted two girls. Patricia came from Botswana. Her parents had drowned.

'Where are my real parents?' I asked.

Karen recoiled from the question as if wounded. 'We don't know.'

My young mind leapt to a wildly accurate conclusion. 'They're dead aren't they?'

'Truly Sonya, we don't know. You were found escaping from a war-torn country. We don't know where you came from or how you got here.'

'Sonya?' I replied. 'Who's Sonya?'

'Paul and I have decided to give you a new name, for your new beginning.'

I gave an obstinate stamp of my feet and stated, 'My name is Isabella. I am five years old. I am NOT Sonya!'

The next day I found myself back with the woman in sensible shoes.

'Have I been un-adopted?' I asked as Karen and Paul sped off into the distance.

The woman knelt so that she was at the same eye level as me. 'Don't be sad. We'll find you some nice parents.'

'I'm not sad,' I replied. 'They were horrible. They wanted to rename me Sonya. I told them that I was Isabella.'

'So I've heard,' the woman said with a sudden flourish of laughter.

'And that if they were going to call me Sonya I was going to call them Philip and Agnus!'

'Did you really?'

'Yes . . . you're lovely . . . what's your name?'

'Rosemary.'

'Pleased to meet you, Rosemary, I'm Isabella.'

'I know.'

'You could be my mum!'

'I'm flattered, but I'm far too old to be looking after a mischievous little girl.'

'I'm not mischievous.'

'Oh, is that right?'

'Yes, can I be adopted by poor people? My real parents were poor. Poor people appreciate life more.'

Rosemary gave me a hug. 'I'll make it my mission in life to find you some wonderfully poor parents, OK?'

'That would be great. Thank you, Rosemary.'

'My pleasure, Isabella.'

And so the adventure began.

Isabella, 26th May

5.

With the greatest care and attention Carlos placed Isabella's journal on the floor. He had ceased to squint, and now stared wide-eyed into his quivering hands. There was an uncomfortable sensation of having shaken his mind into sobriety only to find it still trapped within a drunken body. He listened to the sound of his own breathing, like nothing he had ever heard before, a wild animal, something possessed of a furious energy.

This changes everything.

Like Isabella, Carlos had been orphaned by the city. Unlike Isabella he had a clear recollection of his parents. On reflection he considered her to be the more fortunate, not to know what she was missing.

Life had taught him that it would not be tamed, would not be placed in predictable, easily manageable order. It would spin and turn and thwart and evade, sometimes all at once. You had no choice but to go with it. He'd seen and experienced more than most people did in ten lifetimes, and like Isabella he owed it all to Jonathan Pemberton.

You have to help her find him.

You of all people know that this is not possible.

What of your own search? Its ramifications are far greater.

He has waited all these years. He can wait a few more days.

Carlos tapped out a tune on the floorboards. The makeshift rhythm helped rally his thought.

Life does not exist to serve me. I exist to serve it.

Isabella's journal was like a box of delights unexpectedly flung open in the midst of a dark dream. It was an account of triumph over adversity, of promise and destiny realized, of glorious experimentation, of risk taking, of honesty and expectation. It made Carlos want to laugh and cry all at once. It was astonishing to behold and yet he had only caught a glimpse of her full story.

Carlos reminded himself that he was trespassing over private memories.

Just one more page. What harm could it do?

If you only knew Jonathan.

6.

'The World'

I realize this is a pretty vague title, but I could think of no better expression for what you have given me. I wrote a list of all the countries I have visited in my short life – twenty-six – a lot more than most. I am very privileged.

I never feel guilty for my exuberance. It would be criminal to squander what you have given me, and so I fill each day to the brim.

I rise early. I make a list. I take my time. I enjoy each and every thing that I do, even arduous or boring tasks such as cleaning or gardening. I lap them all up with equal relish.

The people that I love in life I really love. I devote the best of my time to them, make sure that I remember their birthdays, build lasting, fruitful relationships, share in their successes and hardships, and they share in mine.

I play several musical instruments – the piano, flute, violin, ukulele and oboe.

I speak four languages – English, French, Spanish and Russian.

These last few paragraphs read as bragging. They are not meant to be. What I am trying to say is that you have given me a sense of perspective, of what is important and what is merely background noise. At all times I am acutely aware of the gravity of both my own actions and those of the people around me. It has made for an extremely fulfilling life so far.

Meeting you and giving you this book would make the fulfilment complete and whole.

When I think of you I think of all the fantastic places I have seen, and imagine you next to me savouring the exquisite sights cast before your eyes:

- *Corcovado mountain, Brazil – standing beneath the statue of Christ the Redeemer, staring down at Rio de Janeiro.*
- *Red Square, Moscow – Knee-deep in snow gazing at the dazzling Kremlin building.*
- *The first glimmer of the Arctic tundra – seen from beneath innumerable layers of clothing at the bow of a ship.*
- *Reaching out and touching giant sea turtles in the crystal clear water of the Yucatan Peninsula, Mexico.*
- *Manhattan's skyline, New York, New York.*

Just a few of the images I would have you enjoy.

In recent years I have used the pretext of coffee to come to South America with increasing frequency. It has been frustrating cruising around Corderro's borders, denied access and knowing that the tiny principality may house you.

May?

The cruellest word I know.

Maybe you are well travelled? Perhaps you have seen the same sites as I. Maybe we have passed each other in the streets and byways of this planet countless times. I hope not. For my own selfish reasons I hope that you have stayed right there, held safe and sound for the day when I will find you.

Isabella, 27th June

7.

Carlos wiped the tears from his eyes. What he had read opened doors of ecstasy and agony within him. It left him with a difficult choice, what to reveal and what to hold back.

In one respect the task is a simple one, a singular truth. It would take less than a minute to relay in its entirety.

. . . But the implications of that truth?

Carlos shook his head.

Not an easy decision.

There was a faint knock and from a wooden trapdoor in the centre of the room a maid appeared. She was dressed in a black shirt and blouse with white apron tied at the waist, similar to the description of Isabella's coffee house.

'I have bought you some wine, Señor Neblina,' she said, angling her head with an expression of coyness.

'This is very kind . . . and unexpected.'

The maid's face reddened. 'I took the liberty.'

Carlos rose clumsily to his feet. 'As you can see, señorita, I am . . . engaged in research so to speak . . . and am somewhat half-cut . . . I do apologize for my dishevelled appearance.'

'Not at all, it is very becoming of you.'

'Mm,' he pondered, 'so, you are saying that a drunken stupor suits me? Well . . . I shall take that as a compliment.'

The maid giggled.

'For your insolence I would have you partake in a glass with me.'

'I'm sorry but I can't drink on duty.'

'Ah . . . this is unfortunate . . . you leave me no choice but to drink it all myself . . . I fear I might not be man enough for the task in hand . . . but I shall endeavour to . . . oh . . . what on earth am I talking about?'

The maid giggled once again. Her laughter tapered away to a sublime silence. She ignored the natural cue to leave, lingering half in, half out of the room. Carlos sensed that the woman before him was having difficulty summoning the words from her throat. He wanted to help, but decided not to try soliciting the message for fear of having already made a big enough fool of himself. Instead he displayed a dopey-looking smile of approval. The seconds passed. Finally she spoke.

'Would you like to . . . go for dinner with me?'

As the words registered with Carlos he realized how stupid and inappropriate his facial expression was. He tried to appear flattered but instead looked bilious. Careful to protect the woman's pride he gently raised his left hand revealing a wedding band.

'Alas for me, given your devastating beauty, I am married . . . I shall find solace in alcohol for the opportunity that has passed me by.'

The maid nodded in appreciation of his response. 'You even make rejection sound poetic. Your wife's a lucky woman, Señor Neblina.'

'Please, call me Carlos.'

'Enjoy your wine, *Carlos.*'

She winked at him and closed the trapdoor.

Carlos was overcome with homesickness. Mention of his wife made him sad for the distance between them. Inspired to fill the gap he dug around in his suitcase for a pen and paper, and hastily scrawled a letter:

To my darling Clarina,

How I miss you – the most amazing woman I have ever met. You glorious goddess, mother of my children, keeper of my heart, possessor of world-class thighs, arms, hands, buttocks, breasts, neck, and as for your face – Oh my Lord!

But enough compliments or you shall become as arrogant as I am.

Suffice to say your absence leaves a huge hole (an emotional hole you understand, not a physical one. Maybe I will rewrite this letter before sending).

Well, I have arrived here, found good food and music, found lodgings, but you will not believe what else I have
found . . .

Carlos placed the new bottle of wine in his suitcase. He had no intention of drinking it just now.

What I need is to regain the coordinated control of my limbs.

Shiny pipes ran along the soot-blackened walls. He followed them until he reached a tap jutting out over a bucket. Carlos let the water run and placed his head under the flow. The freezing cold liquid trickled into his ears, down the bridge of his nose, his neck, his back, soaking his shirt and trousers, his socks, the floor.

Now I'm awake!

He filled his mouth and took several large gulps interspersed with deep intakes of breath.

Go and get some food, go for a walk, work it out of your system.

Carlos moved the bucket out of the way and knelt in the gathering pool.

This decision is bigger than me.

Across the room, nestling amongst crumpled clothing, Carlos could see two other manuscripts.

The weight of history is upon you.

He did not consider the thought pretentious or overdramatic. He was a link in a chain of events spanning centuries. What he hoped to achieve, the reason he had come to Corderro, many others had attempted in the past. All had failed. That failure had *always* cost them their lives.

Carlos turned off the tap and crawled over to the suitcase, shedding a trail of water in his wake. The single manuscript was a dog-eared and disintegrating paperback. Its spine had fallen away and been replaced with a bulldog clip, and its front cover had been worn and sun-bleached so that its bold red title was now a barely visible yellow smudge: *Corderro's Legacy.*

The book had been out of print for over a decade. It was renowned amongst scholars as 90 per cent historical account, 10 per cent propaganda. The latter could all be found in its final chapter.

Water dripped onto its cover. Carlos stepped back to save it from further decline.

Jonathan.

You are bound up within the pages of this book, just as I am.

Carlos dried his hands on a t-shirt, snatched up the manuscript and made his way towards the trapdoor.

Chapter 7
Corderro's Legacy

1.

Corderro came violently into being one blood-soaked morning in May 1507. Before then its disparate fishing communities had been content to exist nameless and without form, bound by the necessity to hunt, and trade, and live.

The day started as any other with the thunderous footsteps of men running along the hills that flanked the ocean inlet. They laughed and joked as they jostled for position, fighting for the honour of being first to reach the top.

Each man carried a spear – 2-foot long and self-crafted with intricate design.

Towards the summit their strides became measured, moving as one. No one faltered. They had learnt to trust in their abilities as well as in each other. Powerful limbs that had known only sports and sunshine propelled them to the edge of the precipice and launched out into effortless freedom. For a moment they seemed to float, suspended in mid-air, before gravity snatched them aggressively from grace and thrust them down towards the unforgiving rocks below.

Arching their back as they had been taught by their fathers they drifted outwards in their descent and cleared the obstacles, plunging deep down into the serene blue waters.

Beneath the calm surface a ferocious current took their limp bodies and formed them into contorted shapes. They were slammed against the seabed sending up a cloud of silt and shale, before being picked up once more and fired like arrows from a bow. Emerging elegantly from the underwater storm they became as statues, seemingly innocuous. A minute passed, then two. As the seconds drifted by the surrounding marine life lost their initial fear, moving in closer and weaving amongst their limbs.

And then the men struck.

There was no signal given, no command. The thought to act was far more instinctive, far more primal. The tranquillity was momentarily interrupted by the thrashing of fish impaled on the ends of spikes, and then they were rising, bringing their quarry to the light, a catch for every single man.

They broke the surface to behold a small boy standing on a rock pointing feverishly out to sea. His cries marked the end of everything. They turned and followed his line of site.

A Spanish galleon was entering the bay, its gigantic bulk squeezing through the narrow channel, mottled pitch-covered cannons cutting a groove in the rock face, and sails billowing proudly with a coat of arms below a crow's nest that stood higher than the cliff tops.

The fishermen had never seen anything like it. To them it resembled a leviathan, blocking the exit and invading their homes. But they were warriors. The possibilities of encounters with sharks and barracudas were risks they took daily. Whilst bigger in size the threat was the same. They huddled closer together to give the impression of a single, more formidable entity, their arms interlocked, spears pointing outwards.

The vessel came closer, its dagger-shaped bow slicing the aquamarine and spilling white squalls in its wake. The deck was empty save for a solitary figure, standing majestically at the stern. He was clothed in a long-tailed magenta jacket adorned with silver buckles and dazzling medals, a frilly lilac cravat, and navy-blue britches meeting at knee-length black leather boots. His long grey hair was tied in a loose bow and a curved sabre hung from his side. The man's name was Ramon Esteban Corderro.

Bathed in the sun's rays he looked like a sculpture of shimmering silver and glorious gold, like a god.

The fishermen changed from fearful to mesmerized. Their precise formation became ragged as they stared in transfixed wondrous awe at the approaching deity.

Ramon's eyes moved within a frozen face of regal indifference and saw the figures in the water. His features gave nothing away as he issued forth course, gravely commands. Immediately afterwards an imposing anchor exploded through the surf and disappeared from view. The deck was suddenly awash with stooped and subservient beings scurrying up ladders, pulling in fabric, lashing ropes to cleats and shouting out incoherent messages.

The hulk groaned and lurched to a halt, pulling the fishermen up in a swell and forcing them away from harm. When Ramon moved he was like a sleeper awoken from centuries of slumber. He walked the length of the vessel, stern to bow, following the most direct route, his crew skirting around him and avoiding his Medusa's glare. Reaching his destination he peered over the side and regarded the natives with disdain.

One of the fishermen moved ahead of the rest. He placed a hand on the vast wooden hull to steady himself in the choppy waters and with the other hand offered up his catch, a broad smile etched on his smooth black face.

Ramon pulled out a pistol and shot the man through the heart.

The sharp crackle of gunpowder and the trailing scent of cordite stunned the fishermen into confused silence. Their friend bobbed lifeless on the surface. The ocean turned crimson. In the next instance they were gazing up at a long line of soldiers cocking pistols and firing into the sea at will.

They had never encountered hostile humans before. They were accustomed to squabbles and tribulations, but never unprovoked, unadulterated violence. Several of their number were cut down before they broke free of paralysis and dived for the sanctuary of the reef.

Below the galleon the waters were crystal clear. Lead shots pierced the waves and found their targets with devastating accuracy, riddling muscular torsos with hideous abrasions.

The first 30 feet claimed most of the fishermen. The few who made it to shore were picked off by long-range sharpshooters. Several savage seconds later the world returned to stillness.

Ramon's face revealed neither elation nor disgust. He replaced his pistol and barked a series of short orders. The anchor was withdrawn, the sails hoisted and they continued their skulk towards the shoreline.

Dragging behind the galleon a solitary fisherman clung to a guide rope. His name was Viracocha. Inland he could see his wife, Inguill, washing clothes in a stream. Gentle wisps of smoke were rising from their home, the dying embers of the previous evening's fire. His children were playing outside, watched over by his elderly father. They were out of earshot. They hadn't heard the gunfire, would not have known to run if they had done. Agonizing, impotent dread gripped him as he watched the soldiers running down gangplanks onto the fine white sand.

They reached Inguill first, clubbing her on the back of the head and swarming over her falling body like ants. Viracocha tore at his hair, scratched at his skin, and screamed gut-wrenching curses that escaped as bubbles. His wife's washing flew up into the air and spread out over the bone-dry dirt. They ripped the clothes from her waist and beat her about the face. Viracocha wanted to look away but he was hypnotized. Life was over. Nothing could give back what was being taken away.

They were moving up the hills now, dragging people from their homes, hacking the men and boys to pieces with machetes, raping the women and girls, torching the buildings, howling and thumping their chests.

Ramon strode down the gangplank, its old wood bowing reverently to his might. He reached down into the surf and gathered up a handful of wet sand. The hills were ablaze. Birds were scattering. Back-breaking screeches and dull sobbing filled the air, and thick black smoke rose into the bright blue sky.

'I name this place Corderro,' he declared.

The morning dragged into afternoon and finally to evening. The sun seemed reluctant to relinquish its hold and hide the day's atrocities within the blanket of night.

'A lord needs his manor,' Ramon whispered. He looked around for a suitable spot. No one place stood out above the others. 'Let the people decide.'

His marksmen were on the beach roasting a pig and drinking rum. Though deeply inebriated they each found a regimented sobriety when the General approached.

'I have an important task for you,' he growled. 'Take ten of the girls and place them at the bottom of the hill.'

When this was done he picked two of the marksmen and handed them their weapons.

'You have two minutes. I will reward the one with the most kills.'

He stepped back.

The men knew better than to contest decisions or ask questions. They each knelt, looked down their sites, fighting the nausea of alcohol, and took aim.

When the first girl fell without sound the children did nothing. A spilt second later the deafening sound caught up with them and they all ran in different directions, screaming their parents' names as they did so.

The marksmen, both fathers, worked with the meticulous robotic efficiency of ones who have learned to choke down emotion. They fired, watched, noted, reloaded, aimed, fired, watched, noted, reloaded, until it was over.

The last girl to fall made it to the top of the hill.

'*There*!' the General shouted with feverish excitement. 'That is where you shall build my home.'

It took a decade to construct his manor house.

Four hundred years later El Rey's palace would be built upon its ruins.

The next day the raiders realized their mistake. With the male population decimated there was a much-diminished means of manual labour. Ramon set the women to work gathering wood for a bonfire and founded it on the bodies of their loved ones. The women were mostly catatonic, having shrunk back from their unfathomable grief. They obeyed their new masters without question or hesitation. It was a few weeks before the true cost of that day was revealed to them.

The first child, a boy, was delivered six months later – a premature stillbirth. It was clear to all that the child was a Mulatto – a half-breed, part native, part invader, an abomination.

The women worked furiously to resuscitate him, unsure as to why they were doing it. When they finally forced air into the baby's lungs its mother, Inguill, wept for her husband lost to the ocean, for the son they had already lost, and for the son who would never be his.

'As you are the spawn of a monster I shall name you Ramon,' she decreed. From that day forth she only ever spoke once more.

By the end of the year there were forty such children.

Viracocha had established himself in the hills. He fished in the evenings when the soldiers were drunk and ate his food raw so as not to risk drawing attention to himself with a fire. His hair had all fallen out and his body was covered in self-imposed wounds, but his eyes were still good and he watched his wife during the day – washing, carrying building material, growing fatter, cradling another's child in her arms. One night he sneaked down to the beach, lay beside the woman and gently stirred her from sleep.

'My precious wife,' he sighed, 'I am alive.'

Inguill held his gaze lovingly for a few moments before her look turned cold. 'My husband is dead,' she replied, 'and so am I,' and with that she closed her eyes, shutting him out for ever.

2.

Sixteen years passed. The fishing community was transformed into a farming belt. Huge forests were felled in order to build housing, and crops were harvested on the fishermen's graves. The mothers placed all of their hopes in the thought that one day the raiders would pack up and head back to wherever they had come from. With the passing of the seasons hope waned to a sliver.

The women had decided from the very beginning to tell their children the truth. They grew up with the knowledge of their twin bloodlines, of the history and the violence. As the boys developed muscles and the women curves, Inguill and the other mothers worried for their safety. In the eyes of the raiders they saw a growing lust. In the young men they saw a swelling rage.

It came in the seventeenth year.

Terezza was a woman of unsurpassed beauty. The drunken old man who approached was her father. She knew this. He did not.

'I've been watching you for some time, my sweet,' he slurred.

Terezza smiled. The gesture was neither welcoming nor flirtatious. She managed to remain supremely neutral without appearing aloof. She could see that the man was looking for a reason to strike her.

'You have something I want.'

'I am just a peasant girl, sir–' she kept her eyes on him, refusing to be the victim '–I have very little to offer.'

'Ah but you do.' He swayed and steadied himself by grabbing her arm. 'Come here.'

Terezza took a step back. 'I'm fine here, thank you.'

Her father tugged her back. 'Don't be that way, angel. I can give you your freedom.' He placed his other hand on her thigh. Terezza kicked out and her eyes flashed with fire.

'It is not yours to give. What you offer I already possess. *Take your hands off me.*'

What happened next has almost certainly been embellished over time. What *is* known is that Ramon was alerted by Terezza's cries and found her on the beach writhing beneath the weight of the invader. There is a conjecture that they were lovers, but this may well be folklore spun down the centuries.

Whatever the truth of the matter, what is known is that upon seeing the debasing of the young woman Ramon became his father's son.

He dragged Terezza's father down to the sea and drowned him.

Many hundreds of years later Cristof's famous illustrations would show Terezza looking at Ramon emerging from the water, her face a tantalizing mixture of fear and gratitude. If indeed they *were* lovers as some historians have speculated, then murder had set them apart for ever.

'You must run, Ramon,' she begged. 'They will catch you.'

Ramon shook his head. 'I have set wheels in motion that cannot be stopped. I would not wish to stop them if I could.'

He gathered the young men and told them what he had done.

'I will *not* run. I will strike down every last one of them as they sleep. Will you join me, or am I to complete this task alone?'

Ramon was the spitting image of the General. Joining him was like being in league with Lucifer. Ribcages rattled with almighty fear as men shook hands in the darkness.

'Speed, stealth and finality, these are the words that *must* resound in your minds this night. Spare no one. Come, I will show you.'

He led them silently through streets that had until recently been undisturbed woodland. They stormed into the first home, through its lavish lounge, down a hallway and into a bedroom. Ramon did not wait to identify the person sleeping. Mercilessly and without sound he slashed the man's throat, pushed the blade down into the lungs and was leaving the house before his victim began to gargle in his death throws.

'Do as I do,' he uttered demonically and disappeared into the night.

The General was awoken by a blade at his throat. He pushed back the silk sheets and saw a younger version of himself.

'At your service,' he greeted eloquently.

'On your feet,' his son replied.

The General rose and beheld a band of dishevelled, wild-eyed savages.

'You have spawned a city of *bastards*, my lord. Your followers . . . they're all dead . . . you are all that remains.'

In all of his time on the continent the General had never been known to smile, but now, in the closing moments of his life, a hideously broad grin spread across his face. 'I salute you for your audacity. Such a trait is extremely rare.'

'I curse you for yours,' Ramon replied. 'I curse your bloodline, I curse your city, and I curse your soul.'

They locked the doors and proceeded to beat the old man so badly that his face became unrecognizable. They gouged his eyes, stamped on his fingers, tore at his cheeks and ripped out his hair at the roots.

'Don't die, your grace,' Ramon spat, 'and whatever else you do don't beg for mercy.'

At first light the barely breathing General was paraded through the streets on the back of a cart, down to the sea and to his galleon. No one mocked him as he passed. The community was reeling in shock from the actions of its children. Ramon took the ship out into deep waters.

'This city has remembered the sins of the father, and permitted its sons to replay the debt.'

He pushed the General overboard.

Ramon Esteban Corderro had been dressed in the full military regalia in which he'd arrived sixteen years earlier – knee-high boots tightened over broken legs, the magenta jacket fastened across cracked ribs. The layers weighed him down and for a few moments he sunk below the surface before re-emerging and uttering a single word.

'*Please!*'

A lead shot passed through his heart. The General slumped forward and his coat tails billowed out behind him. His offspring jumped from the deck and swam ashore. Moments later a fire caught the sails and the galleon was engulfed in flames.

The next evening Ramon was walking along the beach alone. They had elected him leader that morning. It was a responsibility he neither wanted nor considered himself deserving. His hands felt strange. He had killed many men with them and couldn't reconcile the softness of touch with the brutality of memory.

Looking up from his thoughts he saw someone emerge from the trees. The man was clearly a native of the island although Ramon had never seen someone so old. 'Good evening,' he greeted.

'You have no idea how long I have waited for this moment,' Viracocha growled before plunging a decorated spear into Ramon's neck.

Ramon fell backwards, the echoes of his own voice ringing around him.

'I . . . am not . . . who you think I . . . am,' he managed before slipping away.

Viracocha bent down to retrieve his spear and in the pale moonlight saw the boy's youth. The full horror of his mistake revealed itself.

'I have killed my wife's child,' he cried.

Without a second thought he fell on his spear.

The two men were found the next morning, slumped in a lover's embrace.

Without Ramon there was no obvious leader. Every man left alive was a murderer, every mother a victim of rape, every daughter steeped with guilt at their own unwanted existence.

And so they did what they had been conditioned to do. They fought each other for supremacy, dominated the weakest amongst them and coveted what was not theirs to own. The distrust and alliances, strikes and reprisals, claims and counter-claims lasted 300 years through fifteen generations, until the time of Santos.

3.

The world was diminishing and expanding at the same time, the old making way for the new. In neighbouring territories, later to be christened Venezuela, Peru, Bolivia, Chile and Argentina, the Incas and Aztecs were quietly slipping into legend. Those not decimated by the Spanish joined the civilized societies in newly formed cities. Their skills were watered down by the industrial age, their bloodlines lost within a handful of generations.

North American Indians migrating south to escape the wrath of bloodthirsty European colonies passed through Mexico. Here they mixed with the Mayans before continuing down across Panama and arriving at a horse-shoe-shaped coastline.

Later, between 1860 and 1865 the American Civil War accelerated the migration. With virtually no border controls in place hoards of soldiers and civilians sought sanctuary in Latin America, arriving minus limbs and half their minds.

Corderro welcomed its hapless victims like a Venus flytrap. They were quickly subsumed within the city's dark underbelly, some surviving as beggars, most perishing in back-alley knifings, their bodies thrown into *El Rio Amargo* ('the Bitter River'), and drifting through La Fantasma out to sea.

El pote que derrite ('the melting pot') was a phrase born in the gutters, a means of encapsulating how people felt when at their lowest ebb. It gave them a physical picture with which to ascribe blame, a focal point for their fury. Corderro was imagined as a cauldron suspended precariously over a furnace, bubbling away, swirling and churning like a vortex. Into the mix came the incessant flow of raw ingredients – flesh and bone, bad luck, fate, greed, ambition, apprehension, opportunism, every fearful and degraded thought known to man, and blood, so much blood the cauldron could barely contain it.

Street stories of the time talked of life in the city being like falling overboard in a raging storm and finding that the ocean was on fire. The water boiled and retched and stripped the skin from your back before you had the chance to drown in a manner befitting a mariner.

Other tales described it as like being kneaded within the folds of unbaked bread, sticky and suffocating, or as a vacuum, absolute in its hollowness, but it was the image of the melting pot that endured. It would later be immortalized in an analogy given as part of Santos's infamous speech – *La naturaleza de un maldición* ('The nature of a curse').

Little is known of the man in question. Though Spanish in name, he is thought to have been either Indian or French. He arrived in Corderro some time between 1876 and 1884 (historical accounts vary), and brought with him a Latin phrase he is believed to have learnt whilst in Europe – *circulus vitiosus* ('a flawed or vicious circle').

Santos was a historian. He'd studied many civilizations and had chronicled every known atrocity for the last thousand years, but what he saw in Corderro changed him irreversibly. Never before had he seen such a blind willingness for self-destruction. Over and over he witnessed it repeated throughout the centuries, growing in savagery and sadism with each rotation.

One night he sat down at his desk to write an account of Ramon's murder, but instead found himself penning a plea to a nation.

The Vicious Circle

At first there was harmonious community – we fished together, lived together, and enjoyed one another's company.

Then came a great violence which, in its wake, caused discord amongst us. We sought to purge the source of our discord with acts of even greater violence. The results were even greater dissension.

We reasoned that the answer was to overthrow, to cleanse, expel and eradicate the source of our sorrow. But as each new generation rose up to tear out the sins of the old they gave birth in themselves insatiable monstrous desires – desires to reign in that which they had only just freed, desires to seize control, to seek unjustifiable retribution – each time stronger and more potent than the last.

    We are in a spiral, plunging down and down and around and around.

    We must stop moving forwards, step back, open our eyes, learn from our mistakes. Then and only then will we break free of the vicious circle.

He wrote the statement in a single breath. Feverishly he snatched it up from the desk and ran out into the street shouting that he had found the cure for Corderro's illness. A bewildered crowd gathered around him and stood transfixed as a series of revelations spilled from his lips. When he finished speaking some cheered, others wept. He quickly became established as a spokesman for peace. People compared him to the prophets Mohammed and Elijah. They approached him with hushed, sombre words of reverence. Mothers asked him to pray for sick children. The true message quickly became lost.

Some time later Santos was speaking in the Plaza d'Armas when the crowd became agitated and mobbed him. Used to demonstrations of this kind he continued to talk and raised his voice above the dim. Just as he reached the pinnacle of his speech a dagger pierced his stomach. The assailant was unseen. Santos stood silently watching the throng of arms and legs, the anxious faces and child-like eyes. He asked himself how he had ever hoped to rectify the situation all by himself.

'This is madness,' he whispered and dropped to the ground.

At his funeral Santos was commemorated with a drink concocted by his son and named as the new national cocktail. He christened it the Dulce-Amargo ('Sweet-Bitter'). It later became as whisky is to Scotland, or vodka to Russia. The Dulce Amargo was made by mixing tequila, lime, lemon and tomato with sugar sprinkled upon its surface. The recipient would experience a sweet froth that was quickly replaced with the bitter sting of citrus. The drink's appeal was widespread, but the name felt cumbersome. In time it became known simply as the Santos.

4.

On 24 February 1895 El Ejército Libertador de Cuba ('the Cuban Independence Movement') published their manifesto entitled *Independencia o Muerte ('Independence or Death')*. A fledgling uprising was violently quashed by Spanish forces that same day. The incident was one of several disastrous policy decisions that contributed directly to US President Theodore Roosevelt's intervention and the ensuing Spanish-

American War.

Perversely it was during this conflict that Corderro enjoyed its greatest days of peace. An early newspaper of the time published a cartoon of a supposed postcard from Beelzebub. On it he sat perched upon the turrets of Ramon's palace, his eyes fixed across the ocean to the bloodshed in the Caribbean. The caption read: 'Gone but not forgotten'.

The people were under no illusions. It could only be a temporary respite.

In 1899 the war ended. Hoards of American troops set sail from Havana bound for Miami. Many more remained behind to nurse their wounds amid rum-soaked slumber. A third group felt the pangs of inaction and hungered for adventure. Their commissions over they began to spread out and seek fortunes elsewhere. Amongst them was a lay preacher called William T. McCafferty.

McCafferty followed an extreme form of legalism and his views on the world were absolute. *A man must earn his way into heaven, and seek forgiveness from God in the continual physical purging of iniquity.* His ruddy complexion and quivering lips had been cultivated in the Midwest pulpits over a lifetime of bullish evangelism.

He rode into Corderro on the back of a mule, his followers furnishing the pathway with palm leaves. Most people saw the disconcerting similarities to Jesus's entry into Nazareth.

McCafferty quickly establishes himself as a street preacher of unbridled ferocity. No passing stranger was spared the pointing fingers and accusations of unwashed guilt. His approach was at first rude, then invasive, then oppressive. He declared himself 'benefactor', and set about surrounding himself with men of influence – the bankers and power brokers. Dubious in their methods, they usurped and tore down every governmental body in turn until there was no one left but themselves.

McCafferty quickly did away with the men who had helped him ascend to power, replacing them in back-alley treaties with men of more durable stock. 'Cancer cannot be cured,' he boomed, denouncing the financiers for their greed. 'It must instead be cut out.'

A kangaroo court assembled on the beach where, in the pitch black of night, their culpability was confirmed. The financiers were flogged, lashed to the underside of a boat and drowned. The next day their assets were seized under emergency laws.

'We will have peace at all costs,' McCafferty lambasted from the steps of the city hall, the blood on his hands a distant memory. 'Let those words of freedom be carved in letters ten feet high for all to see the glorious path of light.'

His men worked through the night carving the slogan into a great marble plinth that sat above the pillars of government. The next morning McCafferty strode majestically from his beach-front home, eager to behold his words venerated and emblazoned.

Beneath his declaration 'We shall have peace at all costs,' someone had added the words, 'whether we want it or not!' in blush-red paint.

The preacher stared up at the amendment for several minutes, his face thunderous.

'My first commission as your *patron* will be to bring the perpetrator of this atrocity to justice.'

It was news to all present that they had acquired a patron. The graffiti itself was generally regarded as a mildly amusing piece of satire. The spectacle was largely dismissed as theatrics.

The next morning Corderro arose to find that a group calling themselves the 'Parliament for Purity' had seized control of the city.

McCafferty had learned much in his time as a general in the Santa Clara uprisings. He considered the most important lesson of all to be that 'in sparing the rod we let the sin fester and spread.' He had seen many cases where gangrene and trench foot had been halted by garish and brutal amputations. He saw no reason why this principle could not be applied to spiritual matters. Sometimes zealous measures were the only way to safeguard the greater good, the limbs sacrificed in order to revive the body.

A twelve-year-old girl was found guilty of the graffiti offence. McCafferty ordered that she be branded on the face with a red-hot iron and thrown into prison for a year.

'You may think my methods unduly harsh,' he bellowed as the girl was dragged from the gallows screaming and clawing at her burning flesh, 'but there are some evils in this world that can only by cleansed in the flames of judgement. So too with fire will I purge the city of its pestilence.'

McCafferty's ideas of virtue quickly became established as more sadistic and sanctimonious than any vice Corderro had ever known. More kangaroo courts were established haphazardly throughout the lower quarters. Trials were held for suspected petty criminals and murderers alike, with instantaneous mob lynchings conducted upon the thinnest of evidence.

As unpalatable as his approach was no one could dispute its effectiveness. Six months after his Christ-like arrival crime has been virtually eradicated.

The problem now faced was one of choice.

There had been no epidemic of goodwill and McCafferty had not given Corderro the peace he promised, only a benign sense of punishment and attrition. As the little girl's graffiti had foretold, the people *were* forced into holiness, whether they wanted it or not.

Those who would wish to rob, to lie, to covet, to kill, to do anything even subtly amiss were obliged to leave their dark desires unfulfilled, letting them hibernate, grow, spread, sharpen and incense. 'Peace at all costs' wound the city so tight it couldn't breathe.

A second issue of equal weight and importance was one of double standards. Drunk with power the Parliament for Purity had passed a motion decreeing their exemption from the laws which they themselves enforced. For all his pomp and ceremony McCafferty turned a blind eye to the nightly orgies of women, gambling and wild abandon held by his men. It was common knowledge that he himself was embezzling large sums from the coffers and sending the money abroad.

Early one winter morning the patron of Corderro emerged dishevelled from the city hall to find the building surrounded by women. They stretched back as far as the eye could see – stoney-faced and immobile, arms linked, forming an impenetrable barrier.

McCafferty could see his breath in the December dawn, rising in cavorting wisps. His shirt was unbuttoned to the waist. Lipstick and spilt whisky stained his collar. Two days' stubble growth covered his face. There was no shame, only surprise. He'd been convinced that the people had embraced humility and subservience, but saw in their eyes only defiance.

Something inside told him to taper his authoritative roar with a more conciliatory tone, but opening his mouth he found no words, and no voice with which to utter them. Unsteady on his feet from the night's excesses he was propelled clumsily down the steps into the courtyard.

It started to snow. The air was bone dry. Within a matter of seconds thick fat flakes painted the world white.

Someone stepped forward from the crowd – a young girl with two deep scars across each cheek. McCafferty recognized her as the urchin whom he'd branded on his first day in power. She moved slowly and purposefully towards him, half his height, a quarter of his size, salient nevertheless.

Without speaking she pointed up over his shoulder. Behind him, scrawled across the giant marble plinth was the phrase: 'You have turned my father's house into a den of iniquity.'

McCafferty turned back, his face red with furious indignation. In contrast the girl's face remained calm and composed, a smile of satisfaction lurking at the edges of her lips. When she spoke her voice was abrasive.

'Lift a finger to strike me, your grace. Punish me for my offence.'

His fingers curled into fists, but he dared not attack. The crowd tightened.

'Call out your men. Punish us all. We each here present had a hand in defacing your palace.'

Now McCafferty saw the truth in full. It was insurrection, an uprising. *Where are all the men?* he thought. *How can they hope to succeed without brute force?*

The question warmed him but still his confidence remained illusive.

The girl had lowered her guard. Her face broke into a sneer. 'No? Then we shall punish you for yours.'

The women behind her parted to reveal a black metal barrel filled with white-hot coals glistening and sizzling under the barrage of snow.

McCafferty finally found the strength to speak. 'I am your patron,' he whispered.

'Since when?'

'How dare you!'

'How dare I *what*? What is it that aggrieves you? You've lost your way. Surely you are happy that we came to save you?'

'For your insolence—' The patron fell silent.

'My name is Marie. I am the granddaughter of Santos. See how history conspires against you, *your grace*. Corderro is circular in its affairs. Here a person can be sure of repetition. If you had taken the time to understand its people you would know this.'

Before he had a chance to respond Marie raised her hands and an army of women swarmed over the preacher, pulling his feet out from under him and binding his torso with their collective weight.

'We must have *peace at all costs*,' Marie scorned as she took an iron from the furnace and pressed it against McCafferty's forehead, branding him with an 'L' for Ladron ('Thief'), 'therefore your scarred and shamed face will never see the light of day again, as an example to others of what becomes unwanted patrons.'

The latter half of her sentence was lost beneath the preacher's screams. His cries alerted the other members of the parliament who emerged from their slumber and into the cold unforgiving light of day to receive similar punishments.

The incident sealed Corderro's reputation in the eyes of the world as a place where no one escaped retribution for their actions.

5.

It never became clear why the uprising had been orchestrated by women only. Hours later husbands, brothers, fathers and sons awoke bewildered to find that the universe had moved on.

'Corderro will never again recognize an autocratic rule,' Marie addressed the masses. The statement was met with wild, unrestrained applause. 'The route of our continued failure to find a resolution lies in having always placed our faith in one man. Subsequent corruption has always ensued. We must remove the temptation from our midst, and to that end we propose to elect a body of representatives with joint responsibility for the welfare of our citizens.'

Consigned by the preacher to a windowless room for a year Marie had had much time to formulate her views on the world. In later decades the cell in which she had blindly scratched the words 'Mirror of Judgement' became a tourist attraction.

The principle of the mirror was simple. Commit a crime and the same crime would be committed against you:

 – *If you kill – your life will be forfeited.*
 – *If you steal – that which is most precious will be taken from you.*
 – *If you beat a man, woman or child – you yourself will be beaten etc.*

There were fifty-seven such edicts covering every conceivable offence.

Though still a teenager Marie was wiser than her years and not afraid to make bold decisions. She knew better than to enforce her beliefs on the people. The Mirror of Judgement was put to the vote, a practice hitherto unknown. It was met with unanimous approval.

Marie and the other members of the committee acted firmly but also compassionately. Over the next few years they pulled the city up out of the

McCafferty era and allowed the formation of discrete districts – the port, the Market quarter, the affluent hillside suburbs, downtown, the lakes, Liberacion and the industrial hub. Out of the hands of megalomaniacs Corderro began to fashion itself into somewhere truly beautiful, and seemed to have finally found a system of governance that suited its unique composition.

The year was 1902.

6.

In 1948 a book illustrator named Cristof Verdin arrived in El Puerto de Las Ondas Verdes with his wife and child. Five years previous he'd been a colonel in the German Army, and was involved in the occupation of both Poland and France before a shrapnel injury cut short his military career.

Hospitalized for several months he'd spent his days listening to the radio. In time he came to see the propaganda for what it really was – a smokescreen to mask a nation's approaching defeat. Cristof had been a Nazi sympathizer since the mid-1930s. When the end came he felt certain the hammer of reprisal would fall heaviest on his kind.

As soon as he was able Cristof discharged himself, gathered his family and fled.

Unemployed and soon to be disgraced as a deserter he fell back on a childhood talent for painting. Cristof took his family south to Africa – through Albania, then west to Morocco, down into Mauritania and finally to Senegal, selling paintings as he went.

He purchased a small studio with a balcony where he could display his work. His skills were considerable and in no time at all there were more commissions than he could physically accommodate – family portraits, shop signs, menus, murals and books. It was the latter that Cristof enjoyed the most, bringing an author's words to life and enhancing the narrative. It was also good for his wife and son who were given access to such wondrous literature – novels of profound depth, poetry of desperate beauty, encyclopedias of glorious facts and mind-expanding philosophies – far more than they could otherwise have discovered or afforded.

One day he was approached by a short, beady-eyed Spaniard.

'I am looking for Cristof Vair-deen,' the man said.

'I am Cristof. How may I help?'

'You are German?'

'Siberian.'

'I see.'

The Spaniard nodded purposefully as if he had gleaned a great secret from the painter. 'A pleasure to meet you, sir. My name is Marcus. I have purchased much of your work over recent months. You have a great gift. Your illustrations capture a marvellous joy. They pull enchanting characters and colours from the pages.'

'Thank you.'

'I wonder though,' he continued, 'whether or not you would have the same skills with the antithesis, painting pain and contempt, giving form to atrocious and unspeakable acts.'

'I work mainly with children's literature, sir. My affairs have never brought me into contact with such opportunities.'

Marcus's face came alive, his features sharpening. 'I have one such opportunity if you would care to know?'

'By all means.'

The Spaniard reached into a leather satchel and pulled out a 3-inch thick manuscript. On its cover, in beautifully stylized lettering, was the title: *Corderro's Legacy.*

'This is my life's work,' Marcus proclaimed proudly.

'Who or what is Corderro?' Cristof asked.

'A city, great and ghastly. It lies across the waters, on the east coast. By rights it should never have existed. Its inhabitants call it 'The Melting Pot'. It is a place steeped in culture and tragedy.'

'I have never heard of such a place.'

The Spaniard looked horrified. 'To have never heard of Corderro is to have never faced your demons, or stared into the blackest corner of your soul.'

Cristof felt general unease come to rest on their conversation. 'What is it you would have me do?'

'This book is a lesson to the world, a morality tale if you will, a plea to learn from history and embrace one another as brothers. But in itself it is only words. Men are fickle, they need to be enticed, ensnared, mesmerized. For that I need a master artist, I need *you*. You will be to me as electricity was to Frankenstein's monster!'

Cristof could not have thought of a less appropriate analogy. 'What kinds of images?'

Marcus cast his arms wide, mirroring the frenzied stance of William

T. McCafferty. 'Bloodshed, genocide, desperately dark ingenuity, the very bowels of human corruption.'

Cristof weighed up the enthusiasm with the mania.

'My book is a veritable cornucopia of grief, misery and victimization. Why, even the word itself – Corderro – spells out the country's torment. Lose one of its Rs and you have *cordero*, the Spanish word for 'lamb'. When Ramon's galleon appeared on the horizon there could have been no better title to bestow on its accursed shores? Corderro – a lamb to the slaughter.'

Cristof had never heard of Ramon, nor knew why a galleon should be associated with slaughter. It was clear from the Spaniard's attire that he was wealthy, and such a commission could yield considerable financial rewards, but he was also eccentric and a little sinister. Cristof was cautious.

'I'm not sure,' he answered, instantly regretting the weakness conveyed in his voice.

'I would pay handsomely.'

'I don't doubt your generosity. Can you give me one month with which to familiarize myself with the text, and a further month to prepare preliminary sketches?'

'Oh good Lord no!' The Spaniard shouted and clasped both hands to his temple. 'No, you must see the city first-hand to truly grasp its insidious nature.'

Cristof laughed. 'I couldn't journey across the Atlantic. I have a wife and child!'

'They would accompany you obviously. I would have you all come and live with me. After all, the project will take many years.'

'I cannot just leave. I have several jobs to finish, four months to run on our lease, and my son is nearing the end of his studies. What you ask is impossible.'

The Spaniard was undeterred by the obstacles. 'Nothing is impossible, as you will see when you read my book. I will compensate you in full for your lost earnings and rent, and as for your son, he will thrive in Corderro's university . . . and . . . besides . . . I would imagine it wise for a man of your allegiances to be mobile in this current climate.'

Taken at face value the comment appeared harmless, but beneath the warm tones of concern Cristof thought he detected a guarded threat. It was 1947; the Second World War had been over less than three years.

Throughout Europe and further afield scores were being settled. The Nazi party had become a symbol of hatred and evil. Cristof held out little hope for a fair hearing and reasoned that Senegal was a safe place to hide, but the world was becoming smaller by the day. It would only take one suspicion, one phone call, to bring the whole house of cards crashing to the ground. Perhaps Marcus would be the one to provide it? Cristof couldn't take the risk of declining the Spaniard's request. They set sail with all their earthly possessions two weeks later.

During the crossing Cristof had little chance to read *Corderro's Legacy* as it was monopolized by his son. The sixteen year old spent many choppy, stomach-churning hours with his face buried in tales of malice, sorrow, loss, revenge and consequence. He marvelled at the possibility that it could all be true and was enraptured by the city's ability to obliterate those who tried to conquer it.

His son's name was Emile.

Corderro was not how they imagined it would be. Marie, now an old woman, still sat on the elected committee of representatives. The mirror of judgement had been in force for over forty years. The city was calm, safe and tranquil.

Emile hated it.

The Spaniard installed them in a luxury apartment in the hills overlooking a fabulously exuberant district.

'Well,' Cristof proudly asked his family, 'what do you think?'

'I think that the devil has just shown you Babylon,' Emile replied. 'Paint for me and all this could be yours.'

When Cristof finally managed to prize the manuscript away from his son he realized why Emile had been so reluctant to relinquish it. Its stories were astonishing, the chapters well written and it all knitted together into the coherent narrative of a cursed city.

He set to work right away, making preliminary sketches of the various characters and key events, but quickly became disenchanted with his own talents. He couldn't seem to bring his images to life in a way that satisfied his high standards. Cristof's first batch of paintings were bland and uninspiring, his second even worse. He had never experienced a creative block of this kind. It took many sleepless nights before the answer to re-releasing his abilities revealed itself.

Cristof realized that he could not illustrate a book so dark without first freeing himself of his moral constraints. His last job had been bringing life to a family of squirrels lost in a wood. Now he was contemplating the raping of innocence, the disembowelment of children and the loss of sanity. He was convinced that it could not be done in a rational frame of mind.

That evening his wife cooked a glorious meal. Cristof ate in self-effacing silence, cleaned his pallet with a glass of water and announced, 'I'm afraid I have an appointment with the Spaniard. I shall be home late. Don't wait up.' He grabbed a coat and hurriedly left.

Cristof hated lying, but in an abstract way the deceit helped open a door into a dark place within him. He took his first step down.

Cristof returned four days later – emaciated, unshaven and sunken eyed. His breath reeked of alcohol, his clothes of smoke and body odour. Clutched within a clawed hand he gripped a collection of crumpled sketches.

'My God, Cristof,' his wife cried as he stumbled into their home in the early hours, 'what the hell have you done to yourself? Where the hell have you been?'

He couldn't quite focus on the woman in front of him and so directed his response in her general direction. 'Discovering the true nature of debauchery. *Now* I can work.' He dropped onto the sofa and slept for three days.

When he awoke Cristof was feverish with excitement. He wasn't sure why he had set himself so methodically and obsessively to the task in hand. All he knew was that he had to support his family and avoid detection.

The Spaniard had annotated which dramatic scenes he wanted bringing to life. The first was entitled: 'Massacre of fishermen at the hands of Ramon Esteban Corderro'.

'All pictures have their centre,' Cristof declared and rose from his stool to pace the boards of the makeshift studio, 'a place from which everything else flows.'

He considered several different ideas – the contrast in expressions between friend and foe, the arms holding up their catches versus the arms holding guns, the prowess and splendour of the General. They seemed too obvious, too ordinary. Finally he decided that it was the crimson water, bearing away lifeblood in its undulating currents.

'There, that is *it,* the moment when the circle found its form.'

He began to paint.

7.

Slowly but surely Emile dropped out of site. With his mother suffering from ill-health and his father lost within work, he found that he was left largely to his own devices. He walked the streets trying to recover the sensation he'd experienced within the pages of *Corderro's Legacy*. He sought out famous landmarks – the beach landing, the town hall steps where McCafferty had been branded, the dilapidated remains of Ramon's palace and the Market place where Santos met his demise. It was awesome to behold.

A favoured pastime was hanging around the lower quarters watching the street hustlers at work. The confidence-tricksters left him spellbound with their lightning reflexes and sharp minds. He learnt their slang, ran errands for them and rapidly developed an invaluable incite into the real workings of the city.

Emile enrolled at the university where he studied history and politics. Wherever possible he chose periods of conflict, dissecting the rhetoric and daring of figures such as Garibaldi and Napoleon.

He quickly tired of studying theory and longed for practical, hands-on experience. Without his parents knowledge he abandoned his education and enlisted in the army. Emile used his street contacts to gain forged documents – a birth certificate stating his age as twenty-three, and a first-class degree in mechanical engineering, both of which allowed him to enter in the rank of Lieutenant.

During the next six months his dogged and zealous approach found both shape and style. He discovered that it was easier to be taken at face value when you were well turned out; easier to be accepted when you had earned your place. One by one he watched his fellow academics incur the scorn and contempt of the lower ranks. Emile saw that, whilst position could be easily attained, real power and respect only came with hard work.

He threw himself into the task, attending basic training and sitting with the grunts during mealtimes. To his superiors he presented a flawless picture of lateral thinking and ingenuity. Through grit and flare he managed the unusual feat of appearing both an everyman and a star. Promotion soon followed. His rise through the ranks was exponential.

While Emile was ascending his father was descending with equal savagery and speed. The task of illustrating *Corderro's Legacy* had claimed almost every waking moment for two years. He'd lost the sparkle from his eyes and over 3 stone in weight. A shadow had crept across his face and his spirit was broken. The need to paint was like a parasite consuming him from the inside out. He was surrounded at all times by macabre imagery: McCafferty branded in the snow – Santos knifed in the market place – Tragedy on the beach/Viracocha mistakenly kills his wife's son – The public flogging of Marie – The beating and execution of Ramon Esteban Corderro, and several dozen others. They had the combined effect of a psychological prison.

Somewhere amidst the two men's opposing transitions their wife and mother passed away. They hardly noticed. Her cause of death could be attributed as much to loneliness and neglect as it could to the respiratory infection that had filled the house with inhuman, guttural crowing for over a year. Emile had rarely been home to witness her decrepitude, and to Cristof it was as if the volume had been turned down on the world. All he heard were the faint brush strokes on canvas and the distant echoes of ancient tragedy.

Like Santos before him, Emile saw patterns in the city's life. No matter how busy his day he would always find time to sit alone and write down his thoughts and experiences. Sometimes the pen would rip through sheets of paper with such gluttonous pace it was as if he were merely the scribe for some supernatural power. The views and philosophies came thick and fast. Each day he rose a little in stature, respect, knowledge and power. He honed his views into a fine point and recorded them on a single side of parchment.

The Spaniard visited every few days and was always elated by what he found. The quality of Cristof's work made him blind to the artist's physical deterioration.

'You are a master of your craft,' he would bellow emphatically. 'I chose well in commissioning someone of such staggering talents.'

On one occasion he arrived to find Emile waiting for him in the garden. Without greeting him, the young man handed him the parchment.

'What is this?' The Spaniard inquired.

'The final chapter of your book,' Emile replied.

'My book already has a final chapter.'

'You will revise your thoughts when you read what I have written.'

The look on Emile's face was deeply unnerving in its intensity. Reluctantly the Spaniard cast his eye over the document.

8.

'Summation'
     by Emile Verdin

A vicious circle exists in Corderro to which no one has ever escaped. History teaches us that from Ramon's time to this the unkindness of men has always been revisited upon them tenfold, and the good intentions of women repeatedly undone by outlandishly poor fortune and wild cards.

I am not a superstitious person, but the sheer weight of evidence over the centuries has convinced me that the city is indeed cursed.

It was no easy feat for a faith-less man to accept an otherworldly quality to existence, but great discoveries require an even greater pragmatism.

Against this ethereal backdrop I set about answering a deceptively simple question: how might a man break free of the circle?

The journey of discovery that I took is a tale within itself. Suffice to say that it led me wayward down seldom-trodden paths. My mind travelled to the ends of the earth before finding the solution right back where I'd started. The secret to unlocking the conundrum lay in understanding the nature of the entity.

A vicious circle is by its own nature vicious.

Why did McCafferty fail?

Because he gave the people too much leeway.

When confronted by Marie and her women in the snow he should have gunned them all down without hesitation, not flounced around demanding respect and honour.

He simply wasn't vicious enough!

Therein lays the crux of everything.

Elated and euphoric I took my conjecture to the academic community. It was met with widespread scorn and derision. My conclusion was deemed to be ridiculous, and at every turn I was presented with volumes and volumes of counter-argument. The phrase that most often barred my way was that of Lord Action – 'Power corrupts, absolute power corrupts absolutely.'

I agree wholeheartedly with this deduction, but also believe that its meaning has been taken woefully out of context. The modern-day viewpoint is founded on the belief that corruption is a bad thing. As I have pointed out to many a straight-laced scholar – morality is not scientific.

One man's vice is another man's virtue. What could possibly be wrong with surrendering to temptation? It is the most basic, honest means of achieving your ambitions and becoming what you set out to be.

This is what Corderro has been trying to teach us.

9.

The Spaniard clutched his forehead in bewilderment. 'You're joking.'

Emile looked confused by the question. 'I am deadly serious.'

'My word! This is amazing, and awful, and tragic. You cannot *possibly* have taken this hokum to heart? To say that a man was not vicious enough is tantamount to saying that not enough evil exists in the world!'

'No, no, no, I am sorry to correct you, señor, but you are quite wrong in your view. As I have stated, 'Morality is *not* scientific.' There is no such thing as too much or too little evil, only fulfilment and failure. The latter is the cause of Corderro's troubles. My epilogue will crystalize what you have set out.'

'This will not be the epilogue, merely another repetition. You have made yourself rather than the city the central focus. You have established yourself as another would-be tyrant waiting in the wings. Your argument is disjointed and skips about haphazardly, and your conclusion is hopelessly flawed. In short, you have taken a real-life epic and reduced it to a poor man's fiction.'

Emile stared at the Spaniard for a long time. He was shocked at the critique his theory had received, but mostly he was outraged. He found himself feeling intense hatred towards the man who had fed, clothed and housed his family for the past two years. He wanted to threaten him and do him physical harm in some way, but Emile resisted. He could see that the timing was inappropriate. In the eyes of history it would not afford him the proper sense of occasion. He realized that his response simply didn't matter. No one of any consequence would ever hear it.

'How dare you reject my findings so casually? The next time we meet I shall remind you of this conversation.'

To the Spaniard the comment sounded like the empty threat of a sulking teenager. He remained silent as Emile snatched back the parchment and stormed off down the garden path.

Emile had barely left the front door when he broke into uncontrollable floods of tears. His body began to shake.

'What is happening to me?' he asked, stumbling into a side street and cowering in the bushes to hide his weakness. He was accustomed to being heaped with praise. His actions were never challenged as they were always so insightful to begin with. But now some common, unqualified serf had taken his most prized work of philosophy and tried to reduce it to sham and mockery.

He realized now that his swelling tumour of ambition had grown beyond the armed forces, far beyond even the confines of his own body. The tears were born of frustration.

How dare he ridicule an intellect so obviously superior?

How dare he stand in the way of my glorious ascension?

He cannot see what I am to become . . .

. . . El Rey ('the king').

And how could he? Emile hadn't even seen it himself until that moment.

This must be my destiny. I can have been born for no other purpose.

Despite its Spanish heritage the country had never had a monarchy. Ramon had seen fit to remain a general after conquering the coastline, and subsequent rulers had used either religious or governmental structures with which to dominate.

But to be the king! The unequivocal, unquestioned monarch – who could contest such a man? Surely any person even conjecturing a notion of defiance in the deepest recesses of their mind would shudder violently under treasonous indignation?

Emile was a soldier in the midst of an unprecedented rise into the echelons. He saw no reason why he shouldn't continue on his heady journey until he reached the summit.

The obstacle that Emile faced was one of motive. There was no crisis to be addressed, or cancer to be cured. Marie's mirror of judgement had worked well for almost half a century. The city had never been so prosperous. In order to save the people Emile would first need to place their lives in danger.

In battle it was important to know your enemy, to study them and understand what it was you were attempting to destroy. Emile's enemy was a mirror.

He erected *it* in the basement of his father's house – 7 feet tall and 3 feet wide. He looked back at himself in the glare of a naked light bulb.

Revelation should never be forced. It must be given the space to reveal itself.

Emile waited, and waited, and waited, his eyes fixed upon his own face.

In time he noticed that his nose was ever so slightly crooked. Not so much that anyone would notice in the course of conversation, but flawed none the less. There was also the beginning of a blemish forming on his cheek. His skin was greasy to the touch and just within his hairline Emile could see a tiny scar. He could not recall how it had occurred.

A reckless childhood act, no doubt.

The mirror reflects my every blemish and imperfection.

That is it!

The mirror must judge everything it sees, no matter how petty.

Marie's council has never been truly tested.

Emile went about his task with ferocity of focus. He started with the beggars, shelling out money with wild abandon and whipping up a frenzy. More riches were promised upon completion of a task. The task was specific to each person.

He provided them with clean clothes, soap, shampoo, scissors to trim beards and temporary identities, and once they were looking half respectable he sent them into the town hall and to Marie's mirror of judgement.

Their complaints varied in detail but each was equal in its contrived stupidity, and each required some of Marie's time in order to rectify:

'This man stopped my daughter in the street and shouted "Whore". I must be allowed a public gathering to call his *daughter a whore.'*

'My neighbour's son kicked a football at our house and shattered a window. I in turn wish to shatter one of his.'

'A dog bit me in the park. I demand the right to bite its owner.'

'This man sits next to me on the bus each morning and deliberately passes wind. I demand the right to empty my bowels in his home.'

Most of the people Emile chose were alcoholics. They remained drunk throughout their appeals for justice and often argued more fervently as a result. The courts quickly became backlogged with fictitious squabbling, and despite Marie and the council's best efforts to implement emergency measures, the wheels of justice ground to a halt. Seeing the chaos and breakdown of law and order that ensued, the city's underbelly once against seized its chance to flourish. Day by day, Emile's motive for seizing power took shape.

There was a balance to be struck. He had to wait until Corderro had reached a state of degradation worthy of being rescued. At the same time he needed to be wary that the noble intentions of others might step in and steal his thunder.

The moment came a few months later. A series of riots and murders had shocked and appalled the city's ruling class, and people had begun to take to the streets in protest at Marie's inadequacy. They held banners and placards denouncing the mirror of judgement as a dated and ineffectual means of maintaining law and order. The time to strike was at hand.

In secret Emile arranged a meeting of some of the most influential military men in the principality. They crammed into a tiny basement room in the small hours of yet another lawless evening. Emile called the meeting to order. Every man in the room outranked him, but no one dared to question his authority.

'My fellow men at arms, the vicious circle is at work once more. This country of ours has gone to the dogs. The mirror of judgement has failed us all. Marie and her council sit slack-jawed and impotent while the dregs of society rampage through the street unchecked. It is high time we took matters into our own hands. I therefore propose to stage a coup d'etat and take the country, if necessary, by the most extreme of force. Are you with me?'

The meeting was over in a matter of minutes. The verdict was unanimous. Emile had already devised a plan. He issued orders there and then, and sent his subordinates out into the city to seize control of key installations – the port, the city hall, the electricity, the communications, and the police – swiftly, coolly and clinically.

Emile did not join them. He had a separate task to complete, one of infinitely more weight and importance.

10.

The Spaniard met with Cristof as he did each week. As always the results of the artist's sacrifice were spectacular. The Spaniard had begun his usual torrent of praise when Emile entered unannounced.

'Give me my manuscript.'

There was no introduction or explanation. Emile looked as pale as his father.

'*Your* manuscript?' The Spaniard replied. 'I don't understand.'

Emile calmly drew his weapon. 'I told you that I would remind you upon our next meeting. My book, *Corderro's Legacy,* give it to me.'

The Spaniard chose his words carefully. 'Emile . . . it is not you book . . . it is mine . . . taking it by force won't change that.'

'Then it should be no burden handing it over.'

At the back of the room Cristof rose wearily to his feet and stumbled

105

towards his son. Emile raised the weapon in line with the Spaniard's chest.

'Come now, do you value the book over your own life?'

Still no response.

Emile cocked the trigger.

'I won't ask again.'

He didn't have to. The book was in a leather satchel. The Spaniard carried it around with him at all times. Slowly and with obvious agony he retrieved the large volume and placed it on a table in front of him.

'I paid for your education...gave you access to my life's work...and this is how you repay me?'

Emile was unrepentant. 'As I said in my epilogue, if you'd had the intelligence to grasp my argument, what the people of Corderro lack is the courage of their convictions.'

He shot the Spaniard dead in his own house.

Cristof stared at the floor in disbelief. 'My God, Emile–' he had to take a deep gulp of air in order to finish the sentence '–what have you become?'

'A butterfly, Father,' he replied sarcastically, his eyelids fluttering. 'How are the illustrations coming along?'

Cristof may have been weak but he still had the foresight to see where their conversation was heading. He was crushed. Everything ceased to matter.

Had I never set foot on these shores would I still have sired a monster?

He steadied himself and stood up straight, pulled the creases out of his sweat-incrusted shirt and wiped greasy moisture from around his eyes. As they looked at one another Emile silently began his 54-year reign.

'I had hoped to be finally rid of *Corderro's Legacy*, but it appears I have one more tragic scene to illustrate – 'the Nazi sympathiser's son, overcome with foolish ambition, takes the life of a simple businessman.'

Cristof searched his son's face for signs of remorse. He found nothing.

'Mmm.' Emile mulled over what his father had just said. 'It lacks the bravado and pathos of its peers.'

Without energy for tears Cristof cried from dry eyes.

'Are you with me or against me, Father?'

'You are my son.'

'That is no answer.'

'We are *blood*. I raised you! What nonsense is this that you should question the allegiance of your own blood?'

The Spaniard's blood flowed out across the floor.

'I shall not ask again, Father. Are you for me or against me?'

Cristof looked down and saw that the encroaching crimson pool had almost reached his feet. There was a paintbrush lying on the floor in its path. Cristof stooped down and picked it up. The brush had a thin head of fine bristles. He ran it over his tongue as he'd done countless times before, making it finer still, working it into a point.

'Can you do me a favour, Emile?'

'For you, Father, *anything.*'

'Fetch me a bowl of water.'

Emile nodded, lowered the weapon and stepped past the fallen Spaniard into the kitchen. He returned with a bowl, half full and tepid. Cristof placed both hands in the water. He washed between the fingers, beneath the nails, rubbed his palms and worked rings around his wrists. Finally he removed them and dried the digits on his trousers. The symbolism could not be clearer. Emile smiled broadly.

'If you are Pontius Pilate, what does that make me?'

'Barabas,' Cristof whispered turning away.

Emile's smile disappeared beneath a mask of rage. A blow to the back of the head sent his father sprawling to the ground. As he fell his shoulder glanced off the desk sending his paintings flying into the air. They came to rest all around his dormant form.

Later that same day Emile walked unchallenged into the city hall clutching his father's paintings in one hand and the Spaniard's book in the other. As he strode down the corridors of power uniformed men saluted him. In the main hall he found Marie and her council being held at gunpoint.

By now Marie was in her late sixties. Her hair had turned silver and her face had grown more and more angelic with the passing of the years. When Emile looked at her he saw no fear, no regret and no malice. It unnerved him.

'Finally,' she uttered, 'another rotation . . . I had thought . . . and hoped it would never come . . . but alas . . . history is bigger than all of us.'

Emile sat facing her and leant so close they could have kissed. 'You've been complacent, old girl, all this acrimony and legality, so much paperwork mounting up.'

'I take it you had a hand in increasing my workload?'

Emile put a hand to his breast. 'Such slander! I am saving the people from your inadequacy.'

Marie saw the book in his hand. '*Corderro's Legacy!*' she gasped.

Emile's hand recoiled as if from a fire. 'What do you know about this book?'

'I helped Marcus with his research. You have usurped his work just as you are usurping the city?' Marie's eyes bulged wide and she placed a finger to her lips. 'Shhh, whoever you are, listen, if you have read Marcus's account then you will know that you are about to repeat the mistakes of your forefathers. Open your eyes, your mind, your hands. Step back from your intended actions. For the love of God show some sense.' Her voice dropped beneath a whisper. 'Look at my face. It still bares McCafferty's scars, even though I have placed a lifetime between then and now.'

Emile leaned in even closer than before. Their noses touched. 'I am going to place you within a transparent, spherical prison so that all may see the vicious circle in action. See how it traps even the most sycophantic of its inhabitants.'

Marie did something he did not expect. She winked. 'What's your name?'

'El Rey.'

She looked amused by his answer. 'Well, El Rey, let me leave you with an analogy. If this is a relay race then you have just been handed the baton of stupidity. *Congratulations!*'

That night Marie died peacefully in her sleep. Her passing was such an affront to Emile's sense of spectacle that he rampaged through the parliament building pulling paintings from the walls, ripping ornaments from shelves, smashing vases and slashing at the wallpaper with his ceremonial sabre.

Marie's body was placed at the centre of the main chamber. Emile sat beside it for many hours. Her final words haunted him. The sun rose. Outside he could hear Corderro's people cheering at the dawn of a better day. One of his generals arrived and suggested that he address the nation. Emile gave his assent and the event was arranged for seven o'clock that evening.

'Can you hear me, I wonder?' he addressed the corpse. His voice reverberated around the empty stone room. 'If you can, then know this: I am going to systematically tear down everything you worked so diligently and foolishly to build. It will almost be as if you never were.'

He placed his hand on her face. It was soft and cold.

'I say *almost* because I shall remember you. You have taught me two invaluable lessons. Firstly, that chance has no master. I shall be wary of that in future. Secondly, the importance of symbolism. Long after you are forgotten there will still be the mirror. I imagine that it will morph into some kind of gothic fairy tale. How does it feel, I wonder, to have your beliefs reduced to pantomime? Shall I tell you my symbol? A clock face. Ingenious isn't it? I imagine you're kicking yourself for not having thought of it yourself.' Emile's shoulders shuddered with an unexpected chuckle. 'At seven o'clock this evening I shall bring both fists crashing down on the time of Marie. Your mirror will be shattered; your council disposed of.'

Emile ordered that the body be cremated, her ashes taken out to sea and thrown over the side. He could not bear the thought of her physical form being received by the earth. She needed to be banished in her entirety.

At seven o'clock sharp Emile 'El Rey' Verdin walked out to a pulpit at the centre of Parliament Square. He was dressed in a loose-fitting blue linen suit and open-collared shirt. Everything about his appearance was deliberate. He had distanced himself from the military uniform of his youth, avoided the many colours associated with Ramon Esteban Corderro, shunned the cassocks famously worn by Santos, and stood juxtaposed against the double-breasted power dressing of McCafferty.

Even the simple act of his appearance sent the crowd into a frenzy. His smile had the perfection of a chameleon. Emile put aside the bloody acts of mere hours before and initiated the expressions of sincerity.

'My friends,' he spoke softly, 'I am so excited at the possibilities set out before us—' His voice was lost under raucous applause. He waited. The noise subsided. 'I am *not* a religious man, but I *would* like to make comparison between this moment and the very first passage of the Bible.'

There was some unease at his words. He was edging dangerously close to McCafferty's territory. It was unavoidable.

'In the beginning God created the light. He separated the light from the water, and He saw that it was good. If our land had a moment of birth, of light, then it was the moment a Spanish galleon appeared on the horizon and prepared to bathe the beaches in blood.'

A pause. This time there was no sound at all.

'It was midnight, the beginning of time.' He cast his arms wide like a messiah, and then cupped them to his breast; his voice dropping to a whisper. 'The hands of the clock face began their slow and painful rotation, their cycle of repetition – Ramon, his son, Santos, McCafferty, Marie, over and over without learning from their mistakes. But I say to you, with equal trepidation and pride, that the hands of the clock have reached 23.59. We are *teetering* on the brink of a new day. We have only to show the daring to reach out and claim our inheritance and the shroud will fall!'

Emile had prepared a lengthy speech, but was not afforded the opportunity to finish it. The deafening applause that swept through the plaza continued for many hours. In all that time he stood perfectly still, his face a flawless facsimile of grace and humility. Beneath the mask he told himself:

You have become an icon. You have become an icon. You have become an icon.

A few days later Emile was sworn in as El Presidente. He had yet to reveal his regal intentions to the nation, but his inauguration had all the pomp and ceremony of a coronation. The event was presided over by the Archbishop of Peru. His presence represented a newfound cooperation between Corderro and her continental cousins. He presented Emile with a crown, a sceptre and a scroll recounting the verse of Corinthians 13 concerning the nature of love.

11.

The final page of *Corderro's Legacy* concludes with a description of El Rey, clothed in a golden cloak and waving to the masses. The last sentence reads: 'As the people cheered their king and saviour the circle was finally broken.'

Marcus would no doubt have been appalled to witness his painstakingly accurate historical account doctored and compromised as a platform to self-serving ambition.

The book was published within weeks of the President's inauguration and became an instant bestseller.

Emile was careful to omit the events immediately preceding his ascension and was quick to do away with anyone even remotely associated with the coup. The disappearances were veiled in anonymity. No one was clear as to who had been taken, why, or by whom.

It was 1950.

12.

Years later a man named Oscar Arenal published his memoirs in which he claimed to be the soul surviving general in Emile's coup d'etat. He detailed the killings and disappearances of his colleagues and accused the then king of having plagiarized the writings of a Spaniard.

We were told that the circle was broken, but we were lied to. Even as Emile began his first day in power we were trapped within repetition. When Ramon Esteban Corderro was overthrown by his son every one of his followers was a murderer. So it was with us'

At the time Oscar's memoirs were largely dismissed as fiction. Exiled in Ecuador no one could be found to corroborate his testimony. Later his opening paragraph would come to define the city.

I was sitting in my study when I heard a knock at the door. My wife answered it, and an emotionless voice asked 'Would you come with us please?'

When she inquired as to the reason she was taken by force. Armed men entered the house and seized my children. They were at the bottom of the stairs calling my name. My wife and children were screaming. I looked out of the window and saw a long black vehicle, the first of its kind.

I was a general in the Corderrian army. I had thousands of men at my command and many medals on my chest, but to my eternal shame, upon seeing the machine parked so obtrusively on our lawn . . .

. . . I ran.

Chapter 8
The Trojan Trick and Everything Thereafter

1.

The last item on Kelly's roster read: 'Pantomime horse'.

The goods beneath were all fairly lacklustre – tea-towels, cook books, hats, scarves, bin liners – but it was the horse the checkpoint guard focused on.

'Is this a joke?'

'In a way, yes.' Kelly watched the guard's eye for indications of his mood and intent.

'What on earth would you be doing with a pantomime horse?'

'It's for El Teatro de la Luz ('The Theatre of Light') on Southside.'

'What happened to their old horse?

'How the hell should I know?'

El Teatro de la Luz had been closed since a fateful night three months earlier when all of its actors had disappeared on their way home. Most of the guards in El Puerto de las Ondas Verdes were mercenaries from surrounding principalities and had little knowledge or care for the concerns of Corderro. Therefore the chances of being caught in a lie were minimal. Nevertheless Kelly was always careful to reduce the risk to a negligible level.

The guard was from Nicaragua. The accent was a giveaway as were the brand of cigarettes he carried in his top pocket. He was ignorant of the city's sudden shortage of actors. Kelly was safe.

'I wonder what would happen if we called them and checked if they'd *really* ordered your horse?'

Kelly shrugged as if the threat meant nothing. 'They'd probably say, "Oh no he hasn't!"'

The comment was a joke, but the delivery was aggressive. Kelly could see that the man's strength came from his uniform, not his character. He wouldn't overly push the advantage, but to act subservient in the presence of weakness was suspicious in its own right.

'It's a big box for a horse costume?'

'That's marketing for you! It's probably mostly packaging. Take a look if you'd like?'

Kelly had caught a whiff of the man's breath – Cheva – a locally brewed beer. He appeared sluggish, and had little or no interest in investigating the cargo.

'No, that won't be necessary. I have no regard for novelties.'

Kelly feigned offence and got back behind the wheel without asking permission.

'Move on.'

2.

The first thirty-eight years of Kelly's life had been abandoned. Thoughts of his old life always caught up with him by late afternoon when there were no longer people around to provide useful background noise.

He turned on the radio.

There were two radio stations in Corderro. Both were owned by El Rey and both were manned by DJs who weren't allowed to speak. The Emperor saw radio as the first line of attack in any planned coup d'etat. All announcements were heavily censored and pre-recorded to prevent any spontaneous acts of revolt, and the body of music played was generally military in nature. Kelly was presented with a choice between two separate dirge-fuelled marching bands. He switched off and drove in silence.

Curfew was an hour away.

Thirty-eight years – a long time to write off.

Kelly was pragmatic about such losses. They were important only as a lesson learnt. It was the following four that counted. Four years with which to rebuild and reshape a life in tatters. One thousand, four hundred and eighty six days so far, one thousand three hundred and seventeen of them spent in Corderro.

How much longer?

Soon.

Each day brought him closer; the margins of deals made and opportunities taken. His progress was slow but methodical. It was a false economy to acquire too much too soon. Alerting the authorities would mean losing more than his fortune, and it *was* a small fortune, amassed abroad and earning sizable interest.

From the moment he left El Puerto de Las Ondas Verdes to the moment he awoke each morning Kelly was alone. He loathed the company of others and abhorred their need to bond with one another. To the smuggler rapport was functional, something to aid the flow of information, nothing more.

3.

El Sacramento was humming with activity. Alfonso sat as always in front of the reception desk. He was dressed in a lilac suit that looked as if it was made of crepe paper. Behind him the roofless building teamed with ripples of movement. A hat stand glided by an upper window, its carrier unseen. A piano rolled past a lower level opening. A man bent double beneath heavy sacks trudged up an open stairwell. Engines fired into life and doors slammed.

'Mr Kelly!' Alfonso greeted with a high-pitched squeal of delight. 'I do so love our daily chats, so full of warmth and vigour.'

'Hello,' Kelly responded dryly without a hint of irony.

'Javier, Manuel, *AQUI*!' The hotelier yelped and clapped his hands dramatically as if he were about to break into a dance. His oversized lacey sleeves hampered the clean crisp slapping of flesh upon flesh. Two weary looking boys appeared from the shadows, their shoulders slumped and faces resigned to a fate as beasts of burden. Alfonso pointed towards the van and snapped his fingers. The boys began unloading without question. Alfonso turned aside and whispered through the corner of his mouth. 'I pay them in petras. Sometimes the value drops so much in one day that their wage does not even cover the bus fare home.'

Kelly couldn't tell whether the comment was intended as comical or tragic.

'Leave the large box at the back.'

'Why Slim! Holding out on us? Trading your best goods elsewhere?'

'It's a present.'

'But of course! For one of your wide array of friends no doubt.'

The comment drew a wry smile that lasted the length of a single breath. 'What's with all the commotion?'

Alfonso became agitated, strutting on his heels like a bull getting ready to charge. 'That *hijo de puto* – El Comedin! He's declared that at midnight tomorrow all vacant buildings will fall under the ownership of El Rey by default. I have no choice but to open for business. Governmental officials are coming to inspect the "hotel" first thing tomorrow.'

'You have no roof and no guests!'

'The lack of roof is a feature – open air terrace! As for the guests, I have called in many favours and purchased a going concern. It has cost me an arm and a leg.'

'My heart bleeds.'

'Thank you. Your empathy astounds me. Can I tempt you with a continental breakfast tomorrow, free of charge?'

'Mm, appealing offer, but I'll pass on this occasion. Let's settle up.'

'Slim . . . always to business!'

'Always,' the smuggler echoed.

4.

He stopped outside El Banco Nationale and watched the cashiers through floor-to-ceiling windows. Miguel was nowhere to be seen. It was a Wednesday. Miguel always worked Wednesdays.

Kelly wasn't sure why he had stopped. The two men had concluded their business dealing twenty-fours hours earlier. The bank had what they called a 'policy of transparency'. There were no back rooms. All public affairs were conducted in glass booths. If the clerk was there then he would be in plain sight.

The smuggler imagined the accountant, old before his time, following his advice and sneaking out of Corderro with his family, hidden within a crate of manikins. With a one-in-ten chance of being caught the odds were favourable. Kelly had duel thoughts on the matter, each cancelling out the other.

Good to see someone put their money where their mouth is.

Given enough time, everyone lets you down.

He pulled away.

5.

It was dark when he returned home. Kelly reversed the van up to the stairwell and turned off the engine. The cab provided perfect silence, the first sense of peace he'd had all day. It had been a good day.

Then why do you feel so low?

He shook himself free of self-pity. Such thoughts served no purpose.

There was a thick coil of rope beneath the driver's seat. Kelly took it and climbed into the back. Working in darkness he tore an opening in the large box and fixed one end of the rope to the object inside. Next he unlocked the double doors and ran the rope up the stairs, looped it through the bars at the top of the walkway and back down again, forming a primitive pulley. Kelly worked fast, leaning back, bending his knees and pulling the rope through his hands. The item in the box was extremely heavy and required great force in order to dislodge it. Kelly guided it up onto the twin railings, tying off every few feet in order to rest. Eventually he managed to heave the object into his apartment.

Once inside Kelly slipped into his routine. He boiled a kettle, ran a bath, opened a bottle of wine, heated a pan and threw in some onions. Strings and brass filled the dead air. He dropped a steak into sizzling oil, crossed the room and tore open the package.

It was a sofa – seven feet long, deepest aubergine velvet, polished mahogany arms with a subtle ripple of purple running threw the fabric.

It was unusual for Kelly to enter into flights of vanity. His tastes were specific and it was rare that he found anything to his liking.

He'd seen the package being unloaded in the early afternoon. An officious-looking man had stood sweltering in a three-piece suit as guards prized open the crate. Even from a distance the sofa looked magnificent. A thorough inspection had taken place before it was moved into a large cardboard box and placed in the back of a truck. Kelly followed at a safe distance as the vehicle weaved its way through the port, and was surprised to find the sofa moving from truck to crate to van to trolley, each time with a new owner. It was sometimes the case that buyers wishing to remain anonymous would ask for goods to be transferred mid-crossing, but never to this extent. Kelly was intrigued. Still he remained cautious. Smuggling was 99 per cent planning and 1 per cent opportunity. As much as he liked the item it wouldn't pay to get carried away.

The moment came when they reached the outskirts of the inner circle. The package was loaded onto a forklift. The driver took a pack of cigarettes from his pocket, found it empty and went off in search of a fresh pack. Kelly drove the forklift back to his own van, deposited the sofa and stowed the stolen vehicle under one of the immense tarpaulins.

His bounty inspected Kelly crashed down in his armchair with his steak and a copy of *The Bridge of San Luey Rey*. Besides music Kelly's other love was literature. His reasons were as much functional as they were emotional. A person who creates has made something of their life. To read a passage or hear a signature tune affirmed in him that escape *was* possible, that hard work did eventually pay off.

The back wall of Kelly's apartment was crammed to bursting point with books. All were fiction, all dog-eared with use and notation. They were his most prized possession.

There were no book sellers in Corderro. To El Rey they meant arming the people with learning, aspirations and stirrings of defiance. Kelly considered the Emperor foolish in this belief. *He* used books as patients used morphine – to deaden the pain and drive away the demons.

Some time later he realized that he had ceased to read and was merely scanning from left to right. Kelly put down the book, undressed and got into the bath.

The water was uncomfortably hot.

How much longer?

Soon.

6.

The next morning he left the house a little after 5.00 am. *El Torbellino* ('The Whirlwind') was due to dock in less than an hour. It was not common knowledge and there would be easy pickings for the early bird. He got as far as the alleyway before a poster stopped him dead in his tracks. It was tacked to a telegraph pole and featured a large photo of an aubergine-coloured sofa with the word 'Recompensa' ('Reward') written above in bold. Beneath the photo were details on what to do if you had any information.

You're an idiot!

One slip-up is all it takes.

Similar posters adorned every telegraph pole as far as the eye could see.

Kelly turned and sprinted back to the apartment.

Walk, no one knows.

The Nicaraguan port guard?

Alfonso?

It wouldn't take a genius to make a connection between the stolen item and Kelly's pantomime horse.

Got it get it back to the port.

Too risky. Dump it and phone anonymously.

He took the steel steps three at a time and jabbed at the lock with his key. Inside, the sofa that had previously instilled such joy now sat lodged in the entrance hall gloriously proclaiming Kelly's guilt. Thoughts of *El Torbellino* and its bounty were abandoned.

What to do?

Before he knew it he was back in his routine – the music, the running water, the pan. The moronic nature of his actions made him shiver.

Forget about the port for a day. You're in no fit state of mind.

At least fourteen hours till dark.

7.

'Hey Slim!'

Arty was pounding on the outside door. Kelly was instantly on guard. The café owner never visited his home. His appearance and the sofa's disappearance may not be an unhappy coincidence. He knew Arty to be a man of deep cynicism and greed who wouldn't think twice about turning him in for the reward.

'What do you want?'

'I want to come in.'

'Why?'

'I'm running out of coffee. I need you to steal some for me.'

Arty's voice rose in pitch as he accentuated each word. It infuriated Kelly that the café owner should so openly threaten his anonymity. But he saw it for what it was, a cheat trick designed to entice him out into the open.

'You're the most well-connected man in Corderro. How can *you* have run out of coffee?'

'My seller got himself black-sedaned.'

'That's too bad. I'm just a humble dock-worker. You know that. Go and buy some.'

'At those prices? I'd as soon as serve up my own head on a plate.'

The comment sparked an awful premonition.

Arty has led men to my door. They know.

He moved back from the door and made his way to the window. There was a clear view of the walkway and the street below – empty.

That means nothing. That could as easily be crowded around the entrance.

'Slim? Are you still there?'

'Yeah, I'm here.'

'I said "What good is a coffee house without any coffee?"'

'What do you need?'

'Let me in. I have a list.'

'Slip it under the door . . . I've just got out of the shower.'

'I'll wait.'

'Arty, I'm a busy man. Slip it under the door and sod off. I'll see what I can do for you later.'

'I need it by lunchtime.'

'Not a chance. Bye.'

'Kelly . . . *Kelly* . . . oh . . . *hijo de puto!*'

Arty thumped the door. His footsteps led away down the steps. Kelly watched him traipse along the walkway adjusting his braces and cursing under his breath. As he squeezed into the driver's seat of his car, the whole chassis dropped several inches. A few misfires and bouts of swearing ensued before the car lurched away.

Kelly's nerves were shot to pieces.

That settles it. I can't just sit here stewing. I need to put this right before it gets out of hand.

The roster!

It'll clearly state 'Pantomime horse'.

OK, the Nicaraguan, then Arty's coffee, then Alfonso.

8.

It was ten o'clock by the time he reached El Puerto de Las Ondas Verdes. *El Torbellino* had long since been and gone.

The entrance gate was saturated with blood, oozing and congealing within its mesh frame. The guards offered no explanation. Kelly knew better than to ask. The occupants of the outer bartering dens were having a hard time concentrating on their scams. Kelly saw unease on each and every face.

Do they suspect me?

No, it is merely fear of the unknown.

What could be more fearsome?

The guards to the inner circle presented him with similar walls of silence.

If they knew they would act.

Kelly parked up and took a look around. He could see Paolo and Raoul at work, the former checking a palette of eggs, the latter shrugging and gesturing in the heat of a deal. A necessity for answers overwhelmed the hatred he felt towards both men. He walked over to them.

'What's with the gates?'

'My word, Slim, it's a miracle!' Raoul replied. 'You know, in all my time here I think this is the first time *you've* ever approached *me* for anything.'

'Don't be an asshole. What's going on?'

'We'd love to tell you,' Paolo interjected, 'but we've got to look out for number one . . . sorry.'

Paolo turned back to the palettes. Kelly was incensed by the rebuttal and grabbed him by the wrist. 'Hey, I asked you a question.'

Paolo responded with equal aggression, grabbing Kelly's throat and squeezing. '*Get your hands off me!*'

Kelly's grip remained firm.

'You've far more to lose from a public scuffle than I do,' Paolo spat. 'Tell you what, as a professional courtesy from one smuggler to another I'll let you throw the first punch. What do you say?'

Kelly marvelled that he could inspire such animosity. He let go and raised his arms as if to say 'forget it'. Paolo shouldered past him into the crowd. Raoul discarded his deal and followed suit.

9.

Jerome had worked in the port for two and a half years. Like Kelly he was overdue for the black sedan. He was an American – sun-kissed and unhinged by too much California sun. Kelly avoided him wherever possible due to his erratic personality. Today was an exception.

'Hey, do you know why the gates are covered in blood?'

Jerome spoke in a monotone and let his beady eyes provide the intonation. 'They killed one of their own. No one's really sure why. It might have something to do with the theft. Whatever the case I'm outta here on the next boat to the Bahamas!'

Despite feeling deep-seated anxiety Kelly chuckled and shook his head in mock indignation. Jerome had been threatening to leave every day for well over a year. Kelly said as much.

'I'm serious this time, Slim,' Jerome protested, tugging nervously at his feathery hair. Fingernails that had been bitten down to the quick dug into his greasy scalp. 'Take a look around you. The serpent has a hold of its own tail and has begun to gorge upon itself. Look . . . there.' His hand shot out towards a guard hut towering high above the port on imposing black stilts. 'There.' The hand swung to the left where two men stood on a raised platform brandishing bloated-looking chain-guns. 'There.' A second tower with snipers. 'There.' A speedboat patrolling a few hundred feet from the sea wall. 'One bad night's sleep and El Rey could pick up the phone and have us all cut to pieces! It used to be a calculated risk . . . now it's just plain lunacy. Time to go, my friend.'

Without another word Jerome vanished. The two men never saw one another again.

10.

Kelly made several other inquiries and discovered that the man currently adorning the gates was none other than the Nicaraguan guard. At eight o'clock that morning Eleanor Blake had arrived with a convoy of trucks. A strange contraption was unloaded from the last vehicle in the convoy. The Nicaraguan guard (who was just coming to the end of his shift) was forcibly thrown into the machine which shredded him alive and sprayed his liquefied remains out over the gates. Eleanor had then driven away without a word of explanation.

So it definitely is connected to the theft.

Kelly felt a palpable sense of relief.

Only in Corderro could it be fortuitous to find that a man had been brutally executed.

That still leaves Alfonso.

First things first – Arty's coffee.

Purchases that should have taken moments instead took several hours. Kelly couldn't seem to focus. Throughout the day additional security flooded into the port; most of the regular clientele disappeared into the woodwork. Eventually Kelly found someone willing to trade a wide selection of coffee beans, but the prices were not favourable. Arty would no doubt squeeze the margins down to zero. No matter, today there were greater considerations.

In order to pacify Alfonso he needed to find a package similar in size to that of the sofa, which he found it in the shape of an extremely ugly and low-quality ottoman. The hotelier would probably struggle to sell it on and might even become suspicious of Kelly's lapse in judgment. Once again, it was the lesser of two evils.

His business concluded he wearily took his wares back to the gates. Beyond the macabre mesh of wrought iron and bloodied entrails Kelly could see a man pleading with an official. As Kelly watched a black sedan pulled up behind them. The official knocked the pleading man to the ground. The doors of the sedan snapped open and shut like the jaws of a wild beast – he was gone

We are parasites.

This is madness

Kelly felt sick. He tried to imagine what it must have been like for the Nicaraguan, knowing with a choking certainty that his life was coming to a close. On any other given day he wouldn't have entertained a concern for others, but the immediacy of his predicament demanded attention. There was every chance that he too could be unceremoniously snuffed out at a moment's notice. It could come at any time, from any angle. The closed existence he had strived for so long to protect had been flung wide open. There was nothing to be done but wait and hope.

A fool waits. A wise man plans.

He couldn't breathe. Kelly got out of the van and sat down on the curb taking huge gulps of air. As he did so, a phrase sailed unsolicited into his mind.

I ceased to care, and in doing so found peace.

And then another.

The most destructive weapon at man's disposal is conscience.

Kelly shook his head. He'd suppressed his emotions for so long that they had built into a tumultuous swell. He could feel the dam about to burst.

Pull yourself together. You look suspicious.

It was no use. Kelly bowed so that his welling eyes were hidden in shadows. Instinctively he took a notebook from his inside pocket and began to write.

11.

Excerpts from 'Thirty-eight' (Unpublished)

This is the story of my death and resurrection.

No, too inflammatory, unnecessarily controversial and pretentious.

This is the story of an ascension.

Better.

It is a forecast, a carefully calculated prophecy, meaning that it hasn't actually occurred yet. At this juncture I am at the base of an exponential curve pointing upwards, languishing in god-awful squalour, but poised on the brink of escape.

Kelly looked down at what he had just written with an abstract sense of detachment. The intimacy of his words unnerved him. There was something deeply disturbing in giving over such personal details. It was almost a forbidden notion, but it was also compelling. He continued to scrawl, bent double over the notebook.

The thinnest thread of hope holds me anchored to a patch of land in Staffordshire, England. I have a brother there who I desire to become reacquainted with in time.

How much time?

Soon.

We lost touch through immeasurable degrees of misfortune. He once offered to help me build a house. The plot is waiting patiently for our duel efforts, should I be able to flee this place, find him and seek his forgiveness.

He stopped writing.

'Not feeling' was what had carried him through the last four years. To suddenly relapse into recollection and soliloquy would be his undoing. He couldn't help himself.

At this point in my introduction I have already become something of a cliché – the man who rides his luck far beyond the point of no return, into the ridiculous. I will not bore you with tales of my unhappy past. There is only one story to tell of my exploits before the age of thirty-eight. Everything else I will gloss over with echoes and whispers, leaving behind the vacuum of a ghostly presence, passing pathetically into obscurity. It is a simple story, not very exciting, stupid really, but important in so much as it sets out the example that my life has followed.

As a child I played many games, but the one I remember most vividly was called 'Centrifuge'. We were all so young none of us even knew what a centrifuge was, or why the game was named as such. It involved tying a length of rope to the outside rung of a roundabout and coiling it tightly around the central axis. Two kids (usually boys) would take their places at either side facing each other and grip the rung tightly. The rest (usually boys) would take the other end of the rope and begin to pull. As the rope uncoiled it turned the axis, gathering speed with each increment until one of the boys lost his grip and flew off leaving the victor to enjoy the spoils of glory.

It was such a dangerous game that most of the players would surrender their hold on the carousel long before their fingers were forcibly prized away.

I always won.

My secret was painfully simple.

I never let go.

12.

Kelly drove to Alfonso's with the notebook burning a hole in his pocket. He was disturbed by the sudden and unannounced outpouring, but also felt a certain pride. It wasn't the best thing he had ever read, but neither was it the worst.

Where did it come from, and what should I do with it?

Throw it away? Build upon it?

I just don't know.

He found El Sacremento as a fully functioning hotel. Alfonso was in high spirits. He had been able to convince the officials that he ran a legitimate business.

'Mr Kelly,' he bellowed. 'See how I have eluded the grasp of that clown El Comedin.'

'So you're a going concern now?'

Alfonso dabbed the corner of his mouth with a handkerchief and laughed feebly. 'You jest? I shall of course close down at the earliest opportunity. This is costing me an arm and a leg. None of those vultures are paying customers. But enough of my woes, I am skirting around the verge of a rant, so to speak. What of you? What delights today?'

Kelly got straight to the point. 'That item I held back yesterday, you can have it.'

'I thought you said it was a present.'

'They already had one.'

13.

Arty was not appreciative of the smuggler's efforts. Kelly had not expected him to be.

'I told you I needed it this morning!'

'And I told you that it was not possible.'

'You know how many people have stormed out of my establishment in disgust at being served instant coffee?'

'No, nor do I care. Forward planning, Arty, it's the key to everything.' Kelly could not afford to show weakness. 'Here are the beans, everything you asked for. Here is the price. It is in dollars. It is non-negotiable.'

Arty absorbed the aggression without batting an eyelid. He adjusted the braces around his mighty girth.

'I hear you've been hanging around with that Esperanza girl?'

'Who the hell told you that?'

'Paolo dropped by, said you were in need of cheering up.'

'That vindictive little shit. If you tell anyone—'

'Relax, I know a wind-up when I see one – unlike you, my friend.'

'What business do you have with Katrina?'

'On first-name terms are we?'

This time Kelly answered with more restraint. 'If ever there were a person with a target drawn on their forehead . . . and Paolo's the one you want to watch.'

'I watch everyone, Slim, you know that. This is how I know so much.'

14.

He didn't make the call that night. He couldn't face any more revelations. The rest of the routine remained unchanged – the bath, the coffee, the pan, the wine. When he crashed down into the water with Sammy Davis Jr playing in the next room it was clear that the day had taken more than mere energy from him.

I am unravelling.

He saw himself in autumn, trying to hold all of the fallen leaves within his hands. As the season passed the burden became too great. The bounty grew heavy – rotting, dissolving and disintegrating.

You need to get out before you drop everything.

Not yet.

When then?

Soon.

That no longer holds weight. You must act.

Arty is pacified, Alfonso is not suspicious, the Nicaraguan is dead. There are no more loose ends.

You really believe that?

Sammy Davis was singing 'Mr Bojangles'. Kelly let himself become lost in the surge of big-band horns, and slowly dropped beneath the surface.

Chapter 9
Hope & Expectancy

1.

Katrina Esperanza's real name was Kathryn Hershaw. Her father was an earl who owned a large part of Buckinghamshire. Over the years he sought to shower his only daughter with every material gift imaginable. She in return became increasingly aggressive and insular, lashing out with a rage born of the frustrations in a life not earned.

At first it was simply a notion that something was missing, something passing by that should be grabbed hold of, but it quickly grew to be the only thought worthy of contemplation.

She spent her days horse riding, reading and playing backgammon with other ladies of leisure. At all times the sensation of unease lurked incessantly at the back of her mind.

Nothing carried the weight that it should. Nothing seemed important enough.

She took up archery and quickly found that she was a natural. She entered a local competition and won easily. The next day she gave it up. The thrill of achievement had evaporated before her eyes.

The same was true of everything she touched. Kathryn cruised through her school years, eating up qualifications and accolades with dispassionate ease. She drifted through a degree in Latin and promptly returned home to stagnation.

The next few years were a heady blend of social climbing and uneventful tedium. Shortly thereafter her father began pressing her to marry.

'It's about time we found a man to take you off my hands,' he stated one evening with his usual overstated sarcasm. Kathryn retired to her room without response and sat in front of a floor-to-ceiling mirror for the rest of the evening. She knew that she was not a particularly attractive woman.

Most of the men she met had the look of a predator about them. They stalked from function to function sniffing out the wealthy and the available. She had no intention of ransoming herself to the highest bidder.

She was trapped.

In conversation Kathryn began to find her party crowd dreary. She longed for substance but found only gossip and slander. She also began to wonder if her own existence fell woefully short of the mark.

In the winter of 1989 Kathryn turned twenty-one. Her father chose to mark the occasion with what he called a 'banquet to surpass all other banquets'. In the weeks leading up to the event he cancelled all of his business affairs, cleared his diary and devoted himself wholeheartedly to the task in hand.

Hundreds of people were involved – an army of hired help assembling tents and marquees, decking out the walls with well-wishing banners and trains of tinsel, carrying behemoth-sized bottles of champagne, mowing acres and acres of grass, mixing potent-smelling punch, delivering geese, duck, venison, multi-tiered gateaux, trifles, an endless flow of booze, fine wines, cognacs and boxes of cigars.

The day before Kathryn's birthday a procession of trucks arrived in the courtyard, and a swarm of roguishly dressed men and women began to feverishly assembly a circus on the front lawn – a big wheel, dodgems, merry-go-rounds, flashing lights and the whooping sounds of canned laughter.

Kathryn watched it all build before her eyes with a horrific sense of bloated excess. Her father's excitement made her feel guilty. She found it impossible to summon even the merest hint of enthusiasm and struggled to portray gratitude whenever in his presence.

The grandiose moment trudged sluggishly and unwanted to its arrival, staggering under the weight of its own affluence, and encroaching upon her without permission or apology. Peeking through drawn curtains she watched the guests arriving, most of whom she didn't recognize. Out in the courtyard Rolls-Royces and Bentleys lined back along the driveway as far as the eye could see. The sparkle of jewelry blinded her like a sea of photographers vying for supremacy.

Kathryn realized that she hadn't chosen a dress to wear. As the centre of attention the expectations bearing down upon her were unbearable.

She picked out a high-cut, pastel-green ball gown with dark emerald heels. It was an outfit Kathryn had worn on countless occasions. The colour complimented her red hair and brought shape to her otherwise bland figure.

People will expect something new. They will look down on me for my

127

repetition.

The anxiety and paranoia of youth had grown as tiresome as everything else in her life.

Let them think what they like. I no longer care.

No one noticed her entrance. She opted for a side door over the sweeping spiral staircase that had been used to spectacular effect by many of the other women. A passing steward handed her a glass of Buck's Fizz without making eye contact. Out in the main hall alliances were being formed and deals made. A pianist in a dinner jacket several sizes too small parodied various jazz styles – Joplin into Hancock, to Brubeck, to Monk.

She watched with a sense of detachment and prayed for it all to be over.

'So you're the birthday girl!'

Kathryn beheld pinpoint eyes within an oblong face. The man invaded her personal space with all the finesse and fortitude of a marauding Viking intent on pillage. She stepped back, giving ground to his boney arm flicking out like a forked tongue. 'I'm Philip. Pleased to make your acquaintance.'

'Likewise.'

Inwardly Kathryn asked why she allowed herself to be sucked into the façade of diplomacy.

Philip had a rodent's face – narrow pointy nose, tiny chin hidden below pencil-thin lips, greased back hair and bad skin.

'Quite a party you've put together,' he commented. His eyes scanned her body. His face revealed disappointment.

'It was my father's handiwork mainly,' Kathryn replied, trying to remain buoyant and upbeat.

'Mm,' Philip sighed dismissively and signalled a waitress to bring him another drink.

'So, how do I know you, Philip?

'Ah,' he rocked back revealing his paunch, 'it's complicated.'

Did he avoid answering as he wished to spare her the dull details, or was it, as his tone implied, that he considered her incapable of grasping the complexity of his lineage? Kathryn suspected the latter.

'Enlighten me. I have a degree in Latin so I can probably grasp a family tree.'

The sarcasm was lost on him. 'Oh, you know, so 'n so marries his

second cousin twice removed, goes to school with the great uncle . . . and
. . . etcetera.'

'Doesn't sound desperately complicated, but I'll take your word for it.
What is it you do for a living, Philip?'

He laughed. The sound left his throat as a stifled, high-pitched warble.
'Little of this, little of that, horse rearing–' a lengthy sip of his drink mid-
sentence '–livestock . . . bit of . . . farming.'

Nothing then.

'Tell me, has your father come to any decisions on that unit trust
venture?'

'I'm afraid my father and I don't discuss—'

She stopped. Philip didn't appear to be listening. Something up on the
balcony had his attention.

'Right, right,' he nodded, detecting a break in the conversation. 'OK, I
must get back to him on that.'

Back to him on what?

A thought lodged itself at the forefront of her mind.

You epitomise everything I loathe in the world.

She stifled laughter with a sip of her drink.

Philip began to regale her with an obviously fictitious tale of a
mountaineering expedition, blissfully unaware that he had silently lit a
fire within her.

'We reached the . . . tor . . . on the sixteenth day, by which time I was
the only one without frostbite.' Philip was momentarily distracted by a
low-cut top. Kathryn was incensed.

Worse than talking into my cleavage is talking into someone else's!

'I had to construct a primitive . . . shiv . . . and lower them down one
at a time—'

'You must be very brave!'

'It was nothing really.'

'Where did you say it was again?'

'Himalayas.'

'North or east face?' she guessed.

'North.'

'I've climbed the north face,' Kathryn lied on impulse, 'without oxygen
. . . very dangerous . . . we had to eat the huskies.' She giggled at her own
spontaneity.

Philip had not heard her response. Having noticed a stain on the lapel of his dinner jacket he was busy dabbing wine on the offending mark. Once again sensing a gap in the conversation he looked up with dull vacant eyes and said, 'Really? You're an amazingly interesting woman.'

The comment struck Kathryn as exceptionally smug. Philip's eyes wandered, following a passing derrière. It was such a small act of arrogance and yet she boiled over, angered that someone should so blatantly flaunt their condescension and disinterest.

How dare my special day be used as a platform for jackals and vultures?

There is an absence of intimacy.

Something monumental is missing.

Philip has just given you a compliment, however lame the delivery may have been. Protocol dictates that you thank him with a coyness and grace.

Protocol is a cage.

'What *exactly* do you find interesting about me?'

She was careful to keep any semblance of hostility out of her voice, opting instead for a firm, inquisitive force.

'Well–' Philip looked away, more out of embarrassment than distraction '–your ancestry is . . . what was it you said you did?'

'I didn't.'

'Well . . . your family has a lavish and satisfyingly full history–' the words tripped clumsily off his tongue '–especially on your mother's side.'

'Do you know my mother?'

'A fine woman!'

'She's been dead for eight years.'

Philip guzzled the rest of his drink. He looked angry at the glass for being empty. Kathryn felt emboldened. She leaned in closer, dominating the space between them.

'Philip, is it fair to say that you have come to my birthday celebration knowing nothing about me whatsoever, and that you have approached me out of some inane sense of furthering yourself rather than any real desire?'

'Well . . . I wouldn't say that.'

'What *would* you say?'

'I . . . appear to have finished my drink . . . I should really be going.'

'No, don't go. This is how conversations should be – engaging, exploratory, challenging, honest.'

Kathryn felt electrically charged. She knew that her conduct would be considered disgraceful by her peers, but to her it was like the shedding of a tight and oppressive skin.

'So tell me about yourself, Philip. What makes you tick? What gets you off, so to speak?'

Philip turned ghostly pale. 'If I have offended you in some way . . . I . . . Happy Birthday.'

He made a bolt for the door.

Kathryn had wished to make a swift exit there and then, but was grabbed by her father who whisked her down through a whirlwind of handshakes and well-wishers. Drinks were given and taken away, presents forced into her arms and passed to waiting servants, she was outside, she was inside, upstairs, downstairs, upstairs again, round and around and around. It was several hours before she was able to extricate herself and drop unseen into one of the back corridors. It was still relatively early. There was no point retiring to her room. They would only seek her out. Kathryn chose one of the many unused attic rooms in the forgotten heights of her father's house. The mattress was bare but she was too tired to find sheets or blankets. Kathryn lay down in her ball-gown dress and drifted off.

2.

She awoke before the sun to the sound of a cockerel crowing. Downstairs the party was in its death throws. Through the attic window she could she dishevelled-looking stragglers being ushered into the courtyard by her father, his ever-present grin showing signs of battle fatigue. Kathryn threw on a dressing gown and crept along the narrow corridor and down into the main body of the house. The repugnant stale odour of tobacco had snaked its way into the carpets. Somewhere far away she could hear the dull mumblings of drunken conversation and gravel scrunching beneath tyres.

Kathryn entered the banqueting hall via one of its many balconies. Beneath her the newly arrived day staff were taking down banners, and sweeping up champagne corks and streamers from the polished-oak floor. Within a matter of minutes there was no evidence the party had ever taken place.

Kathryn felt wretched, thoroughly ungrateful, self-pitying, morose and confused.

Why does this bother me so much?

What more could I possibly want?

She imagined a bottomless pit opening within her that no amount of pampering could fill.

Get away for a few days. Get some perspective.

Without further deliberation Kathryn ran to her room and packed a small suitcase. Before she left she wrote a brief note to her father. It read: '*I am going to find myself.*'

She booked a flight from the car on the way to the airport – Paris – no particular reason. A few days sipping red wine on the Champs Elysées left her restless, so Kathryn travelled to Barcelona and hung around La Rambla soaking up the coffee culture and mime artists. Once again she quickly became bored with her surroundings. A few days swelled to six weeks as she trekked from city to city – Rome, Venice, Prague, Lisbon, Berlin, Budapest. In the latter she witnessed a beggar being unceremoniously ejected from the foyer of a five-star hotel. Kathryn was appalled by the act. Her mind became filled with romantic notions of charity work and saving the world.

Perhaps this is what I am lacking, a consideration for others?

She chose a country at random – Sudan. As a token gesture Kathryn travelled economy class and donated the difference in airfare to an orphanage, vowing she'd never to do so again. The service was terrible.

On the streets of Khartoum she observed the most extreme forms of poverty and famine known to man from the tinted windows of an air-conditioned 4x4. She offered to help build a school, but quickly found that physical labour was not to her liking. Instead she wrote a cheque for a suitable sum and moved on.

A thirst for new culture and experience led her to South America and to El Salvador. She established herself in a hotel that was a virtual fortress shielding her from the outside degradation. Twice a day she withdrew low- denominational notes from an ATM and distributed them to the waifs and strays who loitered at the hotel's perimeter, before returning to the lavish creature comforts within. Her actions gained notoriety and the number of people waiting for her arrival grew to a mob. They were joined by low-income families who put on torn clothes in the hope of snaring her attention. Kathryn became known a La Chica Dinero ('The Money Girl').

One morning the cash machine refused to give her any money. Somewhat perplexed she phoned her father and discovered that he had stopped her considerable allowance. Kathryn was furious.

'What is the meaning of this?' she demanded and launched into a tirade of shamelessly sanctimonious accusations.

Her father laughed heartily. 'It's good to speak to you too, *dearest*.'

'Don't patronize me,' she snapped. 'I've just had my credit card refused in a restaurant. It was embarrassing.'

'Didn't you check that there were sufficient funds left?'

'Of *course* I didn't.'

'Well how did you think the money got there, by magic?'

'Oh God,' she scoffed. 'You've humiliated me in public and you simply don't care.'

'My poor baby, of course I care.'

Kathryn had never heard her father talk in this way before. He was usually so malleable and passive, agreeing to anything for a peaceful life, but now his voice was steeped in sarcasm. He seemed to be finding her whole predicament hilarious. Kathryn was incensed, but didn't dare hang up. She needed her allowance.

'I'm sorry if I appear overzealous. I am stranded several thousand miles from home with no means of getting back. *Please Daddy*, I need your help.'

'Perhaps I have been a little overgenerous with you. It's not healthy for someone to get everything they desire. It breeds ingratitude and a lack of understanding in the true value of things. What I'm doing is teaching you a little bit of humility, darling.'

Her softly-softly approach having failed Kathryn reverted back to an aggressive one. 'Give me my allowance this minute. I *need* money!'

'Tantrums are for babies,' her father replied. 'Anyone would think that it was your God-given right to receive handouts from Daddy.'

'How can you treat me with such contempt?'

'By learning from you.'

'How the hell am I supposed to live?'

'I thought you had gone to *find yourself*, my sweet. What better way than earning your own keep? In order for gold to be purified it must come through the refiner's fire. It must be beaten out on the hot plates and suffer flames of obscene temperatures. But when it has come through the refining process it shines exquisitely, even though it is surrounded by embers and charred impurity. Only now is it ready to ascend to its true purpose in life. Call me in a couple of weeks and let me know how you're getting on. I love you.'

And with that he hung up.

Kathryn stood dumbfound in the reception listening to the dial tone. People were staring at her. She wasn't aware of how loud she had been.

'OK,' she whispered 'OK.'

She checked her wallet for funds – 100 dollars in traveller's cheques and another eighteen in change. The hotel in which she was staying cost 300 dollars a night. Reality hit home hard.

I can't even afford to pay the bill.

Her first inclination was to call her father back, but she was too proud to beg. Kathryn burst into tears. It was the first time in her life she could ever remember having no one to lean on.

The hotel has my passport details. I can't leave the country with unpaid debts.

Kathryn retired to her room and made several extortionately priced international calls. She found that when it came to lending money most of her so-called friends were unwilling to part with even the most modest slices of their fortunes. Eventually she tried one of the predatory suitors who had been dogging her for months. Amidst snarling sexual advances he offered to wire her one thousand pounds, the loan conditional upon Kathryn agreeing to a dinner date upon her return. Reluctantly she agreed and the money was sent. There were sufficient funds to pay the hotel bill and purchase a flight home, but Kathryn couldn't leave.

Returning to England means failure. I know that much even if I cannot fathom an end goal.

In Buckinghamshire she would find only subservient lackeys and paralyzing inertia.

Her Spanish was passable and in the next fortnight she was hired and fired from a succession of bar jobs. Reasons varied from refusing to empty the drip trays to being obnoxious to customers and pouring herself excessive amounts of alcohol in order to get through the shifts.

She moved out of the hotel and into a hostel. Her upbringing had not prepared her for the enthusiasm of back-packers and the cramped realms of necessity. Each night she feared for her safety amidst the sleeping strangers. Each day she worried about how she would fund the next meal. Circumstances forced her to choke down her squeamishness. She managed to hold on to a job preparing food in a hotel kitchen, and slowly but surely began to put some savings together.

3.

One night she overheard a conversation between a Bolivian and an Italian in the bunk beds above her. They spoke in broken English of a city named Corderro, and used phrases such as 'glittering prize', 'vicious circle' and 'the melting pot'. Whilst both women were clearly embellishing their respective stories, Kathryn was enthralled by the thoughts of a principality bubbling and swirling with the hopes and aspirations it had ruthlessly consumed over the centuries. She felt certain that it was here that she would truly find herself.

4.

Later Kathryn realized that even as she was stepping off the boat, the city was marking her with its curse. With her meagre savings Kathryn had a week or so before she would need to seek employment, time in which to get acquainted with the place.

It was dark when she arrived. She ducked into the first place that crossed her path. It was a bar in the loosest sense of the word – bottles on shelves, scratched glasses to pour them into and makeshift furniture to sit upon. Six months later the nameless building would be lost beneath rubble and consigned to bitter memory. Kathryn would always remember the excitement that turned to dust, the moment she stepped off the path.

She had read about the infamous national cocktail Santos in a guidebook during the crossing. It was described as 'a gulp of joyous disappointment'. Kathryn ordered from a barman who smelled as though he drank as much as he served. The first sip was sickly sweet. She didn't see what all the fuss was about.

'Fsss,' she winced as the bitter half of the experience assaulted her taste buds. She looked around. A number of people, mostly men, seemed to be laughing at her expense.

So much for blending in!

She took another sip. It was surprisingly addictive.

I could get used to this.

One hour and a few Santos's later the world looked a far rosier place. It wasn't so bad that she had no one to talk to. It was quite peaceful in fact. Kathryn looked up from her thoughts.

Two men nearby were staring at her. They glanced nervously away, their noses buried in glasses.

Strange.

It was probably nothing. You're in a public place. Nothing can happen to you if you're careful.

'*Hola, mi chica bella.*'

A mountain of a man was standing besides her, a gigantic hand offered in greeting.

'Hello,' she replied.

'Ah . . . you English?'

'Yes.'

'Ah . . . pleased-to-meetchu. My name is Balthasar.'

She shook his hand. 'Kathryn.'

'In Espanol . . . *Katrina* . . . *Katrrreeeena*, eh.'

Kathryn giggled. Balthasar was more than a little drunk himself and his bumbling hospitality eased some of the tension she felt at being in a foreign place.

'*Como bebibe*? What would you like to drink?'

'I already have one, thank you.'

'Oh, *come on!*' Balthasar grabbed his chest. 'A pretty girl like you, it would be a disgrace not to fulfil my duty. Santos?'

'Please.'

Balthasar signalled the barman and sat down beside her. 'So, what are you doing here?'

Kathryn once again found herself under the watchful eye of the two men loitering near the exit. They looked away.

'I don't know really.'

'You have come to Corderro with no reason? This is unheard of.'

The barman placed two drinks in front of them.

'*Gracias, amigo.*' Balthasar took a sip. 'Ah, the Dulce-Amargo – sweetbitter. This was the drink's original name, the Dulce-Amargo, you know?'

'Really?'

'Truthfully, it was deemed too cumbersome and replaced with the great man's name.'

'I didn't know that.'

'Would you like me to furnish you with tales from some of Corderro's more colourful moments?'

'Please, that would be very kind of you.'

Balthasar told her of Ramon, McCafferty and then Emile. With each chapter came another Santos. Kathryn felt the room begin to spin.

'Why has no one ever learnt from the mistakes of previous generations?' she asked.

'Human nature, my sweet. Have you learnt from your father's fathers?'

'I guess not . . . those men have been watching me since I arrived.'

Balthasar turned and squinted into a dimly lit booth where two figures sat skulking in shadows. 'I know those men, trouble-makers both. Don't worry though, they will not move against you whilst I'm here.'

'Thank you. I'm very grateful.'

'Would you like to move bars and give them the slip?'

'If you don't mind?'

'Not at all. Anything for a new girl in town. Just let me use the bathroom. I'll be right back.'

Balthasar rose from his seat like Atlas bearing the world upon his shoulders. Kathryn was left alone once more.

I have not found a hotel.

Perhaps Balthasar will be able to suggest one?

'Señorita?'

Kathryn turned. One of the skulking shadows was by her side. 'My God,' she gasped.

'I am sorry to bother you, señorita, but I must warn you. That man is playing a game with you. It is called *esperanza* – in English, expectation. Do you understand? You are in great danger. You must come with us.'

'Are these guys bothering you?'

Balthasar had returned with lightning speed. Several others were with him.

The man Kathryn would come to know as Paolo turned to face the group. A cursory glance told him all he needed to know. They were poised, looking for even the slightest excuse for violence. He smiled softly and let his shoulder sag.

'I'm sorry, gentlemen. We didn't realize this lovely lady was with you, our apologies.'

He and his friend bowed and stepped backwards towards the door, leaving their drinks unfinished.

Balthasar put his arm around Kathryn. 'You OK?'

'A little shaken.'

'They're gone now.'

'Thanks again.'

'Come on. Let's get out of here.'

He led her out of the makeshift bar and into a part of the city he referred to as Liberacion. The buildings looked as if a giant had bitten mouthfuls of brick and mortar from their bodies.

'Where are we going?' Kathryn asked more than a little sluggishly.

'There's a great bar just round the next bend.'

'OK . . . but just one more . . . I need to find a place to stay.'

The ground beneath her feet was broken and uneven. She was concentrating on not stumbling and didn't notice Balthasar lead her off into a side road. When she looked up Kathryn found herself in a dead end. She felt hot breath on her neck.

'What are you doing?'

Balthasar's hands were on her hips. 'Welcoming you to Corderro, my sweet.'

Kathryn struggled to free herself. 'No, get off me. I'm not interested.'

'Oh come now, Esperanza. You let me buy all those drinks and then you don't put out.'

'I would have bought you drinks in return had you let me.'

'Let's not split hairs, *mi chica bella*.'

'You didn't buy my favour, and you can't have it.'

Balthasar struck out with malicious accuracy, catching her across the cheek and sending her sprawling to the ground. 'Let me be the judge of that.'

Kathryn's mind leapt from image to image – the fields of Buckinghamshire, horse riding, her father's manor house, the lecherous suitors who so desperately wanted to get their hands on her inheritance. It all now seemed so safe and secure.

Balthasar fell upon her, his hands tearing at her clothes. Kathryn tried to defend herself but her arms were prized apart and pinned beneath her. Unable to move she let out an angst-ridden howl that was immediately snuffed out by a sweaty palm.

The old world became a vague dream, the merest notion of a memory. She began to spiral into detachment and paralysis.

'The vicious circle.'

Her mind dredged up the words. They stopped her attacker in his tracks. He came closer, his pupils dilating.

'What goes around . . .' she continued.

'. . . Has already come around,' Balthasar finished. His hand moved from her chest and formed a claw, contorting so that only the digit sporting a wedding band was visible. There were tears in his eyes, but they were as much for rage as they were for sorrow. 'Corderro owes me, not the other way round.'

'You've lost something . . . so you're taking something . . . is that it?'

Balthasar face bulged with confusion and lust. He ripped at her jeans but then seemed to hesitate. Kathryn filled the resultant space with her malice.

'Your wife would be ashamed.'

The statement did not have the desired effect. Intended to provoke sleeping virtue it instead unleashed a barrage of explosive blows to the head. Kathryn felt herself blacking out and fought hard against the delirium. A single thought repeated itself over and over.

Corderro is having its way with you.

Corderro is having its way with you.

Corderro is having its way with you.

'Let her go.'

There was an arm around Balthasar's neck. His features were losing clarity, dripping off his shoulders into the earth. The ground itself began to swirl, churning her over, kneading her into the folds, spitting her back up.

A circle . . .

A hand grabbed Balthasar's hair, pulling it roughly back from his shoulders.

'This is no way to cope with grief. It won't bring her back.'

She recognized the voice. It belonged to the man who had warned her back at the nameless bar. For the first time Kathryn noticed just how silent it was. Later she would learn of the curfew and the dangers of impinging upon its inflexible boundaries.

Balthasar roared like a wild animal, reached behind and threw Paolo over his shoulder. A second pair of arms pitched Balthasar back into the dirt, crushing the breath from Kathryn's lungs. A brick struck her attacker's forehead. Once again he rose up. Kathryn saw the flash of a blade and heard something scream at the end of itself.

'Tomas . . . TOMAS!'

She faded away.

5.

A vicious circle needn't exist merely within the single rotation of a circumference. There is no reason why it cannot loop around a second, third or infinitive number of times. It may chose to vary the theme and adapt to maintain its own interest, or perhaps as in Kathryn's case repeat itself as a carbon copy, adding a sense of monotony to its list of dark delights.

She awoke in a room where three months later she would stand as Paolo now stood, looking upon her patient with equal loathing.

It was a small room; besides the bed it was devoid of any furniture. Paolo lingered by the door, her suitcase in his hand.

'Here are your belongings,' he stated coldly. 'Go back to England, you silly little rich girl.'

Paolo tossed her suitcase into the room and closed the door.

The events of the previous night came to her. Kathryn closed her eyes as she relived every naïve and terrifying moment. Opening them she saw a picture hanging above her bed. The picture was of a satellite.

Tomas . . . TOMAS!

Kathryn got out of bed and examined herself. Barring a few cuts and bruises she appeared to be OK. Hurriedly she got dressed and gathered up her possessions. The room led to a circular stairwell overlooking a lower floor.

She found Paolo in the kitchen. He was talking with the man she would come to know as Raoul. Both looked up from their conversation and took a step back as if repelled by her presence.

'Tomas?' she asked feebly. 'What has become of Tomas?'

Paolo was too disgusted to speak.

'*Somos de la tierra, señorita,*' Raoul replied. 'We are of the earth. Let it prey upon your conscience as is good and proper.'

'I don't understand.'

'Corderro has enough parasites without importing them from oversees,' he continued. 'My friend has called you a taxi. It is waiting to take you to the airport. If you deviate from this course you will die. Corderro will devour you. It is that simple. Be grateful I give you even this much advice.'

6.

Kathryn found herself standing in a vast and impersonal airport terminal.

How did I get here?

She could scarcely remember the taxi journey.

What did I say to those men?

How did I repay them for saving my life?

Nothing, you said nothing. You just left, fled with your tail between your legs.

Kathryn looked back at the past few months and saw in full the vast, blinkered arrogance of her actions.

I thought I was helping, but it was all for me.

I am responsible for a man's death, just as surely as if I'd plunged the blade into his heart myself.

I never even asked for their forgiveness; never said sorry.

I must atone for my transgressions.

The vicious circle . . . has already had its way with me. Perhaps I am immune?

Yet more arrogance?

No, defiance. Immune or not, it makes no odds. I must do something to justify my existence, justify the price that has been paid, the blood that has been spilt on my behalf.

Kathryn stumbled wearily through the terminal to a wall of payphones. She inserted a handful of petras into the coin slot and dialled a number. After a long wait the purring tone gave way to a wonderfully familiar voice.

'Hello.'

'Hello Father.'

'My dearest, it's good to hear your voice.'

'You too–' she trembled '–I think I've found myself.'

'That's good to hear. You sound like a different person.'

'I've been really ungrateful . . . and unreasonable . . . thank you for sticking with me.'

'My pleasure. What are fathers for! Where are you?'

'On the other side of the world.'

'Are you coming home?'

'Not yet . . . there are a few things that I need to do first . . . but I will . . . soon.'

'Are you OK?'

'I think I will be . . . yes . . . I think so.'

She heard the beeps go.

'I'm sorry . . . I haven't got any more change . . . I'll have to call you back.'

'That's OK. Call me when you can. I'm glad to hear that you're alright, and I love you very much.'

'I love you.'

The line disconnected.

7.

The taxi ride back into Corderro was unpleasant. Only days before she'd traveled the same streets with a sense of excitement and child-like awe. Now, however, those emotions sort to bring into sharp focus just how ignorant she was. They drove around in circles searching for snapshots that would jar her memory as to the location of the Satellite building. The river provided the first major clue. The driver gleefully watched his fare meter clicking away into the echelons as they snaked back and forth over bridges and through tunnels. Eventually they came to a row of dilapidated structures separated from the water by a patch of scrubland.

'This is it,' she cried. The fare claimed the remainder of her savings.

The door was answered by an old woman. Whilst Kathryn didn't recognize her it was clear that she recognized Kathryn.

'I'm looking for Paolo.'

'He's not here,' the woman replied flatly.

'When will he be back?'

'Couldn't say.'

'Do you have a home address?'

The old woman's eyes narrowed. 'Didn't he make his intentions clear enough to you?'

Kathryn put her hands together as if in prayer. 'Yes he did, but *please*, I have something to say to him, something important. I will wait for him here if necessary, but it would be far better for him if we were able to meet in private . . . *please.*'

The woman's eyes softened somewhat. 'I can think of nothing important enough to go stampeding over raw wounds. Are you sure you want to do this?'

'No,' Kathryn sobbed.

The woman offered her shoulder for support. 'Well at least you're honest! Here–' she wrote the address on a scrap of paper '–you didn't get this from me.'

8.

The door opened to a scene of children playing. Kathryn hadn't considered the possibility that Paolo was a father.

Perhaps they belonged to Tomas?

Even worse.

A woman was scooping them up into her arms when Paolo's imposing presence blocked Kathryn's view. She gazed mesmerized into a vacant, wraith-like face. Paolo's sagging features revealed a man who was elsewhere, reliving the moment when life had been pulled out from under him.

'Good morning.'

Kathryn winced. It sounded like a business greeting.

How could he find anything good?

'What I meant to say is . . . I know this isn't what you asked me to do, but I came back because I wanted to let you know I'm more sorry than you could possibly know. I won't ask you again what happened, but I can hazard a guess. I want to make amends and will do everything within my power to help you.'

Paolo made the strangest of expressions, a look of pleading undercut with deep insincerity. Kathryn was mortified to discover that he was mirroring her own beseeching features.

'I counted eight 'I's' in your little statement,' he whispered. 'Go to hell.'

He closed the door.

Kathryn stepped back and fell in the road. She had expected a hostile reception, but the malice conveyed within the softly spoken words overawed her. She moved to the curb and wrote him a note – short and honest.

Paolo,

You're absolutely right – I am a silly little rich girl – but I want so desperately to make amends, and will wait outside your home until you can see that my pledge to you is sincere.

> *Yours with the deepest of regret,*
> *Kathryn*

Moments after posting it Paolo opened the door and threw it back at her. His rejection ignited a resolve within.

'I will wait here until you speak with me.'

Paolo looked at his watch. 'Curfew starts in four hours. If you are here after then the black sedans will take you. Go home.'

Kathryn had never heard that phrase before and was consequently oblivious to the inherent dangers.

The afternoon passed uneventfully. Barring a handful of bemused glances few noticed her silent vigil. The encroaching darkness banished people from the street. The temperature dropped. The lights in Paolo's house went out.

He is testing me.

No he isn't. He doesn't care.

It doesn't matter. Either way I will show him how serious I am. The desire to be something more than myself is voracious.

9.

Her watch told her that it was 4.16 am. Kathryn looked up and saw the curtains twitch. She cursed herself for being caught counting the seconds. Paolo would think that her tenacity was waning. He would wait her out.

I will stay here until I collapse from exhaustion.

At 6.03 the beggars were up with the sunrise. Unlike Kathryn they had learnt to live with perpetual boredom and whiled away their days wearing down the soles of their feet on rapidly diminishing pavements, honing their looks of desperation and shouting, *'Dinero por favor, pero no petras.'* ('Money please, but no petras.')

Kathryn was new to Corderro, but even she knew the risks posed by the dawn folk. The homeless knew all too well that no one would miss them if they vanished. So much so that most were in the service of El Rey, and in return for not being black-sedaned they served up all manner of salacious rumours, whispers and half-truths.

All she had left was a handful of small change. It seemed to pacify them.

They will not be so forgiving tomorrow.

By midday it was raining so hard that her face and shoulders ached from the onslaught. Doubt crept in. She sniffed her clothes. They smelt stale. Maybe she wasn't a changed person after all? Perhaps what she perceived as determination was just another in a long line of tantrums?

Maybe rather than doing the right thing the end goal was merely to win and get her own way.

Peripheral movement disturbed the thoughts of self-pity. She looked up. Paolo was standing in front of her.

'I will not forgive you, Kathryn,' he said. 'You're wasting your time and you look like a fool.'

'I no longer seek your forgiveness. I wish to give my life in service.'

'You have no idea what you're saying.'

'You're right, I don't, but I shall wait out here until you show me.'

'By rights you should have been black-sedaned last night.'

'I don't know what that means.'

'You are an incredibly stubborn woman.'

'It is my best feature.'

'No, your red hair is your best feature.'

The statement did not carry the warmth that it inferred. Paolo was closed to her, now and forever. The rain intensified. 'You'd better come inside.'

10.

Paolo's charity was worse than his scorn. He lived with his wife and daughters in an apartment that would have fit inside her father's study several times over. They possessed very little and existed on the edge of poverty, and yet everything was made to stretch that little bit further with Kathryn's arrival.

She wished for cool contempt but instead received an outpouring of generosity. Paolo joined them for the evening meal but his place was not set.

Kathryn was horrified. 'I would rather go hungry than deprive you.'

Paolo shrugged. 'Food is hard to smuggle. It is easier to steal at source. I eat at the port. I never eat at home.'

In the early hours of the next morning they returned to the Satellite building. Paolo set her to work doing every menial task he could think of – emptying bins, cleaning out the U-bends in blocked sinks, wiping up vomit, changing nappies, bed baths to the elderly, sweeping stairs.

'I have to go to the port,' he said. 'Dinner will be at six.'

Kathryn realized that Paolo had no intention of accepting her help. It was merely a different form of discouragement – soul-destroying work during the day and psychological shame during the evening.

I can do this.

She toiled tirelessly until she was told to leave, and in the evening Paolo sat opposite with an empty plate, watching her eat.

To the rest of humanity Paolo was the best amongst men. Kathryn watched him from afar and saw genuine beauty in his face. He worked tirelessly for the people who arrived at Satellite, never letting them see the fatigue that washed over him in waves. His voice was calm and level, his eyes gave all of their attention and his angelic smile had earned him the nickname 'Santo' ('Saint').

But when it came to contact with Kathryn, a shroud fell. It was as if he was incapable of kindness. His velvet words became a growl that barked orders, his eyes betrayed the loathing that he felt towards her and his angelic smile became a sneer.

She in return gave everything to him, carrying out his commands humbly and subserviently. She choked down her propensity for backchat and worked harder than she'd ever known possible. But it was not hard enough to Paolo's way of thinking. He would deliberately set her tasks at midnight that took her into the early hours of the next morning, and then demand she start work with everyone else. The cumulative effect of sleep deprivation began to take serious hold after the first week. Her skin became yellow and waxy, her appetite vanished and her coordination slipped and slurred into a mess of confused stumbling.

Again the doubt oozed into the cracks opening in her mind, and again she beat them back with gritty fortitude.

It is not called 'endurance' for nothing.

It must be endured.

She did not make a spectacle of the state she was in, quite the opposite. Kathryn tried to bury the discomfort and anguish beneath the mountain of her duties.

Weeks passed with the same repressive routine, and then one day when she was on her hands and knees scrubbing the floor, Paolo was beside her.

'You can stop now,' he said. 'That's enough.'

She rose to her feet.

'You know the word "Esperanza"?'

Kathryn trod carefully. 'Yes, I know that word . . . how could I not know? "Expectation".'

'It also means "hope". For you I think this is a good name – Kathryn

146

Esperanza. No, better still, Katrina Esperanza.'

She understood perfectly. He was wiping the slate. Her eyes welled up. It was all too much.

'I'd like that.'

'You are a woman of privilege and it frustrates you that you do not have a cross to carry. Your lack of angst causes you angst! Do you not find this amusing? No, I can see by your face that you don't. Do not seek such emotions – they will come soon enough. But when they do, do not wear your grief on your sleeve. Let it hone you, but do not let it define you. It is a cruel quirk of fate that over time contentment turns to boredom. You seek excitement and yet when the excitement comes you seek a return to innocence. I do not think that human beings are made for happiness. We snatch glimmers here and there, but that is all.'

'Even now, you are trying to discourage me?'

'Absolutely! You should go back to your affluent life, go with my blessing, go guilt-free. Your only crime was naivety. After what happened I am sure it has been purged from you for ever. Enjoy your wealth and privilege, share it with others as you desire, find a shape that fits your skin and discover the joy that eludes us here.'

'More than happiness I desire purpose. I am too ordinary and clumsy to be a socialite, but if I can just channel my feistiness I know I can be of some use to you here, Paolo. I don't wish to be grandiose, only to make some small difference.'

'You will never gain my affections, Katrina, despite your noble intentions.'

'I wouldn't dream of aspiring to such heights.'

'Has it crossed your mind that, for me, having you around is a constant reminder of a crushing loss?'

Kathryn bowed her head. 'To tell you the truth . . . No, it had not. I am such a selfish person. I will leave.'

'You would leave . . . after everything you have endured . . . because I said so?'

'Yes I would.'

'Then stay.'

11.

That night she insisted that Paolo eat with them. Katrina (as she was now called) bartered her gold watch for a prime fillet steak and presented it to the family as a gift.

'This is not intended as a show of wealth, but of gratitude.'

She hoped they would not find the gesture offensive.

Paolo accepted the gift with good grace. He sat with a daughter on each knee savouring the feast.

'Why do you call yourselves "Satellite"?' Katrina asked.

'Imagine a satellite orbiting the planet earth,' Paolo replied, 'gracefully fulfilling its purpose up in the heavens. By itself it could never have scaled such heights. It is too flimsy, too vulnerable. No, it needs help from a rocket, boosters, fuel and a launch pad. Each in turn is sacrificed in pursuit of the prize – getting the satellite safely to its destination.

'The satellite is a metaphor for Corderro's people, our organization the rocket, the fuel, the boosters. It's a little cheesy as analogies go. We could just as easily have used a diamond – pressure and time producing something beautiful – or a jigsaw – putting things back together again and making them whole – but it was the satellite imagery that stuck.'

They talked into the early hours. Paolo spoke with an informed distance, never injecting the conversation with any warmth.

'How do you maintain such composure in the face of such tragedy?' Katrina asked.

'You cannot choose what life hurls at you, only how you deal with it,' Paolo replied. 'Like you we have each reached a crossroads where a higher purpose was demanded. Each of us in turn has sworn an oath that our lives are forfeit in the service of others. Not a single one of us truly understands the nature of our oath. Each day we experience a new depth, a new fear, a doubt, an elation. I think this is what it is like to be a *real* person . . . you understand?'

'I think so . . . and I'd like to make it.'

'*No* . . . don't rush . . . take your time . . . an oath can be made . . . it cannot be unmade . . . or it was never really an oath.'

Chapter 10
Carlos Offers an Olive Branch

1.

Isabella's first day in Corderro had been a disaster. From the moment she left Café Sal de la Tierra things had gone against her. First the taxi driver had ripped her off and then the hotel she'd been recommended turned out to have been derelict for over a decade. Sitting down in a bar to contemplate Plan B a group of local men had been overzealous with their advances, forcing her to leave and seek an alternative venue. The men proceeded to follow her around, wolf- whistling and shouting comments that she didn't fully understand before finally losing interest.

The only hotel within her price bracket not raised to the ground was The Phoenix. From its state Isabella presumed that it was yet to rise from its own ashes. There were bullet holes over the reception desk, and the man behind its counter was a clichéd vision of greasy hair, outrageously unkempt moustache and string vest with tufts of chest hair poking through. He shamelessly ogled her breasts before handing over a key ring featuring a well-endowed man holding his scrotum and grinning inanely.

'My name is Ronaldo. Anything you need. *Anything*. Ask Ronaldo,' he rasped as seductively as his sweaty features could muster.

Ronaldo did not offer to carry her bags. He led Isabella up three flights of stairs and stood outside the room with his hand outstretched waiting for a tip. Isabella slammed the door in his face.

The room itself had a terminally ill air-con unit that spluttered in its death throws when she switched it on. The bed smelled of unwashed linen and humidity and the bathroom featured a 5-inch hole over the toilet into next door's shower.

But worse of all – her journal was missing.

The journal meant everything. It wasn't just a diary of events. It was a list of achievements, a raison d'etre, the crux of her journey. Without it she was bereft of purpose.

It *had* to have been Carlos. She would never have been so careless as to lose it. He'd taken it. Isabella was certain of it. Alone and deflated she felt tears well in her eyes.

No, you can't let it get on top of you. Not so soon.

Isabella grabbed the phallic key ring and left the room without another thought.

'The room is good, no?' Ronaldo snorted as she passed, giving her breasts another thorough perusal.

The comment compounded her already considerable anger. 'Its disgusting but thanks for asking,' she beamed sarcastically before staring in revulsion at his gut. 'You should be ashamed.' She did not wait for a response.

Salvation came in the form of Feliciano's Late-night Bistro. With a large glass of red wine and a roast chicken sandwich Isabella began to see events in a rosier perspective. Losing the journal wasn't the end of the world. She'd reread it so many times that she could practically recite it from memory. If pushed she could write it all out again. After all, no hardship was too great if it brought her into contact with Jonathan Pemburton. And the hotel could be endured. So the sheets teamed with unwelcome life – she had a sleeping bag in the case and a jumper would suffice for a pillow. It wasn't so bad.

Next morning she was awoken by the hum of an electric shaver emanating from next door. As she stirred a deep voice boomed, '*Bienos dias,*' through the 5-inch hole.

Isabella was surprised to hear herself reply with, '*Y tu tambien.*'

2.

The Pheonix hotel stood at the corner of a particularly run-down neighbourhood. A disintegrating road stretched out in three different directions.

Left, right or straight ahead?

The choice was immaterial. They were all foreign to her. She chose left. The full extent of her daunting search quickly became apparent. Isabella's Spanish was passable and she was able to speak with relative ease, but inquiring after Jonathan she received a host of counter questions.

'What does he look like?'

'How old is he?'

'What does he do for a living?'

'Where did he live when you knew him last?'

Her response to each one: 'I don't know.'

His name and a single conversation – that was all she had.

By midday she found herself back where she'd started. Her hope was waning.

Isabella walked down towards the port. An armada of ships of all shapes and sizes waited to dock. She stood for a time watching the pinpricks on the horizon morph into people.

Will they all feel the same disappointment that now grips me?

They came teaming up the hill in search of accommodation and answers. Isabella ducked into a high-walled side street and lost herself within the maze of the Market quarter.

How will I recognize him, it's been so long? More to the point how will he recognize me?

Nothing's to say he's even still alive!

Amidst the stalls and barbecues she saw a tiny coffee house called 'Cup o' Joe.' Its brightly coloured sign and simple décor called to her in its normality. She ducked inside and found a seat by the window.

A combination of aromas helped to lift her spirits. There was the earthy fragrance of ground beans, a tang of potpourri and the sweet smell of baked bread.

All those years waiting for the sanctions to lift.

Such blind optimism, such a lack of real planning.

Why didn't you make better provisions?

'Good morning.'

Isabella looked up from her unforgiving conscience. A middle-aged woman with piercing green eyes smiled down at her.

'Is it?'

'Oh dear, having a bad day?'

Isabella sat up straight. 'Something like that. Sorry, where are my manners?'

The woman raised her hands as if it was nothing. 'That's OK. Corderro is renowned for giving people bad days – and worse besides. How about a slice of Gabriel's carrot cake and a mug of the best coffee in the city?'

'That sound's divine. Gabriel?'

'At your service.'

'Isabella – pleased to meet you. You sound English.'

'It's my adopted home.'

'You have a British passport?'

'For the last fifteen years.'

'Then what on earth are you going here? Surely you have exemption from the sanctions?'

Gabriel wrote down the order, pulled up a chair and placed the pen behind her ear.

'Seeing as you ask, seven years ago I was travelled up through South America on my way to Mexico but didn't quite make it. I had every intention of leaving but something about this city's chaos appealed to my nature. I could open up a coffee house anywhere in the world, but here I got to open a sanctuary. Anyway, this place had been derelict for quite a while, previous owner black-sedaned.'

'Black-sedaned?'

'Sorry, you're probably too young to remember the term – abducted by El Rey's men and tortured to death, very commonplace, even now. I take it you're new here?'

'New and old! I used to live here many years ago, but I only arrived yesterday.'

'Welcome back. What are your plans? Looking to stay?'

'No, I'm just here for a short while, till I find someone.'

'Someone dear to your heart?'

'Yes.'

'I have one of those. This place is named after him.'

The object of Gabriel's affection way well have been in the kitchen cooking an omelette or out running errands, but something in the way that her face altered told Isabella the man in question was dead.

'Let me get you that cake and coffee.' Gabriel got up and walked behind the counter. Isabella watched her as she took the cover off the cake, cut a generous slice and gathered up the ground coffee in a scoop. Her face appeared at ease. There was a light, effortless quality to the way she moved.

She has chosen a path similar to my own, opening an establishment and tying it inextricably to the past.

In any other part of the world losing someone would make your tragedy unique. Here it makes you ordinary.

But she seems to have come to terms with whatever it is that happened. Perhaps there is hope still for me?

Isabella chanced her arm. 'Ever heard of Jonathan Pemburton?'

Gabriel thought for a moment. 'No . . . I'm sorry.'

'That's alright. It was always a long shot.'

'Is this the person you have come here to seek?'

'It is.'

'Have you tried the library archives? They have records from the census.'

'I thought most people gave false names?'

'Some, but not all – you might be lucky.'

Isabella appreciated the optimism, however tenuous. 'Thank you. I'll give them a visit.'

'No problem. How about public records at the town hall?'

'What would I find there?'

'All kinds of information – income tax records, births and deaths certificates, passport applications. Come over here. There's a map on the wall. I can show you some other places.'

Isabella got up from her seat and joined Gabriel by the counter. In addition to the library and town hall she was shown the location of various hostels and soup kitchens where the homeless and abandoned now dwelled. Isabella remembered Jonathan as a strong, self-sufficient man. She could not imagine him ever falling into reliance upon others, but noted down the buildings' positions regardless.

Returning to her seat Isabella received a shock. On the previously empty table lay her journal.

Carlos! How did he find me?

Has he been following?

Where is he now?

There was no sign of him from the window.

Why would he steal my journal and then return it anonymously?

Gabriel brought across the coffee and cake. Isabella took her time over them.

If he's lurking outside, let him wait.

When she had finished she thanked Gabriel for her help and hospitality, settled up and left. Outside Carlos was nowhere to be seen.

Isabella travelled deeper into the Market quarter. She chose the busiest streets and weaved between the traders, masking her trail with the crowds. Her journey took her down into the bartering dens where many years previous Emile Verdin had honed his skills and dreamt of becoming an emperor. Frequent glances over her shoulder failed to reveal her illusive spy.

Perhaps he'd simply left the journal and fled?

She emerged from the side street into one of Corderro's many plazas. Carlos was seated directly in front of her with his feet up on a table. He was dressed in a Hawaiian shirt, shorts and flip-flops, and appeared to be doing a crossword.

How did he get ahead of me?

Whatever the answer Isabella was livid. She stormed over to him and knocked the puzzle out of his hand.

'How *dare* you!' she shouted. 'You don't know me.'

Carlos looked up and greeted her aggression with a smile. 'Ah, *mi chica bella*, sit down, let me buy you a drink.'

'Turn off the charm. I can see right through you.'

He took his legs off the table and frowned. 'I can assure you my intentions are honourable.'

'Ah yes, I forget, you're a family man!' Isabella spat sarcastically. 'A doting wife and kids.'

'That's right, two girls and a boy.'

'Swear to me. Swear on their lives that you did not take my journal.'

Carlos shook his head. 'Alas, I cannot.'

Isabella turned to leave.

'*Wait!*' Carlos stood up and lightly held her arm. 'Please, hear me out. Look, I know my actions up to this point have been questionable. I have been foolish and I'm sorry. I've made a bad start and I need to regain your trust, but truthfully, I would like to help you search for this man Jonathan Pemburton.'

Isabella freed herself from his grasp with a sudden jerking motion. 'Why would you want to help me? Why should I even trust you?'

'Because I brought the journal back, which proves that I am only half-rascal, because I have contacts and an intimate knowledge of the city which would come in handy, and because I genuinely want to see you reunited with this man.'

'Swear on your children?'

'Yes.'

'How can I be sure you even have children?'

Carlos gave an exacerbated chuckle. 'Well, what chance does that give me?'

Isabella's harsh expression softened a little.

'I tell you what,' he continued, 'if you would be kind enough to sit down and grant me a moment's leverage I have thought of a way in

154

which to make recompense.'

Isabella kept up the pretence of stubbornness, but her resolve was slipping. 'Why should I?'

'Because you are intrigued. I can see it in your beautifully inquisitive face.'

She sat with her arms crossed and her face scrunched in a scowl. Carlos summoned a waiter. 'A latte for the lady, *gracias*.'

'How presumptuous of you!'

'Would you like to change the order?'

'No.'

Carlos straightened his shirt and tidied his hair, making himself as presentable as his dishevelled features allowed. 'OK, so I have gleaned somewhat underhandedly four important pieces of information about you. I know of Peter—' Isabelle's face immediately flushed red with embarrassment. 'I too know what it is like to have loved and faltered. On balance I am happier with the echoes of loss than to have never experienced such dizzy heights. Secondly, I know of your coffee emporium – an achievement for which I am astoundingly envious. Thirdly, I know of your travels – an impressive feat if ever there was one. Like you I have stood beneath the concrete Christ on Corcovado and gazed down at Rio de Janeiro, an awesome experience. Fourth and finally, I know of your exodus from this city fifteen years ago. Therefore I am in debt to you for the grand total of four questions. Ask me any four questions you like, then we shall be quits, then I shall help you find Jonathan Pemberton.'

Isabella looked away so as to avoid eye contact.

You're letting your guard down, woman. Something isn't right.

Maybe you're just being cynical.

Nothing is for nothing.

The plaza was saturated with musicians and mime artists. People sat around drinking and applauding. Instead of giving money they gave food.

Take a chance. He seems harmless enough.

'OK,' she sighed, 'for what it's worth, question number one. What's the weirdest job you've ever done?'

'That's easy – lion tamer.'

'Yeah, sure.'

'In truth, señorita, *con mi corazon*, in a circus just outside Moscow. Alas it is also a piteous profession. Lions are born to be kings, not put on pedestals, and you will never truly tame a wild beast. All you succeed in doing is whip-cracking until its resolve is broken.'

Isabella laughed. 'This is ridiculous.'

'No it is not, next question.'

'OK. Why have you come to Corderro?'

'You mean besides aiding damsels in distress?'

'As I said yesterday, I am not in distress.'

'I too have come to find a man, a very important man.'

'Who?'

'Is this question three?'

'This is a subset of question two.'

'Oh I see. His name is inconsequential.'

'What relation is he to you?'

'He isn't.'

'Then why do you wish to find him?'

'To give back something that I stole from him, and to take back something that he stole from me.'

'Care to elaborate?'

'No señorita, I would not. Another?'

Isabella leaned forward. 'Have we met before?'

Carlos winced, and then grinned. 'Ah my clever one, I have already stolen your book – to lie to you would add insult to injury. Yes, I believe we have met before.'

'Where?'

'Alas this is question number five. You only had four!'

Isabella's latte arrived. Carlos paid the waiter and jumped to his feet. 'Good! Then it's settled, I shall meet you here tomorrow morning at eight-thirty.'

'What's wrong with now?'

'Regrettably I have pressing business elsewhere.'

Isabella arched her eyebrows. 'Depriving widows of their life savings?'

The comment elicited a wink. 'A tempting offer, señorita, but on this occasion I must decline. Incidentally, does your book have a name?'

'Are you deliberately trying to disorientate me with your bizarre, jumpy behaviour?'

'Not at all, this is how I normally am. Does it have a name?'

'No . . . not really, I was thinking of maybe calling it *The Book of Life*.'

Carlos frowned. 'I don't think so. This is a very cheesy title and does not do it justice.'

'I suppose you have something better in mind?'

'Seeing as you ask, yes, how about *Isabella's Odyssey*?'

'Odyssey is specific to Odysseus.'

'This is true, alright then, what about *The Isabossy*?'

'Oh, ha ha! You know, for a self-styled Lothario you haven't got this social interaction thing nailed at all. You never insult a lady after leaving halfway through a drink after stealing from her!'

'My apologies, it is not a scenario I have encountered in the past. It cannot be helped, time is pressing. Oh, there is one final matter. Have you heard of *Corderro's Legacy*?'

Isabella nodded. 'I've read it every year since I was a child.'

'This is excellent news. I would like you to have my copy, a book given for a book taken.'

She shrugged. 'OK.'

Carlos made no move to produce the promised gift. An uncomfortable silence formed between them.

'Well?' Isabella prompted.

'Well what?'

'The book? *Corderro's Legacy*?'

'Oh, I placed it in your bag.'

'When?'

'Whilst we were talking.'

'Is this a joke?'

'See for yourself if you don't believe me. Corderro has many pickpockets, but only one put-pocket!'

Isabella reached below the table and rummaged around in her bag. Sure enough she found a mass of disintegrating pages blotched with copious notation and dubious-looking stains.

'Is this a first addition? It would be very valuable if you'd taken care of it.'

She looked up. Carlos had vanished into the crowd.

Chapter 11

The Plague of Lethargy

After more than thirty-five years in power the unfulfilled artistic pangs had become unbearable. In recent weeks *Corderro's Legacy* had reached the impressive milestone of having sold ten million copies worldwide, but having not penned the original text the Emperor derived little joy or satisfaction from the achievement. In the days that followed, a niggling sliver of doubt grew into an all-encompassing obsession. The accolades and praise were all a sham. There was only one thing for it. A sequel was required.

El Rey wrote in his leather-bound journal: *'I am constantly amazed by the sheer randomness of life.'*

As if to emboss the statement he pulled out a revolver and shot the man nearest to him.

'Yes,' he declared, mulling over what had just transpired. 'Yes, I think that this is a most accurate reflection of the mortal coil.' He underlined the sentence in thick black ink. 'Did he have a family?'

The second soldier stood uncomfortably on the balls of his feet. Next to him his colleague slid down the wall, clutching the wound in his chest with one hand and grasping for support with the other. The soldier knew better than to offer assistance. His colleague was beyond help now and acts of compassion were usually rewarded with extreme measures. It felt wretched speaking in the past tense about someone who was not yet deceased. He swallowed down the bitterness and accepted the absurdity of his predicament.

'Yes sir, a wife and daughter. Their names were Lo—'

'No names! I have no wish to clog my mind with widows and orphans.'

El Rey returned his attention to the journal, blocking out the sounds of gargling and rasping that emanated from across the room.

I have chosen to call this account 'The Plague of Lethargy' as I feel it elegantly and succinctly captures the essence of my observations, namely that for the vast majority of people on this planet, life consists of bobbing around directionless in a sea of mediocrity.

Given that 'this is not a dress rehearsal' (to use the parlance of our times), it is with a morbid and astounded hilarity that I have witnessed the widespread squandering of existence. How is it that so finite a time can be so foolishly frittered away, especially if, like me, you believe that death marks the end to all things? No satisfactory answer has ever truly presented itself. The only way I can rationalize this most absurd phenomenon is by referring to it as a plague.

The Emperor placed the pen between his teeth and ran a finger over the finely grained paper.

Yes, a strong, bold opening, a clear outlaying of purpose.

The rasping sound had stopped.

'How many more sessions must I sit in this ridiculous position?' he shouted.

The question was directed at an artist standing at the far side of the room. The man, whose tiny stature was further dwarfed by a gigantic easel, opened his mouth to speak but found no words forthcoming.

For the past five mornings El Rey had sat in his full military regalia – uniform, stripes, medals, sabre, polished knee-length boots and a fedora hat. During that time the artist had captured the unearned paraphernalia in its full glory, brush-stroked a good 50 lb from the Emperor's midriff and had been putting the finishing touches to his face. But now on this sixth day El Rey had emerged dressed in a toga with sandals on his feet, a crown of laurel leaves on his head and a purple velvet cape that reached down his back and wrapped around both arms.

Was it a joke? A test? A change in direction? The artist wasn't sure, but knew better than to seek advice. He was the fourth person commissioned to paint the Emperor's portrait. The previous three had been shot during the sitting.

Faced with an impossible dilemma he decided there and then to finish the session, collect his daughter from school and go into hiding.

'I should be finished by tomorrow morning, Your Highness,' he squeaked.

'I will hold you to that, painter.'

El Rey returned to his journal.

A plague needs a cure. It strikes me that a cure for lethargy is an influx of energy; a cure for meaninglessness is purpose. To this end I have devised what I modestly like to refer to as the 'one true religion' – a belief system simpler and more honest than anything that has ever gone before. It is founded upon a duel premise:

> i. *All theories religions and philosophies on the reasons for existence are (without exception) utterly and hopelessly flawed.*
>
> ii. *Pleasure, however fleeting, is the only real truth.*

El Rey remembered the source of his anger, causing his inspiration to vanish into the ether. He tore a sheet of paper from the journal and hastily scrawled a note.

Eleanor (dear),

Some puta has stolen my sofa! It cost the earth, weighed a ton, and was the size of a small elephant. Is it too much to expect the port guards to detect a theft of this magnitude while in progress and deal with it accordingly? Is this not why I pay them so handsomely? (Please) find the person responsible for this lapse in duties, shred them alive and have their remains sprayed out over the entrance gates as an example to the others. As for the perpetrator of this outrage – I would very much like to see him or her alive and in person.

(Please) see that the theft is suitably publicized.

I am, as always, eternally grateful for your skill and dedication.

> *Much love,*
>
> *Emile.*

A ring of a bell summoned Cheech. 'Send this to Miss Blake–' a thoroughly wicked idea crossed the Emperor's mind '–and then hurry back. I shall have a further task for you.'

The servant boy bowed. 'Yes, Your Highness.'

To elaborate:

i. *All theories, religions and philosophies on the reasons for existence are (without exception) utterly and hopelessly flawed.*

I have spent my life reading the findings of great men throughout the ages – Aristotle, Plato, Nietche, Socrates, Machiavelli, Marx, Confucius, Jesus, Mohamed, Maynard-Keynes, Martin Luther, Freud, Tao.

All have promised so much and yet all in turn have failed to deliver. At each attempt at enlightenment I have been left equally disappointed.

Aristotle famously wrote: '(i) Every Greek is a person. (ii) Every person is mortal. (iii) Every Greek is mortal.'

To me this supposed 'great man' was little more than a great stater of the obvious. *Of course every Greek is a person, just as every banana is a fruit! I could stake my name on the revelation 'All trees are made of wood,' but this would not give credence to my self-proclaimed genius. To give him his dues he did give us rudimentary mathematics and scientific axioms, but credit must be limited to these achievements.*

Machiavelli was a pragmatic man – focused and single-minded in his unashamedly selfish dogma that 'a prince should do all within his power to maintain that power.' I myself have followed this course of action for some years now and find it an essential part of my happiness. But really, the man was a coward, switching allegiances all the while, making truces – a man who so gutlessly failed to live up to his own premise.

Jesus: interesting fellow, set out some incredible teachings, but burned a little too bright in the early years, and ultimately didn't last the course in my (humble) opinion.

Martin Luther: German. Copied Jesus!

Freud: Claimed that the mind was made up of the id, ego and superego. I for one am missing two of these devices. I leave it to your imagination to deduce which two!

As stated in my previous book Lord Acton came up with an interesting phrase: 'Power tends to corrupt. Absolute power corrupts absolutely.'

I think it's fair to say that I hold a position of absolute power, and if it follows that what I feel is deemed to be absolute corruptness, then corruptness feels pretty damn good! But then, if pleasure is the only truth (and truth is a good thing), how can the pleasure that I feel be corrupt?

In addition to my superior standpoint Acton stole his sentiments from Homer, further discrediting what was essentially a weak argument to begin with.

All of which may well simply be an elaborate, roundabout means of showcasing my immense knowledge, which in turn derives pleasure, further supporting point ii.

In short, I am a simple man of monstrous ambition.

Indeed, what better reason could there be for possessing power than enjoying the inevitable corruption that accompanies it?

Couple that with the crushing boredom of unswerving loyalty and all manner of vociferous vices can be brewed, be it drinking ass' milk from the navels of vestal virgins, or sending snipers into the hills with fictional assignments. I have sampled every disgraceful thought imaginable and made it a reality. One man's demise is another man's light entertainment.

Pleasure.

Say it.

Close your eyes, let go of every sanctimonious scruple and embrace the bloated, debauched desires that flood over you. Breathe them in, breathe deep, take them to the back of your lungs, feel them surging through your veins. You have just been given a glimpse into my world, which brings me nicely to . . .

ii. Pleasure, however fleeting, is the only real truth.

There is pleasure too in being famous, or infamous, or notorious. It matters little to me how I am remembered as long as I am remembered. Rank me alongside Hitler and Pol Pot, for all I care. Drape the words 'genocide' and 'dictator' over my corpse, as long as the words 'Emile "El Rey" Verdin' are etched inch deep into the tablets of history.

The sheer audacity of my arrogance makes me squirm with joy.

Cheech re-entered the room. 'You wanted to see me, Your Highness?'

'Yes.' The Emperor pointed his pistol at the boy's chest. 'I have a question for you. Answer incorrectly and I shall kill you. What do you think of Machiavelli?'

The boy straightened his back and met the Emperor's gaze. He watched as El Rey took his eyes away to a bowl of grapes; the weapon remaining trained upon his stomach. There was never a right or wrong answer, only chance. He chose his words and spoke them with confidence.

'I think he was a gutless coward, Your Highness.'

The Emperor choked on a pip and started to cough. He thumped at his chest as the spluttering rolled into howling laughter. '*A gutless coward . . .* that's priceless . . . and quite correct. How old are you, boy?'

'Twelve, Your Grace.'

'Where does a twelve year old learn of Machiavelli?'

'From my father, Your Highness. He was a history teacher.'

El Rey sat forward on the edge of his throne, elated. The very deliberate use of the past tense told him all he needed to know about the boy.

He has hidden his defiance in plain site for many years, magnificent!

It was so very rare that the Emperor found anything even remotely interesting.

'Well then, as you are no doubt aware, Machiavelli was the ultimate pragmatist, but that made him inconsistent. One should never shy away from disdainful acts, wouldn't you agree?'

Cheech didn't reply. Whatever thoughts swam behind his eyes were not revealed. El Rey was impressed.

'Maybe I should put you in charge of my soldiers?'

'I am just a humble servant, Your Highness,' the boy replied, the momentary flicker of animation fading to dull servitude. El Rey's excitement turned to disappointment.

'I was of course joking . . . never mind.'

The dead soldier was now surrounded by a thick treacle of life-blood, congealing around a body frozen in a stance of bemused horror.

'Take it away,' the Emperor commanded.

The other guard moved to retrieve his fallen colleague.

'NO!' El Rey boomed. 'Not you . . . *you*.'

Once again he pointed the firearm at Cheech. 'Since you exercise for mind and tongue so exquisitely, let's see if we can't also work on that puny body of yours.'

'Yes, Your Highness,' Cheech replied. He did not ask for help. None would be forthcoming.

As the boy struggled out of the room clutching the soldier by his feet El Rey was struck by a new line of thought. He wrote:

It is very rare that I meet someone with the courage of their convictions. They generally don't last long, consumed by the surrounding imperfections that refuse to allow their murky blackness to be compared against spotless white. When someone of that ilk does come along it is important to observe with a sense of awe. Such people are glitches in evolution – they are not normal – they do not belong.

El Rey was disturbed and annoyed by what he saw before him, a knee-jerk response to a boy's insolence. He very nearly called him back for an impromptu execution. Ironically it was lethargy that deterred him from the decision causing his further consternation. With an angry swirl of ink he concluded:

Ultimately their occurrence is utterly insignificant. The good and the evil alike travel down the conveyor belt together, side by side, waiting to be received by the earth. Be it selfless or selfish – 'Love your fellow man as you yourself would be loved' or, 'whoever dies with the most toys wins', we are all destined for dust. Now is all we have.

Chapter 12
Fiscal Policy

1.

The residents of the tower block stared down with a surreal sense of foreboding as the men below calmly rigged their building with explosives. A ring of sedans had rolled into position forming an impenetrable circle. The revving of engines disguised the sound of industrial drills boring holes into the concrete struts that supported the upper floors. They were packed moments later with dynamite. An elderly caretaker went out to see what all the fuss was about and was promptly executed.

Though just a spec on the distant ground everyone recognized the woman responsible. Inappropriately dressed in seductive attire, trademark claret-coloured lipstick, low-cut blouse and hair loose in black ringlets, Eleanor Blake glanced up at the petrified residents, giggled and blew them a kiss.

'Such tiresome work,' she sighed. None of her men risked showing signs of either agreement or dissent. 'Hurry up, boys. I am not renowned for my patience.'

I white flag appeared from the main entrance, closely followed by an extremely large man dressed all in black and sporting a dog collar.

'How splendid,' Eleanor grinned and waved for him to approach. With an arsenal of firearms trained upon his body the man made his way across the concourse with excruciating caution.

'Oh come, come, come, Padre,' Eleanor shouted. 'Time waits for no one.'

Clearly used to being shown reverent respect the man looked deeply shocked, but picked up his pace none the less and lumbered with an awkward waddling limp.

'You are . . . Miss Blake?' the man wheezed.

'At your service.'

'Father Medici.'

'Delighted to make your acquaintance.'

Father Medici glanced around at her faceless henchmen, features hidden beneath goggles and dust-masks, palpable tension in their limbs.

'Likewise,' he murmured.

'As you can see, Padre, I'm a busy girl at the moment. What is it I can do for you?'

The priest glanced back to the figures behind him leaning over balconies. 'Isn't that obvious?'

'No, it is *not* obvious. I'd like you to spell it out for me.'

'Well . . . I'd like you not to blow up this building.'

Eleanor shook her head as if she were genuinely aggrieved at having to disappoint the man. 'Sorry, I'm afraid I can't do that, Padre.'

'Oh . . . well, in that case . . . can you let the people leave the building first?'

'No, I'm afraid I can't do that either.'

'But *why*?'

'I am not inclined to explain myself to civilians, however, you as a holy man can obviously go free.'

Father Medici stared at her for what seemed to him like for ever. His heart and mind told him that it was pointless to argue with the woman no matter how high the stakes.

To find genocide nothing but an inconvenience is to have irretrievably lost your way.

There is a force at work here so evil it isn't even aware of its own abhorrence.

There is no hope of compassion. You must act upon her pitifully playful nature.

'Can I exchange my own safe passage for one of the others?'

Eleanor looked nonplussed 'Suit yourself, it's *your* life.'

Once again Father Medici paused for thought. 'As you can see, I am a large man. I think I am worth at least . . . three children?'

At this Eleanor lips parted in a succulent smile. 'Ah very good, Padre! I admire an audacious man. Very well, three children it is, but be quick about it. I haven't got all day.'

'Yes–' the Priest gasped in horrified disbelief '–and thank you,' he added in barely a whisper.

'Don't mention it.'

Father Medici began to walk away and as he did so he prayed.

'Dear Lord, everything under the sun belongs to you–'

I am walking into a tomb.

'–Show your power and mercy. Soften the heart of my enemy. Grant me a miracle, I pray–'

The doors will nail shut like a coffin, incarcerating you in a maddeningly oppressive hell of man's own making.

'–If it be your will. Amen.'

Both sets of thoughts were perfectly calm and reasoned, his footsteps uniform. He had not awoken that morning with a sense of the eternal, quite the opposite in fact. Life in humble servitude had slowly eroded his pride and the streets of Corderro had stripped him of his earthly hope.

Life is cruel. Paradise awaits.

If that is true then why attempt to save anyone? Surely it is cruelest on the ones you leave behind?

Father Medici genuinely had no answer to his own question.

The caretaker lay in front of him on the steps, pools of blood congealing around his head.

The dead and the soon to be dead.

He moved back into the foyer, quickly now, finding a strength previously absent. The reception was full of people, held back from the door by an invisible line. An old lady peering from a ground-floor flat asked in a frail voice, 'What's going on? I heard shots.' Every face he saw echoed her concern.

'All is well,' he said, his voice warm and composed, his eyes searching frantically through the crowds. Within a split second he found what he was looking for and politely pushed people aside to reach for the prize.

Suffer the little children to come unto me.

'Come here beautiful,' he said to a pretty girl in pigtails as he lifted her from her stunned mother's arms.

And forbid them not, for such is the kingdom of God.

'You too, handsome,' he called to a boy dressed as a fireman, his smile waning fast. He met the eyes of the boy's father and saw that he understood the full gravity of their situation. The man pushed his reluctant son towards the priest and took a step back.

Father Medici would've liked to have acknowledged the staggeringly selfless knee-jerk gesture but there was simply no time.

'And you.' Another girl – big wild Afro, tatty green dress.

He gathered them up and dashed back into the open air.

'God bless you,' one of the parents called after him.

'I'm truly sorry I couldn't do more,' he replied.

Out on the concourse and away from their parents all three children began to cry. Up ahead of them Eleanor tapped her long fingernails against the bonnet of a sedan.

'Can't you shut them up?' she scoffed.

'They are scared and soon to be orphaned.'

'My heart cries a river of tears on their behalf. Now go back inside and join your friends.'

'And you will look after the children?'

'Certainly not, this is not what we agreed.'

'But they will perish.'

'Perhaps – your god and the city will decide.'

'You are a disgusting human being.'

'Brave too . . . I have killed for less.'

'So kill me and end this pathetic little charade. I go to be with God. For those such as you hell awaits.'

'All in good time, Padre, all in good time, now . . . *start walking.*'

Father Medici began pacing towards the high-rise.

I don't understand, Lord. If I am to die, then let it be in place of the people, not amongst them.

'Padre?'

Father Medici turned, expecting either a bullet or a miracle. Instead he saw the children being dragged from the street into a black sedan. Eleanor's face quivered with forbidden pleasure.

'For you I think remaining alive is more painful than receiving your heavenly rewards.'

She gave a nod to her right and the building collapsed in on itself with an almighty, ear-rupturing boom. Father Medici was thrown forward by the force of the blast. He landed face down on the broken paving stones. A secondary shockwave sent a ripple through his body. Thick black clouds enveloped him.

I am at the Presbytery, getting ready to go out and administer to the sick – I am giving communion to those not able to venture beyond their four walls church – I am placing the Eucharist in a woman's mouth – offering her the chalice when the drilling starts – even as I am placing the sacred cup to her lips.

What does life amount to?

All things come to an end.

Yes, but the manner of that end, the deliberate pointlessness.

The detonation had deafened him. Fragments of stone and glass started to rain down.

Father, give me the courage to act upon the things I can change, the serenity to

accept the things I cannot change, and the wisdom to know the diff—
Something heavy struck his head. He blanked out.

2.

The phone rang in Tito's office. The brass handles of the receiver reflected an unflattering picture of middle age back at him. Annoyed, he snatched it up. 'Yes?'

'Some more coppers for your piggy bank, El Comedin.'

'Eleanor, a pleasure as always. The operation was a success?'

'In a manner of speaking.'

'How do you mean?'

Eleanor decided that now was the most opportune moment to spring her surprise.

'We were somewhat hampered by all the people trying to get out. It took us a while to subdue them. The methods were crude but the results spectacular.'

Tito's body temperature dropped several degrees. 'The building was full?'

'But of course it was full. It was a residential area. This is why the operation took so long.'

'Naturally, they were never going to be ecstatic about being moved on.'

'You never said anything about moving them on.'

'Well no . . . but I assumed that—'

'Assumption is the behaviour of fools, El Comedin.'

'Yes . . . but you did move them on, didn't you? I mean . . . basic human decency dictated that—'

'Again, El Comedin . . . assumption.'

'*Mi Dios.*'

'Not God, Tito, these are *your* doings.'

'What? How can you say that?'

My hair – mustn't panic.

'You think I don't have better things to do than blow up buildings?'

'No . . . but the people? You did—'

'Tito, your instructions said nothing of the people, only the building.'

'BUT IT'S OBVIOUS!'

'Do not raise your voice to me again, Majagranzas. I have heard this word many times so far today – obvious. Obvious to you maybe, politician. I am a soldier. I follow orders and make snap decisions in the heart of battle.'

Tito placed his head on the desk.

We are only at war with ourselves.

What have I done?

How many times has this happened before?

'One more thing, El Comedin. I am not a mathematician. I do not possess a mind as grandiose as your own, but by my crude calculations I cost our operation this morning at roughly twice that of what we'll make on the insurance claim.'

Tito was thankful Eleanor was not standing in front of him to witness all the blood drain from his face.

'You are too kind with your praise,' he mumbled into the receiver. 'Unfortunately, you are not taking into account the fiscal shift this morning's operation has instigated. The resultant macro-economic pressures on industry to meet its production quotas, coupled with that of the micro-economic pressure on civilians to pay more representational taxes will more than compensate for any shortfall . . .'

He petered off. Eleanor was not immediately forthcoming with a response. Tito closed his eyes which sought only to magnify the silence. He hoped beyond hope that she would not realize the statement made absolutely no sense.

'Fascinating, Tito, fascinating. I have always looked upon economics as being one of the dark arts, like sorcery in many respects, conjuring something from nothing. I must drop by your office one evening and trouble you for an explanation in layman's terms.'

'I'd like that.'

Eleanor was no longer there.

3.

Paolo found Katrina sitting amidst the rubble with her arm around a clergyman. The tops of their heads were chalky white with the slow descent of dust.

'You shouldn't be here, Esperanza. It's not safe.'

'Then what are you doing here?'

'I blend in. I am Hispanic. I don't have red hair.'

'What would you have me do? I live a block away. The blast knocked my breakfast off the table!'

169

Up above the birds were circling. They could smell fresh carrion.

'These people are dead, Katrina. I would have you worry about the living, yourself included.'

'We need to start moving people out of the high-rises.'

'Are you listening to me?'

'Of course I'm listening to you, Paolo. I always listen to you. I hang off your every word, but in this instance I simply don't agree.'

'In a city this size we're talking tens of thousands. It's a logistical impossibility, not to mention the attention it will bring, and the fact that many people won't want to come but *will* want to inform upon us.'

'You have to think bigger than this, Paolo. We have to be bold. The city has set us a challenge. We need to break free from the vicious circle.'

'Listen to yourself, Katrina. You sound like a woman suffering from delusions. What we need to be is discrete, small, unnoticed.'

Behind them the remaining pillars crumbled.

'They took children,' the priest murmured into the dirt.

Katrina's frustrations boiled over. 'This is *unacceptable*! El Comedin – that, incompetent, murderous imbecile. I'd like to slit his throat.'

Paolo fixed her the most intense of stares. 'You are being serious?'

Katrina was unashamed. 'Absolutely! One life for thousands makes perfect sense to me at this point in time.'

'No.' Paolo shook his head violently. 'You have to stay behind a moral line. Once you cross it you lose the high ground. You lose your basis for being in opposition.'

'Forget morals, think of the mathematics. There are degrees of right and wrong, Paolo.'

'No, complete rubbish! Ask Raoul, he will tell you better than I. There are no degrees. There is only right and wrong, black and white. Don't try to be a crusader, Esperanza. You don't have the stomach for butchery, and you'll be dead long before you fulfill your potential. Stealth and compassion are the best ways.'

'And do what? We took in a dozen people yesterday whilst El Rey's men killed hundreds.'

'Yes, but think of the dozen, a dozen more today, and tomorrow, and the day after. Think of the little victories. Any more and you will undo everything we have strived to achieve.'

'OK, then what little victories can we gain here and now?'

Paolo couldn't tell whether or not she was being sarcastic. He looked around him and answered as best he could.

'What I suggest is this. First and foremost, that we uncover as many people as possible and bury them. We give them a resting place and we mark that resting place so that it can be visited by their loved ones. We need to form two groups, one to commandeer a van and load the bodies, the other to find a spot in the hills and start digging. We should wait till after curfew to drive the van to the grave . . . and we should douse the van in petrol so that if the black sedans see us we can cremate the bodies . . . and we should remove all of their shoes and jewellery – the shoes for the poor, and the jewellery to barter for food and provisions . . . have I missed anything that you can think of?'

Kathryn was crying. 'Oh God, what a mess. I'm sorry for shouting. It was so inappropriate.'

'It's OK. It's a natural reaction. You're only human. As I keep telling you, you can't change the world all by yourself, all in one day. We have to work together – and in increments.'

Father Medici had begun to rock backwards and forwards.

'We need to think about getting you out of the country, Padre,' Katrina suggested.

Medici made no indication that he'd registered her comment.

'Breathing is excruciating, suicide an unforgivable sin. I can neither live nor die.'

'Padre?'

'I prayed for a miracle and yet still they perished.'

'*Padre?*'

'I fell short in some way and the Lord forsook me.'

'Hey!' Katrina brought him to his senses with an abrupt slap across the cheek. 'Stand up.'

Medici was so shocked that he obeyed without protest.

'You are God's mouthpiece,' Katrina continued. 'There is no higher office. Promise me you'll take something from this experience and use it for good.'

Medici brow furrowed so that his expression changed from disillusion to desperation.

'How can any good possibly come from this?'

'I have no idea, Padre, but you are the only one left alive to work it out.'

Medici closed his eyes. 'I'll try my best.'

'That's all any of us could ask for.'
Katrina turned to Paolo. He looked impressed. She nodded.
'Little victories.'

4.

Next morning the site had been sprayed with a large 'A', the tail of which broke the circumference of a circle.

Chapter 13

Events Conspire

1.

There had been strings and woodwind, sailing over a mind that had momentarily allowed itself some much-needed respite, but now Kelly was on his feet, alert and electrified. Wagner masked his footsteps as he tiptoed over polished floorboards into the kitchen. The drawer slid silently open. He reached in and took out a steak knife, turned on his heels and headed back towards the front door.

There had been a knock. No one ever knocked. Very few people even knew he was here.

Could be Martine about the rent?

Unlikely, he already left a note.

He opened a window. There were no obvious signs of movement. The street was empty. He watched the LP spinning and heard cymbals crash. The apartment had been Kelly's shelter for as long as he cared to remember. Never in all that time had he felt threatened within its walls.

And now even that's compromised.

There was another knock, firmer, more definite in purpose.

Arty?

Already seen him twice today.

Kelly flipped the knife over in his hand so that the blade pointed behind him, and took three large catlike steps that brought him up against the wall. Like most buildings in Corderro the outer door was fitted with a peephole, but Kelly knew better than to use it. The black sedans had been known to wait for a flicker of light before discharging shotguns into over-inquisitive eyes.

Whoever it is, they know I'm here – the music.

A quick glance at his watch revealed that it was ten minutes till the beginning of curfew.

They're taking a risk visiting this late in the day.

Unless . . .

He crouched in the corner, making himself as small as possible.

Another knock.

173

Persistent.

Decision?

Kelly looked around at his environment.

Open the catch, step back and pick a middle point. If they're harmless step forward and greet them, if not, close and bolt the inner door, run for the open window.

Not ideal.

It'll have to do.

The knife looked feeble in his hand. It would be of little use. He placed it on the ground.

If I die in the next instance then my final act will have been to run a bath.

Nothing poignant materialized to replace the ridiculous thought.

He rose to his feet, stepped back and undid the lock.

'Oh, it's *you.*'

Raoul smiled awkwardly. 'Charming as ever.'

'What do you want?'

'A few minutes of your time.'

The door was already closing. Raoul blocked with his foot.

'I'll be brief.'

'How did you find this place?'

'You're fat friend, the café owner.'

'What did it cost you?'

'Twenty US and a bottle of Scotch.'

'Not all bad then! Make it quick.'

Kelly marvelled at how quickly the childlike hope to live another day had been replaced by mundane reality. His movement was purposefully intimidating. He walked backwards so as not to take his eyes off Raoul. Kelly could see what his unwanted guest was doing. It was what came naturally to a smuggler. Raoul casually glanced around the room, assimilating all of the information into an appraisal and judgement.

Steak sizzling in the pan – the rich aroma denoting its high quality – simple, elegant hi-fi – equalizer bar rising and falling with the music – bottle of red, the only item on a spotless worktop – no clutter – no non-essential items – steam rising through a door at the back of the room – the sound of running water – beautifully minimalist furniture – a large, out-of-place cardboard box pushed into the hallway.

In the unseen confines of his head Raoul made his summation.

You live in an empty, functional space. Despite dwelling here for years you have never made it your own. There is nothing here that you wouldn't happily abandon in the blink of an eye. A few luxury items to keep you tethered to sanity – the wine – the steak – but nothing that you truly love or appreciate.

He didn't wait to be offered a seat, knowing that no such gesture would be forthcoming.

'Make yourself at home,' Kelly responded.

'Thank you. Someone's got to,' Raoul replied with equal sarcasm.

'Coffee?'

'Do I get one if I say yes?'

'Cute.'

'OK then . . . yes . . . black, no sugar.'

Kelly turned his back and reached into a cupboard. Raoul noticed that the only other item on the shelves was an upturned picture frame.

'You live well.'

'I live frugally.'

'I'm sorry if Katrina offended you. She's an idealist.'

'She's an idiot.'

The comment seemed the final word on the matter. Raoul let it drop. 'What's in the box?'

'*Nothing*, forget you ever saw it.'

Raoul raised his arms. 'OK, it's forgotten.'

The coffee grinder omitted an unpleasant gargling growl as it chewed the beans into aromatic dust. Kelly made his discomfort known.

'Where there was once an orchestra we now have a dirge. Seems every time we meet you're unimproving my existence in some way or other.'

'Ever thought of granting someone a little hospitality?'

'No, the privileges of being a bastard.'

Due to the open hostility, neither man felt perturbed by the ensuing break in conversation. They were both accustomed to long vacuous pauses interspersed with momentary outbursts – watching the ships come and go, waiting for the opportunity to strike. Kelly left the grinder running far longer than was necessary. Whether it was to postpone an unwanted conversation, to contemplate his words or simply to annoy Raoul could not be fathomed. Eventually he depressed the switch and the nauseating swirl was replaced with the majestic marching of brass.

'Julian was black-sedaned today,' Raoul announced.

Kelly summoned the image of a tall, blond man, bright features, Steelers baseball cap, wispy moustache.

'They picked him up right outside the port, *right outside*. His van was empty, he had no US dollars, but they took him regardless.'

Kelly filled the kettle. 'Did you know him well?'

'Unfortunately no.'

'Neither did I, so why should either of us care?'

'You're unbelievable.'

'I don't remember falling over myself to gain your approval.'

'Don't you at least feel some empathy? Or pity? You worked in the same space as the guy for over a year.'

'Not one iota. The man was a fool.'

'What?'

'Why do you never see Columbian drug barons?'

Raoul shrugged, his face a picture of disgust. 'I give up . . . no idea.'

'Because they know that if they get caught with anything more than a handful of cocaine in their possession they're facing the death penalty as a default. This makes getting caught a moot point. If cornered they always coming out shooting. Columbian drug barons are either living the highlife free and easy, or else they're dead. There is no middle ground. What the hell was Julian thinking getting into that car?'

'What would you have had him do, go out in a blaze of glory?'

'I wouldn't have him do anything now. Right about now they'll be running electrodes over the soles of his feet and getting him to cough up everything he knows.'

Raoul shifted uncomfortably in his seat.

'He should have run for his life. Either that or else beat the guy to death. Anything but humbly accept his own murder in broad daylight.'

'Not everyone's as callous as you.'

'Callousness has nothing to do with it. This is the continuation of life. What else does a man have?'

Evidently the question was rhetorical. Kelly turned his back and poured the brown powder into a circle of filter paper.

'So, enough pointless chatter, what can I do for Paolo's little errand boy?'

'I'm not here on an errand. No one knows I'm doing this.'

'Have you formed a break away faction of . . . that was it . . . Satellite?'

'Come on, Slim, give me a break.'

Water boiled in the kettle. Kelly took a cafetiere from a second equally barren cupboard and poured in the liquid.

'Fine, what is it that you want?'

'We could really do with your help.'

Raoul regretted the words as soon as they were uttered.

'What part of our last conversation did you not understand?'

'That's not what I meant. I phrased it badly, sorry. OK, forget humanitarian reasons. I know I can't appeal to your better side as you don't have one! So let's look at it from a purely selfish perspective.'

'What did you think I was doing?'

'I think that you've been working alone, putting all your eggs in one basket and taking an immense risk. You have no support network to look out for you.'

'Oh very good, playing the insecurity card. You'll go far.'

'I'm serious. What are you gonna do when you get into trouble?'

'I have a British passport.'

'Come on, that means shit and you know it. When this place falls, and it *will* fall, El Rey will take as many people with him as he can. You think the embassy will step in to help a smuggler? They'll be fighting off women and children to be the first out of the principality. What you'll need is a safe house, people who you can trust, who can hide you.'

Kelly pushed down on the plunger forcing hot water through tiny perforations. 'So you've selflessly come here to offer me help and assistance?'

Raoul had expected his rival to be difficult and did his best to remain upbeat. 'I could never carry off a lie that big and you know it. What I'm offering is a mutually beneficial arrangement.'

He was presented with a small cup of sweet-smelling, thick, black coffee. It was the first time he had ever seen Kelly offer anything to anyone. Raoul saw no joy within the man's eyes, only the surging energy of a relentlessly calculating mind.

'Let me ask you something,' Kelly said, fixing Raoul with a piercing stare. 'You, like me, are a smuggler, correct?'

'Yes.'

'So, amongst your day-to-day activities is it fair to say that you regularly steal from people, that which does not belong to you?'

'You could say that.'

'I could and I do. So, at what point in the day do you rise above the quagmire of your own actions and attain grace?'

Raoul frowned. 'I'm sorry, you've lost me.'

'I'm just trying to ascertain whether or not you know why it is you're doing all this. Katrina told me that you're a humanitarian organization. Founding the operation upon theft doesn't sound very humanitarian to me.'

'There's a greater good at stake.'

'So, hardship justifies daylight robbery.'

'When it gets bad enough, yes.'

'What's the tipping point?'

'*What?*' Raoul showed signs of becoming flustered.

'The tipping point? The sliding scale? At what point does hardship justify theft? How bad does life have to get before you can put hand on heart say it's OK to walk down to the port and take as much as you can get your grubby little paws on?'

'It's not like that and you know it.'

'Yes it is, and no I don't. It only took one bite of the apple to bring the downfall of man. How many picnic hampers full of goodies have you pilfered so far, Raoul?'

'Preventing murder justifies theft. It's obviously the greater good!'

A wickedly sly smile spread across Kelly's face. 'Well, now you're into weighing up sins against one another. It's a moral minefield out there.'

'Yeah, well at least I've put a stake in the ground.'

Kelly shrugged. 'The point I have now successfully made is that you can't in fact quantify why it is you do what you do. You have some kind of glorious notion of goodness, but it's at best contrived and at worst imbecilic. I don't *care* about any of that and my reasons for not caring are none of your business. All I care about right now is, 'why is this incompetent bunch of supposed humanitarians hounding me when I've explicitly told them to leave me alone?'' Kelly ran a hand across several days' worth of stubble. 'So, you still want to pitch me that business proposal?'

Raoul cradled the small cup in his hands, raised it to his lips and used the coffee to swallow down his pride. Kelly's quick wit and clever use of language had tied him up in knots. By rights he should leave, fling the drink over one of his precious chairs and finish with a choice insult, but he couldn't get up.

I took an oath.

So what if I'm not as great an orator as you. My heart is in the right place. I'm trying to do something important, serve something bigger than myself.

He started again. 'Though it pains me to say it, you have proven yourself time and time again to be the best in our rarefied profession. You can remove items from El Puerto de Las Ondas Verdes that none of us could ever dream of.'

'You want to *pay* me to steal stuff?'

'Yes.'

'It just gets better. You dark horse! And there was I thinking you'd touched rock bottom. You really are jumping into bed with the devil, aren't you?'

Raoul struggled to maintain his composure.

Damn you. You make me doubt my own good intentions.

'If you say so, Slim.'

'Indeed – what kind of stuff?'

'Medical equipment, vehicles, furniture—'

Kelly flinched.

Raoul stopped mid-sentence. Nothing was ever without purpose.

Furniture.

The penny dropped.

He spun around in his seat and glared at the large cardboard box. 'Is this what I think it is?'

For the briefest moment Kelly was lost for words. It was all the proof Raoul required. The power passed from one man to the other. Raoul got to his feet. Kelly shrank back against the worktop.

'What was that you were saying about getting into bed with the devil?'

Their conversation was disturbed by a repugnant smell wafting across the room. Thick smoke rose from the pan. Kelly's steak was burnt to a crisp.

One of the few pleasures in life.

He ran to the stove, picked up the saucepan and dropped it into the sink. Tap water fizzed over the cold rubbery remains.

'This is what happens when I involve people,' Kelly whispered, more for his own benefit than for Raoul's. 'Everything turns to shit. Thanks for thinking of me, but the answer's no, now *get out!*'

Raoul laughed and shook his head in disbelief. 'You're joking. There you were, all high and mighty, talking about how incompetent *we* all are when *you've* endangered the lives of every man in the port. Of all the stupid things to steal!'

'Keep your voice down,' Kelly snapped.

'I'LL TALK AS LOUD AS I LIKE! Moral sliding scale? Such a show of intelligence to mask your own futility. I'll give you a sliding scale. This–' Raoul pointed at the cardboard box '–is more important than *you*, and if *you* won't help *me*, either by choice or by money, then I'll have to encourage you by some other means. Seeing as you have no cause, I'm sure you won't object to me giving you one!'

Kelly struck him across the jaw and followed up with a barge that sent Raoul sprawling to the ground.

'You presume to threaten me, in my own home? *Me*, minding my own business, getting through, and you, relentlessly pursuing me, getting lower and more debased with every turn.' Kelly wiped phlegm from his lips. 'Blackmail *and* theft! You're not a moral man, Raoul, however much you purport to be. Well, now that you're finally revealing your true colours let's follow this line of argument through to its conclusion. You leave here now and give me up to the authorities – one insignificant smuggler. I in turn will give up every orphan and widow in your care. You know I'll do it so don't try entering into one of your pitiful little pitches. You don't even know which side of the fence you sit on anyway. I'm going to take a piss. Show yourself out and don't feel compelled to finish your coffee. Oh, and while we're threatening one another, contrary to what Paolo argued last time we spoke, you *are* both finished at the port. I see either of you there again, I make a phone call.'

Kelly left him cupping his hand under a bleeding nose. Raoul felt pathetic. Not only had he failed to enlist Kelly's help, he had also succeeded in placing his colleagues in jeopardy. The conversation had simply run away from him.

What next?

He had no intention of blackmailing Kelly. It had been an empty threat.

Becoming an informer really would mean crossing over.

Raoul picked up his half cup of coffee and carefully placed it on the worktop. He resisted the urge to peek inside the box and opened the front door.

A man was standing in his way.

'Oh,' was Raoul's final word.

Belatedly his mind registered the man's uniform and what he was carrying, and then there was a deafening boom and he was falling. Muddled thoughts flashed before his eyes.

Good intentions.

Getting into bed with the devil.

A satellite slipping out of orbit, plummeting to earth, crashing into the sea.

2.

Kelly was at full sprint before he was even aware of himself. As he re-entered the lounge he caught his shoulder on the door frame. Something to his left was collapsing. Several dark shapes moved into view. His body span off kilter. He tripped, fell and scrambled back to his feet, the shot ringing in his ears.

Katrina's fault.

Without hesitation Kelly dived through the window. Something grabbed one of his ankles as he was in flight.

'Wait, we just want to—'

Talk?

Like you did with Raoul, or Julian?

His face crashed against the metal walkway. Kelly kicked for all he was worth and heard someone cry out. His shoe came away. He scrambled to his feet and flung himself over the railing.

The images came clearer now – the previously empty alleyway, the remorseless black sheen of the vessel beneath him, impenetrably vacant glass, the slow-motion descent.

This is going to hurt.

The bonnet bowed as he punched down into it. Kelly couldn't feel anything. The front door began to open. He slid off onto the floor and launched himself at the emerging passenger. The force of his charge slammed metal into flesh and rebounded back into his stomach. The wind was driven out of him and he dropped to his knees.

This is really happening. This is my time.

No, I'll be the exception.

Just like everyone else!

Kelly struck at his chest, willing the air into his lungs. The passenger was crawling out of the sedan nursing his head. He heard heavy footsteps on the walkway above him. Rage forced him to his feet. He yanked off his other shoe and threw it at the man on the ground, and then he ran.

His eyes captured staccato images of rushing colour – an upturned bin spewing fluorescent foulness from its mouth, the light playing tricks in the alleyway, distorting shadows into slim-line giants and pulling the walls in close, the open road that stripped away all of his protection.

Kelly doubled back into a parallel street. A glance behind him revealed aggressive movement. He veered to the right, under an archway, a courtyard, a garden, over a low wall.

The world was shrinking, closing and evaporating. The apartment was gone forever. He could never set foot in the port again. The Market quarter rushed past – a stall for every cubbyhole, the wild, pale, statuesque expressions of vendors. Above him wooden shutters closed, the inhabitants of Corderro turning a blind eye.

How many times have I myself stood impotent and watched people run for their lives?

How many times have I sat in darkness, the curtains drawn, waiting for the chase to end?

How many of them ever truly escaped?

Do I wear that same stupid look, searching the faces of strangers for a miracle, looking for what is so painfully absent?

Is this to be my final inspiration?

Is this all it amounts to?

The money – was it worth it? The patch of land, the brother reconciled, the book, thirty-eight years lost, the four that count?

Julian.

What possesses a man to give in like that? Or was it that he simply never gave his life enough thought? Never had a plan? Never saw the consequences of his actions, or inactions?

The chemical stimuli for flight and fight were waning, replaced with pain and fatigue. His bare feet ached as they pounded the pavement.

I am unravelling.

There was someone in the street behind, someone with shoes, making ground on him with every stride. Kelly thought of Raoul, talking passionately mere moments ago, now broken in a way no rhetoric could ever mend.

In a way I sent him to his death.

Fingertips snatched at his shoulders. Kelly lashed out blindly. His fists made contact with something soft. He could hear the other man's breathing, smell his sweat, see his shadow in the road ahead.

You come into this world kicking and screaming.

Kelly stopped dead and threw himself into a backwards charge. His pursuer careered into rising elbows that dug deep into his gut. As the man doubled up Kelly grabbed him by the hair and wrenched back his head exposing the jugular.

No one ever fights back. Didn't see that coming.

Kelly noted the dementia in his own thoughts and embraced it as a vampire welcomes a juicy throat. His fists found the Adam's apple, the chin, the cheek, the bridge of the nose. The man brought up hands to guard his face. Tinted glasses buckled under the blows. Kelly heard rasping and coughing. He kicked the man to the ground and dropped down on his belly. His knees encountered little resistance.

'Why?'

The word stopped Kelly in his tracks. Was it his voice or the others? He couldn't be sure. In that moment it encapsulated everything he had ever thought or experienced. An engine roar denied him the luxury of contemplation. He got back on his bare feet and stumbled onwards. The man did not follow.

Kelly found himself in a graveyard. The ground was uneven and most of the headstones had been unearthed. His senses heightened.

Over a free-standing stone wall, across a road, through a gate, into a park. Overhanging willow branches whipped at his face. Kelly punched through into a green expanse. Up ahead he could see a bridge. Another backwards glance revealed nothing. His pounding heart begged him to stop. Kelly dragged himself over a fence and up onto the bridge.

A black sedan was parked at the bottom of the slope. Several men were rushing towards him.

In a final desperate act Kelly climbed up onto the railings and gazed down at the river.

Something ripped through his shoulder, spinning him a full revolution. There was no pain.

This is it. I am at an end.

Kelly thought of the plans that would now come to nothing, hopes that had never been shared with a single soul. Delirium took him and he experienced a sensation of floating.

More shots rang out. All Kelly could see was sky, swirls of maroon and magenta having their moment amidst the encroaching black. His head struck something that gave way and embraced him. In the failing light his lifeblood appeared as a violet cloud, billowing out into the surrounding water.

Get to the surface.

His mind envisaged gunmen on the bridge, waiting for their target to re-emerge.

Let the current take you.

Can't breath.

You'll never breathe again if you ascend.

And then the pain came, suddenly and remorselessly, surging over him, terrible and absolute. He felt himself fading.

Don't. . . ..

3.

'Can you hear me?'

Yes I can

Are you real?

'Hey, say something.'

The voice was strange. Kelly couldn't discern whether it was male or female.

'Yes . . . yes I can hear you. Who are you?

'My name is El Ambiente.'

Kelly looked down. His chest was awash with blood. He heard wheels rattling over cobbles and the sound of running water. Street lights illuminated a narrow walkway. He was lying in a wooden cart. The person pulling him along wore a hooded coat that hid their features.

'Where are you taking me?'

'You have a bullet in your shoulder. You need someone with medical expertise.'

'No . . . hospitals.'

'Give me some credit. I'm taking you to a safe house.'

'Let me see your face.'

'That would be in neither of our best interests.'

Kelly tried to raise his head. Searing pain tore up his spine.

'Be still,' El Ambiente commanded. 'You have fallen into the hands of chance. You have an open wound that has been exposed to the elements. You will need all of your strength to fight the infection.'

'Why are you helping me?'

'If our situations were reversed, wouldn't you help me?'

'In truth, no.'

'Then I have done the right thing. You cannot be allowed to die a wretch. You must first be redeemed.'

Chapter 14

The Golden Envelopes

1.

El Ambiente first came to prominence in a full-page advert taken out in the last of the country's national newspapers, *La Tierra* ('The Earth'). In it he introduced himself as 'an ordinary person who had grown tired of tyranny', and went on to deplore and condemn the actions and very existence of El Rey, citing him as a 'malignant and bloated vermin scavenging for scraps on the emaciated husk of our once great city'.

The advert also set out a series of beliefs entitled 'The manifesto for basic human rights', and declared El Rey's claims to the throne to be null and void.

Shortly after the article was published Eleanor Blake arrived at the offices of *La Tierra* with an armed contingent and executed the chief editor. To add insult to injury it was later found under investigation that the proofs for the advert were paid for by the office of El Rey's Chancellor, Dimitri. Shortly after this revelation Dimitri was asked to call Tito Majagranzas and appoint him the new Chancellor, whereupon he subsequently disappeared.

That was thought to be the end of it. There was no almighty uprising and no one stepped forward to take responsibility for the article. Never the less El Rey's paranoia heightened and tensions over what might happen grew to almost unbearable proportions.

The Emperor surrounded himself with a tightly knit inner circle of advisors and protectors, but even they were regarded with disdain and scorn. Life within the walls of his palace spelt immediate prosperity for its favourite sons, but could just as easily denote sudden and absolute oblivion. The will of their leader spun sporadically on the head of a needle.

Winter passed into spring without incident or reprisal. A limited sense of strength flowed back into the barrios. It was a strength of defiance rather than replenishment; the gritty residue of having survived.

In an unusual display of kindness El Rey declared his fifty-seventh birthday a national holiday.

He started the day as any other, being awoken by the bells of San

Sebastian at 7.30 am. It was the only time of day or night they were permitted to ring. The double doors to his penthouse suite opened and the servant boy Cheech entered carrying a breakfast tray. He placed the tray by his emperor's bedside, bowed and made a swift retreat.

El Rey smiled. In addition to his usual cooked breakfast, espresso and glass of orange juice, there was also a plethora of different-sized envelopes. It amused him no end to imagine the host of grovelling well-wishes that waited within, pale-faced, spineless subordinates parting before him like the waves before Moses.

A whimper disturbed his moment of contentment and he turned to glare at the bound and gagged woman lying beside him. She was immediately silent.

Later that day a carnival was to be held in his honour, a venture so big it would take up the whole of central Corderro. There were to be street performers, acrobats and floats of every description, all culminating in an hour-long fireworks display.

Enthused and invigorated he wolfed down his breakfast and went to shower, leaving the letters untouched.

When he returned the woman had been removed from the room and the bed made. El Rey took the envelopes out onto the veranda that overlooked the city.

The first card was from Pablo Maracito, the Minister for Public Works. It read: 'To his Excellency El Rey. Happy Birthday, Your Highness! May this year bring forth countless blessings and approbations as befits your glorious name.'

The Emperor held his nostrils to prevent the espresso from coming out of his nose. Pablo could always be relied upon to stoop lower to the ground than anyone else and today was certainly no exception. He ripped the card into tiny bits and dropped them over the balcony.

The second card was from the Chancellor: 'Your Highness, my sincerest hopes for a prosperous year ahead. Tito. P.S. Everything's going well here.'

He recognized Eleanor's handwriting amidst the pile: 'My Lord – I am wearing your present. You will need to unwrap it slowly. Happy Birthday, Emile!'

He chose the next one at random, a small golden-coloured envelope with a smudged postmark. Instead of a card the Emperor discovered a letter.

2.

To his Excellency El Rey on his birthday,

It was with much sadness and regret that I viewed the innocent slaying of La Tierra*'s chief editor Margot Maurice, and of your previous chancellor Dimitri. I shall add their names to the list of the unavenged.*

I feel an unmeasurable anguish at having in some way contributed to their deaths, but I realize too that this anguish must be weighed up against the actions of the man whose will caused them to lose that which they held most precious.

These actions are unforgivable and compound the already insurmountable body of shame for which you will someday be held to account. Of that I will make certain.

Yours is the sort of laughable, pathetic character that feeds on the misfortune of others; a wretched, vacuous vessel that finds my hatred and contempt where only pity is deserved.

Today, on the commiseration of your birth I shall rechristen March 15th as a day of celebration, a day when the walls of your reign started to crumble.

I take on this role reluctantly and with a heavy heart. I do not underestimate you as an adversary, nor the task that lies before me. At the same time the very nature of myself assures me that you will never find me. I will never be where you look, for you do not have the eyes to see me.

Though I consider the asking fruitless I implore you to cease all of the killing, the disappearances, the fear and irrevocable loss. No good can come of it. Surely you must see this?

In closing I will say this. You are exposed and weak, like the jugular of an antelope to a lion, I have watched you from afar, watched you cloth yourself in the spoils of the victor, watched you alone at night, wearing the vacant look of a man hopelessly incapable of grasping his own arrogance and stupidity. If I weren't a peaceful person you'd be dead already.

Having said all this – Happy Birthday your Excellency!

Regards,
El Ambiente

3.

El Rey dropped the letter in utter bewilderment. It immediately blew off the balcony and sailed out on the wind. In reaching desperately to grasp for the paper the Emperor very nearly plummeted to his death. His legs buckled beneath him and he dropped heavily to the floor. The elation that he'd felt upon waking vanished, and in its place grew the desire to commit unspeakable acts – to rip out the throats of children, to rape a thousand virgins, to torch hospitals and schools, to release murderers from prison and have them prey upon the disobedient and heretical inhabitants of his unworthy city.

Crawling on his hands and knees he returned to the bedroom and rang the servant bell. Cheech was first to answer the call. Seeing the Emperor's face and general demeanor he approached with extreme caution, knowing that his life might depend upon it.

El Rey pulled himself sluggishly to his feet using the boy for support.

'Get Eleanor,' he growled, 'and cancel everything.'

4.

The crumpled letter flew over El Puerto de Las Ondas Verdes and out to sea before a change in the wind altered its direction and sent it back into central Corderro.

Far below, the tens of thousands of people beginning their national holiday were oblivious to the treasure passing overhead. It continued east, over the industrial district, dancing and pirouetting between the thermals of smelting forges and furnaces that could so easily have hidden its message.

It arrived in the suburb of Liberacion where the wind died, causing it to fall onto a cobbled side street and into the path of a passing priest.

Lost in the pages of a book entitled *The Conception of Grace,* the priest slipped on the letter as if it were a banana skin and fell on his backside with a thump. He collected himself and inspected the cause of his sudden humility.

The priest stared at the words for a long time, glancing up periodically towards El Rey's palace many miles away and trying to fathom how the letter had come into his possession. He composed himself and reread it several times. A smile spread across his face and he bent over to kiss the cobbles before laying prostrate in prayer for over an hour.

Rising sometime later he found that a crowd had gathered around him.

'Are you OK, Father?' one of them asked. 'You were mumbling. We were afraid to disturb you.'

'I am ecstatic, thank you,' he replied. 'I am exalted, I am raised up, overjoyed, *elevated*, empowered, euphoric, elated, glorious, jubilant, thrilled, delighted and tickled pink. God has shown me the way, the way to a printing press.'

The only printing press in the city suitable to his needs could be found at the offices of *La Tierra*. The priest flashed his crucifix and Bible at the security guard as if they were business credentials.

'Can you tell me where I might find the editor?' he inquired politely.

'Do you have an appointment?'

'Not at all.'

'Then I'm afraid it won't be possible. The editor has a very full diary. I'm sorry.'

'That's OK,' the priest replied handing him the letter, 'read this.'

Somewhat cynically the guard took the piece of paper. As he scanned the lines his eyes began to bulge and an involuntary smile spread across his face.

'Gold dust, isn't it?'

'I'll buzz you right through.'

'How kind.'

By the time he reached the editor's office pandemonium had broken out. News of the letter was spreading through the building like wildfire. A board meeting was in the process of being unceremoniously abandoned with journalists diving at the nearest unused phone.

The editor welcomed the priest into his office as if he were handling volatile chemicals.

'News of your arrival precedes you, Padre.'

'Wonderful! Then the good news is spreading?'

'Yes . . . with dangerous ferocity, Father. May I see the letter?'

'Of course.'

The editor groaned as he read El Ambiente's words. The analogy that presented itself was of a man who wins the lottery and finds out he is terminally ill all within the same day.

The most fantastic scoop I could ever attain, and yet if I print a word of it I'm a dead man.

For once he chose sensibility over sensation.

'Padre, you have to be careful. El Rey's spies are everywhere.'

The priest waved his arm dismissively. 'I don't care about all that. I'm a man of the cloth. God has granted me immunity from such worldly trivialities.'

'What is it I can do for you, Father?'

'Time is short. I need . . . ten thousand copies in the next . . . thirty minutes . . . more if you can manage it.'

'I'm afraid that's impossible.'

'Nonsense, it's easy . . . print one, double it up, print two, double them up, print four, etcetera. You'll be there in no time at all.'

'No, I mean the print rolls are in use. We have a paper to get out by six o'clock.'

'You're joking! Have you never heard of "Stop the press"? You're the editor, for crying out loud. This is dynamite, once in a lifetime . . . er . . . two fingers up to the establishment – pardon my language, a chance to show our malefactor in a less than favourable light.'

'What if we're caught? Eleanor Blake executed my predecessor only a few months ago.'

'You shall receive your reward in heaven.'

The editor went ghostly white.

'That was a joke . . . never mind . . . well, if you don't want to get caught, work incognito . . . I don't know . . . use anonymous paper.'

'Anonymous paper?'

'Yeah, stuff without a watermark . . . you tell me, you're the expert!'

The editor leant forward and took a long-drawn-out breath. 'To tell you the truth, Padre . . . this scares me. Don't get me wrong, it's a wondrous opportunity. I can see that. It's just that . . . I'm just . . . afraid of the consequences . . . I don't believe as you do—'

The priest sat down. He tried to weigh up the disappointment against his pledge of humble service. His smile was forced.

'That's OK . . . Perhaps I am being overzealous . . . It is wrong of me to put you in this position.'

'I'm sorry, Padre . . . if Eleanor Blake ever found out—'

'I understand. I have heard of this woman . . . most unfortunate . . . a sheep who has wondered from the flock.'

The editor's mind seethed with confliction. It went against the grain to pass up such an opportunity. More than that it shamed him to think he should so dishonour the memory of his predecessor by rolling over for El Rey's regime.

Freedom of speech?

Whatever happened to telling it how it is?

You can twist and turn all you like. The decision has been made for you.

The editor sighed and placed his head in his hands. 'If I do this and it goes pear-shaped, will you vouch for me, Padre?'

'Vouch?'

The editor lifted his head and looked towards the ceiling.

'Oh! Yes of course.'

'Then let's get to work.'

The priest jumped up from his seat and clapped his hands with glee. 'Splendid. This day the Lord has bestowed upon us a magnificent bounty!'

'I prefer to think of it more as a poisoned chalice,' the editor edited. 'Right, first things first, how are you planning to distribute them?'

'I hadn't given it much thought really. It's all a little overwhelming . . . perhaps a van?'

'Mm, a bit risky – if you're spotted you won't get very far.'

'As I've said before, earthly issues do not concern me.'

'I understand that, but I was thinking more of the fact that you won't have delivered the letters.'

'Oh I see . . . well then, how about a plane?'

'Know anyone how owns a plane?'

The priest frowned. 'No.'

'How about a hot-air balloon?'

'You know of someone?'

'Yes, we've hired him for press stunts in the past. I could give him a try?'

The priest's enthusiasm returned. 'Fantastic! May God forgive all of your slanderous lies over the years.'

'Thank you . . . most *charitable*.'

The editor stood with his legs spread wide, placed his fingertips on the desk and leant forward so that he loomed like a tyrant.

'Excuse my stance. I do my best work from a position of smug, overbearing authority.'

'OK, it's your office.'

'That it is. Now, what is the fastest-known phenomenon?'

'The speed of light?'

'Wrong, Padre – *gossip* – it's far faster, and if you and I are going to have any hope of getting ahead of the game we shall need to be faster still. Bear with me whilst I make a few calls and apologies for the offences I shall no doubt commit in the next few minutes. It's a devious profession and I find your presence more than a little disconcerting.'

'I shall take that as a compliment,' the priest beamed with delight.

'Take it however you like.'

The first call summoned a runner.

'*This*,' the editor bellowed dramatically handing him the letter, 'is the most sacred article known to man . . . no offence, Padre. Take it to the print room as fast as your little pixie legs can carry you and tell them to print twenty thousand copies.'

'I only need ten,' the priest protested.

'Best to be over rather than under-prepared, Padre. Tell them to ensure they are printed as fast as is humanly possible, even if that means delaying the evening addition of *La Tierra*. GO!'

The second call summoned a gang of dogged hacks.

'Phone anyone of note you can think of. Offer obscene amounts of money for the letter's whereabouts. Throw up a smokescreen. Deny everything. GO!'

The third call confirmed the priest's means of distribution.

'You are in luck, Padre, if indeed it can be deemed "luck". The balloon operator lost his brother to the black sedans last winter and is more than happy to oblige any acts of subterfuge. I should inform you that he has a somewhat kamikaze nature about him. I imagine you'll be like blood brothers!'

5.

Shortly after their departure the offices of *La Tierra* were raided. Eleanor strode along the corridor, an ankle-length leather jacket billowing out behind her revealing thighs and suspenders. The staff were herded three deep against the far wall.

'Where is the editor?' Eleanor asked.

When no one answered she fired a single indiscriminate shot. It hit a young woman in the shin. She dropped to the floor and began writhing in agony.

'A wound like that left untreated can cause fatal loss of blood in a matter of seconds, and if you do not inform me of the editor's whereabouts in a matter of seconds you shall all join her on the floor, sharing in one another's demise . . . *now* . . . I ask you all a second and final time . . . *where is he?*'

The first few seconds of silence were understandable. Eleanor knew their expressions well enough.

Poor, forlorn, little lambs. It's not everyday someone calls you to account in so absolute a fashion.

'He's out to lunch, Miss Blake.'

The voice belonged to a weasily looking man in a tweed jacket and comb-over hair. Eleanor glided to within an eye-lash of the man. He leant backwards so as to prevent their lips from meeting.

'Three o'clock in the afternoon? Odd time for lunch, wouldn't you say?'

'We work unusual hours . . . never know when a story might—'

'*Break*?'

'Yes.'

'*Yesss* . . . I imagine it must be one, long, continual adrenaline rush working here.'

'It has its moments.'

'Why don't you tell me where he really is? And be quick about it.'

The man laughed, a reaction born entirely of nerves. Horrified, he tried to stifle the noise but instead forced a loud 'pah' of hot air straight into Eleanor's face. 'Oh . . . my God . . . I didn't . . . you made me . . . that is to say—'

Eleanor wiped the moisture from her cheek, ran a forefinger along the man's brow and tasted his perspiration. 'Mm . . . you're *delicious* . . . I might have to *devour* you . . . *the editor*?'

'He's . . . gone to . . . he went to investigate a story . . . a hot air balloon . . . distributing a letter . . . a letter from El Amb—'

'Please,' Eleanor interrupted, 'do not mention that name out loud. It makes me nauseous . . . you are telling me the truth?'

'Yes.'

'There, that wasn't so hard was it?' Eleanor cupped her hands beneath the man's throat.

'No.'

'One minute you're being a *naughty little liar* . . . and the next—' her hands fanned out wide, fingers contorting like a flamenco dancer '–you're a reformed citizen . . . do you like my new nail polish?'

The man was phased by her sudden switch in conversation. He looked at her hands and saw that they were dripping. He tried to say 'I don't understand', but found that he was unable to speak or breathe. He clutched at his neck. It was awash with blood. Eleanor stepped back out of the reach of flailing arms, and sighed.

'Oh, the world loathes an informer.'

6.

The editor was having trouble weaving through the traffic. He was so anxious that even his hands were perspiring. The wheel slipped through his hands causing him to oversteer and brake with every turn. By contrast the priest was utterly relaxed, seat back and window rolled down.

'Funny how things turn out, isn't it? There I was struggling for inspiration with a sermon. It was a fairly lack-lustre piece on grace, a near impossible task to make something so amazing sound so dull, and yet I had managed it. I felt so down in the dumps and now look at me!'

'Careering recklessly towards your, and my, death,' the editor replied.

'Oh come now, I wouldn't say that.'

'Well, what would you say?'

'I would say that you cannot choose what life throws at you, only whether or not you throw it back.'

'And you live by this motto, do you?'

'No, I just made it up.'

'I was being sarcastic.'

The road became clearer as they made their way into the hills. The editor could see the entire city in his wing mirror.

Dare I go back after doing this?

Corderro had steeped him in cynicism to the point where he could no longer see the good in people. Everything was regarded with suspicion. Now he found himself in the company of a charismatic and hopelessly naïve man to whom the rules of engagement seemed not to apply. As nonsensical as distributing a photocopied letter was, it made him feel as if he'd been dragged from a deep sleep and doused with ice-cold water.

They pulled into a field. Ahead of them a giant marshmallow of fabric was spreading out and expanding under the influence of an intense flame. The operator stood by his balloon dressed like the Red Baron in a leather cap, goggles and bomber jacket. His face was ruddy and inebriated.

'Good day to you,' he shouted aggressively, 'Ready for a mid-morning raid?'

'It looks a little flimsy,' the priest commented.

'Nonsense, safe as houses, let's get loaded up.'

As large as the basket was, twenty thousand fliers filled it to the brim.

'How about a photo?' the operator suggested.

'I don't have a camera,' the editor replied.

'What kind of journalist are you? Here, I've brought one along.'

The priest and the operator scrambled on top of the basket, gave the thumbs up and smiled. The editor took their picture.

'Should make a good front cover for you!' the priest proposed.

The editor laughed. 'You know I can never use this without implicating myself.'

'This is true,' the operator agreed. 'Still, you'd best keep hold of it. Don't think I'll be having much use for it anytime soon.'

'Good luck to you.'

'You too, *adios amigo*.'

Their goodbyes were premature. It took another half an hour to get off the ground.

'You're going to have to get out, Padre,' the operator conceded. 'If I put any more air in the balloon it will explode!'

'I'm not going anywhere. God has charged me with a sacred duty. I cannot fail him.'

'If this balloon pops we're both likely to be incinerated.'

'Go ahead, keeping filling her up, I have faith.'

The editor took a few more photos whilst surreptitiously retiring to a safe distance. Eventually the balloon began to drag along the field and gain some lift.

'Start unloading,' shouted the operator.

'We haven't reached civilization yet.'

'Yes, I know, and we won't at this rate. Have you seen how close those rooftops are?'

'Oh my.'

'Oh my indeed.'

The priest untied the first bundle and began to share El Ambiente's message with the world.

7.

Eleanor watched the clumsy looking object making its way across the skyline.

'How amusing . . . that sweaty little man was telling the truth after all. Pull over here.'

The convoy of black sedans came to a halt. Eleanor got out of the car and saw that the balloon was haemorrhaging paper. Though she would never knowingly show anger for fear of corrupting her face with lines, Eleanor was livid.

'They're moving west to east. Get sharpshooters on the hills over there and bring them down.'

8.

'What was that?'

'What was what?'

'That swishing sound.'

'I didn't hear anything.'

'There it was again!'

A bullet whistled past inches from the priest's face.

'My Lord, they're shooting at us!'

'Quick, unload the rest of the fliers.'

'Are you kidding? We're in enough trouble as it is!'

'No, the weight, we need to lose weight.'

'OK,' the priest replied. He genuflected, knelt and closed his eyes.

'Get off your knees and help me unload these sandbags,' the operator screamed.

'You take care of our physical welfare, and I'll take care of the spiritual welfare.'

'Well, if you're going to stay on the floor make yourself useful and increase the size of the flame. We need to get higher.'

9.

One of the fliers fluttered down into the hands of its owner. El Ambiente read the letter with perplexed amusement and looked up. The sky was full of falling paper.

I write a letter, send it to the Emperor, it multiplies a thousand-fold and finds its way back to me!

Circles.

The silhouettes of two figures were visible high up in the heavens. There was the sound of gunfire. One of the silhouettes disappeared from view.

'Stay.'

Another volley of shots and then there were none. El Ambiente looked at the men lining the hillside.

'Have you any idea what you've just done?'

10.

'I'm feeling a little heady,' said the priest. 'I think I might be wounded.'

'This is perfectly normal,' the operator replied. 'We're at a far higher altitude than we should be . . . the air's thin . . . it promotes sluggish behaviour.'

'Ohhhh . . . how far can bullets . . . travel?'

'How should I know?'

The priest peered over the edge of the basket. The soldiers were smaller than ants. 'Praise God . . . I think we're going to be—'

The operator had fainted.

'Oh dear . . . Oh deary dear, dear,' the priest giggled before joining his new friend in unconsciousness.

11.

El Rey was not the only person to receive a golden envelope that morning. Across the city dozens of people – men and women from all walks of life – were visited with messages, requests and suggestions from their anonymous host.

One of those people was Tito Majagranzas.

El Comidin,

It is no secret that you have been using taxpayers' money to finance five-course meals and luxury hotels with your mistress, Maria Clott (a woman whose ironic name has not gone unnoticed), certainly not by your wife who this morning received a copy of the accounts detailing your embezzlement and betrayal.

I sense that, whilst your economic condition is somewhat tenuous, we may well have only just begun to scratch the surface of your incompetence.

I very much look forward to seeking out the truth.

> *Yours,*
> *El Ambiente*

12.

Another recipient of a golden envelope was Marcela Rosier, a widow and retired teacher whose one and only child had been black-sedaned three months earlier. Since that day her life had become a hellish slurring of nonsensical time, stumbling from one moment to the next, shrouded in black, face hidden beneath a veil. In her heart she knew that her son was dead, and her only true wish was that her grief should catch the attentions of those who had done this terrible thing, that she may at least be whisked away and freed from the relentless anguish.

Madame Rosier,

It is with great delight that I bring news of your son David's well-being. He has for the past three months been hiding in a safe house near Castillo de San Michelle. I last saw him two nights ago when he was smuggled out of the city, over the border and out of harm's way. He looked healthy and in good spirits.

During his time in the safe house David wrote you many letters. Unfortunately there was a fire and they were lost. We moved him too quickly for him to compose another, but he did ask me to tell you that he loves you very much and hopes to see you soon. He also gave me a lock of his hair, which I enclose.

He is a very brave young man and you should feel very proud to have brought him into this world.

Yours affectionately,
El Ambiente

The letter caused Marcela to weep tears of joy. She lifted the veil and revealed hair that had turned purest white, shouted thanks and praise over and over to this wondrous stranger who had brought happiness and purpose back into her life.

El Ambiente had not seen her son two days before. In truth, the last time they had seen David was the previous December when El Rey's men had dragged him away to be tortured to death.

Marcela Rosier was one of eight widows written to with good intentioned lies. Even now the revolutionary questioned what was the greater good – a hopeful fallacy or the desperate truth? The answer had once been certain, but the blacks and whites were now infinite shades of grey. El Ambiente prayed that it was not a despicable thing to play God with an old woman's emotions.

13.

The priest awoke. It was dark, wet and smelly.
Am I dead?
He heard the sound of chewing, a loud and sloppy munching. There was a rustling of light and movement.
'Hello?' he muttered. 'Is anyone there?'
The chewing persisted.

'What are you eating?'

There was no answer, only chewing. He laughed, still drunk from oxygen deprivation.

'Look what they did to my balloon,' the operator groaned.

'I can't see anything. Is that you chewing?'

'I thought it was you.'

'Someone's outside. Where are you?'

'Over here.'

'I think I'm upside down.'

'Well turn over then. *Honestly*, men of the cloth, no common sense!'

With some considerable difficulty the two men wriggled and writhed their way to the edge of the fabric and emerged into the light of day.

They were in the middle of a vast field surrounded by cows. Behind them a timid-looking band of country folk huddled together and peered at them from the cover of foliage.

'Excuse me,' the priest inquired, 'could you tell us where we are?'

'Earth,' one of the men replied.

'Yes . . . could you be more specific?'

'Bolivia.'

'Bolivia? *Bolivia?* Oh. My friend, we've escaped . . . this is fantastic . . . this is Bolivia . . . *Boh-live-ee-ahh* . . . my sister lives in La Paz . . . *Bolivia!*'

'What are you rabbiting on about, Padre?' the operator scoffed.

'We're in Bolivia!' the priest repeated.

'We're in *Bolivia?*'

'Yes, *BOLIVIA!*'

'This is *wonderful*.'

The priest and the operator began to dance around in the mud.

14.

The editor had not submitted his own copy in years, but the day's extraordinary events brought him out of his creative retirement. He locked himself away in an office and constructed a sensational narrative.

Under the pretext of being utterly horrified, he denounced El Ambiente as a ruthless terrorist and menace to society. This then afforded him the luxury of legitimately recounting the details of the letter and the subsequent aftermath in all their bloated and graphic glory without appearing to gloat (which was the sole reason for writing the piece). To the reading public the article would act as a ray of light.

The piece was entitled: 'Cowardly intruder *ruins* emperor's birthday'.

The editor found that the most effective way of getting his true meaning across to the reader was to write each sentence as he would ideally present it, in all its sarcastic mocking ridicule, and then carefully translate it into the antithesis. In this way he ended up with an account so sycophantic and toady that it could only be satire, and yet it wasn't!

15.

Excerpt from 'Cowardly intruder ruins *emperor's birthday.'*

The fat tyrant sat in bed gorging himself on a banquet, contemplating what unspeakable acts to unleash on the hosts to which he was attached.

'Our illustrious leader gallantly sat overseeing the affairs of Corderro.'

The portly imbecile was under the continued delusion that people wished him a happy birthday when in fact they all wished him dead, and was therefore shocked when confronted with this harsh reality.

'Amongst his overflowing sack-full of birthday cards he discovered treacherous hate mail from an evil charlatan.'

El Ambiente calmly held a mirror up to the fool. The fool in turn was revolted by his own grotesque reflection.

'The scurrilous rogue showed complete disdain for our glorious king with a barrage of hurtful, dastardly lies.'

A mild breeze teased the poetry from his feeble fingers.

'The diabolical dialogue was ripped from his mighty hand by a vicious storm.'

The wind carried the letter into the hands of a humble priest.

'The wind carried the letter into the hands of a demented religious zealot.'

Two unnamed heroes attempting to spread El Ambiente's message were shamefully fired upon by bloodthirsty ignoramuses.

'The perpetrators of this outrage received their just deserts. The hot-air balloon in which they were escaping was riddled with bullets.'

Despite their quarries being unarmed and practically stationary El Rey's feeble band of monkeys missed with every single shot. The priest and his colleague later telephoned from Bolivia to report their magnificent escape.

'Unfortunately the balloon drifted out of range. Both men were believed to have died, but later telephoned to boast of their despicable act.'

16.

The new addition hit the streets at 5.00 am the next morning. By lunchtime *La Tierra* was reporting record sales. The office was being run on a skeleton staff. Following Eleanor's visit many of the employees had resigned with immediate effect.

Just after five o'clock she walked into the building for the second time in twenty-four hours.

'It appears you are flourishing at the expense of your master's humiliation,' were her opening words.

The editor considered his response carefully.

Has she already made up her mind, or is it possible to talk my way into tomorrow?

'A most unfortunate turn of events. I can only hope that my piece has helped to lessen the impact of a story that was already running rife.'

'I see . . . you were providing a public service?'

'As much as is in my professional capability, yes. Would you have me write an additional article?'

Eleanor's glossy lips revealed a pearly white smile, a gesture that intimated she was amused with the editor's maneuvering. 'No. . . I think you have done more than enough.'

Eleanor took out a coin, tossed it into the air, caught it mid-flight and placed it on her overturned palm. She examined the exposed face for what seemed like for ever.

'Tell me, would you knowingly embarrass your emperor?'

'No, *of course* not, Miss Blake.'

Eleanor winked. 'Well then . . . continue.'

'OK . . . thank you.'

He didn't dare turn his back on her.

'Don't stand on ceremony. I shall show myself out.'

The editor stepped back, bowed and slipped through the nearest doorway. From there he made a series of random choices, zig-zagging from office to office, putting as much distance between them as he could.

He ended up in a makeshift storeroom on the eighth floor. The editor battled his way though boxes of paper and redundant machinery to a tiny window at the back of the room. From here he could see Eleanor sauntering down the steps to her car, eliciting lustful stares from men and women alike. As she reached the curb she turned, picked out the editor with a precision glare and blew him a kiss. He stumbled over himself and was instantly buried beneath stationary.

17.

That evening the editor arrived home to find a golden envelope on his doorstep.

To the editor of La Tierra,

Sir, I am impressed! Suffice to say I should hate to ever become embroiled with you in a battle of words.

You have done me an immense service, and lived to tell the tale. This is no mean feat. I sincerely hope you feel thoroughly refreshed by your actions. It is a wondrous thing to act selflessly. It leaves your pockets empty but your soul full to the brim. Long may you continue in this vain.

Bless you sir.

Regards,

The 'Scurrilous Rogue' El Ambiente

Chapter 15
Echoes of Jonathan

1.

'Reflection'

I remember so very little of that day, but one thing I do remember is your directness. For some reason your time was desperately short (hopefully you will one day be able to explain what it was that put you under such immense pressure). Your words resonate with me always, as does your warm smile. As important as what you said was the way in which you said it – firm, ordered, black and white. I imagine you as a man who has always known where he's going. I too have made direction and achievement my dual goals throughout these years apart. Some say I am a little too feisty as a result, others that I am a force to be reckoned with!

I think a lot of people find it hard to accept male traits when displayed in a woman.

As for me? I think they suit me just fine.

Your traits.
Isabella, 30th November

2.

Isabella wore the most shapeless thing she could find – a smock-like dress tied loosely at the hips, but Ronaldo still found what he was looking for.

'Sleep well?' he spoke into her chest.

'The air con's broken and there's a large hole in the bathroom,' she replied.

'Oh,' Ronaldo muttered dismissively whilst scratching his stubbly chin. 'That's too bad.'

'I expect both to be fixed by the time I return,' she countered without blinking.

'I'm sorry. Is no good. Man on holiday.'

'I'm sure that you're more than capable of the task.'

'I would have to charge. You take the room as you find it.'

'Do you know the phrase "I wasn't born yesterday"?'

'No.'

'I didn't think so. Let me put it this way. If you're not going to lift a finger to help me and address what is a basic requirement for a hotel then I have no choice but to deduct the inconvenience from your room rate. Shall we say fifty per cent?'

'Oh no. I'm afraid is not permitted.'

'It's already done. *Buenos dias*, señor.'

Isabella left The Phoenix with a skip in her step. She'd met men like Ronaldo all over the world. They presumed that women existed solely for their own purpose, and that they were the weaker sex in every aspect.

How wrong you are!

Isabella could have looked for a different hotel, but there was a principle at stake and she always relished the opportunity to challenge a chauvinist. She wasn't confident that Carlos would turn up. His actions to date had been unpredictable and dishonest. She made her way down into the Market quarter with the ongoing suspicion that her self-appointed tour guide had omitted something vital.

Carlos was waiting for her just as he'd promised, still dressed in the Hawaiian shirt, but now also sporting a gold pendant that was so big it was teetering on the verge of becoming a medallion.

'*Hola, mi chica bella,*' he greeted.

'Good morning, book snatcher!'

'*Oh*, give a *ladron* a break. It's a beautiful day, you're beautiful. Why be spiky with me?'

'What would your wife say if she knew you were complimenting another woman in this manner?'

'Oh good God, she'd beat me black and blue. Shall we start with a drink?'

'No thank you, Casanova. I'd like to get straight to it if you don't mind.'

'Fine with me, you're the boss. Before we do however, as your guide I feel duty bound to point out something truly awe-inspiring. This is Plaza Viejo ('Old Square'). The great Santos was stabbed just over there. The wooden table on which he was standing is preserved in a museum in the next street. Isn't that amazing – Corderro's most renowned citizen met his untimely demise mere feet from where we now sit?'

'Corderro's most renowned citizen was Ramon Esteban. The city is named after him!'

'Ah, I see you are a glass is half empty kind of girl.'

'Not at all, I just don't believe in looking at the world through rose-tinted glasses.'

'Life for you must be very abrasive.'

'Life for you must be very naïve!'

'How abrasive of you!' A grin flashed across Carlos's face to show that his antagonism was meant only in jest. 'Santos is the yardstick by which mortal men should judge themselves. Corderro was merely a pirate.'

'Whatever you say,' Isabella replied, closing down the conversation.

'Come now, whatever happened to the lost art of banter?'

'I have no interest in flirting with you, Carlos. Besides your *apparent* married status, I find you a little overbearing, not least of all because you won't fully explain why it is that you want to help me.'

'Is it so hard to believe that a man's intentions could be noble?'

'Not when confronted with clear evidence, no.'

'Wow señorita, you are a hard nut to crack! But I'm sure that I am up to the task. I tell you what, I shall let my actions do the talking, and if you are not one hundred per cent satisfied I will give you your money back.'

'What money?'

'*Exactly!*'

3.

Carlos flagged down a taxi and asked to be taken to El Campo de Marcadores. Isabella was suddenly hesitant.

'Why can't we walk there?'

'It's several miles out of town and would take a couple of hours.

Secluded.

Previously there was one unknown man. Now there were two. It didn't feel right.

Did that taxi just drive by, or has it been waiting for Carlos to give the signal?

You read horror stories of women getting into cars in foreign countries and never being heard of again.

So what if he's offended. Better that than making the biggest mistake of your life.

Besides, if he's a gentleman (which he's not) he'll understand.

'What will we find there?' she asked, stalling for time in which to think.

'Answers hopefully, and a chance to prove my intentions.'

She didn't move. Carlos nodded despondently as he realized the cause of her reluctance.

'Are you coming? I can assure you I have your best interests at heart.'

Isabella remained rooted to the spot.

How can you take the word of a thief?

There is no way to be sure.

Carlos frowned. 'Suit yourself, señorita. I could not be any more friendly if I tried, but if this does not allay your suspicions then I would rather you stay here and not burden me.'

Isabella considered the comment to be a double bluff designed to entice her into the vehicle.

'There'd be no point going without me,' she responded.

Carlos laughed. 'As surprising as you may find it, señorita, not everything in the universe revolves around you.'

He did not wait for a response. Carlos slipped into the passenger seat. The taxi pulled away and out of sight.

Isabella was impressed.

A man who does not panda to my every whim, this is rare!

What to do?

You are being paranoid. It was probably a perfectly innocent proposition.

Probably?

You are alone and you know no one. What harm can it do to follow him at a safe distance?

If it looks dubious you don't have to leave the car, just turn around and come back.

It is still a risk.

Think, woman!

Isabella sat down on the curb, blissfully unaware of the true gravity inherent in her decision.

4.

La Fantasma chased the vehicle as it snaked its way into the hills. Isabella gazed through the back window and witnessed Corderro vanish beneath a blanket of mist.

Where are you Jonathan?

You must be so close.

If I could only send my thoughts sailing over the breeze, we could be together within the hour.

The last site to disappear from view was that of the port. Ships saturated the horizon.

Perhaps you are boarding a vessel at this very moment, taking a long-sought opportunity to leave?

Do not dwell on such a thought. Surely fate would not be so cruel as to deny me after all these years?

The taxi came to an abrupt halt. Isabella saw that they had joined the tail end of a traffic jam stretching up out of sight. Within a matter of seconds several more vehicles joined the queue behind. La Fantasma rolled relentlessly over them and the world was subsumed within smoky swirls.

How stupid – rather than worrying about accompanying Carlos, I'm now worried about not being able to find him.

The queue showed no sign of moving. Isabella made a snap decision to get out of the taxi.

'Keep the change,' she uttered to a driver who was clearly furious at being abandoned mid-fare. Outside the temperature had dropped dramatically. Isabella could hear footsteps all around. Most of the cars she passed were empty. As she ascended the fog became thicker still. The road widened and disintegrated, growing sticky beneath her feet. There were whispers and sounds that could possibly be crying, and then, out of the murk loomed a sea of giant wooden posts driven haphazardly into the earth. A flicker of movement up ahead was instantly swallowed up. Isabella had just decided to retrace her steps when a hand grabbed her shoulder. She screamed.

'So, you deemed to grace me with your presence!' Carlos greeted cheerily.

'My God,' Isabella sighed, 'Are you always this dramatic?'

'Always.'

More noises, this time behind her.

'Who is with you?' she asked.

'I am alone,' Carlos replied.

'Don't lie to me. I can hear someone nearby.'

'Señorita, I would imagine that right now we are surrounded by anywhere from fifty to two hundred people.'

'What is this place? Why have they left their cars by the roadside?'

'It is called El Campo de Marcadores. In English: 'The Field of Markers".'

'*Markers*? Markers for what?'

'You are familiar with the term black sedan?'

'Yes, I am familiar with it.'

'Each marker represents a person black-sedaned. It is not a cemetery. There are no bodies buried here.'

'It a place of the dead?'

'It is a place of uncertainty,' Carlos corrected. 'People come here for one of two reasons – to weep or to reaffirm pledges.'

'You seem to know a lot about this place.'

'I spent many occasions here as a child.'

'Why have you brought me here?'

'To see what we can see?'

'You think Jonathan is dead?'

'This field is fifteen years of vanishing. The dead reside elsewhere. We should look.'

Isabella noticed his face for the first time. He looked distraught, his features tired and distended.

If Jonathan taught you nothing else then it was to face whatever comes head on.

If he's dead I don't know if I can handle the loss.

If he's dead then this is all pointless anyway.

'OK,' she replied, 'Show me what I must see.'

Carlos led her through the markers. Shapes and shadows rose and fell around them. Some of the posts were marked with names, most were unsullied.

'This is a corner of Corderro that El Rey has never touched,' he told her. 'It is a mystery as to why. Perhaps from his ivory tower it cannot be seen, or maybe he deemed that we needed a pressure valve to avoid exploding? I don't know. Whatever the case he never grasped how important this field is. I remember the man who established it. His name was Salvatore. He whitewashed the walls that surround us and encouraged mourners to write poetry on them. Look closer and you will see the "prose of the people".'

They came to the boundary. The whitewashed walls that Carlos had spoken of were lost beneath thousands of messages, painted or scratched into the brickwork. He scoured the surface with a new-found enthusiasm.

'Here's a good one,' he said, and read aloud what was written.

> *'I took a piece of oak*
> *And drove it through the good green earth*
> *That I might safeguard the beauty of life's love*
> *And hide my defiance within a mask of mirth.'*

'As poetry goes it's not very good. The lines have differing lengths and numbers of syllables. It doesn't flow, but it doesn't matter. All that matters is that whoever wrote it poured out their soul. And another . . . '

> *'A thousand epitaphs will not suffice*
> *To tell the world what I have lost*
> *But with this mark I recognize*
> *The impossibility of my task.'*

'It doesn't quite rhyme, but so what!'

Isabella watched Carlos's animated expression and soaked up his words like a sponge.

Perhaps I have misjudged you. Beyond the bravado there may well be something genuine after all.

'El Ambiente wrote something here once. Would you like to see it?'

'Please.'

'Just let me get my bearings. I think it's over here, but I might be wrong. It's been a long while.'

They followed the wall around to the right. In time they came to a section that was cleaner than the rest. The overlaid scrawl gave way to a neatly written statement surrounded by a halo of unblemished white:

What is there left to say of war?

Down through the ages men and women have plundered their souls, and dredged the depths for the perfect summation of all that is bound up within conflict.

I could speak of my immeasurable grief, of the day the bottom fell out of my world, of the loss, of the voices and faces I will never see again.

I could make some attempt at giving shape to the unquenchable rage that I feel towards my oppressor, the aggression that bends the boundaries of my conscience to near breaking point.

What of hope, the promise of a brighter tomorrow? Surely this is what flourishes in the darkest hours? Or perhaps faith – the good will out, the desire to rise above, to even forgive?

Perhaps I should abandon reason, and embrace the nihilistic urge to hate. Throw my cards in the air and spit vehemently that war mirrors the true nature of men's hearts?

But what would be the point of revisiting such notions?

They have each been said far better, far too many times before, by far greater people than I.

And so I chose the road of mischief – playing pranks on my enemy, daubing my name on walls, becoming a nuisance, and acting

   Like a child

      Who believes the horrors that surround

         Are just a game . . .

El Ambiente

'Again, not a spectacular piece of literature, but because of who wrote it this area has become a shrine of sorts.'

La Fantasma closed in further still and the wall vanished. Carlos became a murky silhouette.

'This is so disorientating,' Isabella complained. 'I've no concept of size or location. How many markers are there? How big are its borders?'

'There were over ten thousand markers last time I ventured here,' Carlos replied. 'I'd hazard a guess that it has at least quadrupled in the last fifteen years.'

'How on earth can we search for someone in these conditions?'

'Slowly, *mi chica bella*.' Even in the poor visibility Carlos could see the look of disapproval. 'Are you in a hurry to get back to anything in particular?'

The comment acted as a pressure valve. Isabella laughed and felt her pent-up tension ebb away. 'Ask a stupid question!'

They made their way along the wall, veering away each time a marker came into view. None were scribed with Jonathan's name. After what seemed like an eternity they reached a corner, moved a few paces to the right and began to walk back. As Isabella searched the encryptions Carlos counted the rows.

When they reached the seventh turn a shadow passed across his face.
This is it.

He couldn't remember how far up they were. There was a tree of some description but it would not be visible to guide him. He shuddered with anxiety. Isabella was oblivious to the change.

Carlos was so distracted by his nerves that he almost missed it. The marker was a carbon copy of all the others. He recognised the handwriting as his own.

Raymundo Neblina.

Isabella didn't make the connection with Carlos's surname. Her mind was fixed upon finding Jonathan. Carlos dropped back, raised a hand to his lips, kissed his fingers and ran them across the head of the marker.

'*Padre,*' he whispered softly.

He passed by without breaking a stride. A few more steps brought him to Valeria Neblina. Isabella had forged off ahead.

'*Madre.*'

A kiss.

A few more steps.

Melissa Neblina.

'*Hermana.*'

A kiss.

Tears streamed down his face. The misty air froze them to his cheek. Isabella thinned to a sliver and became vapour. Hate welled in his heart.

I am coming for you. Your time draws to a close.

Don't let her see you like this.

Carlos stopped and composed himself. He considered all that had been achieved in the years since his departure, and then envisaged the markers standing idle during all that time. He shrugged off the hostility with the silent reaffirmation of a pledge, wiped his eyes and rejoined Isabella.

They searched El Campo de Macadores for several more hours, but never found any signs of Jonathan. Isabella felt frustration and elation in equal measure.

'Come on,' Carlos reassured her, 'by the time we have walked back into Corderro the restaurants will be serving their evening menus – my treat.'

5.

ty was branded a thief right on this spot in 1902.'

tomach full with *casadas* and the best part of a bottle of wine ained much of his buoyancy.

d to have died under his own chastisement, purging his

sins with a whip and stripping the skin from his back so that he bled to death.'

'That isn't in the book,' Isabella queried.

'The Spaniard was a stickler for proven fact. I imagine he left out some of the more unscrupulous parts of the preacher's downfall due to lack of evidence, but it was common folklore when I was a child.'

Isabella had drunk two Caiprinas with her meal. The cocktail was deceptively intoxicating, hiding its potency beneath copious amounts of sugar and lime.

'You still haven't told me how we know each other,' she said.

'If you can't remember me, then maybe we never met.'

'But we did.'

'How do you know?'

'Because you told me.'

'I might have been lying. I am a book thief after all! You know what? I would very much like to hear another entry from your journal.'

'I don't think so,' Isabella scoffed. 'You have learnt quite enough by underhand means as it is.'

'Well in that case, how about I make you a deal. I'll tell you a story and then you tell me one, deal?'

'It depends on how sensational yours is. I might not find it interesting enough.'

'Now you're just being plain awkward! Very well, I have the utmost confidence in my own sparkling wit and oratory ability. Here goes.'

Carlos made a showpiece of clearing his throat.

'How I met my wife (who is not, as has been inferred, a fictional character).
By Carlos Neblina.

I'll try diarizing it. I was in the chorus line of a Broadway musical. She sold ice creams in the interval. I'd often see her in the wings during a performance. She made me forget half of the lines.

Through a bit of subtle digging I acquired her name – Clarina. She was (and is) stunning beyond words. I ate so much ice cream, every night, just to be around her. I put on half a stone in a matter of weeks!

Shortly thereafter the choreographer started shouting at me on a nightly basis. I was overweight, clumsy, distracted and forgetful. On each occasion I would always promise to buck up my ideas, but my heart was no longer in it. It was elsewhere.

Brief pause to build unbearable suspense.

So, one night I was queuing to buy my ice cream (to date it had cost me an absolute fortune), when Clarina took my hand and said, "I cannot wait any longer for you to ask me out. I fear that your teeth will all fall out and your belly will swell to bursting point."

I realized that if I could ensnare the emotions of so fine a woman I must be one hell of a catch, and so began my ascent into staggering arrogance (and brilliance).

We were married within a year. I proposed underwater using sign language (another story), and we got hitched at the top of a mountain. Many, many children and much happiness ensued. The end.'

'You were never in a Broadway musical,' Isabella said disparagingly.

'Of course I was.'

'Alright then, what was it called?'

'The Laurel-Canyon-Shuffle.'

'Never heard of it.

'That's because it ran out of money in less than a month.'

'It bombed?'

'Only commercially, romantically it was a raging hormonal success.'

'None of which tells me where we've met before.'

'God, you're such a *woman* about things, all indirect and implied. A man would just come right out with it.'

'OK. How do we know each other?'

'Not telling you.'

'Oh, you're impossible.'

'Yes I am. So, we have established that I am an exciting and engaging storyteller.' Carlos filled his glass with the remainder of the wine and ordered another Caiprina. 'I have clearly earned the right to know more about you. What is it you have to tell me?'

Reluctantly Isabella took out her journal and leafed through its pages until she found an entry she was willing to reveal. 'OK, don't you dare laug'

' be as sober as a judge,' Carlos slurred.

'Man-hattan

Today I walked through Central Park. It is autumn. The world is steeped in leaves of golden rust and amber glow. I was being childish, kicking and swishing my way through the undergrowth when a jogger, drenched in sweat, ran up to me and offered a handful of grass.

"If I'd known you were going to be here I'd have brought roses," he said with a smile, part cheek, part nerves.

I laughed. "A very noble gesture."

Beneath the red face and the hair caked to his brow I saw just how good looking he was. I practically forced my phone number onto him. I had a pen but neither of us had paper. We used his skin. Even as I was writing, the digits were blurring with perspiration.

The man slapped himself. "I didn't expect this to pan out so well . . . My name's Simon, by the way."

I pointed to my own name. It was underlined with a kiss.

"Wow . . . I've got to memorize this before it fades . . . I'll call you later . . . once I'm a little more presentable . . . wow."

"I'd like that."

"Wow . . . OK . . . I gotta run."

"Thanks for the grass," I shouted after him.

The sun was setting. All around me the squirrels were once again reclaiming their kingdom.

And then I thought of you.

I realized it had been over a year since my last correspondence (!) I desperately wanted to tell you about how wonderfully surreal I felt at what had just transpired – a moment that would not have been possible without you.
Thank you.

Isabella, 23rd January'

Isabella was surprised at how openly she divulged private and intimate details of her life. Carlos listened intently throughout, the corners of his lips curling slowly into a broad grin.

'He sounds like an amazing man this Jonathan.'

'He is.'

'And you say you've only met him once?'

Isabella leant forward in her seat. 'I know how it sounds and I can see where you're going with this. You think I'm deluded.'

'I think you are a romantic. There is a world of difference between romance and delusion, but it's a phenomenal leap of faith to write a journal and travel halfway round the world in order to present it to a man you saw briefly as a child over a decade ago. I just don't want your hopes to be dashed.'

His concern was clearly genuine and his argument was difficult to refute.

'If you'd met Jonathan you would not speak of him in this fashion.'

Carlos looked away, across the plaza to a patch of grass where two children, a boy and a girl, were having a race. They ran and giggled their way towards a woman who was crouched on the floor, her arms cast wide awaiting their arrival. The scene reminded him of a time long ago. It made him smile.

I have met him.

Chapter 16
Tito and Maria Partake in Genocide by Proxy

1.

Señor Majagranzas,

We here at Phantom Pharmaceuticals were both thrilled and honoured to discover that we had such an esteemed gentlemen as yourself on our books. Hair loss is often seen as a 'humiliating, emasculating condition'. It is refreshing therefore that you should so publicly reveal your identity to us.

We cannot deny that we were somewhat dismayed at your threat to 'kill us' (paraphrasing the distasteful term 'black-sedaning'). We can only presume that the stress brought on by your 'debilitating baldness' has in some way unbalanced your brain. Please accept with our compliments this free thirty-day course of mild sedatives (enclosed).

As you can no doubt see we pride ourselves on our customer care. At the thought of your 'unhappy scalp', we leapt into action, and an emergency meeting was hastily called where the following was agreed:

- *To point out to you that you had misquoted us in your complaint. Our actual claim is to 'show significant follicle rejuvenation . . . in 99% of treated cases'. Congratulations, El Comedin – you are unique!*
- *To liquidate the company with immediate effect and relocate to Honduras where we are told the Chancellor of the Exchequer is in possession of (i) honesty, and (ii) a thick head of Afro.*
- *To make copious copies of your original letter and deliver them to every street corner in Corderro on our way out for the city's amusement.*
- *To give you this sachet containing the 'prototype' version of our latest hair cream. We sincerely hope you agonize over whether or not to apply it. Who knows what our intentions could've been?*

There you are, probably not what you were looking for, but on the bright side it <u>does</u> give you an empty building to insure and blow up.

Yours irreverently,

Señor Valere
Phantom Pharmaceuticals (deceased)

217

2.

Your Grace,

I write in reference to your recent request for the establishment of private limited companies 'Spiderman' and 'Hercules' respectively. This correspondence also covers your three previous memos:

> *02/08 – Re: 'Barbie' and 'Skeletor'.*
> *24/08 – Re: 'Don Quixote' and 'Captain Fantastic'.*
> *04/09 – Re: 'Doctor Octopus' and 'Huckleberry Finn'.*

The reason for my lengthy preamble will shortly become apparent. Suffice to say that I and the remainder of my colleagues not killed in last month's explosion have worked diligently to forge a new home for ourselves amidst the rubble of our once great edifice.

The typewriter on which I am composing this letter was found in a tree two hundred yards from the office. Though badly scratched in the incident the word 'Philippe' is still evident on the underside (though it now lacks both a '#' and a '&' key (written in by hand after the event)). Philippe was a rather camp legal secretary who worked opposite me. He enjoyed fishing and ballroom dancing. He's dead now.

But to the matter in hand (is it proper etiquette to began a sentence with the word 'but'? I have never been entirely sure). Perhaps with all the stresses of mismanaging a country's finances it has slipped Your Grace's mind that the legal department is no more (it certainly slipped your mind to inform us of said demolition in which you were personally responsible for the extinction of seventeen men '&' (hand written) twelve women).

At 20 petras per word perhaps you found our documentation an unwelcome expense (?). (Under legal guidelines the '?' symbol can be classed as a word and charged accordingly). To write to us on numerous occasions asking for help after attempting (unsuccessfully) to annihilate us demonstrates a level of idiocy hitherto unknown, but entering into the spirit of things we have endeavoured to furnish you with a comprehensive answer:

- *Your request cannot be acquiesced as the chosen names are already legitimately copyrighted entities.*
- *Even if they weren't copyrighted we would not be in a position to help you, finding ourselves as we do, homeless, jobless and hopeless.*
- *Even if we were in a position to help you we wouldn't (slightly immature, I*

realize, but under the circumstances wholly understandable I'm sure you'll agree).

With that in mind I have, with a thoroughly irresponsibly uneconomical use of language, set out several reason why your request remains unfulfilled (see above).

The total word count for this correspondence is 504 which equates to 10,800 petras. Having said that I fully appreciate:

   i.   *That the petra is now virtually worthless, and*

   ii.   *That you would never in a million years pay us.*

But (there I go again) it provides us all here with some limited amusement to think that this letter will provide you with yet another sordid secret to conceal to your bottomless pit of empty promises.

You are destined for a very dark hot place, El Comedin.

     Yours concisely,

         Anonymous surviving lawyer

         Legal department (no more).

3.

Tito tried to remain calm, fearful of the impact anxiety would have on his hairline. 'Goddamnit, no one in this rancid cesspool respects me!'

Maria Clott leant back, draping herself provocatively over the chaise longue. 'Raise taxes, darling,' she replied with nonchalant ease.

'I cannot make macro-economic decisions based on mild annoyance,' Tito chastized. 'Besides, I wouldn't have thought you could afford a raise given your astronomical outgoings!'

'Oh calm down, Minky. It's not as if anyone pays their taxes. I certainly don't!'

Minky – a new pet name that had crept into Maria's limited vocabulary in recent weeks. How Tito despised those two syllables, joined loathsomely together with seemingly no reference back to him.

God, it's worse than El Comedin.

Perhaps it's a generic term?

Maybe she has a string of men all called Minky for simplicity?

Perhaps the term links back to an original Minky, someone for whom the word had meaning, or even intimacy?

Tito once again worked himself into an unnecessary frenzy.

Pet names, nicknames. Why can't people call me by my real name?

'How am I supposed to maintain a position of authority when even my own lover doesn't abide by the rules?'

Maria puckered her lips and blew Tito a voluptuous kiss. 'Really dear, don't take offence. With the combined factors of 70 per cent tax and a devalued currency, the average family would have to earn in excess of 30,000 petras per week in order to live within the law. The numbers simply don't stack up.'

Tito was astounded by Maria's sudden show of acumen. 'Where on earth did you learn that?'

'El Ambiente told me,' she answered proudly.

'El Ambiente?'

'Yes, he wrote it on a wall outside our gym.'

'Darling, El Ambiente is a terrorist.'

'Only one of you blows up buildings on a regular basis, sweety.'

Tito pretended not to have heard her cutting remark. 'You shouldn't pay him the slightest attention.'

'Or her.'

'What?'

'He could be a her?'

'Unlikely.'

'Why ever not?'

Tito wasn't about to reveal his deeply sexist views on society, even to a woman he considered his intellectual inferior. Life had taught him that it simply wasn't worth the hassle. He opted instead for a safer response.

'Because he chose a masculine noun as a pseudonym – "El" Ambiente – not "La" something.'

'Oh my dear gullible one,' Maria patronized much to Tito's vexation, 'that could easily be a double bluff. No, I think he or she is more likely a poet or a teacher than a terrorist.'

'Maria! Don't you see what's happening here? Only rich people can afford gym membership in this day and age. He's mocking you for your wealth and trying to make you feel guilty.'

'Oh.'

'*Oh* indeed . . . I don't need advice from the Scarlet Pimpernel! I need a sustainable economic policy.'

'How about . . .' There was a pregnant pause whilst Maria's mind caught up with her mouth.

Oh here it comes.

Tito placed his head on the desk.

Is it not enough that I suffer the humiliation of office. Must I also endure the dregs of human contemplations?

'Instead of taxing people for what they have . . . taxing them for what they *don't* have.'

Oh mi Dios!

'How do you mean, my darling?' he asked whilst inwardly thinking *Don't encourage her*. 'There are many things people do not have. Surely we cannot tax them all?'

'No silly, I don't mean what they *don't* have. I mean what they wouldn't *want* to have.'

'I don't follow.'

'Well . . . for example . . . the air is pure and fresh, and the drinking water is clean . . . what if the air *wasn't* pure, and the water was filled with . . . ooh, I don't know . . . all kinds of nasty things?'

'You mean like Blackmail . . . or Extortion?'

Maria's vacant expression momentarily became vibrant. 'Exactly.'

Oh well, it's back to the tried and tested method.

Tito unlatched the window and together they gazed out on the city. There were an awful lot of blots on the landscape where buildings had once been.

'Wow, it really sneaks up on you, doesn't it?' Maria gasped with the marvel of a child.

Tito was overwhelmed. 'That's one way of looking at it.'

How can we be so deep in debt with so much insurance revenue coming in?

'OK, how shall we choose this time?' he asked. 'Toss a coin?'

'What about that large building halfway up the hill with the green roof?' Maria replied.

'That's my house?'

'Is it?'

'Of course it is. How many times have you been there?'

'It looks a lot different far away, doesn't it?'

Tito took the opportunity to peruse his mistress's curvaceous form, reminding himself why it was he had cheated on his elegant, charming, intelligent wife for the past three years.

'Well, how about just blowing up your wife's side?'

'*Really*, Maria! Such comments are beneath you.'

'That's where I like to be, Tito – beneath you!'

4.

Later that day Tito took out his journal and wrote: *I am not so much scraping the barrel as burrowing beneath the barrel towards the earth's core.*

Six days later he would amend the entry with the words: *Perspective is a wonderful thing!*

There was a knock at the door. Cheech the errand boy entered the room, his head bowed, a note in his hand. 'Excuse me, Your Grace – a memo from Ms Blake.'

Tito snatched the note from his hand and shooed the boy out into the corridor without a word.

El Comedin,
> *My expenses for the month – progress with all speed.*
> *Eleanor Blake*

Another straw for the camel's back.

Wrapped within the note a thick roll of scented paper spilled endlessly out across the floor. The list of expenses included shoes, lingerie, make-up, bullets, wallpaper, a fireplace, a kitchen renovation and countless other inadmissible items.

Tito hated the way Eleanor took such liberties, hated the fact that he must always pay her in full without question, hated the way that she addressed him by his nickname, hated her insistence upon sending the bills to him personally when one of his lower clerks could easily have processed the payments for her, and hated her insistence on being paid in US dollars, a currency that was both illegal and costly to convert.

All in all he hated *her* and felt certain the feeling was mutual.

It took the Chancellor three hours to process Eleanor's expenses, by which time Maria had conceived another idea.

'Come with me to the rooftop,' she said.

It was dusk. Autumn colours were beginning to impinge upon daylight.

At this time of day the city could almost be beautiful.

Maria laid out a large map on the floor and held it down with empty wine bottles.

'Angel, my head is aching from all that number crunching and it's time for my early evening cognac. What are we doing up here?'

'You'll like this,' Maria giggled. 'It takes all the thinking out of decision-making. I've christened it "Playing God". It's simple really – you close your eyes, I spin you round three times to disorientate you and then you point in whichever direction you feel like. Next, you open your eyes, follow the line from your finger and whichever building it points towards you blow up!'

It was the worst idea Tito had ever heard, but desperate times called for even more desperate measures. 'OK dear,' he agreed wearily.

'Great, I'll go first.'

5.

At three in the morning Tito lay staring at the ceiling with Maria snoring beside him.

That damn miracle cream!

The sachet was in the next room calling to him, preventing sleep. With every passing moment he was getting balder and balder and balder. There was no denying it.

Maybe it can cure everything?

They wouldn't have sent anything genuine, not after you threatened to black-sedan them.

Maybe they would, knowing that I wouldn't dare use it?

No way to be sure . . .

. . . but to try it.

The circular thoughts went round and round for hours until finally he jumped from the bed and dashed across the bedroom like a man possessed.

Don't think, don't think, don't think, don't think, don't think, don't think, don't think.

The sachet was in his sweaty hands, slipping through his grasp. It wouldn't open. He tore at it with his teeth.

Come on, come on, come on, come on, come on, come on, come on, come on, come on, come on.

It ripped. Pungent pearly cream was on his lips. He spat it into his palm. The substance looked just like shampoo.

A good sign?

Don't think, don't think, don't think, don't think, don't think, don't think, don't think.

Tito strode to the bathroom breathing heavily, stood in front of a full-length mirror and watched himself massaging the unknown fluid into

223

his scalp.

What are you . . .

Don't think, don't . . .

It felt good, refreshing, reviving. He breathed a sigh of relief. Everything was going to be alright.

6.

A little after four Tito and his mistress threw themselves out of bed in response to an almighty boom. The blast was so loud that it sounded as if it emanated from within the palace walls. The Chancellor's first thought was that they were under attack. The phone rang.

'Good morning, El Comedin.'

It was Eleanor. Her velvety voice oozed vindictive pleasure.

'I'm just ringing to inform you that the demolitions went off without a hitch. Sorry about the hour. It was deemed the most cost-efficient time of day.'

The line went dead.

Goddamn that woman! Her sole purpose in life is to taunt me.

Maria scrambled clumsily to her feet, pulling at various corners of a skimpy negligee and trying in vain to preserve some dignity. 'What was that noise? What's that smell? MY GOD, TITO . . . YOUR FLUFF HAS GONE GREEN!'

'MY FLUFF!' he shouted, suddenly enraged.

'Hair,' Maria quickly corrected, recoiling into the quilt.

'You said *Fluff.*'

'I meant hair.'

Tito ran to the bathroom for the second time that morning.

Don't think, don't think, don't think, don't think, don't think, don't think, don't think, don't think.

His hand lingered on the light switch, fearful of what ghastly spectacle would be revealed. Outside, the rumbles of aftershocks rippled up through the foundations. The room began to vibrate and the silence was broken by a choir of car alarms. Dogs started barking. People started screaming. Tito was oblivious to it all.

Click.

An unnatural mist was rising from the top of his head. The Chancellor's drooping quiff resembled a radioactive rodent – bright lime in places, tinged with tangerine in others, and through the dazzling array of colours his ever-present scalp continued its quest for freedom.

Damn you Señor Valere and your mythical elixir!

Tito took the used sachet of miracle cream from the bin. On contact with the air the remnants of the cream had changed composition, morphing from a shiny shampoo into what looked like dull mayonnaise interspersed with globules of vinegar. The smell was unspeakably vile.

Excrement mixed with bleach?

Rotting meat and damp rot?

Egg nog and spoiled sprouts?

For a maddening second he considered sending Eleanor to Honduras and paying the owners of Phantom Pharmaceuticals a little visit.

No, I could never tell her about this, and besides, she pays no attention to me at the best of times.

He imagined a room full of managers all howling with laughter at a joke well executed. There was nothing to do but accept the blow as part of a painfully slow, certain, continued, unrelenting humiliation.

Tito jumped fully clothed into the shower, eager to wash out the cream without further delay. He watched the floor in horror as clumps of dead, mossy hair congregated around his feet. A whimper escaped his lips.

Is there no end to the torment?

He emerged naked minutes later, a towel wrapped around his head like a turban. He could tell instantly from Maria's face that something was up. On any normal day the spectacle of his naked form would have sent her into fits of hysterics.

'What it is?'

Maria handed him a note, her face pale.

'It was pinned to the outside of the bedroom door.'

Your Grace,

While you slept peacefully your conscience jumped from your body, unable to tolerate the filth a moment longer.

It wandered lonely into the palace corridors where it met me.

We shook hands, and together we crept to your bedside and stood over you. Watching.

In time your ghostly hands rose from slumber, took a transparent box of matches from the table beside you, struck one and lit a fictitious fuse. We gazed in horror, your conscience and I, as a tiny spark travelled across the floor, out through the open window, down the outside wall and into the city. As it did so we jumped up and down, kicking manically at the trail, hoping to extinguish the flame before it fell out of sight, but to no avail.

We took flight. I became El Ambiente – the very atmosphere, smoke and ash, bitter vapour. Our screams could not be heard as we tried to warn the people below. Like you, they slept. They would never wake.

As they were <u>ripped limb from limb</u> their souls burst forth into the night air. They were confused, angry and bewildered at your actions. They demanded answers from your conscience. It had none to give.

I begged it to return, to try and talk some sense into you, but it replied that in doing so it would have to put on the garments of a murderer, of a clumsy coward who puts his own vanity above the sanctity of life. It said that your cause was lost.

I am a great believer in the human spirit and I still have faith that you will do the right thing, but I cannot permit you to pursue this destructive course of action any longer.

> *You have been warned.*
> *El Ambiente.*

'Oh for crying out loud!' Tito shouted, clutching his towel turban. 'Am I to be patronized to death?'

'I told you, darling,' Maria declared excitedly, 'he's a poet.'

'His text is tawdry,' the Chancellor replied dismissively, 'as is his clichéd view on morality. I will have to double the guards within these walls'. And with that he screwed the note into a ball and threw it out of the window.

Chapter 17

In which El Rey Discusses
'The Art of Corruption'

El Rey gazed at the naked form of Eleanor Blake, sprawled out on the king-size bed beside him, and considered with lustful relish all he had successfully coveted from the world.

It was the middle of the night, but he found sleep impossible. There was so much to do, so many earth-shattering thoughts to capture on paper. The *Plague of Lethargy* lay open before him.

It is without a doubt that corruption is our true nature. Who can say with heartfelt conviction that it is best to leave the apple ripe and unplucked on its branch? If we are truly infected with a disease, then it is the disease of morality – confusing our base instincts and causing us to fall woefully short of our true selves.

Who can deny the orgasmic surge of black delight that accompanies sleeping with another man's wife, or the nucleus of energy that follows giving yourself over to rage and throttling the life from a sworn enemy?

In Old Testament times King David looked out from his palace rooftop and saw the goddess-like Bathsheba bathing in an adjacent building. Not one to shy away from conquests of this magnitude, David had her soldier-husband placed at the forefront of battle so that his death would be assured. He then took her for his own and drank from forbidden streams.

Even as I write these words I lie next to my own Bathsheba; beheld as a trainee cadet, seduced with gifts and promotion, and ensnared when her fiancé died suddenly and violently at the hands of smugglers in El Puerto de Las Ondas Verdes. His death invoked in her a desperate need for companionship, a need I felt more than qualified to fill, having sent the unfortunate soul to his death in the first place.

Doubly delectable is the realization that having sampled all that her body has to offer I now seal her fate with the previous paragraph. Upon reading my words Eleanor would no doubt reward me with the cruelest retribution her savage, formidable mind could muster. No, if I am to publish my legacy to the world then she too must meet an untimely demise.

But for now at least I most certainly will have my cake and eat it!

El Rey put down his pen and walked over to the easel where his portrait lay waiting for its finishing strokes. The artist, his fourth, had vanished before the job was complete. It seemed to the Emperor that he had sat in that regal posture for an eternity. He stared at the vibrant swirls of oils.

What does that expression convey to you?

He looked deep into his own eyes.

Power, virility, justifiable arrogance, nobility, intellect.

And yet the fact remains, despite all your power you have been denied the simple wish of a satisfactory conclusion.

There was no refuting it. His pride was bruised and demanded a disproportionate punishment for the insult. The Emperor moved to the next room and snatched up his phone. A faceless servant answered. 'Yes, Your Highness.'

'Three things: firstly, find the man who painted my portrait and bring him to me minus his hands. Secondly, commission another artist and send him or her to me within the hour. Their sleep patterns do not concern me. Thirdly, I would like fresh lobster delivered to my room as soon as is humanly possible.'

'But it's three o'clock in the morning.'

El Rey considered the man's response for a moment. 'Is there a guard near you?'

'No, Your Highness.'

'Go and find one. Call me back once this is done.'

He hung up.

Eleanor stirred in the next room. From where he stood only her thighs were visible. El Rey fixated upon them.

You are near physical perfection, but you could never be my equal.

Nevertheless, I shall cry the day that your throat is slit.

The phone rang. 'Yes?'

'I have located a guard, Your Highness.'

'Good. Please relay my three instructions to him.'

There was a moment of mumbling before the servant returned. 'As requested, Your Highness.'

'Let me speak with him.'

A deeper, gruffer voice greeted him. 'Sire.'

'Soldier, are my wishes clear?'

'Crystal, sire.'

'Good. Be so kind as to kill the man who handed you the phone and bring his head to my room. Before he dies, tell him that *I will not be questioned.*'

'Yes, sire.'

El Rey replaced the handset, closed a partitioning door so as not to disturb Eleanor and sat in an armchair facing the corridor. Over the next ten minutes three guests arrived. The first brought him a human head, the second fresh lobster and the third news of a fifth artist's imminent arrival.

He returned to Eleanor and his writing.

Like all great men my weakness is in soliloquy. The incessant monologue required to outline the colossal ideas of a dictator's mind is a time-consuming and tiresome affair.

As with so many of my tyrannical brothers around the world I have commissioned over the years a plethora of paintings and effigies that play to my ego – shapes, contours and colours that strip twenty years from my face and hide the paunch, the sagging jowls and the general onset of time.

My hair is bleached black, my face is clean shaven. In the event of a coup I could let my vanity go and be a wizened old man within a few days. I could work on a market stall selling broccoli and aubergines amongst the proletariat. I could stand humbly next to a statue of the pompous and exiled dictator in a crowded street and be recognized by no one.

But I would be remembered.

Oh my, my!

They would write songs, hold banquets, make tall stories taller still, and slowly but surely I would slip into legend. Retiring to my hiding place I would usurp the reputations of trolls and goblins. Mothers would say to their children, 'Don't go in the woods or El Rey will get you.'

'What does he look like?' the overinquisitive children would ask.

'He's eighteen feet tall with purple hair and fangs as long as your arms,' the mothers would reply.

A man can dream, can't he?

However, in the unlikely event that I am forced into this position sometime in the distant future, I will act as the Egyptian pharaohs of old – gathering up the slaves and servants who have built and run my kingdom, and scythe through them in one gloriously callous moment, the secrets of my life buried amongst the remains.

Chapter 18

The Story of the Sofa

1.

They waited on the bridge until they were sure that he had drowned. The sun had completely vanished from the sky, and water that had previously run red with Kelly's blood now flowed black and impenetrable as an oil slick. They drew straws to see who amongst them would be the one to phone Eleanor Blake. The loser dialled the number, his voice shaky and his top lip moist with perspiration.

'It is done, ma'am,' he whimpered into the receiver.

'What is your name, soldier?' came her velvety response.

'Alessandro, ma'am.'

'Congratulations Alessandro, you are now on my radar. As I'm sure you're aware, this is a double-edged sword.'

'Yes I am, ma'am, thank you.'

'Not at all. Search the apartment. Let me know when you find the names of his associates.'

With Eleanor there was never any uncertainty. When Alessandro searched the apartment he *would* find the information he sought, whether or not it was actually there. Soldiers finding themselves falling short of Eleanor's expectations were left with a difficult decision. Did they do the honourable thing, relay the facts as they were and hope for leniency, or, as was more often the case, fabricate the details in a way that made their stories plausible? The latter option had the unfortunate consequence of incriminating innocent bystanders and sending them to the palace sub-floors to receive any number of garish ends. Alessandro had seen it happen many times and had even been responsible once or twice. He wasn't a bad man, he was just weak, and haunted, and afraid, and acceptant of his lot in life. In a peculiar way he considered his position a fortunate one.

After all, the one thing worse than being a soldier is being a civilian. At least in the military you have some say, however limited, in your fate. As a civilian you effectively enter into a lottery, every day a new roll of the dice, your chances equally bleak.

He ended the call with a heavy heart.

230

The walk back to Kelly's apartment was pleasant enough. The fresh evening air gave his mind a moment's respite from the pressures of duty. The journey took him through his own neighbourhood, a place where he was regarded with utter contempt. Soldiers did not live in separate barracks as in other countries. In Corderro the wolves lived amongst the sheep.

Curfew was in force. There was no reason to take the closed shutters and whispers as a personal affront, and yet Alessandro felt an acute sense of detachment. His thoughts turned to an incident several weeks previously, a single event that had polarized the community with him on one side and everyone else on the other.

He had just completed a double shift – sixteen hours straight through. He parked his car in the driveway and switched off the ignition. It hurt to use his eyes. He closed them. Alessandro felt the searing heat of the sun burning through his eyelids. He opened them.

Outside it was a lazy Sunday morning. The old man who lived next door was weeding his garden, children were spraying each other with hosepipes and men congregated around a barbecue. It could have been a utopian picture of suburbia were it not for the huge plumes of smoke rising from the city and the distant scraping of sirens.

He never discovered what had triggered the old man's outburst. All he knew was that as soon as he got out of his car he was subjected to a sudden and savage barrage of verbal abuse.

'Hey you – *soldier!* I have a quotation to share with you. Something that I hope spurs you to react, or else keeps you awake at night. It's from a historian called Edmund Burke: "*All that is required for evil to triumph is for good men to do nothing.*"'

Alessandro was the only person in the street who was armed and in uniform. By rights he should have held the higher ground, but upon seeing the old man's face he forgot all of his training. The threat posed was cerebral, something a gun could not alter. The men around the barbecue had stopped talking. The hosepipes lay trickling water onto the lawns.

The old man walked with a stick, was stooped in posture and clearly found it difficult to place one foot in front of the other, and yet he was menacing.

'I think it's high time someone stood up to the likes of you,' he continued, 'and explained in the simplest terms possible that your actions are *disgraceful.*'

Alessandro recalled his feeble response with a sense of shame.

'Sir, I don't think you want to be having this kind of discussion in public.'

'Oh don't you? I think you'll find that I do. I very much want to have *this kind of discussion* in public.'

Alessandro realized that he had taken a step backwards.

'My words are a long time in the making, they are considered and measured, and if no one else has the courage of their convictions then it falls to me to utter them. I wish to draw good and evil into sharp contrast. We here are good–' he waved his hand to indicate the people around him '–El Rey is evil . . . and *you*? What are you?'

Alessandro said nothing. He simply stared at the man, his whole body frozen with impotent fear.

'Pah,' the old man scoffed, dismissing him in his entirety with a single syllable.

The next day he and his wife vanished.

It was a stain that he couldn't wash away, a blemish on the horizon, an ever-present, unhealable tear in the fabric of his world.

2.

The process of sifting though Kelly's possessions was slow and laborious. Despite the smuggler having owned very little in the way of personal effects, every item was poured over with a focused fanaticism.

One of the soldiers found the crumpled note left by his landlord days earlier.

Slim,
Your rent is due. (PANG).
It's my daughter's birthday next week. She could do with a gold necklace.
Martine

The note gave no reference to or indication of, any terrorist activities. Alessandro sighed and told himself that he was the victim and not the instigator. Eleanor expected results. He had none to give.

'It looks like we've found our scapegoat. Find him and bring him in for questioning.'

The last room to be checked was the hallway. It was here that they discovered the sofa.

At first Alessandro was elated. Whilst the reward for its safe return was next to worthless, the prestige and kudos earned in the eyes of El Rey would be priceless. Alessandro would be granted an audience with the Emperor, he would be praised for his efforts and elevated to a higher office. His face beamed with pride.

It was then that he saw the bullet hole in one of the arm rests.

His bubble didn't just burst, it imploded, sucking all the air from the room. Alessandro loosened his collar and ran to the window. It would matter little to El Rey that his prized piece of furniture had been damaged in the course of discharging responsibilities. He would take it as a personal affront and act accordingly. Alessandro had seen him kill without reason on many occasions. If the truth was discovered his life would be snuffed out.

His initial thought was to torch the room and destroy all of the evidence, but then he reflected upon Eleanor's command. She had specifically told him to clear the room's contents and bring it to the palace. To disobey or deviate in anyway could bring down a far more exquisite end than the Emperor was ever capable of devising.

Alessandro thought fast.

'Load *everything* into the trucks – the carpets, door handles, shelves, light bulbs. Leave nothing – except this box. Leave this one to me. Go.'

3.

The knock was answered by Rafael, a greengrocer by trade. He took a moment before turning the handle. No one was expected. This usually meant bad news. Each of them had their own little mantra for such moments. Rafael's was: 'If it ends now, it's been swell.'

It was nothing earth-shatteringly poignant. He'd found from bitter experience that events of gravitas rarely were. He opened the door.

A narrow pathway led up from the basement to the street level via a stairwell. Draped over the top step he could see a hand.

A trap?

A choice.

He approached the hand with caution. Daily life in Corderro had taught him that a hand needn't necessarily be attached to a body. On this occasion is was – a middle-aged man, soaking wet clothes, bloodied shirt and neck, sharp scruffy dishevelled features, eyes wide open, glistening rather than opaque, hanging on to existence.

'Thirty-eight,' the man groaned, and tried without success to lift his head.

'Hang on,' Rafael replied backing away, '*hang on.*'

What little first-aid training he'd received told him that the man's wounds were beyond his skills. He made his way up to the first floor and awoke his colleagues. Sixteen people emerged haunted and dream-ridden from the dormitories. Amongst them were Katrina and Paolo.

Silently they carried the man into the kitchen and placed him on a table.

'Thirty-eight,' he slurred once again, thick crimson saliva running down his cheek.

Katrina entered the room and instantly recognized the man as Kelly. It was like an electric current had passed through her, a sudden, violent influx of conflicting thoughts.

Did I lead them to him?

A horrible, spiteful, selfish man who loathes me as much as I loathe him.

Am I responsible for another man's death?

Paolo had opened Kelly's shirt and was surveying the full extent of his injuries. He looked up into Katrina's eyes. His face was strained.

He advised me against this course of action.

He is reminded of Tomas – of my hand in his death.

I never listen; never learn.

How many more rotations must we endure?

'Boiling water, towels, the sharpest knife you can find,' Paolo instructed. Katrina obeyed without hesitation.

They had no doctor or surgeon amongst them. Nothing like this had ever happened before. Members of their group had disappeared in the past, falling prey to the black sedans, but no one had ever escaped.

Paolo took the lead as he so often did, speaking quickly and confidently, addressing the group as a whole. 'OK, in the absence of any informed opinions I'm going to suggest a course of action. This man has been shot. I can't see the bullet but it must be in there somewhere, and it will have to come out or he'll die. I propose to dig it out with a red hot blade, cauterize the wound in some way . . . or maybe stitch it if that doesn't work . . . not sure if that's going to be enough to ward off infection. Anyone have a better idea?'

No one spoke.

'*Come on,*' he snapped, 'how about a sense of urgency?'

Kathryn found her voice. 'It's as good a plan as any.'

'OK then. Someone fetch me some oil or paraffin or something flammable, something I can light on his chest.'

'You . . . did this to me.'

Kelly was staring up at him, eyes not quite focused.

'How did you find us?'

'You . . . son of a bitch.'

'Yeah, right Slim, that's why we're helping you when you refused to help us.'

'This is . . . guilt . . . not charity.'

'I'll show you just how guilty I feel. It's important that I ascertain how you found us. Others' lives may depend on it. It you don't tell me I'm going to lift you off this table and throw you in the street to die, which, considering you have yet to achieve anything worthwhile in your miserable subsistence would be a crying shame . . . for you.'

The others were shocked. They had never heard Paolo speak in this way, nor had Kelly. The smuggler coughed, inadvertently spraying Paolo with flecks of blood.

'You're a dark horse.'

'I am many things, but you, my friend, are slipping away with each breath. How did you found us?'

Begrudgingly Kelly summoned a response. 'El Ambiente.'

A surge of excitement rippled through the group at the mention of his name. 'You know him?'

'No...'

'How did *he* find us?'

Kelly's eyes became as opals, his pupils rolling upwards and out of site. Paolo grabbed his face and squeezed the flesh between his fingers so that Kelly's lips formed a hideous pout. His pupils reappeared and he growled like a deranged animal.

'That's right, Slim, you hang onto that hatred. It'll see you through.' Paolo released his face. 'El Ambiente?'

'I don't know . . . I . . . knock at the door . . . bridge . . . shot, fell . . . heard a voice . . . that's all . . . I swear.'

Katrina returned with a knife and a pan of boiling water. Rafael had located some white spirit and a tea towel. Paolo took the blade.

'I'm not going to lie to you, Slim. This is gonna hurt like hell.'

Kelly reached up and grasped at Paolo's shirt. 'I cannot die. I need forgiveness.'

'From God?'

'From my brother.'

Paolo let his guard down. 'Me too, Kelly, me too.'

Katrina passed him a wooden spoon. 'To bite down on.'

Paolo placed it in Kelly's mouth.

'Close the doors. It'll keep some of the sound in.'

The two men locked eyes.

'Who'd have thought it would ever come down to this.'

Evidently Kelly had no more to say.

'OK, everyone take a limb and hold him down.'

Paolo pulled open the wound and dug deep.

Kelly bit through the spoon as if it were made of matchsticks and his piercing screams roared out into the night air. Few people heard his agony and those that did buried their heads beneath pillows. Sounds of suffering often filled the hours of darkness. The people of Corderro had long since become conditioned to turning a deaf ear to those in need.

4.

The sofa was discovered a little after 4.00 am. Some of the dock workers had been locked within El Puerto de Las Ondas Verdes all night unloading a vessel that had arrived late the previous evening. They'd finished their chores over two hours beforehand, but were forced to remain within the port walls until the curfew was lifted.

Reaching the exit they found the gates open and the guards seemingly oblivious to their presence. One of the giant searchlights cut a sharply defined circle of light ahead of them. Within its intense glare Raoul sat upright with his legs crossed and arms folded. Rigor mortis had frozen him within a staged pose.

The dock workers all recognized him. Each one of them had exchanged greetings and handshakes with him over the years, helped him load and unload goods, bartered deals and shared jokes. The contrived congeniality fooled no one. He was clearly dead.

But what did his staged appearance signify? Why had the guards placed him there in full view? Were they hoping to invoke a reaction? If so, which one? Each man suffered his own internal deliberation. Ultimately they were forced into the most unnatural of responses – they acted as if he simply wasn't there.

As they passed beyond the circle of light one amongst them whispered, 'I'll phone Paolo.'

5.

Phone calls in or around curfew usually meant that someone had died. Paolo's wife approached the receiver as if it were a viper. She told herself that if she moved cautiously and didn't take her eyes of it she wouldn't feel its fangs sinking into her flesh and hear venomous words that poisoned the life out from under her.

'Hello.'

The caller correctly read the anxiety in her voice. 'It's not Paolo.'

'Thank you.'

'Is he there?'

'No . . . he's . . . away . . . who is it?'

'Raoul.'

How awful that I should feel so relieved.

'Where?'

'The port gates.'

'I'll let my husband know.'

'For what it's worth . . . he was a good man.'

Click.

6.

After the operation Paolo's hands shook so violently that he couldn't hold the bottle of unnamed liquid that was handed to him. He placed his head under a tap and drank from the water spilling down the bridge of his nose. His jaw ached. During the proceedings Kelly had broken free from his restraints and struck him.

He dropped down soaking wet into an armchair. The others kept their distance. Paolo had yet to relinquish the blade; his nerves were wound so tight that the slightest comment could trigger an explosion.

Katrina took the call. Besides a greeting and goodbye she said nothing. She just listened and felt the light within her fade a little more.

'It's Raoul.'

Her face portrayed the rest of the message.

Paolo crossed over. Something demonic was taking place behind his dead eyes. He rubbed sleep from his face.

'What time is it?'

'Ten past four.'

He was up out of the chair. 'Sun will be up soon.'

'Where are you going?'

'To get his body.'

'Paolo, you can't, you'll be marked.'

'I've worked with him for four years. We're like brothers . . . thick as thieves. You think I'm not marked already after this? I'm not leaving his flesh to those bastards. He deserves better.'

'OK, then let's go.'

'You're not coming.'

'I'll drive. You're in no fit state.'

'*I'm* driving.'

'Paolo, *no*, I took an oath just as you did.'

'This is not up for discussion.'

'Finc, then I'll be your passenger.'

'No.'

'This is not up for discussion.'

7.

The van approached the gates at speed. The guards were armed and curfew was in place. Their course of action should have been obvious, but they could see who was behind the wheel and the look in his eyes left them immobilized.

'My—' Katrina began, her heart in her mouth.

Paolo swerved at the last moment.

'No, too quick a death,' he replied. 'I would not grant them such a service.'

He pulled hard on the handbrake and the van spun to a halt.

'May God curse your blackened souls,' he howled as he exited the vehicle.

Behind the wire mesh the guards took a startled step backwards.

'*Hijos de putas*! I cannot even look at you, I am so consumed with vehemence at your pathetic cowardice.'

Katrina was more conciliatory in tone. She had only ever seen her friend like this once before and the memory of it conjured images she would rather forget. 'Let's just do what we came here to do.'

Paolo's eyes welled up. 'Do not burst as teardrops,' he commanded, 'or I shall see that which I cannot bear.'

'Let me guide you,' Katrina offered. She led him to Raoul, still posed awkwardly on the sofa.

'Can you do something about his posture?'

Katrina tried to move the cadaver's arm, but found it to be the texture and temperature of ice. 'Let's just get the sofa into the van. I shall make him more presentable when we get home, I *promise*.'

Paolo nodded. 'OK.'

'We'll do this in a single lift, all of your efforts on the first attempt.'

The guards shuffled uncomfortably and kicked at the dust to fill the silence.

Katrina grunted as she bore the weight. She gritted her teeth and forced the furniture up through the open doors of the van. Raoul fell forward onto his face, his rigid arms holding his body off the ground in an unnatural shape.

She looked up. Paolo had walked over to the port gates.

'Don't!'

Katrina began to run towards him, hoping to pacify his intentions. Ahead of her Paolo calmly drew a line in the dirt with his foot and spat over it.

'When your time comes I hope they dress you up as clowns.'

One of the guards poked his gun barrel through the wire mesh. 'You're a marked man, amigo.'

'So are you,' Paolo responded, 'marked with shame . . . and disgrace.'

Katrina began pulling him away.

'Stench . . . dishonour . . . betrayal . . . blood.'

She forced him into the passenger seat still cursing, and drove away.

8.

The three men's absence did not go unnoticed. They were the longest serving and most experienced amongst the smugglers of El Puerto de Las Ondas Verdes, and now, just like that, they were gone – Raoul (dead), Kelly (black-sedaned), Paolo (missing, rumoured to have confronted the guards in the early hours of the morning).

The day passed like any other with all the scheming and waiting for opportunities to present themselves, but most found it hard to maintain their concentration.

At midday the dock workers who had worked through the night returned to the port, and a vital piece of information was relayed to the smuggling community – the sofa.

The news spread like wildfire and it wasn't long before it reached El Café Empressario and the ears of Arty Bey. He did what any good informer would and started making phone calls.

9.

Alessandro received a message summoning him to a meeting at the palace. He never arrived. During the journey one of his own men clubbed him over the back of the head. When he awoke Alessandro found himself bound and blindfolded. Though he couldn't see, it was clear that he was somewhere outside. He could feel the wind on his naked body, and hear the sound of birds and distant traffic. The ground beneath him was soft.

I am sitting on a sofa.

The message was clear.

They know.

Alessandro rocked himself into an upright position. He felt strangely relaxed. Having been caught there was nothing left to agonize over. His worst fears were already upon him. He heard the sound of high-heeled shoes drawing nearer and felt someone sit down beside him.

'Comfortable, isn't it?' Eleanor asked.

'You'd kill me over a piece of furniture?'

'My dear boy, I'd kill you over far less than that!'

Alessandro felt one of her talons touch his thigh.

'If it's any consolation to you, let me just say that I know what it feels like to lose everything, but unlike you I don't have the luxury of dying and being spared the daily torment of life.'

'Please, don't do this.'

'Pull yourself together, man, you're a soldier!'

Alessandro thought of the old man who'd accosted him only weeks before.

I wish to draw a clear distinction between good and evil.

Isn't that what he said?

I don't feel evil . . . nor do I feel good.

Neither one nor the other.

I have turned a blind eye for years. Now Corderro is turning a blind eye to my own demise.

Full circle.

Circles . . . always circles.

The port guards who had shone the searchlight on Raoul's grotesque manikin had been called in as the firing squad. They lined up 50 feet from Alessandro and took aim – the head, the heart, the stomach. Eleanor silently mouthed 'Three . . . two . . . one . . . fire.'

They fired.

Nothing happened.

They inspected the guns and found them to be unloaded.

'Gentlemen,' Eleanor half spoke, half laughed, 'what kind of guard stares at an emperor's prized possession watching it being defiled by the bodily fluids of a rotting cadaver and does nothing about it?'

'READY!'

The men turned.

'AIM!'

A second line of gunmen stood behind them.

'FIRE!'

A thunderous whip-crack reverberated all around. It was immediately followed by several dull thuds. Alessandro himself remained unharmed. He couldn't understand. Regimented footsteps marched away from him . . . a door slammed . . . a vehicle's engine roared into life . . . all returned to silence.

He had expected his skull to implode under the awful, awesome weight of merciless projectiles, and his heart to be reduced in a flicker to scorched and mangled meat. Instead the wind touched his sweat-ridden body and showed him that he was very much alive.

'Hello?'

His voice faded away without reply.

What is happening?

Through his blindfold Alessandro caught snatches of light. His hands were bound tight with course rope that dug deep into his wrists. Despite his restraints he found that he was afforded ever so slight movement. Alessandro relaxed as best he could and tried to rotate his palms. Even a single revolution caused him intense pain. He stopped, gathered his nerves once more and repeated the exercise. Time ebbed by with only the sound of undulated breath and twisting of twine. The rope slowly began to slacken and after what seemed like for ever the loops slipped over his fingers and he was free.

'You clever little monkey.'

The sound that accompanied Eleanor's voice was like an arrow in flight.

'Oh my—'

Alessandro felt the world spin off its axis. He reached down. His stomach felt sticky.

'I've seen it a thousand times,' Eleanor announced. 'First there's the thousand-yard stare. You should know all about it being a soldier – that you-haven't-faced-your-demons-until-you've-seen-combat look.'

Alessandro reached up and carefully removed the blindfold.

'Then realization sets in. I'm told you experience a sudden drop in temperature.'

He was in a quarry filled with sand-coloured rock.

'Each time it comes I learn a little more of what it must have been like for . . .'

It was flowing along his thighs, his knees, trickling down his calves, congealing around the ankles.

Eleanor trailed off.

Alessandro turned towards her. She was unscrewing the silencer and placing it in the pocket of her dress suit. For himself he felt nothing, but for her he reserved regret, sorrow, loss, even vulnerability.

. 'You're right . . . I do feel cold.'

Eleanor took his hand in hers. Was it possible to feel empathy towards your assassin? Alessandro decided that it was. Her touch was tender.

'Why are you so—'

'*Abhorrent*?'

'Yes,' he slurred, his vision tinged with sepia.

'Well, seeing as you're not in a position to divulge my little secret, I'll tell you. I'm on a quest.'

'A quest?'

'Yes.'

'To do what?'

'To avenge a death.'

'Whose death?'

'Oh, now that I can't say.'

'Who sent you on this quest?'

'I did.' Eleanor's face revealed a sudden innocence that was almost angelic.

'Is this how a man enters your confidence, at the cost of his life?'

Eleanor retracted her hand and lit a cigarette. 'You needn't be so polite, Alessandro. Most men curse and scream at this point, calling me a murderous whore and worse besides . . . and why not? After all, what hold do you have over someone after you've all but despatched them on their way?'

Alessandro thought about it as best he could. He felt certain that some sort of universal truth should reveal itself, but all his mind conjured was three words, repeating over and over.

This is ridiculous.

'What would be the point of all that?'

'Exactly! You're an astute fellow Alessandro . . . pity.'

'You know . . . the fires are reserved for people such as yourself.'

Eleanor blew a smoke ring and watched it rise and expand. 'You too, my lukewarm little friend!'

'Do you believe in the vicious circle?'

'I most fervently do, yes.'

'Then you must know that this . . . will . . . come back at you?'

'Ah, but it won't.' Eleanor tapped her nose with a fingernail. 'I've entered into a pact with Corderro. I'm quite immune.'

Alessandro slumped forward and rocked back, shaking himself awake. 'You're insane.'

'Quite possibly, yes . . . grief does that to you.'

'It's not the brutality of your actions . . . it's the arrogance . . . furniture more important than flesh.'

'Well that's the travesty of it . . . aubergine hides all manner of sins. You could have got it cleaned, found a good tailor to patch up the damage, even claimed the reward, but instead you're sitting here on a sofa, washed up, the blood of all those soldiers on your hands, an innocent landlord condemned . . . Oh how I would weep if only I had the conscience for such things, but that's the thing, you see, Alessandro. How can you feel for others when—'

Next to her the soldier fell from his seat into the dirt.

'Oh,' Eleanor sighed, seeming to show genuine remorse. 'Just once it would be nice to reach the end with the attention of a captive audience.'

She thought of the life that had been, and the life that now was.

Sweet memory – you exist merely to taunt me with what can never be again.

She rose from the sofa and stepped between the bodies, suddenly reverent in her treatment of death.

Such finality – can they really be gone forever?

243

Have they gone where he went?

And if so, when should I follow?

Eleanor got into her car and drove out of the quarry. The road was uneven and flanked on either side by imposing hulks of rock, rising steeply to the cliffs and beyond that the sea. The ritual was always the same – stopping the car, stepping out onto the patchy grass and staring out at the rolling waters.

The circle comes in a wave and I am riding it, sweeping inevitably towards the shore and on to my retribution.

How much longer?

As with Kelly, the answer left her perpetually languishing in limbo.

Soon.

10.

Kelly's ascension took place over several days. It was a slow muggy rise into cohesion formed from uncomfortably disjointed snapshots. First there was the notion of space travel, then dreams of metallic spiders. In time his mind grabbed at the imagery and formed some limited clarity.

They're not spiders, but the antennae of something man-made – an old television? No.

A satellite.

For many nights it was his sole contemplation.

A satellite drifting through space.

He opened his eyes.

A musty nondescript room – yellow curtains drawn – underground? A picture in a wooded frame, hanging lopsided on the wall – a satellite.

Gone.

The next image was of a helicopter gunship, hovering above him, huge rotary blades sweeping in powerful rotations, stirring the dust at his feet into spirals. The sound was deafening.

Vvou . . . Vvou . . . Vvou . . . Vvou . . . Vvou . . . Vvou . . .

He stepped back and found himself on the edge of a parapet.

Vvou . . . Vvou . . . Vvou . . . Vvou . . . Vvou . . . Vvou . . .

The sound became a pulse, the ground thumping, swelling and subsiding in rhythmical surges. The air was sucked from his lungs and forced back down his throat – in, out, in, out, in, out.

He awoke.

The gunship had been fiction. The pulse was real. His chest was on fire. He reached for the source of his agony. His hand made contact with flesh.

'It's alright.'

A woman's voice.

Gone.

The room again – alone – the satellite hanging from the far wall – a bedside cabinet – an open bottle of tequila – an unhealthy slug poured in a glass – a note.

Slim,

We have no anaesthetic. It the pain gets too much to bare, drink all that you can.

Paulo

'Raoul.'

He heard the women's voice again. 'What?'

'You were dreaming. You said it was Raoul's fault.'

Now he remembered.

'What do you know about him?'

There was heavy anxiety in her voice.

Esperanza?

He rolled over, away from her unspoken accusations.

'Don't you turn your back on me.'

Already done.

Gone.

'I know you.'

The man before was thin as a rake with a patchy beard and unkempt hair.

'Yes you do, Slim?'

'Ernesto?'

'At your service.'

'You work for—'

'Arty?'

'Yes.'

'What are you doing here?'

'I work here.'

'You're a waiter.'

'On occasion. Mostly I listen to guys like you and pass on what I have learnt to those less fortunate than myself.'

'A regular Samaritan!'

Ernesto smiled. 'There's no longer any need for you to hide behind your mask. It is clear to me that you are a man without a purpose.'

'You're a poor judge of character, Ernesto! So where am I?'

'Somewhere safe.'

'In Corderro? I doubt it!'

Chapter 19

Tito's Continued Economic Misfortune

1.

The Chancellor's week had not gone well – a slow, frustrating, incompetence-laden, will-sapping descent into God-awfulness.

It had started with a phone call on Monday morning informing him that several of his insurance reclamation teams had reclaimed the wrong buildings over the weekend. Amongst the casualties were a gasworks, a hospital, several churches, a power station and a shoe warehouse.

Each team had filed separate reports blaming the others for the mistake that now left a third of the city without heating or electricity.

On Wednesday the various areas of scalp burnt by his use of the so-called Miracle Cream all joined together in a gigantic crater of shiny shame. Tito wrote in his diary: *You have ceased to be a man. Why don't you just cut off your balls and be done with it?*

And then on Friday came the stinger, the encore, the straw, the grenade over the wall – a letter from his wife. It arrived by special delivery in the early afternoon, hand-delivered by a motorcycle courier who had no concept as to the gravity of his actions. Tito couldn't remember the last time his wife had written to him. It had been some time since they'd even spoken. He opened the envelope with fear and trepidation and was not disappointed by its contents.

Mr Majagranzas,

My, my Tito, you <u>have</u> been a busy boy, haven't you!

I must say, for all the bad things I hear about this illusive 'El Ambiente' character, he seems to have done me an immense favour.

I take it you will be making no pathetic attempt to deny the infidelity for which you are so magnanimously guilty? The sheer audacity of your deception staggers even me.

No words can adequately sum up the emotions that I felt in reading the lies so clinically recorded before me – to choke back the hate and accept that I have wasted twenty years of my life with a man I have never truly loved – to commit to duty over passion, only to find that you hold no value or respect for it.

247

In short, Tito, I am crushed.

But how do you respond to such a cunning and devious spouse? That is the question. Oh, how it has consumed me since I first set eyes on the account of your treachery.

My first thought was to file for divorce and take you to the cleaners – all your money (worthless as it is), the house from under you and your self-esteem. But I soon realized the folly of my ways – that in attempting to find justice when my husband lives and breathes a regime of corruption is a fool's hope.

I needed to be cleverer than that.

And so I came up with the following, my dear sweet shit of a partner.

This morning as you left for work I watched eagerly from the bedroom. The moment that you disappeared from sight I phoned the removal company who had been on standby. They arrived in record time. Once inside they worked with surprising efficiency, packing up the more valuable of our possessions, chosen from a list I had carefully compiled over the previous week.

They brought the biggest van they could find and packed it to bursting point with all the wondrous items we have accumulated over the years – the oak dining table, the chandeliers, rugs, paintings, cutlery, china, my clothes, your clothes, the carpets, curtains, light fittings, the baby grand, the taps, mirrors, the four-poster bed, the marble fireplace (which left a terrible mess when they prized it off the wall) and your classical record collection.

I left the photo albums. They mean nothing to me now.

After they had gone I stood in the hallway of our soulless, furniture-less house and wept.

You rancid heap of excrement.

But then, oh joy, the most fantastic idea took shape in my mind. How ironic that my inspiration for revenge should come from my own disgraced husband's underhand activities.

I went down to the garage (do you know, what with all the servants, I don't think I'd ever been in there before!) and found just what I had been looking for, gallons of the stuff, all helpfully labelled with the words 'highly flammable'. It took several trips back and forth, but eventually I concluded that I had enough.

Up the staircase and along the hallway I went, trailing the heady, intoxicating liquid behind me, making doubly sure I visited each empty room in turn – a frugal dab here, a careless dousing there.

My work done I returned to the front door, lit a single innocent-looking match and let it fall to the floor.

You should have been there to see it, my love. It was beautiful – vibrant little arms reaching out, hungry and voracious. Even from the bottom of the driveway the heat was unbelievable.

I took the Mercedes (I presume you can do without the Roller and the Porsche? Bit late now either way!)

As I drove away the intense guilt that I felt at having torched your life's work to the ground was soothed by the knowledge that you would be more than healthily reimbursed by the insurance company (and seeing as you now make a regular habit of blowing up properties you may even be happy at the occurrence).

All of which reminds me – earlier this morning I cancelled our home insurance. The man I spoke to sounded incredibly relieved at my news. I believe they have been making some record payouts recently and one less to worry about can only be a good thing, from my point of view.

At the border I showed my passport to the guard and pointed out that I was the Chancellor's wife. Whilst I could swear the man smirked at my announcement he let me through without further questioning. I smiled. Despite the public humiliation of having taken on a name synonymous with idiocy it seems that there are some perks after all!

Beyond that there seems very little else left to say. I hope it was worth it for you. It certainly wasn't for me. Somewhere in the ruins of our home (if you look hard enough), you will find my wedding ring.

Adios El Comodin.

Elizabeth

2.

Tito was beaten back by the flames before he got within a hundred yards. He'd raced home as fast as the blockades would allow, weaving between burnt-out, unrecognizable vehicles and flashing his credentials at various checkpoints, but he was too late.

Far from exaggerating, Elizabeth's letter had played down the extent of a jilted spouse's destructive capability. Everything they had ever owned was alight. Even the trees, far-flung outhouses and boundary hedges crackled and curled under the intense heat. Nothing was spared.

For the first time in many months Tito's mind was not filled with thoughts of monetary balance. Elizabeth had been his foundation – strong, reliable, *essential*, overlooked, forgotten about. Now she was gone, he was inconsolable. All memories of happiness were at least ten years old.

'What have I been doing for the last decade?' he asked aloud.

More to the point, what has Elizabeth been doing?

The west wing collapsed before his eyes. He could not recall ever having set foot in it. They were his wife's quarters, her realm. When was the last time they had shared a bed? Shared a meal? Shared *anything*?

He was destitute, penniless and without the insurance with which to reclaim his fortunes. He had no clothes save the ash and smoke-filled garments on his back. He had a mistress whom he detested and whose physical charms no longer countered her parasitic nature. He had an employer who was as yet unaware of the financial state of his kingdom, but who would no doubt snuff out his existence the moment that he was. He had the nationwide reputation of a fool. He was abandoned by she who mattered most, and worst of all he had a receding hairline!

No firemen had arrived to fight the blaze – Tito himself had ordered the fire department raised to the ground some months ago.

He looked around him. The house was one of several infernos raging in the city that day. No one paid his crumbling life's work the slightest attention. It had become run-of-the-mill, bread and butter.

Tito got into his car and drove away, never to return.

3.

As he drove back towards central Corderro, El Rey's palace loomed up on the opposite hillside. It occurred to him that if the Emperor looked out of his balcony he would have a perfect view of the Chancellor's blazing estate.

Does he have enough interest in me to know where I live, and if so, what will he make of this latest blunder?

I shall have to make the palace my home for the time being. Will he notice my increased presence?

If not will El Ambiente be kind enough to furnish him with the details in the same way he has furnished Maria?

Maria!

The revelation hit him as he reached the armoured gates.

Maria is El Ambiente. El Ambiente is Maria!

It was so obvious. How could he not have seen it before? She had practically rubbed it in his face over the preceding weeks – implying that the terrorist could be a woman, coming to him with notes supposedly found pinned to walls that he himself had never seen, always in the palace, unquestionable access to everywhere, those moments of clarity where the shroud of docile stupidity fell.

They weren't rarities, they were the norm. She was letting her guard down.

Mi Dios, *what secrets has she gleaned from me over the years?*

More than the anger and betrayal was the fear, fear of what El Rey and his callous concubine would do to him when they found out. He had to come clean, and quickly, so as to limit any further transgressions.

Maria was not in residence.

No doubt undertaking acts of subversion!

Tito snatched up the phone, called Eleanor Blake and relayed to her an economical version of events, sparing the more incriminating details.

'Are you sure?' she asked.

'More or less.'

'*More or less?*'

Eleanor dealt only in absolutes.

'*YES*, yes I'm sure.'

The line went dead.

4.

Away from the harsh reality of his predicament the Chancellor regained some pragmatic distance from events. Not only did he still have to balance the books he now had to somehow finance the rebuilding of his home.

There was no point in ordering the printing of more currency. The hyperinflation of the petra would only be further exacerbated. No, he had to do just the opposite – reclaim the banknotes, burn them, reduce the circulation till scarcity forced the value to return from the arse end of obscurity, making the black market less profitable.

'Etcetera, etcetera,' he mumbled and looked across at the bookcase to *The General Theory of Employment, Interest and Money.*

'John Maynard Keynes, I would happily string you up by your thumbs.'

The only way to reclaim more currency is to raise taxes.

From?

Tito couldn't remember what the current rate was. He looked through a leather-bound journal on his desk.

Seventy-four per cent.

Last raised six days ago.

'*Mi Dios,*' He laughed, 'Seventy-four percent!'

It only took a few seconds to do the maths. He now needed eighty-two percent if he were to meet the outgoings from the month, as well as kick off construction of a bigger, better Majagranzas mansion.

Laughter mixed with tears as he wrote out the memo. It was an obscene and unachievable hike and he knew it.

What else is there to do? There is little left to burn.

He signed the order and rang a tiny bell on his desk. A few moments later the servant boy Cheech entered the room.

'Take this to the Department of Publicity with all speed.'

The boy remained motionless.

'Well?' the Chancellor questioned impatiently.

'I'm sorry, sir,' Cheech replied, 'I have no knowledge of that department.'

Tito closed his eyes, realizing his mistake. 'Oh yes, I remember.'

Insurance claim.

'Never mind, I will deal with it myself.'

5.

Later that afternoon the latest tax rise was sketched onto chalk boards and displayed around El Puerto de Las Ondas Verdes. The announcement was greeted with a duel response. The situation had been ludicrous for so long that most traders stole as much as they bartered. Therefore the farcical tax regime meant little to them. For the others who feared the consequences of unlawful behaviour the announcement was received with horror and disbelief.

Kelly was in the port that day. With less than four hours before a bullet would irrevocably alter the course of his life he quietly siphoned bootleg liquor down a funnel that ran the length of his arm into a rubber sack under his shirt. When the rates were lifted into the air he made eye contact with a soldier walking the perimeter fence. From time to time the occurrence was unavoidable. It was best not to smile, especially when bad news was being broadcast. They always looked upon the gesture as suspicious rather than friendly. Kelly nodded, then shrugged as if to say, '*Hey it's nothing – fact of life.*' The soldier nodded back. The two broke eye contact.

Raoul was also in the port, blissfully unaware of how little time he had left. Unlike Kelly he had failed to master the art of concealment. His face was a direct portal into his emotions, every thought and feeling exposed for all to see. At that moment it revealed contempt.

252

He wasn't to know, but at that precise moment his gesture was noticed and his fate sealed. Authoritative eyes tracked him as he moved through the crowds. They would later follow him to an apartment housing El Rey's missing sofa.

'ENOUGH!'

The voice belonged to a short, rotund fisherman dressed in dungarees, thick woollen jumper and rubber boots. He stood with his shoulders slumped and his arms cast heavenwards.

'This is intolerable. How does El Comedin think we're going to live? By magic? No, no more. El Rey is not my ruler. I owe him nothing. In fact, he owes—'

The fisherman disappeared in a hail of gunfire.

There, it had been said, not as a slogan on a wall, or an anonymous letter, but aloud and in person. There it was – the tipping point. Kelly could see it, they all could: the first open sign of resistance.

6.

Sealed within the bubble of office the Chancellor remained blissfully unaware of the consequences of his actions. The day passed with a slow and laborious drag. He tried to work on the accounts but instead found himself drawing circles and writing the name Dimitri over and over. Thoughts of Maria preyed upon his conscience. He phoned Eleanor for news but received no answer. He then found himself calling the house number that no longer existed.

Go home, you're a mess.

What home? For crying out loud, your home is a pile of hot ash! Pull yourself together.

What are they doing to Maria at this very moment?

Each second was like a drip of water – drip, drip, drip – torturing him with its uniform monotony.

Maria, Dimitri, Elizabeth – the names spiraled around his warped and addled brain.

Nothing is holding you to this place other than greed and fear.

You can leave. You should leave.

But if I get caught?

And if you stay?

The phone rang.

'Hello?'

'El Comedin.' Eleanor sounded more bored than ever. There was a long pause.

'Well?' Tito gasped.

'Well what?'

'How did it go with Maria?'

'Oh yes, *that* . . . difficult to say . . . Maria *did* admit to being El Ambiente, but by the end she would have admitted to just about anything! I must say that I have my doubts, El Comedin.'

How you love your games.

'By the end?'

'Yes Tito, by the end. You know, sooner or later you're going to have to start taking some responsibility for those loose lips of yours. Goodnight, El Comedin.'

7.

Late that night a draught blew in through an open window. The curtains billowed up like ghosts.

'Maria?' he mumbled. 'Close the—'

He remembered.

Tito pulled back the covers of his makeshift bed. 'Not content . . . to . . . betray me . . . now you want to . . . try and freeze me to death!' He slammed the window and turned around. Daubed on the wall were two red handprints, between them a large circle containing the letter 'A'. The message was desperately clear.

You have made a grave error. I am still alive. The blood of an innocent is on your hands.

Chapter 20
Rotations

1.

'Grace'

Last night I finished a really good book. It was one of those stories that are so well written and engrossing that it's almost as if you yourself have been caught up within the struggles and elations of its characters. You wish that the author had continued on after the final page, if only to relay trivial details, just to keep the sensation from ending.

Such occasions make me think of you.

A good book, like the good deed of a stranger, has the unfortunate downside (in me at least) of instilling a sense of shame. Alongside the gratitude there is also a thought that their actions highlight a fundamental lacking in my own self; that I should have aspired to their heights rather than the lesser path I chose.

Perhaps this sounds stupid to you? Over the years I have repeatedly made the mistake of thinking I can earn my way into people's affections or respect by filling my time to the hilt with achievements and accolades. The more I do the more I realize what would have been possible had I started sooner. Rather than satisfy it infuriates and ties me up in knots. Like Corderro it is a vicious circle.

Did what you achieved that day set you up for life, or like me do you still struggle with an ongoing sense of self worth?

I remember your final words. They fill me with sadness. I think you too were trying to earn your way back into favour. You asked me to help you. It has been my sole pursuit ever since.

But I so desperately want to see you and tell you that there is no need to feel lacking or in need of redemption. No one will ever be good enough to satisfy such infinitely high standards. I have learnt that lesson over years of paradox – personal success continuously failing to fill the hole within me.

My favourite word in the whole world is 'grace'. It has many different meanings, but the one I like the most is 'a free and unmerited favour; a gift that you do not deserve'.

It is a concept too fantastical for my feeble mind to grasp, but embracing it has irrevocably changed me. I try to take life one breath at a time. I no longer feel unworthy, I simply feel immense gratitude.

Mostly towards you.

Maybe you learnt this a long time ago? Maybe it still haunts you?

I so desperately want to see you, throw my arms around you and tell you that all is well.

Isabella, 3rd August

2.

On the third day's searching she found her own name in a government census and discovered the name of her mother. Isabella Derecha: daughter of Ash and Penelope. No address was given, but they were able to trace the location via housing records. It pointed them to a one-bedroom upstairs flat in Liberacion. The building that had been her childhood home rang no bells of recollection. Seeing it in its vacant and dilapidated condition was like having someone rewrite her memories.

This isn't the place I remember, and yet this is what it was really like.

They searched every house in the street. When that proved fruitless they ventured further afield, branching out into the surrounding suburbs. They asked in shops, offices, churches and synagogues, tea rooms and coffee houses, parks and schools. They posted messages on every single board they passed with a note to call The Phoenix hotel should anyone have information. They queued at the radio stations to add their names to the ever-lengthening list of recordings beaming out over the airwaves. They filled the day to the brim and were satisfied that they had investigated every available avenue.

No one, neither past nor present, had heard of Jonathan Pemberton.

Carlos did what he had done the previous evenings and suggested that they find solace in food. He took Isabella to a Mexican restaurant in downtown Corderro and quickly imbibed several marguerites. A little loose lipped he began to speak openly of his family.

'Do you see them often?' Isabella enquired.

'Bless you,' Carlos replied with deliberate condescension. 'This is Corderro. They're all dead.'

Isabella reeled from her clumsy question as if she had been struck. 'I'm sorry.'

'Don't be,' Carlos dismissed with a wave. Something over her shoulder distracted him. His mood swung back into vibrancy.

'Ever hear of Enrique Truijo?'

'No, who is he?'

'He's a journalist – just like his father Marcus was.'

'The Spaniard?'

'The very same – he was purported to be the true author of *Corderro's Legacy*.

'Why do you mention him?'

'He's sitting over by the door. I recognize his face from a magazine.'

'Risky being here.'

'No riskier than you or I. He once wrote a paper called 'The Attributes of Perdition' – claimed he could prove not only that Hell existed but that it was circular in all its ways, just like Corderro. It didn't help his father's claim to legitimacy, but a fascinating read none the less.'

Isabella was giggling.

'What's so funny?'

'I had you down as one of those fast-talking machismo types, but amidst all that bravado and testosterone there's *actually* something going on!'

'The more you know the less you need to prove. El Ambiente said that.'

'When do you think he'll reveal himself?'

'Who says he will at all? What's in it for him?'

'Glory? Fame?'

The spark in Carlos's eyes faded and his face sank with disappointment. He drained the remainder of his marguerite and stood up. 'Come on, let's go.'

'Have I said something to offend you?'

Carlos evaded a confrontation with a change of subject. 'You know, this is day three of our little adventure together, and you've still to tell me anything substantial about this Jonathan Pemberton character.'

'That's because there's very little to tell. I've told you pretty much everything I know.'

'Was he young or old?'

'I don't know. I was only seven. Everyone looks old to a seven year old.'

'What did he do that was so great?'

'He took me out of harm's way.'

'How?'

'I told you. I can't remember.'

'If you can't remember, then how do you know that he saved you from harm?'

'Because I just do, alright? The details aren't clear. I remember lots of noise, and running and hiding, and being found, and being safe.'

'And yet you've effectively written a book of thanks to the man whom you only met briefly over a decade ago?'

'I know it sounds ridiculous, but it's not . . . besides, you're a fine one to talk!' Isabella countered. You've been equally cryptic about your own quest.'

Carlos rewarded her with a broad grin. 'This is true.'

'What is *their* name?'

'If I told you that then it would give the whole game away.'

'What's that supposed to mean?'

'It's for you to figure out, *mi chica bella*.'

'Are they famous?'

'It's closer to the truth to say that they are infamous.'

'El Ambiente?'

'Now that would imply that I know their true identity, which is highly unlikely, isn't it?'

Isabella stamped her feet. 'Why won't you just tell me?'

'Do you remember anything at all of your time with Jonathan – colours, objects, people, things said or done?'

'Stop changing the subject.'

'I'm not. It's all one in the same. A quest is a quest is a quest! So, do you?'

'Everything I know, which isn't much, is recorded in my journal.'

'Can I see?'

Isabella shrugged. 'Sure.' She took it from her bag, scrolled through to the appropriate page and passed it across the table:

1. *Bald man with many scars on his face.*
2. *Large room filled with rainwater and branches.*
3. *Voice outside shouting 'A tap-dancing career in ruins!'*
4. *Boy with blankets.*
5. *Jonathan's face – sad.*
6. *Key – the lock box in London.*
7. *'Make something of your life and you will have redeemed me.'*

Carlos recognised each and every recollection. His face remained closed.

'*A large room filled with rainwater and branches*? I might know where that is.'

Isabella looked unimpressed. 'Come on, Carlos, don't play with me.'

'I am being deadly serious. I shall take you there this instant. Come. Be so kind as to pay the bill. It's the least you can do for all my enthusiasm and servitude!'

Chapter 21

El Rey Ruminates on 'The Art of Rumination'

Something eludes me, damn it. Boredom is so much more unfulfilling for having been the product of genocide. My father knew the answer. I saw it in his face as life slipped away. He had been enlightened by a celestial body.

'Tell me what you see!' I shouted, my urgency heightened by his transient status. When he refused to answer I began to throttle him. Shocked that his offspring could be capable of such treachery he choked back his secret and hid it behind eyes that glazed opaque and stared through me. Later, once I had succeeded in quelling the rage, I realized the irony of my predicament and laughed heartily.

You can only kill a man once. To attempt a second foray dampens the impact somewhat.

Something exists beyond the boundaries of death. For the briefest moment I glimpsed into its doorway.

I set my will to the task of rediscovering that revelatory moment. I found as the new tyrant of Corderro that any number of reasons could be used for killing a man. It was as easy as falling off a log – the best ways were a slit throat or a knife to the belly – something where you could see it coming. As they reached the point of paradox I would watch anxiously for signs of euphoria. Again and again I was left disappointed. In time I came to doubt my original recollection.

In recent years I have become like a wizened old seer, searching in vain for the elixir of eternal youth. I can see the comparison clearly. I am not blind to my predicament. Tearing and scratching to remove a layer I find endless layers beneath. Something is mocking me, daring me to uncover its truth. I have no problem in upping the ante. Audacity and avarice have never been my weaknesses.

Perhaps it is my methods?

I have taken to recording the final stages, not for crude posterity, more for research purposes. The enlightenment I saw in my father's eyes all those years ago has never been matched. I have often wondered whether the process of video capture distorts the ethereal. Can something so otherworldly be caged within celluloid?

Last night I sat in the shadows of a cell and watched a man being garrotted. I do it from time to time. I take great interest in a broad spread of my subjects – the old, the young, the sick, the lame – and in all manner of approaches – short and sharp, long and drawn out, and everything in between. I must confess that on this particular occasion my mind had wandered. I was thinking of Eleanor – stunning, sleek and supple Eleanor. The thought of having to kill her at some point in the not-too-distant future upsets me greatly. I have never known pleasure like her.

Having said that, as it was her hands tightening the garrotte, I had to concede to pragmatism over lust.

Lost in cavorting remnants, I suddenly refocused on the man in question and saw a figure beautified in agonizing grace.

'Stop,' I cried, rising from my crouch and charging into the light. Eleanor released her grip and stepped back with feline fluidity. The man dropped forward sluggishly, his face slapping against the concrete floor.

'What did you see?' I screamed, scraping his pathetic carcass up from the dust. 'WHAT DID YOU SEE?'

The man smiled, his teeth dripping black bloody sputum. 'My daughter's face . . . I saw my daughter's face . . . you bastard.'

'Revive him . . . REVIVE HIM!'

But alas, he escaped, down the tunnel of knowledge away from me.

Angry and aroused I grabbed Eleanor by the throat, threw her to the floor and had desperate aggressive sex with her next to the man's corpse.

Where is this going?

My story had most definitely lost its narrative.

Is the end game power, purpose or perdition?

Power, Purpose or Perdition!

What a simply fantastic title! My spirits revived, my creative juices flowing, I ascended to the palace rooftop and looked down on my city. It was like seeing with new eyes. The world was on fire, smoke rising from the ports, flames from the industrial quarter, traffic fumes and the scent of charred flesh.

My first thought was to send for that cretin accountant El Comedin and stick pins in his eyes, but then I took a second look, and the sight that befell me filled my senses with wondrous awe. It was beautiful, a work in progress, a study of suffering, of human endurance. I couldn't believe I had been so obsessed as to miss the transformation that was taking place in Corderro.

This was a pivotal moment. I had to be about my work. This was where lesser men would fall at the final hurdle, failing to fulfill their potential, but not I. The chosen road stretched out before me as clear as day.

Any historian will tell you that every regime falls, given enough time. The plates shift, people rise up, servants betray their masters, any number of pitfalls await, the odds increasing with the passing of the seasons. What I saw before me was a convergence of fear, hunger, brutality, displacement, injustice, desperation and rage. Retribution was coming my way. You could smell the anticipation suspended in the ether. Now was the time to squeeze the hardest.

As I once said to my father – it was as if the devil were stretching his hands out over Babylon.

'All this could be yours forever.'

Chapter 22
Excerpts from 'Thirty-eight' (unpublished)

My life ended on a duel-carriageway on 12 October 1985. Whilst my body remained firmly rooted in this mortal coil, if I had a soul, then it most certainly left town that day.

I held my wife close to my chest. Her chin was wedged over my left shoulder, her arms wrapped around me against the conventions of human posture. We had been strangers from one another for many years and our sudden forced intimacy brought home the absurdity of our fates with crushing clarity.

I whispered to my sons that everything would be alright, but my words were lost beneath the rasping din of cutting equipment. They would not have heard me had there been silence.

What do you say about such a moment? To elaborate is to try and make tragedy seem poetic; to remain brief is to deny loss the gravitas it deserves.

Thankfully I remember very little of my demise. I do recall the moon-shaped face of a white-haired woman glaring inquisitively at me from a passenger window as she rubber-necked her way by.

'Some help would be nice,' I murmured into my wife's ear.

A stream of faces followed suit, that same dumb, disgusting look of pitiful inaction scrawled across each and every one. At some point the world became a sea of lights, and the grinding commenced. My mind conjured images of dentist chairs as I bobbed in and out of consciousness.

'You need to let go, sir,' someone said.

'Let go of what?' I slurred back.

Something sharp and sweet pierced my arm and I began to drift. They prized my wife's fingers from around me and lifted her off. My final recollection was of her coming away in two pieces.

Life is so fragile. We carry it around in sacks of flesh, flimsy membranes that burst at the slightest jolt. Many times since that day I have tried to rationalize events, and the only conclusion I have ever reached is that the past must be put aside in its entirety. Where is it they went? They cannot have ceased to exist? And yet they have. Nothing can be fathomed.

My legs had been reduced to spineless snakes. They were pinned in several places and surrounded by helter-skelter frames. Friends stayed away in their droves. For that small mercy at least I was thankful.

It's one of the infuriating things about men (at any rate in my experience) – the inability to show emotion. I should have been screaming the place down, forcing them to restrain me, or else taper the obscenities with sedatives. Instead I lay motionless, Hell contained silently within.

The nurses bombarded me with blood-curdling kindness, a doctor warned that I might never walk again, my wife's parents refused to visit and amidst the madness I felt as though someone had simply switched me off.

Time slowed to a crawl. I watched fruit rot in a bowl next to my bed, listened to the meaningless ramblings of other people's visitors, wondered why I wasn't dead, wished for sleep, told God that I hated him and that he should visit wrath upon me for my insolence, refused to eat, grew tired, remained awake, began to fade.

When you come through something like this mundane things in life seem offensive – daytime TV, gossip, the weather. I could think of no words worthy of my larynx. Those attempting to fill the uncomfortable silence with their good intentions consigned themselves to my ever-growing list of loathing.

The man who hit us emerged unscathed.

That's the way it rolls!

I later read his statement in which he professed to have 'no explanation for his actions'. I have since come to abhor any and all people who cannot competently quantify themselves, be it lack of a plan or lack of views. None of them deserve the space they occupy or the air they breathe.

His name was Tim – such an innocuous little word. He arrived at my bedside with a cheque and some flowers. I had never seen him before, but knew instantly who he was. He had the weight of dread in his limbs. His eyes were red raw, his skin waxy. For a long while we simply stared, I at him, he at the floor.

'I can never give back what I have taken from you, and I can never apologize enough, but for what it's worth, I am truly sorry.'

Maybe he'd rehearsed those words for a month? Maybe they came to him in the car park? Who can say? To date I had been one of life's victims and look where it had gotten me. Now I found myself in possession of the world's most powerful weapon – forgiveness. I mustered my most demonic tone and slowly uttered the words, 'You came here as an act of contrition, as a means of expunging your own sorrow and wiping the slate clean. You care nothing for me or my family, and this is why I do not release you from your guilt. I wish you a slow and agonizing death.'

He ran from the hospital howling, thus proving me right.

'I should very much like to run and weep,' I yelled after him, 'had I the legs and *the tears you self-effacing son of a bitch!'*

The next three months were a blur of physiotherapy, endless injections, casts and counselling. I returned home to find that I had lost my job and that the bank had foreclosed on my house.

A family home without a family.

I wouldn't wish it upon my worst enemy.

I was only alone for a single night. The next morning my brother arrived at the door with his wife and a bottle of champagne.

'Happy bankruptcy!' he declared and we all fell about laughing. My situation had passed from torment into farce. 'You have one day to pack up your shit,' he commanded. 'You're coming to live with us till you get back on your feet. This is non-negotiable.'

I thanked him from the bottom of my shattered, blackened heart.

The banks moved in with the dispassionate precision of cockroaches to a cadaver. They liquidated everything, sold the house for a fraction of what we'd paid for it, the car for a song, the personal effects that I couldn't bear to look at needlessly thrown away.

My brother dragged me to an auction where he bought back some of my furniture – a sofa, an armchair, the bureau where my wife had brushed her hair. It was safely stored in the attic. I was eternally grateful.

My sister-in-law was called Roberta – a celestial being of long flowing garments and graceful gliding. She worked as a dance choreographer and walked on her tiptoes. In the evening she would read my mind, bringing me cups of coffee before I even knew I was thirsty, and soothing my wretched soul with an expression so beatific it was as if she were in communion with heavenly hosts. The look said to me, 'All is well, all is good.' At times I even dared to believe it was true.

Her mannerisms made me laugh. She didn't mean to amuse but couldn't help herself. She was too pure for this world, but didn't know how to be any different. My wife and children were dead, I was languishing in self-pity and personal hygiene had gone out of the window. Rather than point out my blatant stench she would say things like, 'Your cologne has become overly distinct.' She was priceless.

My brother worked away a lot and Roberta ran a dance studio from within the house. I was left alone for most of the day and in those first few months I turned being a recluse into an art form. I invited grief each morning and let it devour my ever-diminishing frame. I welcomed the day when I would simply waste away, no longer a burden on those around me, not so much out of consideration, but pride.

I wrote poetry – hideously, offensively awful verses; a quagmire of clichés and plagiarism. I walked in the surrounding countryside, I brooded and became something altogether wretched.

One evening Roberta found me drunk and emaciated on the bathroom floor, sobbing like an imbecile. She knelt beside me and kissed my forehead.

'It's OK, my darling,' she whispered with such tenderness that my mind conjured images of my wife. I was wallowing in an ocean of the past and desperately needed company. The opportunity was there and I took it.

Suffice to say I had grotesquely misjudged the situation. Rather than give herself body and soul Roberta pulled back from me with a contortionist's ease. I grabbed a clump of her hair soliciting a precision slap to the face that temporarily blinded me. I struggled to my feet and followed her path of escape, catching her by the door.

Roberta's screams alerted my brother who came charging up the stairs to find her lying next to me, her blouse ripped open and her nose bloodied from a careless lunge on my part. I was slumped next to her shouting that all women were 'sluts' and all brothers 'bastards'.

My brother approached us very slowly. I expected to be helped to my feet, but I had grown too accustomed to donations. Instead he hit me so hard that I was knocked out of my own head.

Next thing I knew, an extremely large Rastafarian was shaking me. I was half in-half out of a taxi, parked up in a motorway lay-by.

'Wake up, sweety-pie,' he grinned, revealing several gold teeth.

'What's going on?' I asked, my swollen lips stumbling over the pronunciation.

'Your man told me to drive north until the money ran out.'

'Where are we?'

'Carlisle.'

'Wow,' I leant back into an incapacitating head-rush, 'he really hates me.'

'Certainly looks that way.'

'Can you give me a lift back?'

'Sorry.'

'C'mon.'

'He paid me extra to leave you here. Besides, he told me that you didn't have any money.'

'This is true, but how about a little charity?'

'No can do.'

'You unethical, opportunistic asshole.'

'That's rich coming from someone who tried to molest his brother's wife.'

I flushed deepest red. 'He told you, huh?'

'Thaaat's right,' the Rastafarian replied with smug relish.

Sheepishly I scrambled my way onto a grass verge and watched the taxi pull away. Looking down I saw that a piece of paper had been stapled to my shirt. The writing was upside down and read: 'You have treated my charity with utter disdain. Don't ever come back.'

My brother was/is a man who thinks through the weight of his actions. I was being abandoned in the definitive, lasting sense of the word.

There on the hard shoulder, with streams of traffic flooding by indifferent to my predicament, the world caught up with me. And oh how I wept – huge, blubbering, gluttonous tears. I could no longer support my own weight. I dropped, not just to my knees but onto my face. The universe was wrong. How could it continue to exist? I felt earth in my clenched fists, saw blades of grass as gigantic green spears before my eyes.

Someone amidst the passing throngs honked their horn. I spun in the dirt and began to hurl abuse at the wind. In drawing attention to myself I invoked a chain reaction amongst the motorists. Their taunts grew in number, my reposts in volume and venom. Eventually my red-raw vision beheld flashing lights.

The officer displayed immense restraint in his attempts to pacify me, but I was a wreck. I confessed all, my pride shot to hell. I gripped at his ankles and wailed for all that was gone. He did the honorable thing and arrested me.

A good night's sleep and a warm meal later, I was deposited on the streets of Carlisle. I'd never been there before. On the border into Scotland my brother had almost succeeded in ousting me from the country.

The only way I can think to explain the next part is simply that 'fate took over', both in the direction of my feet and in the knee-jerk decisions I made thereafter. I came in time to a billboard tied loosely to a lamp post in the centre of town. It read: 'Dock labourers required – Maryport – cash paid.'

In my previous life I had been a history teacher. It was a skill I could no longer fall back on, having lost the impetus to exist within society. The advert instigated a number of resolutions:

i. Not to return to the Midlands.

ii. To apply for the work.

iii. To leave the country at the earliest opportunity.

iv. To never come back.

Suffice to say I was hired, and within a matter of weeks found myself transferring to Dublin. I was posted with a small crew of like-minded individuals. They worked hard and never said anything of any real substance. None of them were short on intellect. Like me they chose to hide their thoughts in routine.

Corderro came to my ears by way of a news report – a forgotten corner of the Americas that had become a black market Mecca. I don't fully understand the choice that I made. It just seemed to stand out. I heard my wife's voice. No words, just the sound. It felt right. One port is much the same as another. I can't explain it any better than that.

During the crossing I found myself in conversation with the boat's skipper. He asked me my reasons for journeying to these parts and I saw no reason to deceive him. When I'd finished my short and pitiful tale he roared with inappropriate laughter.

'There are those who pronounce the city "Caw-deh-rrrro", he boomed, rolling the R's around his tongue with manic delight. 'We mariners prefer to use a more staccato vernacular. The city is a spider, her name arachnid in nature. She casts her web wide and from afar she has ensnared you, my foolish young friend.'

I dismissed his comments as the ramblings of an old sea dog with too much salt in his lungs and rum in his veins.

Before it became the incendiary playground of a chancellor, Corderro was a stunning-looking place. The streets were crammed full of colonial buildings reaching back in history to the time of Bolivar and Cervantes. Like me they have fallen into disrepute. Deep fissures run up and along the masonry like ragged vines. Many have no roofs, no internal walls, no front doors, but their imperfection gives them beauty. It is reassuring to see my ruin in the surrounding environment.

The coastline too is a sight to behold. The land drops away so steeply that you are lost beneath the waves within a matter of strides. Living inland as I have done my entire life I had never seen such vast boundless blue, morphing through shades of purple into wondrous, murky green as it approaches El Puerto de las Ondas Verdes. It would hide any number of sins and sorrows.

Bad things happen to people who come here. It is an unassailable fact. But people are wrong when they refer to it as 'The Melting Pot' – the stirring motion of a vicious circle. The circle is not vicious. It is merely cyclical. Catch it at the end of a trough and you will enjoy a heightened period of prosperity. The secret is to see the downturn and jump ship before you're consumed.

As far as I was concerned the world owed me. I arrived in a defiant rage and swore an oath that I would bleed its lands dry and leave two months later with my ill-gotten gains, scot-free and unblemished. Almost immediately the city obliged me my gluttonous intentions. It showed itself to be a place that understood me, that welcomed me in with open arms. I established myself as a smuggler, but it would be closer to the truth to say that I was a thief. Rarely did I arrange the *complete transport of contraband. It was more usual that I relieved its owners in the final stages of a journey.*

In short, I stayed here because I smelt weakness.

I fully realize that this is no way to ingratiate myself to the reader, but then there is something I should have mentioned at the beginning – I am not a nice person. Barring my wits I have few redeeming qualities. I look neither for acceptance nor compassion. It's not that I'm deliberately bad. This much at least I have derived. No, it is simply that I lack the impetus to be good. I tried filling my life with happy families. When that failed spectacularly I emptied myself and refilled the spaces in my soul with anger. When that too failed to inspire or resurrect me I again emptied myself, but nothing presented itself as an alternative, leaving me as a hateful husk. All I have left is the hope of a brother's love. Everything else . . . well . . . there simply isn't anything else.

I have a theory about this place. The only time people have ever been truly happy here was when they didn't realize their own existence. Fishermen used to hunt and trade without claim to the lands in which they lived. From what I have learnt there was no sense of hierarchy, only duty and camaraderie. The problem came when an invader took it upon himself to assign ownership.

Since that time the city has had to endure all manner of pomp and ceremonious brutality, judgement-crazed evangelists, clumsy coups d'etats, death by condescension, the rape of the land and verbal assaults from the pulpit.

I find it amusing that it takes the likes of me to point out what is right and wrong (even if only to myself). In my extensive experience I find that people on crusades, righteous or otherwise, rarely have the time or inclination to gawp beyond their own bulbous piety. If they did they would see what to me is blindingly obvious.

The purpose of a vicious circle is not to fuel scholarly debate on the ways of chance (to which I am ironically engaged at this very moment). The true purpose is to force an individual to see the farcical folly of continuing down a given route, and to instigate a withdrawal.

The message to me is clear.

'Get out – leave me be – let me return to innocence.'

I for my own hypocrisy will oblige the city her wish as soon as I have plundered, pillaged and gorged myself to bursting point.

Corderro is a place for the cursed. It is not in itself cursed. What incident throughout history has been caused by the city? How many times has man assigned blame to her land when the fault lies squarely with himself?

There is a question I ask myself each night as I lie exhausted in the bathtub: 'How much longer?'

The answer I give: 'Soon.'

'Soon' is no answer at all. 'Soon' is a deferment, a blind gamble on unseen odds. The signs were there, the rotation coming back around, people I knew leaving, disappearances increasing. I chose to presume immunity from it all – a foolish and arrogant claim.

The result – I was shot.

The man who fired the ball of hot lead that ripped through my flesh had the intention of taking away everything I would ever possess. Yet in truth he knew nothing about me, having never met me before that moment. That's not a concept you can grasp upon first reading. It's like 'relativity', or 'quantum mechanics' – you need to mull it over, drop through its various depths of meaning, experience revelation, doubt, nirvana, and even then you may not fully comprehend.

In that simple act of raising his hand and pulling a trigger the man (who remains a stranger) showed me a universal truth – that human beings are animals who clothe themselves in culture and morality to hide the shame of their beastliness – that it takes so very little to chip away the veneer and peer into our own abomination.

And there I was thinking I'd hit rock bottom before!

A story needs a nemesis, a counterpoint, a balance.

Mine is called Katrina.

Katrina is a Samaritan who has yet to become self-aware – ticking off her good deeds at the end of each day and counting herself lucky that she can wallow in this shitty mess helping endless parades of the sick, the lame and the criminally insane who serve to furnish her with purpose.

As can be inferred from my acidic little rant I am not grateful for her presence in my life. She is the worst kind of person. She believes that all things are possible. When she speaks I find myself remembering the man I used to be. I can no longer afford to wear my faith in so reckless a fashion. Once, I placed my faith in that which I deemed most precious – my wife and children – but something unseen had no respect for that faith and took them away from me. Therefore the world and everything in it can all burn. I have no wish to be part of it, and yet my body refuses to throw in the towel.

Why is this?

Have I been spared in order to perform some great act of redemption, or is my torment simply being prolonged?

Who can say with any certainty?

All I know is that no one in recollection has ever survived the black sedans.

I am the first.

Life has something left for me to do.

Chapter 23

Paolo Stumbles

1.

'I didn't think it would feel this way,' Paolo said to the two men opposite. 'I thought I'd be petrified . . . or else hateful, but I'm neither . . . I feel only pity . . . pity for you, for your boss, for *her* boss . . . for the whole sorry affair.'

The two men neither replied nor showed any signs of having heard, but simply continued to stare at him from behind dark glasses.

Paolo looked out of the window at the city speeding by. It had never looked as beautiful as it did in that moment. He found himself wishing he had savoured more of its wonders while he'd had the chance.

Smoke was rising from the busy market district where vendors cooked fajitas and enchiladas on makeshift barbecues. The midday sun revealed every ripple of water across the bay, cargo vessels on the distant horizon and the lower east slums where he'd lived for most of his life.

Up ahead the traffic parted to allow them through.

'This used to be a really amazing place before people like you arrived.'

No reaction.

'Parents used to be able to let their kids play in the street without worrying that some wannabe gangster assholes would turn up and whisk them away.'

Nothing.

'Don't you feel the slightest repulsion at what you do? At what you are? No? Well you should . . .'

He trailed off.

They'd picked him up outside a newsagent in downtown Corderro. It had been an unforgivable lapse in concentration on his part. Paolo would've kicked himself had he not been awash with placid acceptance.

He remembered reaching down to tie his shoelaces, an unlit cigarette hanging from his lips. The car had made no sound as it rolled up onto the curb and glided to a halt. Its doors opened with well-oiled, stealthy precision. A child had been passing on the other side of the road. He had seen the look on their face and known what was behind him even before the calm and polite voice uttered, 'Would you come with us please, Paolo?'

He had always imagined that being black-sedaned was simply bad luck, being in the wrong place at the wrong time, but they were far from random occurrences. They had known his name. He had been targeted.

His first thought was for Katrina, still in the newsagent choosing a magazine. She had always said that smoking would be the death of him and now it seemed that she would be proved right.

How do I get them away from the shop before she walks out into their midst?

He turned. There were four of them, two from the back, a driver, another coming around from the front passenger's seat, all nondescript, neutral faces, dark suits.

'Where is Esperanza?' one of them asked.

'Who?'

'Get in the car please.'

Paolo ran. His intention had been transparent and they caught him before he reached the first corner, taking his legs out from under him and slamming his chest against the pavement with clinical brutality. Dazed and frantic, he was thrust onto a brown leather seat. A door closed serenely. There was movement.

Katrina was safe.

They passed over a huge suspension bridge. La Fantasma reared up into view, casting its ghost-like blanket over the sea. Paolo could smell salt air, petrol fumes, freshly laid tarmac, a rich variety of food, infusions of herbs and spices, concoctions of the city.

'What do you tell your mothers when you see them?'

Nothing.

'How do you look her in the eye? How do you look at yourself in the mirror? How do you sleep at night?'

The car passed out of the city and up into the hills.

'Goodbye,' he whispered, and in the silence of his heart a prayer took shape.

Dear Lord . . . Save my family, my wife, my daughters, Katrina, the people of Satellite.

El Rey's grandiose abode loomed up on the horizon. Paolo had always made a point of ignoring it, considering a dismissive attitude the best act of defiance. Now however there was no choice but to stare in disgust at all its overindulgent glory. It was so vulgar and ostentatious, so unashamed and unapologetic for its very existence. The arch overhanging its entrance resembled a mouth. It was as if they were static on a road being reeled in and retracted like a tape measure.

They turned off the path and into a dense line of trees. Paolo looked at his wedding band.

Bury yourself down deep, far beyond harm's way.

They emerged into an exquisitely beautiful clearing. Twin waterfalls cascaded between a series of elaborately designed rock pools. Vines of darkest green provided the backdrop for an explosion of every conceivable colour. Paolo found himself thinking of the Garden of Eden. At its centre the clearing featured a replica of the Venus de Milo sculpture.

Aphrodite the goddess of love, and Eden the fall of man, the conception of sin.

Why would El Rey build a garden here of all places?

Is it to hide its true nature beneath aesthetic charm?

Does he see beauty in the distended, tortured form?

Or is it simply mockery?

It was such an offensive statement to make to a person in Paolo's position. He had never seen the Emperor's face, let alone heard his voice, but he imagined it now, speaking with an acquired regal snarl.

'Look one last time upon all the things that are passing forever beyond your sight.'

The sedan stopped by an archway. The two men opposite became reanimated. One handcuffed him, the other fitted a blindfold.

'I will never again see the sunrise.'

No response.

They helped him out of the vehicle and over uneven ground. Paolo turned the wedding band between his fingers. Thoughts of what it signified kept him tethered within a cocoon of serenity.

The uneven ground became rigid and flat. Keys groaned within padlocks and doors opened ahead of him. On several occasions a mechanical voice told him to be wary of approaching stairs. They always led downwards. Finally Paolo was seated and the blindfold removed.

He was in a large room with smooth magnolia walls and no windows. Next to him sat another man in manacles. He had jet black skin and a brilliant white shirt with ripped trousers and scuffed shoes. There were many other chairs dotted around, all empty.

'A waiting room?'

No response.

He turned to the man next to him and saw that both his eyes were badly swollen.

'Hello, what's your name?'

'Richard.'

'No talking,' one of the guards commanded sternly.

Paolo fixed him with a piercing stare. 'Given why I'm here, what threat could you *possibly* give me?'

He turned back to Richard. 'Paolo, pleased to meet you.'

Hindered by the handcuffs they made a fumbled attempt at shaking hands.

'What do you do for a living Richard?'

'I'm an accountant.'

'Public enemy number one – I'm surprised they didn't pick you up sooner! They can't have anyone showing up El Comedin. Kids?'

'Three . . . two boys and a girl . . . you?'

'Two girls . . . married?'

'Divorced.'

'Sorry to hear that.'

'That's OK. How are you so calm? We're going to die here, you know that, don't you?'

Paolo let his head fall back against the wall. 'Yes I know, and I'm not calm. I just think that if you're going to be devoured by a beast, at the very least you owe it to yourself to give it indigestion on the way down.'

Richard started to sob.

'This place is so clinical,' Paolo continued. 'It's like an abattoir. What am I saying, *like* an abattoir? It *is* an abattoir! Hermetically sealed conveyor belt . . . heavily sound-proofed underground—'

He noticed a deep gash in his arm.

Must've got that when they restrained me.

Without further thought Paolo stood up and pressed his shoulder against the wall. Stepping to the side he left a thick smear of blood in his wake. Pleased with what he saw Paolo took another step. He heard movement behind him.

'This is what I think of your disinfected dungeon,' he shouted without turning.

A swift crack on the head sent him to his knees.

'Goodbye Richard,' he slurred as he was dragged along the floor by his shirt collar. 'Have I been moved up the waiting list? *How kind!*' He began to laugh and cry all at once. 'How pathetic you all are . . . One shot at life and this is how you choose to live it.'

Another door opened to yet another flight of stairs. Paolo was unceremoniously thrown into the darkness.

2.

Ice water roused him abruptly from sleep. His hands were still bound and he struggled to focus. Something struck him hard in the face, then the shoulders, the ribs and arms. He fell forwards into a volley of blows to the head and legs. There was a snapping sound and he slipped away.

Some time later a shock went through his body that caused him to ride up against his restraints. A hand grabbed a clump of his hair and forced his head back onto the concrete floor. He was upside down and could see a jagged blue light dancing across the soles of his feet. It caused him to convulse so hard that he feared his back would break. Just as the pain became unbearable it stopped. In the moment's silence that followed he heard the intake of breath.

A second shock surged into his legs. He felt hot liquid rise up in his throat.

Blackness.

3.

Paolo awoke with a choking rasp to brilliant white light that stung his eyes. He was sitting on a chair, a noose around his neck, the other end fastened to the wall. The slipknot was already tight around his windpipe and he pushed back from the floor to slacken the rope. The ceiling was filled with high-powered light bulbs that hung without shades every few feet. There were no windows and only one door. Paolo's chest and arms were covered in vomit, his torn trousers felt moist and there was an unbearable stench. It looked as though one of his legs was badly broken.

His thoughts turned to Katrina, standing alone on the street, being told what had happened by the pedestrians, breaking the news to his wife. His eldest daughter Monica would be five in a few weeks. He and his wife had planned a party for her with cakes and balloons. A local magician was booked as a surprise. Now he would never see her face light up as she unwrapped her presents, or tuck her in at night, or watch her blossom into a woman. The loss was too staggering to fully absorb.

They revived him over and over, sometimes beating him, at other times running electricity through him, on one occasion holding his head underwater till he was on the verge of drowning. He had resolved to remain silent and show his contempt with unflinching endurance, but the pain was too great and within moments he was screaming with guttural howls that lurched from the pit of his stomach, begging and pleading with them to stop.

They didn't listen.

There was no indication of whether it was day or night, no sound from outside.

Hours passed.

At some point his restless slumber was disturbed by the turning of a key and high heels on concrete. He looked up as the door was closing. A woman stood alone in the centre of the room. Paolo had never seen her before but knew instantly who she was: the infamous Eleanor Blake.

She was younger than he'd imagined, somewhere in her mid-thirties, tall, very beautiful, cat-like eyes, shoulder- length black hair, hints of maroon, cream suit, empty hands. Slowly and purposefully she moved towards him . . . click

. . . clack . . . click . . . clack . . . the menacing mantra of her feet, balanced by an expression of deep sorrow. She knelt down and reached around his neck, loosened the knot and removed the noose. Paolo slumped forward.

'My God! What have they done to you?'

'You didn't even give a reason . . . or ask a question.'

Eleanor's face was a picture of compassion. 'Oh Paolo, it wasn't me, my child. I'm here to make all these awful things go away. You *must* believe me.'

Paolo looked down at his feet. Two of his toes were missing. He couldn't remember them being removed.

'I'll believe anything you want me to. Isn't that how it works?'

The empathy evaporated from her features. 'Katrina Esperanza? Where is she?'

'Who?'

His voice was so lame he didn't even convince himself.

'Paolo, we need to find this woman. She's a dangerous individual. You gain nothing in protecting her.'

'Have you ever met her?'

'Paolo, it is not wise to play games with these people. I think you should—'

'*Answer my question,*' Paolo interrupted. 'Have you ever met this "dangerous individual"?'

Eleanor stood up and walked away from him towards the far side of the room. She folded her arms and shook her head in disapproval. 'Oh Paolo . . . Paolo, Paolo . . . you are foolish and naïve . . . all they need is her whereabouts . . . give me that small little detail and I can make all of this pain go away . . . I understand that you have a wife and two lovely daughters?'

Paolo reached for his wedding band. It wasn't there. 'Why are you doing this?'

'I should hate to have to call them in for similar questioning.'

'You'd do this to a woman, to little girls?'

'Do it? I've *done* it, countless times. Esperanza? Where is she?'

At the end now the world became simple.

She will kill you regardless. She will kill them regardless. No safe passage can be bartered. They are lost.

'I am a man of peace . . . but as God is my witness, if you placed a gun in my hand I would shoot you dead . . . this is what you have done to me . . . this is what you amount to . . . *puta-madre* . . . devil . . . wretched animal . . . I would die a thousand deaths before I betray a friend.'

Eleanor came in close. 'Before you do I will have your daughters scream Daddy's name within earshot.'

The floor was awash with Paolo's blood. 'Doubtful,' he replied. 'It appears your men have been overly efficient.'

Eleanor stormed out of the room.

Not much longer now.

Please Lord let me die.

4.

'Paolo . . . Paolo?'

The soft voice guided him up from sleep.

'Yes.'

'Your wife and daughter are safe. They will leave the city tonight.'

He was lying where Eleanor had left him. The voice was coming from a sliver of light under the door.

'Cruel trick.'

'No Paolo, the truth.'

'Who are you?'

'My name is El Ambiente.'

'Truly?'

'Truly. They are on a ship called *El Cisne* ['the swan']. It is bound for Venezuela.'

'I know that ship . . . it trades in . . . fruit.'

'That's right Paolo – fruit, and vegetables and sugar – harmless goods that no one would ever think to search.'

Paolo cried with joy. Tears spilled out over his broken cheek and onto the bloodstained tiles.

'My friend . . . I cannot thank you enough.'

'It is *you* who deserve thanks. I am sorry, but I am unable to free you.'

'That's OK . . . I think I'm past the point of recovery anyhow . . . I feel as though your words have released me in some marvellous way . . . my daughters will grow to be women . . . my wife will remarry and be happy again some day . . . these are the things that a man aspires to . . . that you have preserved for me.'

'It's my pleasure,' said the voice. 'Before I go I want to leave you with a promise, an *oath*. One day I will stand before El Rey and speak your name as I strip him of all power.'

'I'd like that.'

'Close your eyes, Paolo. Be at peace.'

Chapter 24
The Cabin in the Woods

As with all the preceding days their search had proved fruitless. They visited the industrial quarter, most of which was burnt out, a library that had somehow escaped Tito's campaign, more schools and endless bars.

No one had heard of Jonathan Pemberton.

They looked at the various 'missing persons' boards erected throughout the city. At each site they found euphoric- looking individuals of all ages handing out photos of their loved ones, exchanging them with one another, and telling anyone who'd listen of their fondest memories.

'They are delusional,' Carlos whispered to Isabella. 'This is on account of the black sedans. Every single person pinned to that board is dead.'

'You can't be sure of that?'

'Yes I can.'

'Then what does that say for my quest?'

Carlos thought for a moment. 'Have you seen his face up there?'

'I'm not sure if I'd know him if he walked right up to me and burst into song.'

'That's enough for one day,' Carlos replied, drawing a line under the conversation.

Isabella wanted to discuss her frustrations over an evening meal, but Carlos was suddenly ambiguous and apologetic. He spoke of a prior engagement, looked at his watch and said that he was late. After dropping Isabella at The Phoenix he made a swift exit.

Carlos walked up through the Market district. Many of the walls were daubed with a large '*A*' surrounded by a broken circle. He ran his hand along one of the symbols, thinking about all that it signified to him. Passers-by regarded him nervously, their staring eyes reprimanding for placing himself so needlessly under suspicion.

There was an undeniable weight about the city, sapping the spirit of even the most energetic of its visitors. Carlos felt his reserves ebbing away with the fading daylight.

Outside the port gates he caught a bus out of town. It was a peculiar contraption – hubcaps removed to accommodate tractor wheels, no glass in its windows, bonnet missing, engine strapped to the roof, all manner of leads and pulleys running along its ceiling, anything and everything to keep it roadworthy.

The driver recognized him from the previous evening and they began to talk to one another. Conversation inevitably turned to the past; what had once been and what was no more. As they spoke Carlos noticed in his companion a habit for competition, a compulsion to outdo whatever was said beforehand. Such insecurities always made him sad. He listened attentively to stories that were obviously works of fiction, allowing the man to embellish his life. He avoided any questions that might trip him up and played down his own vast number of achievements. Carlos had seen this type of behaviour many times since his arrival. Corderro bred it – that lack of self worth, and subsequent desire to compensate with fallacy and mistruth, to portray a person who never was.

He alighted a few hundred feet from the border. It would not do to bring attention to himself, not yet. Hidden within the trees he found the track. His footsteps from previous evenings were still apparent in the mud, showing him which way *not* to go.

The sun was setting rapidly now. Carlos had a torch but did not wish to use it. He moved up through a passageway that snaked between giant roots. He quickly reached a junction. His memory told him that he had turned right on four previous occasions and left on three.

Left it is.

At the second junction he had to rely on a primitive map that detailed the choices and decisions taken so far. At the next fork he reached a new road, a narrow track that plunged down into a dark thicket.

Deeper still – if it were me this would not be deep enough.

Carlos was encouraged by this new course.

Take your time – breathe.

The blackness intensified. Still he refused to use the torch. He reached out his arms for balance and descended along the uneven ground.

Curfew will have passed.

He was due to meet Isabella early the next morning. The sleepless nights were beginning to take their toll.

Am I doing the right thing not revealing what I know?

By rights she should remember herself.

Fifteen years was a long period to wait, to speculate and to hope that events would turn out as planned. It allowed time for doubt to creep in, whispering that ideals were ridiculous, that it had all been a waste of time, and that it was best to cut and run.

With each step he took Carlos considered the possibility that he might be on the verge of vindicating every prayer and oath since his youth. He struggled to maintain composure. He wanted to break into a run. It had been the same the night before, and the night before that, and each time his ecstasy had been met with crushing disappointment.

This time . . .

Carlos had not heard a sound in over an hour – no cars, no birds, not even a breeze. It was beautiful.

If he's here – the silence will be driving him insane.

He took no comfort from the thought.

The blackness suddenly gave way to the moon, illuminating a small clearing. Within the clearing was a log cabin. Carlos felt his temperature drop.

Surely not? This is too perfect.

A strange way to describe the discovery of your nemesis.

There was light in one of the windows. Carlos approached cautiously, using the cover of shadows to draw near. He could see candles, a thick-set oak table, a hand, an arm. He took a risk and moved into open ground so as to get a look at the person's face.

I am exposed.

The thought excited him.

The person at the table had long white hair. He was stooped over a manuscript writing feverishly, his whole body seeming to shake with the pen's movement across the paper.

'Show me your face,' Carlos whispered.

As he watched the man suddenly tore the top sheet from its spine, screwed it into a ball and threw it angrily onto the floor. As he did so his hair parted to reveal a wispy beard, a long, thin nose and small dark eyes.

A great deal had changed in the man. He had after all seen his world fall apart, but the likeness was unmistakable. Carlos couldn't believe the moment was real.

I have found you.

Chapter 25

Satellite

1.

'Hungry?'

Kelly emerged from painful recollection and put down his pen. A scrawny looking man in oversized clothes was standing in the doorway holding a tray of food.

'I know you.'

Ernesto winked. 'We've already had this conversation.'

'Have we?'

'How's your shoulder?

'It smells funny.'

'Well that's not good. I'll get someone to look at it later.'

Kelly scoffed. 'I won't hold my breath. You're the first visitor I've had in days.'

'Yes,' Ernesto empathized. 'This is unfortunate. The others hold you responsible for Raoul's death. It is not easy to shake that kind of animosity, but you should not blame yourself.'

'I don't. I blame Katrina.'

'How did you come to that conclusion?'

'It was her clumsiness that gave me away to the authorities.'

Ernesto placed the tray next to Kelly's bed. 'It was nothing to do with you. They were following Raoul. Arty was the one who gave you up'

'*What?*'

'Why do you suppose I work all the hours God sends wiping tables and serving coffees for that scumbag? It's not for the money, I can assure you. Every snippet of worthwhile gossip and slander in the city flows into that café and then gushes back out of his lips like a geyser. I take that gossip and use it to warn people of impending danger. A few days ago I heard him speaking with Eleanor. Your name came up in conversation. You were marked. I was waiting for you to come back into the café so I could warn you.'

Kelly assimilated this new information with a tensing of his limbs. He had misjudged the café owner and his pride was dented.

Arty.

He locked the name away. The desires it spawned would not help him to heal.

There will be time soon enough.

'So, where's my little red-headed nurse? I'm surprised she's not been round to gloat at my misfortune.'

Ernesto tugged nervously at his beard. 'She's gone to collect Paolo.'

'Got his own chauffeur now, has he? I suppose it gives him more time to heal the sick and turn water into wine.'

'Haven't you heard? Paolo's dead.'

'*What?*' Kelly was surprised at how hard he took the news. 'How?'

'How does anyone die in Corderro? They took him.'

The smell of hot food wafted under his nostrils, but Kelly was no longer hungry. The waiter turned to leave.

'Ernesto.'

The man lingered by the door.

'I used to be a . . . history teacher,' Kelly stammered. 'I have never told anyone this before and don't know why I'm telling you now, except to say that all throughout the ages – the Greeks, Romans, Saxons – leaders have often sobbed and torn their clothes in sorrow at the news that a great adversary had been killed in battle . . . Whilst they were pitted against them in life, in death they realized their true weight . . . That is how I feel at this exact moment.'

Ernesto nodded his approval at the statement. 'No man could hope for a greater epitaph. To have evoked such feelings of love and loathing is to have stirred up the universe.'

Kelly couldn't help thinking: *We are dying in the wrong order.*

2.

It had been two days since she had emerged from the shop to find Paolo gone. There could be only one rational explanation. Katrina felt as if the supports had been kicked out from under her. Paolo was her rock, the foundation on which she stood and survived the city. The silent street spoke of the vacuum left by his absence.

Later she was unable to recall the journey to his house. Katrina had somehow got herself behind the wheel and made all of the choices necessary in navigating her way across the sprawl. The overriding thought was to stand before his wife and relay the dreadful news before her nerve failed.

When she got there Katrina found the front door open. She stepped through the rooms with a growing premonition of foreboding. In the kitchen she found a meal half-eaten. In the lounge crayons and colouring books peppered the floor. Everything pointed towards a family ripped abruptly from daily life.

What would Paolo do in my shoes?

He would hide his grief behind a wall of leadership. He would act to protect the others.

Katrina made her way back through the house, trying in vain to ignore the details that affirmed her worst fears. She urgently needed to warn her colleagues. There was no telling what Paolo would divulge under interrogation.

As she was leaving Katrina was confronted with a piece of paper taped behind the front door. On it was written El Ambiente's tag – the large 'A' surrounded by a circle.

What does this mean?

That his wife and children are safe?

Who could know the intentions of an enigma? Katrina was hopelessly confused.

She drove back to the Satellite building, walked down the steps into the kitchen and sat at the table waiting for the phone to ring. Her actions told her colleagues everything they needed to know. The atmosphere became heavy with disbelief. Somebody placed a coffee in front of her, others offered to share in her vigil. Katrina graciously declined, sinking further and further into a haze of vehemence. She sat through the night and all through the next day before the call came. The voice was unknown, and said only two words: 'Plaza Domingo.'

It was a repetition of Raoul – the anonymous tip-off, the public place. Katrina defied the curfew as Paolo had done so before her. The journey across the dark city was filled with malicious thoughts of what would be done if a black sedan were encountered.

I will ram them off the road, gauge out their eyes, bite and scratch and tear and spit.

She knew that if the eventuality arose she would be unable to do any of those things, but the aggression sought to stave off thoughts of loss and despair.

Plaza Domingo was at the lower west end of downtown, a vast square surrounded by three churches and a cathedral.

Paolo lay Christ-like at its centre. He was naked and his body was riddled with black bruises and hideous abrasions. Katrina sobbed when she saw what they had done to him. He was the best amongst men. No one had ever equalled him in her eyes. The sensation was indescribable.

How can the world continue to turn in the face of such an affront?

She took off her coat and draped it over his body. Through the tears something about her friend looked out of place. Katrina wiped the bridge of her nose on her sleeve and knelt down. It was unmistakable. Despite everything that had been done to him Paolo was smiling.

3.

It was several minutes before he became aware of another's presence in the room. Kelly pulled himself into the upright position and saw that Katrina had silently entered as he slept. She wore a look of revulsion that exceeded his own.

'Though it loathes me to admit it,' she said, 'you and I now have something in common. We both owe our lives to the same man.'

Kelly didn't reply. The woman before him was a different person to the one who had approached him so clumsily at the port. She no longer possessed the superfluous trappings of arrogance. Her words were measured and she looked to have lost a lot of weight from her face. Where there had been presumption there was now substance. Where there had been a flimsy lack of experience, Kelly now saw a desire for confrontation.

'When I first came to Corderro,' she continued, 'I placed myself in a compromising situation. Paolo rescued me at the cost of his own brother. I once lay where you now lie. Whilst I cannot deny the disgust that accompanies looking upon someone so selfish, I am also sad because I see history repeating itself and am powerless to prevent *you* from reliving *my* mistakes. What the hell happened to you? It's not normal to be so hollow.'

Kelly looked away to the picture of the satellite. 'I didn't like Paolo and he didn't like me, but he was a good man and I'm sorry that he's gone. As for your question, I lost my faith in other people a long time ago. It wouldn't be worth my while explaining to you.'

'It is immaterial what worth you find or don't find in explaining. You are alive because Paolo considered it worth his while cutting a bullet from your chest, so choose your next words carefully, Slim. Unless you can be of some worth to us I have no issue fulfilling Paolo's threat and turfing you out on the street.'

'What happened to being a humanitarian organization?'

'Do not try to tie me up in moral knots. We all have a breaking point and I have reached mine. Last time I asked, this time I am telling. You *are* going to help us.'

'What exactly is it you do here?'

'You are familiar with the process of money laundering?'

'Yes.'

'What we do is similar, only instead of money we use people. As you know there are three stages in the laundering process – placement, layering and integration. In placement we move people from their original location and deposit them here. They are then layered by being moved through a series of complex financial transactions, i.e. we move them between safe houses, schools, hospitals and genuine residencies, making subtle changes to their personal details as we go – phone numbers, surname, marital status – until they emerge with a new identity. Finally we integrate, reintroducing them into the system and legitimately moving them out of the country right under the officials' noses.'

'How many?'

'Thirty to forty a month.'

'The black sedans take more than that every few days.'

'It takes time. We have to be careful. It's a lot like fraudulent transactions. Once the deception is uncovered the trail of transactions can often be unravelled. We have to be scrupulous and guarded.'

'Then why tell me?'

'Because no one in Corderro's history has ever been so successful a deceiver as you. I am offering you the opportunity to redeem yourself whilst doing what you do best. Otherwise the city will swallow you just as surely as it has devoured countless others like you.'

Kelly heard what was being said and even agreed with some of it, but his heart and mind were elsewhere.

The only thing in life that can redeem me is my brother's forgiveness.

Corderro and history and the vicious circle can all go to Hell. Nothing else matters to me now.

I simply cannot stay. I have already wasted too much time.

'I'll think about it.'

Katrina rose sharply to her feet. '*Fine*, but don't think too long. Next time you see me you will have made a decision. Otherwise I will make it for you.'

Chapter 26
Cheech's Exodus

1.

Cheech stood over the sleeping form of El Rey as he had done on many nights before, a knife drawn at the dictator's throat, arms tense, eyes wild in the dark, breath held.

In the beginning his intention had been to kill the man, to gut him like a pig and watch his severed body rise up from the bed, flailing uselessly about, not realizing that it was dead.

But that was a long time ago now, back when his murderous rage had been at its sharpest, honed to a fine point. Now the thought seemed abhorrent to him and filled his heart with shame.

It should be so easy to push the cold hard steel into soft surrendering flesh. Think of all the suffering you would save in that one brief malicious moment.

The simplicity of theory however was infinitely countered by the crushing weight of reality. Standing over the defenceless, dormant figure Cheech had tried many times to contemplate the sheer boundless implications of his actions, that to kill a man, even a man wholly evil such as El Rey, was irreversible, final and absolute.

Over the following days, weeks and months spent in awful deliberation Cheech had realized what kind of person he was, and more importantly, what he was not. The nightly ritual now stood as an affirmation, each time revealing afresh that his humanity was still intact, whispering softly in his ear that the ludicrous direction his life had taken was a worthy and legitimate one, that the lies he spun daily had cause and purpose.

El Rey stirred in his slumber. The fear and excitement of being caught was exquisite, the heightened awareness of how real and fragile existence was. Slowly and silently Cheech exhaled.

In the not so distant past there had been parents, a sister and a home in the hills. Now there was only the desire to safeguard in others what he himself had lost. On good days it made all the sense in the world. On others, like today, it made no sense at all.

2.

Cheech's father had been a carpenter, his mother a chef; their house was filled with the most fantastic culinary smells and equally fantastic furniture. His sister sported pigtails and teased him incessantly about girls.

One gloriously sunny summer day a black sedan rolled into their neighbourhood. It stopped at the edge of their driveway and its doors opened onto a couple lounging under golden rays. Cheech was upstairs doing his homework – *plate tectonics and seismology* – subjects never to be forgotten again. In the still, lazy air he detected the sound of feet on grass, the gate opening, the words spoken in calm monotone.

'Will you come with us, please?'

His mother issued a startled cry. A man's voice reassured her, 'There's no reason for alarm.'

'What's the matter, Mummy?'

His sister appeared at the front door. His mother's voice ascended in urgency. 'Go back inside, dear.' There was the sound of struggling, his sister crying, mother screaming, father shouting, doors slamming, wheels dropping off the curb, silence.

For a long time afterwards Cheech sat at the desk, pen in hand, his mind blank, waiting for time to begin again.

It was late afternoon when he walked out into the garden. His father's newspaper was draped over a deckchair. A half-empty glass of beer nestled amidst the grass. The day's rising heat had trapped a layer of smog that now hung over central Corderro. Cheech's lasting memory was the view as he stared down the hill into the heart of the leviathan that had swallowed his family whole.

He had been nine year's old.

The next morning as the sun rose over El Rey's palace a sniper radioed down to one of the guard huts that a lone figure was approaching on foot. Looking through their scope they saw a young boy dressed in what appeared to be a school uniform.

They drove out to meet him, weapons cocked, bored fingers itching at the ends of underused triggers.

The tires skidding to a halt sent up a fierce cloud of dust that stung Cheech's eyes. He closed them, knowing that the approaching vehicle might well be the last thing he ever saw.

'What are you doing, kid?' an unseen figure asked.

'I would like to see El Rey,' he replied.

Someone laughed.

'And why would that be?'

'I'd like to work for him, sir.'

Cheech remained polite and unassuming. The sun beat mercilessly down upon him. He prayed for the heavens to open, for a torrential current to surge down the hillside, ripping the estate out at the roots and washing it from the face of the earth.

A forceful hand gripped his arm. 'Get in.'

Cheech thought of the last words spoken to his parents and calmly surrendered.

As his sight cleared he found himself at the main entrance. Its vast archway was interlaced with golden images of gods and philosophers. He was led to an antechamber where he sat silently for several hours.

By the time they finally ushered him up a flight of stairs Cheech had become convinced that his life was forfeit. With each step he expected a bullet to cut his stride violently short.

His tiny unsure presence amongst the grandiose spoils of excess felt ridiculous. Cheech was more than aware of his own audacity. The chances of his survival were minimal. As he reached the landing unharmed he imagined fate as a snarling beast snapping at his heels.

He was led along hallways overlooking courtyards to another stairwell reaching up high into the rafters. At the top he found himself on the roof. Four giant stone pillars formed the base on an immense gazebo.

El Rey was lying across a chaise longue being fanned by a young girl with forlorn eyes.

The Emperor was not at all as Cheech had envisaged – slovenly, garish and obese, spilling out of a toga, pink tree-trunk legs, thick-set arms, long black hair streaked with flecks of grey, pencil-thin moustache and a laurel reef resting on his head.

The scene conjured a picture of Julius Caesar in the boy's mind.

For a time El Rey neither moved nor spoke, underlying that all things rose and fell at his bidding. Cheech remained sharp and respectful, flanked by armed men twice his size, head bowed in patient reverence.

'What can I do for you?' the Emperor finally asked.

'I'd like to work for you, sir,' Cheech responded, eyes averted.

Another brief silence.

'And why would you wish to do that, I wonder?'

Forcing the words through his gums he replied. 'Because I admire you, sir.'

El Rey smiled, baring blunt teeth. Cheech looked up and tried to mirror the gesture but instead found himself thinking of mist over Corderro and the screams of his mother.

'You are a brave boy,' El Rey' responded. 'Brave and stupid, but above all brave. Come back tomorrow and my men will have something for you to do.'

Cheech regarded the distance between them, wondering if he could bridge the gap and strike before he was cut down.

'Thank you, Your Excellency,' he mumbled before being ushered from the roof and back down the stairs.

The next day they started him in the kitchens washing dishes and scrubbing floors. In all things he worked to the best of his ability, striving to be efficient and above all *essential*.

Within a matter of weeks he was moved into the heart of the palace.

He wanted to get close to the Emperor, to understand why he had fashioned Corderro into so disgusting an image. Within the inner circle of El Rey's trusted advisors Cheech witnessed a constant train of excess. Women flowed through the palace gates day and night. Some were willing participants, most were not. He noticed that smoke was always rising from the chimneys no matter how hot the day. In time he came to understand that few ever left the grounds as anything other than smoke and ash.

Life is sacred and cheap – all at once.

Contradictions were everywhere he looked. He quickly became an adult within a child's body.

I want to find my purpose and lose any sense of self.

Ambition swelled beneath humility.

I want to kill the King.

The thought was absurd. He came to work each morning confused as to his intent.

I have held the serpent to my throat and let it sink its fangs deep into me.

Puberty arrived. The most confusing of changes took place within the most confusing of cities. Cheech became convinced that he was losing his mind.

Tito's arrival as the new Chancellor was like a breath of fresh air. In every respect the man was a mess. His marriage was on the rocks, he was hopelessly disorganized, physically he was disintegrating in a stress-induced decay, and at all times he thought only of himself.

Tito was important in two respects. Firstly he made Cheech see the true nature of madness. When the blowing up of buildings became commonplace the boy witnessed a man set against all the conventions of rational thought. As time went by Cheech saw him embrace more and more outlandish beliefs in the pursuit of his unattainable goal. Facts and figures became unrecognizable as they were bent into predetermined shapes. Cheech realized that he in comparison was completely normal. Secondly, working for Tito gave him unprecedented access to the palace. As the Chancellor became increasingly detached from reality his sporadic and demented memos sent his servants further and further afield. The soldiers patrolling the corridors became accustomed to Cheech's presence. They smiled at him and even said hello on occasion.

On one such errand Cheech arrived at the Emperor's apartment to find him raping a young woman. The guards who had previously smiled and greeted now stood idly by the doorway. Cheech found to his amazement that he was allowed to enter unchallenged and gaze upon the grand defilement taking place before his eyes.

El Rey was in the next room. He could see the Emperor beating the woman about the face. A journal lay open before him. Cheech read a passage written in ink that had not yet dried.

There are very few truly evil people in the world, and very few truly good. Mostly the human race is a sea of indifference. Upon their worthless waves I sail majestically.

Cheech fled in tears, past the guards whose blind eyes perfectly illustrated the journal's sentiments.

The words ignited something within him and El Rey unwittingly set his own downfall in motion. The vicious circle began to turn once again.

3.

The *Plague of Lethargy* lay at the foot of the Emperor's bed. Resting on top of it Cheech could see a folded note. He teased open the page and read the message within:

Eleanor,

Over the past few weeks I have become convinced that a traitor is within our midst. I can take no chances. Please arrange for the immediate processing of the

following people.
> *Yours in body and soul,*
> *Emile*

4.

The list was a staff rota. It included everyone currently working within the palace walls – forty-seven people in all. Cheech saw his own name written between the lines, added in as an afterthought.

He had forgotten about me.

But would still have had me hand-deliver my own demise!

The blade trembled in his hand.

Forty-seven people for one. It's a fair trade.

All those meals served, all those subservient errands. They amount to nothing.

El Rey's neck was exposed, ripe for the picking.

You consider yourself royal but I know better. You are lower than the dirt. It shouldn't mean anything to be the end of you. It should even be an honour, a pleasure.

And yet.

Cheech's arm dropped by his side. He did not possess the strength.

If I cannot kill you, then I shall do what I do best – elude and humiliate.

He took the note and journal, and tiptoed out into the corridor.

You need to get everybody out.

How is that possible?

Cheech was so preoccupied with the formation of a plan that he strode around the corner straight into the stomach of a palace guard.

'Easy there, my little one,' the guard chided as he stumbled back steadying himself. 'I could've mistaken you for an intruder and run you through!' His words were harsh, but the delivery was kind.

If I am successful in my escape you will be executed for incompetence.

With the passage of each day Cheech considered himself an accomplice to the travesties taking place far below in the city. He knew that he possessed the means with which to end all of their suffering, but lacked the courage to condemn himself as a murderer. Now he was charged with being the unintentional catalyst in another man's death.

I am just a child. I am not equipped for such measured decisions.

Would a hundred years of wisdom make the slightest shred of difference?

I should not find myself accountable for other people's actions.

The guards know that they watch over a man undeserving of protection.

293

They have entered into a pact. It was their choice.
You will not be the one to squeeze the trigger.
The gravity remained unaltered.

5.

Lucas was the head butler. He emerged with his hair in a mess and his face covered in lipstick.

'You had better have a good reason for disturbing me at this hour, little one.'

Cheech handed him the note. 'I do.'

Lucas's bullish complexion grew pale. His eyes bulged as he stared at the words. 'My apologies . . . I—'

'We are going to play a game of Chinese whispers,' Cheech interjected. 'I want you to take a moment to memorize this note, *word for word*. Then I want you to read it back to me from memory. Next I want you to knock on two doors, pass on the information, and have each person memorize the message as you have. After you are satisfied that they have it in their heads, *word for word*, send them off to inform two people, and meet me in the dinner hall downstairs.'

'Why only two?' Lucas gasped.

'Because then we get a quiet orderly trail of people rather than a stampede. Be deathly still or else you shall be still with death . . . now go.'

6.

The servants assembled in silence. Some had dressed, most remained in their pyjamas. Cheech stood on a table and scanned their faces. He saw varying degrees of disbelief.

'Hands up who wants to die?' he asked.

Their expressions changed en masse to a single look of disgust.

'I'll take that as a no! In that case, do any of you plan to live, or are you going to sit here in shock until they turn up in the morning and kill you?'

Still nothing.

'Come the morning we shall all be rising up the smoke stacks, or else we shall have pulled off a daring escape and be in hiding. This is the stark choice we face. We must decide now, in this moment. *I* have a plan. Would any of you like to hear it?'

They all nodded. No one spoke.

'We cannot sneak away. There are too many of us to leave undetected. Therefore I propose that we abscond in plain sight. My plan is to set off the fire alarms, lie to the guards and walk out through the front door.'

It was a child's plan, uncomplicated by the need to second-guess the cynicism of adults.

'Time is short. Can I have a show of hands?'

7.

When it came to matters of security the Emperor was justifiably paranoid. The fire alarm caused him little in the way of anxiety. All of the necessary precautions had already been taken. He threw aside the duvet, reached under the bed and retrieved a set of clothes that had been stowed there for just such an eventuality. The trousers were coated with a thin layer of dust. El Rey made a mental note to shoot the maid for the oversight.

He didn't notice the absence of his precious journal. All thoughts were focused upon a swift exit. El Rey dressed quickly and moved to the back of the room where an immense bookcase filled the entire wall. The trappings of power had allowed him to indulge a childhood fantasy. He sought out a hardback entitled *Overlooking the Obvious*. Pulling it from the shelf activated a lever. The central section of the bookcase swung open revealing a hidden corridor etched into the rock.

There were no electric lights. The Emperor had opted for Gothic authenticity. At his feet he found a candelabrum. He lit its many wicks, stepped into the corridor and closed the door behind him.

The walls were perfectly smooth, as if they had been cut into the mountain with a giant laser. El Rey walked for several minutes. Up ahead he could see another light.

'Good evening,' he greeted.

'I am sorry for this disruption, Emile.'

Eleanor stood before him in a negligee.

'Not at all, you have just made it worthwhile.'

'Rest assured that I shall find the culprits responsible and deal with them in an appropriate manner.'

'I would expect nothing less.'

Eleanor waited for the Emperor to pass by.

'No, *after you!*'

The exit was concealed beneath a thick blanket of overhanging vines.

They emerged into a clearing half a mile from the palace.

Two black sedans were waiting from them, two chauffeurs standing to attention. The Emperor got into one, Eleanor the other. They sped off in two different directions.

El Rey handed a note to his driver. 'Follow these instructions to the letter.'

'Yes, Your Highness.'

They drove into central Corderro. The Emperor watched the empty streets flash by and marvelled that it was well over a year since he had last ventured from the palace grounds. El Ambiente's tag was spray-painted almost everywhere – walls, bridges, road signs, even the tarmac. They passed through the Market district, Liberacion and back into the hills. As they were ascending the clouds opened and it began to rain heavily. When they reached the highest point El Rey asked his driver to stop.

'Let's just wait here till the rain stops.'

'Very good, Your Highness.'

The downpour intensified. An awkward silence filled the space between them. Beneath the patter of raindrops they both heard a buzzing sound. A fly came to rest on the Emperor's arm. He swatted it away. The sky eventually cleared.

'Where to, Your Highness?'

The Emperor leaned forward. 'I could tell you but then I would have to kill you. Just beyond those trees is my secret hiding place.'

El Rey got out of the car, opened the driver's door and dropped his gun into the dead man's lap. He released the handbrake and watched as the sedan rolled backwards gaining speed. As it neared the bottom of the hill it spun around and flipped over. No flames. The Emperor was disappointed. He stepped off the road and vanished.

8.

Under the cover of night La Fantasma rolled in from the ocean. Reaching the cliff face it climbed along the salt-stained walls, grasping for the summit with vaporous arms. It changed shape, a thin head forming from broad shoulders, rising up under an impossibly long neck and swelling into a monstrous grin. It glided across a road where moments earlier two sedans had passed silently into the valley. El Rey's palace provided little resistance. La Fantasma moved into the cracks in brickwork, the keyholes in doors, filling rooms with its presence and raising hairs on the arms of soldiers. Oblivious to the incessant ringing of an alarm bell it passed over the rooftop. Encountering no more obstacles it began to cascade over itself, falling in tumbles within tumbles. It dropped into the courtyard and began to travel downhill, surging and swelling as it gathered momentum.

At the bottom of the road two guards stood staring up at the approaching mist. They were perplexed. Despite strict palace protocol regarding defense of the Emperor no one had told them anything. The alarm implied that something awful had happened, but their calls went unanswered.

'We should go up there,' one suggested.

'You're joking,' the other replied. 'You know what Eleanor's like. This might all be an elaborate test to see if we can be coaxed away from our posts. Move against her wishes and its certain death.'

'But there could've been a massacre up there?'

'All the more reason not to go!'

The first wisps of La Fantasma touched their skin.

'I don't like this fog. It's a bad omen.'

'It is a meteorological phenomenon, easily explainable – stop being so melodramatic.'

At that moment forty-seven people emerged from the mist like ghostly apparitions. Both guards flinched and reached for their guns.

'Good morning,' Cheech greeted with a careful balance of confidence and restraint.

'What are you doing outside after curfew?' the first guard snapped.

'Someone tripped an alarm. I heard Miss Blake shouting about an assassin. We were told to leave the palace and stay with relatives for the night.'

Cheech used a child's inverse logic whereby the more fantastical the yarn the less likely it was to have been fabricated. The guards exchanged suspicious glances. 'This is highly irregular.'

'You're telling me,' Cheech retorted. 'I was scared to death . . . thought we were under attack.'

Beneath the veneer of adrenaline he was petrified.

If my bluff is uncovered then I shall die knowing that I'd had the chance to kill a tyrant and failed.

'Eleanor spoke to you personally?'

'God no!' Cheech feigned shock, 'One of her men.'

Neither guard looked convinced.

'Why don't you call to verify?'

The question was a calculated risk. He'd seen organized chaos ensue as a result of the alarm. The chances of the men on the hill having any kind of coordinated response were slim.

The notion of disobeying Eleanor filled both guards with dread, but why had she not phoned through to confirm her wishes? It was most out of character and yet the servants seemed perfectly up front and honest. A little nervous perhaps, but then they were facing armed men in front and the threat of assassination to their rear.

A shrug of the shoulders told Cheech all he needed to know. He fought to hide his elation.

'OK, you can go through, but I want all of you to write down your names.'

Cheech nodded. 'Of course . . . thank you.'

9.

They regrouped half a mile down the road. Cheech did a quick headcount and found they had lost three people to La Fantasma.

'They must have walked straight past us.'

To everyone's utter amazement a woman within the group shouted 'Hello' at the top of her voice.

'*Be quiet,*' Cheech hissed, 'Are you a fool? To the guards we are forty-seven, well, forty-four individuals. Why would we be looking for one another if we were separated?'

The woman gave a disgruntled snort to indicate she did not take kindly to being chastized by a child.

'What now?' someone whispered.

'I know a place we can go,' Cheech replied, 'a safe house of sorts.'

'I can't go to a safe house,' a man spoke, 'I have a wife and son to look after.'

'I have no clean clothes to wear,' said another, 'I must go home first.'

'We can't be expected to live in squalor.'

'Then go home and don't live at all,' Cheech scorned. 'Have you learnt nothing from your time in the palace? El Rey would happily murder us all, after everything we've done for him, all that service, on a mere suspicion. Don't go home. That life is closed to you.'

'What are you saying – *leave our families?*'

'Either that or else take them into flight before the sun rises. Be under no illusions. We have escaped, but we are not free. You need to run and hide.'

Cheech was an orphan with the simplistic outlook of a twelve-year-old. He saw no reason why the others wouldn't recognize the sense in his argument and join him.

A woman emerged from the mist and placed a hand on his shoulder. 'I'd like to thank you for informing us of the danger we faced and for leading us out of harm's way, but I cannot be so black and white as to switch off the world. I must go to my children.'

Others came forward with similar well-wishes before vanishing into the murk. Within moments their number was down to thirteen. They could hear the footsteps of their fellow servants, moving away towards their loved ones.

Cheech was deflated by his failure to convince the majority. If they were caught they might well experience a fate far more garish than that which he had spared them.

I pray they heed my advice.

'I take it you all have nowhere else to go?' The question was phrased with unintended harshness. No one replied. 'OK. Let's go. Link arms, I should hate to lose more of you.'

On foot and virtually blind there was a very real threat of being black-sedaned. Cheech knew that if discovered the fog would offer them little protection.

The landscape was unrecognizable. They were in a labyrinth. Open roads appeared closed, trees resembled sleeping ogres, the river a steaming broth of magic potion.

Cheech felt the weight of responsibility closing in on him.

I was spared while my family was taken. That must have been for a reason?

Unless there is no purpose to the universe and everything is the work of chance?

Perhaps my purpose was to kill the Emperor?

Perhaps my compassion is an immense weakness?

Perhaps I am being abandoned as an unfulfilled entity?

He heard the sound of flowing water. It was a marker on an invisible map. Cheech pinned all of his hopes on reaching the river and gaining his bearings.

It was three in the morning. They could descend no further into the recesses of night.

10.

Over an hour later he could feel the group's enthusiasm waning. They had walked back and forth between a confined stretch of buildings. Nothing looked familiar against the alien backdrop of La Fantasma.

'I'm sorry,' he repeated once more, 'we are right on top of it, I'm sure.'

The silence spoke of its discontent.

In the unseen suburbs to his left someone coughed. The group instinctively stopped as one.

Two hours till the end of curfew, unlikely to be a civilian, and yet a black sedan would never knowingly give itself away.

If I don't find it soon more of them will leave to what I'm sure will be their end.

This is your fault. You are the cause of the Emperor's suspicion.

He turned to face the others. Even with their reduced numbers some of them were distant silhouettes.

'I'm going to see who that is. If you hear me scream, *run.*'

The others watched him walk away, marvelling at their own cowardice. Somebody gave voice to the thought. 'Only in Corderro would a group of adults leave a child to the elements.'

Cheech moved away from the river. He felt the presence of walls, of a narrowing and constricting landscape. Most of the stationary juggernauts were without doors or windows. It was an abandoned part of the city; the first of many to come.

Up ahead he smelt tobacco. Cheech stepped carefully over the uneven ground, reasoning that he might be able to retrace his steps in the event of encountering a foe.

It was not a black sedan as he'd feared, but rather a tall stocky man leaning against a broken lamp post. The man saw him, but showed no sign of being startled. He kept his eyes trained on the boy and continued to smoke without a change in expression.

'Hello,' Cheech ventured. He noticed an imposing makeshift axe hanging from the man's belt.

'Hello back, my little one,' the man replied. 'What brings you out in the forbidden hour?'

Cheech chanced his arm.

'We're on the run.'

'We?'

'Myself and a number of others, just back there by the river.'

'You're taking a risk telling a stranger such information.'

'Yes I am, but to tell you the truth I am at the end of myself.' Behind the man he saw a stairwell descending beneath the pavement. '*This is the place!*'

'And what place would that be?'

'Satellite! You are its guard.'

'Nonsense, I live here. Don't like the lounge reeking of cigarettes so I'm outside.'

'At four o'clock in the morning?'

The man smiled. 'Craving's a terrible thing.'

'This isn't a trick,' Cheech pleaded. 'We really need your help. We work at El Rey's palace.' He realized his mistake. Mention of the Emperor instantly put the man on edge. He took an extra long drag on his cigarette and glanced into the fog for signs of danger. 'I found a note. He is planning to have us killed. We set off an alarm and . . .'

The story was ridiculous. He could see that the man would not be convinced.

'We need to come inside.'

'Into my house? Not a chance.' The man was not hostile in his obstinacy, merely cautious. Cheech took a step closer. The man stepped away from the wall, rising in stature.

'You would have thirteen people die because of your neglect?'

The man placed a large hand on Cheech's shoulder and pushed him away with minimal effort. 'You are forgetting, my little one, this is Corderro. Where guilt is concerned I am already full to the brim. I can accommodate no more of its acidic whining.'

Cheech was defiant. He stepped forward once more. 'You misinterpret my statement as a question. We *are* coming inside.'

The man grabbed him by the scruff of his shirt. 'I won't ask you again urchin. *Get lost!*'

Raised up so that his feet did not touch the ground Cheech looked the man square in the eyes. 'Do you know the story of David and Goliath?'

'Of course.'

The man looked down. A blade was poised to plunge into his stomach.

'Guess which one you are, *my little one*.'

Rather than look fearful he roared with laughter. 'A black sedan would never show such mercy. Well, bless me, a soul on fire amidst all this hellish ambivalence!' With a quick flick of the wrist the man swatted the knife from Cheech's hand and held him even higher aloft. 'David indeed, my brave little friend!'

Cheech found the man's euphoria far more disconcerting than his aggression. His voice dropped to a whisper. 'Yes, this is Satellite. My name is Rafael, named after my angelic nature.' He roared once more and placed the boy safely back on terra firma. 'Call your friends. We shall get them some soup and a place to wile away the remains of the night.'

La Fantasma was abating. Rafael patted Cheech's head. 'To conjure another old testament image – if this is the sea parting for the Hebrews then that makes you Moses!'

'The responsibility does not sit well with me.'

'It sits just fine.'

Forty-seven people had left El Rey's palace. Thirteen made it down the steps and safely into the arms of Satellite. It would only be a temporary reprieve.

Chapter 27
Accountability

1.

To his Excellency Tito Majagranzas
Chancellor of the Exchequer
Señor,

I am writing to you on behalf of my husband, Bernardo, who is somewhat indisposed having taken his own life in the early hours of this morning. If my introduction seems overly formal, cold or dispassionate, then it is because I am trapped in a vacuum of sheer disbelief. I dread the moment when this bubble bursts and I am forced to face the true gravity of my loss.

But to the matter in hand – why should my sorrow concern you?

Some details concerning Bernardo – he was fifty-two years old and worked as a lathe operator in the oldest factory in Corderro. It was a small family run business in the northern-most part if the industrial quarter.

Perhaps you knew it, though somehow I doubt it. Men of your stature rarely concern themselves with the affairs of the proletariat.

I say 'knew', and not 'know', as it is now a pile of smouldering detritus, the latest casualty in a financial campaign of terror waged on the good people of this city.

Your people.

Your campaign.

Bernardo was lucky enough to escape the blast having forgotten to set his alarm clock (a Godsend you might say given that it had never happened before in all his years of service). But he was close enough to see many of his lifelong friends being torn limb from limb, and see his own reflection in the tinted windows of the passing black sedan.

The chronology of events leading up to his death is unclear to me. My mind has become turbulent. All I know with any clarity is that the explosion was the final straw, the quivering hand that sent the house of cards toppling.

Do you know the worst of it? My husband has been a devout Christian since his youth, a faith for which suicide is deemed an irreconcilable sin. For this transgression alone Bernardo believed that he would be rewarded with eternal damnation in the sulphurous fires of Hell, and yet he still gave up, such was his

303

despair at this world.

As a man of faith he also believed in obeying the laws of men (as long as they didn't conflict with the laws of God). To this end he was one of the select few who actually endeavoured to pay the taxes requested of them by their Chancellor. By the time it had reached 60 per cent Bernardo was forced to take a second job. At 70 per cent he said to me he could see no way to hang on to the house, or put food on the table each evening.

Though it shames me to say it, you and he had something in common. I would often wake in the middle of the night and find him at his desk, trying to find some way of balancing the books. I imagine this is not all that distant from your own life. The bones began to show in his face, his hair thinned out, he ceased to be enthusiastic about anything, or respond to his wife's affection.

You killed him, Tito.

You killed him.

Just as surely as if you'd thrown the noose over the beam and tied it around his neck.

You killed him.

One of my friends told me of a theory called 'The Butterfly Effect'. The theory states that under the right circumstances a butterfly could flutter its tiny wings and set off a chain reaction that caused a tornado on the other side of the world. It strikes me that if there is some truth to this theory then you are the butterfly Tito, flapping your flimsy membranes and casually wiping out whole generations of men in a single silent sweep of your wings. Whichever way you look at it the trail of devastation leads unmistakably back to your door.

Do you realize this, Tito, high up in your tower?

Do you?

You are the man who killed my husband.

You ripped down half of the city.

Your arms are cast wide.

No one is exempt from your clumsy, inexplicable wrath.

I have one more thing to say to you.

Tito.

Such a repugnant little word.

Do not dare put down my letter unfinished.

People tell me that you are referred to in wider society as 'El Comedin'. If this is true then I have a picture to describe for you.

You are on stage facing a packed audience. They have paid a high price to see you, everything they own in fact (and more besides), but they are not dismayed by the cost as they have been told that you are 'El Comedin' – *the funniest man ever to walk the earth. They are confident that what you have to say will swathe the pain and heartache they feel at their broken lives. They await your opening line with wild anticipation.*

You open your mouth only to realize that you have forgotten your entire act. Not a single punchline presents itself.

What to do?

The audience are expecting everything and you have nothing.

A moment passes, then two, then three.

You begin to perspire.

The front row picks up on your nervousness and their smiles begin to wane. The room becomes a mass of uncomfortable shuffling.

The responsibility has overwhelmed you. You are not up to the task. There is only one option available. You conjure to mind every comedian you have ever heard, every sketch show, every mime and mimic, and you steal it all, regurgitating huge chunks of material, robbing mannerisms, usurping intonations and quirks of speech. You try to form it all into coherent prose, but your delivery is disorganized and your timing is out of kilter. Killer lines go wide of the mark. Your stumbling efforts are met with a wall of stony silence.

You tap the microphone and find to your horror that it is switched off.

There is no set list taped to the floor in front of you as a reminder.

The necessary time and preparation has not been invested.

Hands that should be animating your fantastical stories drop defeated by your side.

Into the oppressive void comes an angry jeer. It is quickly joined by another, then another. Pretty soon the entire auditorium in on their feet shouting and hurling abuse. Where is the laughter they paid so dearly to experience? What are they being given in return for the vast wealth that has been taken?

Amidst the crowds is a small, unassuming woman.

That woman is me.

I look at you dying a metaphorical death on stage, and I think of Bernardo dying a very real death in our basement. Strangely my mind evokes the vision of a disgraced Samurai warrior. He has failed to protect his master from the assassins. The code of honour dictates what his next course of action should be. He should fall upon his sword.

By the time you read these words I shall be dead, reunited with Bernardo, be it in Heaven or Hell.

Do the honourable thing, Tito.

Fall upon your sword.
A curse upon your wretched soul.
   Marcia Massimo (Mrs).

2.

Tito casually folded the letter, placed it on the desk in front of him and took off his reading glasses. He realized that he'd been holding his breath and exhaled for a very long time.

Nothing had ever affected him like this before, neither the abusive letters calling for his head on a plate, nor the razor-sharp satire daubed on street corners, nor Eleanor's constant psychological assault. Marcia's words passed effortlessly through him.

He rose from his desk on legs that were suddenly shaky and walked to the window.

'*Mi Dios*,' Tito gasped as he did so often, only this time he had some inkling into what it must be like to face the Almighty and be forced to account for his actions.

Corderro was the Hell that Marcia had spoken of. Everything was burning.

An idea presented itself – a wonderfully masochistic and self-deprecating notion. Tito returned to the desk, took pen and paper and hastily scrawled a primitive balance sheet – three columns, a fat one for the various entries, and two thinner columns for the assets and liabilities.

The first entry was obvious. He wrote: 'Elizabeth'.

'Asset or liability?' he asked the vacant room.

In the wider context Elizabeth would clearly be an asset to anyone she came into contact with – smart, sexy, witty, good-looking, elegant – but this wasn't a measure of her real worth, it was a measure of her worth in Tito's world. In the liabilities column he wrote: 'Twenty years'.

The soon-to-be-ex-Chancellor could not legitimately claim to have ever really loved his wife, but he did feel genuine remorse at having wasted the best years of her life.

Next he wrote: 'Maria'.

Tito closed his eyes.

Oh my, this is a difficult one.

There was no escaping the truth. He had falsely accused her of a crime she was not cerebrally capable of. El Ambiente was still walking the Earth. She on the other hand was not.

What did I give her?

Moderately adequate sex, constant moaning about my hair, endless brush-offs, unrelenting high-brow put-downs that went sky-rocketing over her head . . . and an agonizing and unnecessary death.

What have I taken?

Tito wrote '1 life' in the liabilities column.

It felt like an abhorrent mark of disrespect to Maria's memory to move on so clinically, but move on he must.

'Something easier,' he muttered.

Tito wrote: 'House (uninsured) + cars + contents.'

A few primitive calculations derived a conservative estimate of three and a half million US dollars. He wrote the figure in the liabilities column.

'Fifty-three insurance claims'.

Now we come to the crux of the matter.

Fifty-three buildings, previously thought to have been vacant – some near-deserted squats, others crammed, high-rise apartment blocks. Try as he might, whichever way the figures were spliced, they still came out with an average of fifty to sixty people per claim.

Mi Dios! That takes me beyond 'serial killer' and into the realms of genocide. History will bundle me with the likes of Pol Pot and Milosovic, 'Tito's Legacy' to sit alongside Corderro's.

He looked down the list of liabilities.

Any assets?

Hah! You truly are El Comedin!

Tito was instantly a changed man. He asked himself how he could have been so wrapped up in the petty trivialities of his existence when so many diabolical debts were stacking up against him.

Right, first things first, let's get rid of this ridiculous hair!

He strode to the en-suite bathroom. Maria's toiletry bag remained unopened since the time of her abduction. The Chancellor ferreted through its contents, retrieved a pair of tiny nail scissors and set about hacking at his moustache and sideburns with gusto. He caught his lip several times, his cheeks, his ears, drawing blood that only made him work more feverishly. The long, grey, brittle hairs collected in the plughole amidst a slur of pink water. Next he went to work on his head. The thin wisps billowed about on the air and came to rest in a wide ark around him. Tito worked a fistful of shaving cream into a thick lather and applied a generous amount to his face and scalp. He was breathing rapidly.

How could I have been so obsessed with such an irrelevance?

He took a cut-throat razor from the cabinet. His hands slowed down, making sure that each swipe of steel was smooth and even – swipe, rinse, swipe, rinse. Tito took a towel and wiped away the residual cream. The results were spectacular, a revelation, a blank canvas. The Chancellor had lost years in a matter of minutes.

Tito liked what he saw. It made him laugh out loud.

To think that this *was so important to me!*

He remembered the balance sheet and his humour vanished.

Time to go.

Go where?

Does it matter? Anywhere.

He covered his baldness with a flat cap. Not out of shame, but so as not to alert the palace guards to the change. Tito didn't have to worry about what to take and what to leave behind. There was nothing left.

A knock at the door interrupted his escape.

'Enter.'

The servant boy was unfamiliar to him. It should have been Cheech, but he had disappeared the previous evening.

'Yes?'

'El Rey requests your immediate company, Señor Majagranzas.'

It had been his custom to snap at the palace staff, but on this occasion Tito smiled. 'Thank you, young man. Tell His Highness that I shall be up in five minutes.'

'As you wish, señor.'

Tito waited until the footsteps had receded and then moved swiftly to the outer door. He turned right in the opposite direction to the Emperor's quarters and headed hastily down a spiral staircase – straight into Eleanor Blake.

She looked him up and down with a mixture of amusement and pity.

'Lose a fight with your barber, El Comedin?'

'Ah, very good, Miss Blake! Perhaps *you* are more deserving of *my* nickname?'

Eleanor was clearly unimpressed with the retort. 'Such insolence in someone so ill-prepared for conflict is inadvisable. Could it be that you have evolved a backbone so late in life?'

Tito glared at the woman.

Why should I try and hide the revulsion that I feel? You disgust me as much as I disgust you.

'Not a backbone no, a *conscience*.'

Eleanor's aggression turned to elation. 'Oh Tito, Tito, you are priceless.'

'You're absolutely right, Eleanor. I am priceless. Only a fool could still walk and talk and breathe with the weight of what *we've* done bearing down on them.'

The flickering of Eleanor's eyelashes revealed how tedious she found his repetition. 'As I have said to you countless times, El Comedin, this was your doing. I am just a soldier. I follow ord—'

Tito had never been a man of action and was amazed at his own reflexes, a culmination of all the animosity that he felt. Suddenly unwilling to let Eleanor pass the buck he lunged forward, cupped her head in both hands and shook it violently.

'NO! NOT ME, *US*, YOU AND I, YOU AND I, ELEANOR. HAVE YOU ANY IDEA HOW MUCH BLOOD IS ON OUR HANDS? HAVE YOU? *HAVE YOU?*'

The Chancellor could not believe his own impudence. He had crossed the line in a way that no man had ever done and lived. There was no way to substantiate the initial outburst. His hands loosened their grip.

Eleanor was momentarily taken aback by the attack. Her only split second of weakness was a thought cutting through the adrenaline telling her that she had underestimated the feeble little man. When she saw the hesitation in his eyes her rage sent her into a vicious counter-attack. She lifted Tito's jaw with one finely manicured hand and punched him in the Adam's apple with the other. The Chancellor fell back against the corridor wall coughing and spluttering, only to be rewarded with a series of blows to the head, neck and groin.

'*Puta madre*,' Eleanor cursed and spat. 'You dare to . . . why the . . . I am speechless.'

Conversely Tito could think of many things to say but chose not to. What was the point of begging for mercy from a woman who had helped him to kill thousands of people?

Pretty soon I shall be dead.

The thought was perfectly calm.

I am coming, Bernardo, to receive my eternal torment.

One of the blows knocked his hat off revealing Tito's bald and

309

butchered scalp. Eleanor was stopped in her tracks by an eruption of hysterical laughter. 'El Com-oh-deen,' she bellowed. 'Now I see . . . not a backbone . . . *legs* . . . legs to run with . . . you are trying to escape . . . you treacherous little cockroach.'

'You're absolutely right,' Tito gasped back at her. 'I am a cockroach . . . and treacherous . . . and all I am good for is stepping on . . . so why don't you, *soldier* . . . after all . . . it's not as if you are *accountable* for any of your actions . . . you are . . . *only following orders.*'

Eleanor slammed her foot into Tito's shoulder and forced him onto his back. Several guards had congregated around them, alerted by the scuffle. Putting on a show for her men Eleanor swept the hair back from her face and ran a hand down the curve of her breast to the hip where she un-holstered a pistol.

'Oh Tito, Tito, how I've dreamed of this moment, vanquishing you from my misery—'

These are not the last words I shall hear, the Chancellor thought, and simply stopped listening.

'To think I have let you live all this time. I should have done this many months ago.'

I am in bed with Maria. I have never been the Chancellor. I never married Elizabeth and consequently never needlessly wasted twenty years of her life. Maria is alive, untortured and in possession of unprecedented intelligence. We enjoy unbearably erotic sex followed by mind-expanding discussions on the nature of the universe.

Eleanor pressed the gun to Tito's temple.

I am far, far away in a simple, modest little house, living within my means, living free, content.

'You know, Tito, I have a better idea. I do not think you are even worth the cost of a single bullet, certainly not one of mine, and so we shall seek out a more amusing demise. Someone fetch me a camera!'

Eleanor's men scattered to the four corners of the palace and returned over the course of a few minutes with several cameras of different shapes and sizes. Eleanor chose one of the more antiquated models with a flash bulb the circumference of a dining plate.

'Smile for me, Tito.'

The Chancellor drifted into delirium. His features beamed back punch-drunk stupidity. The flash captured his gormless expression in all its glory.

'Within the hour I will have this photo at every checkpoint and border crossing in the principality. I shall have it blown up to fill billboard posters and instruct anyone seeing the person fitting its likeness to shoot them on sight. If you can survive undetected for forty-eight hours – which I seriously doubt given your inability to even leave the palace without incident – then we shall begin the door-to-door searches. For every tenth house we come to without finding you I shall personally shoot the youngest member of the household – be they man, woman, boy, girl or dribbling little toddler – one more cadaver to pile upon your mountain of flesh. What fun we shall have, Tito – you and I.

Eleanor blew the Chancellor a kiss and then spat on him.

'You are free to go, El Comedin – *run, run, run.*' She passed the camera to the nearest man. 'Carry out my wishes with the utmost haste.'

3.

Tito came to his senses and found himself alone on the floor. He was not entirely sure what had transpired, how much time had elapsed or what had been said.

How did I escape death?

The last thing he recalled was Eleanor's foot making contact with his genitals. Every part of his body was in pain.

Where has she gone?

Daylight awaited a few short strides away.

Are they lurking outside, ready to pick me off as I leave?

That would be just like Eleanor.

And it would be just like me to cower in the corner and wait for it all to blow over.

The liabilities far outweigh the assets. You have more debts than you could ever repay.

But it would be noble to make an attempt.

Tito got to his feet and limped through the archway into the late afternoon sun. The courtyard was empty. When he reached the gates at the bottom of the hill several palace guards were waiting for him. They each in turn raised their rifles and took aim.

Click.

Click.

Click.

Empty chambers and raucous laughter.

'Good luck, El Comedin,' one of them snarled sarcastically.

Tito passed sheepishly through their ranks, unclear as to why he should require luck when he had survived so long without it. Reaching the main road he was brutally enlightened.

There were posters of him everywhere – small black-and-white photocopies stapled to telegraph poles and huge colour images the size of swimming pools posted up on walls, all promising a huge reward for shooting him on sight and cutting off his head.

Just when you think you can sink no lower.

I am in a box within a box within a box.

A few hundred yards ahead there was a fork in the road, one way leading into central Corderro, the other into the woods.

You deserve everything you get. Let's just see if you can make it to the treeline for starters.

He stepped out of the palace grounds.

The split second he did so a car screamed past him and spun to a halt. The men from the gates emerged.

'Eleanor said to tell you that once you left the boundaries of El Rey's home it was open season.'

Tito saw that one of them was carrying a sword.

'In the interests of being sporting we'll give you till the count of ten . . . ten . . . nine . . . eight . . .'

He ran down the road towards the woods.

I am injured. There is no way I can elude them.

'Six . . . five . . . four . . .'

Tito thought of all the insurance claims and of all the abductions that had ended in the basement rooms beneath his office.

I fed the serpent and yet still it turned on me.

'Two . . . one . . . GO!'

Regimented boots pounded the earth. The ground ahead dropped away into a steep embankment. In desperation Tito threw himself down the incline and began to tumble and roll. Branches whipped at his already heavily lacerated face. His feet flailed forward onto concrete and he heard the screeching of brakes.

Outstanding – I shall either be run over or else the passengers will beat me to death and decapitate me!

Given the choice I would rather be—

There was an abrupt thud and Tito found himself sprawled over a bonnet. A red-headed woman stared back at him from the driver's seat. There was renewed activity behind him, hacking and cursing.

'Help me,' he mouthed to the woman.

'Get in,' Katrina replied.

4.

They drove in silence for the first few miles. Tito sat awkwardly trying to hide his features as they passed endless effigies of himself. Reaching the outskirts of town the Chancellor realized that there was another person in the back seat – a woman, fast asleep, dressed all in black.

'Thank you,' he whispered without intending to.

'I may yet come to regret it,' Katrina replied.

Tito noticed that the driver was also dressed in black and that there was a strong smell of alcohol. 'Your friend is . . .'

'Drunk,' Katrina finished for him. She turned her head to face him for the first time. 'We have just cremated the remains of her brother. She would have liked to bury him, but cemetery space is so hard to come by these days . . . and as for the tax on headstones . . . have you ever heard of something so despicably opportunistic?'

They passed through a burnt-out section of the industrial quarter. Tito thought of Bernardo and Marcia. He had never seen the consequences of his actions so closely. It was a bitter pill to swallow, realizing that the world would have been a better place without him in it.

'So anyway,' Katrina went on, 'my friend back there . . . Alicia . . . since her brother, my friend, was black-sedaned

. . . well . . . she's been drinking a lot . . . to get her through the day . . . and it's just as well for you that she *is* drunk . . . because if she were sober she would tear you limb from limb and gouge out your eyes. I'm having a hard enough time resisting myself . . . *El Comedin.*'

'You recognize me?'

'You really are as dumb as they say.'

Tito bowed his head. 'Yes . . . yes I am . . . dumber in fact. If you recognized me, then why did you help?'

To Katrina the answer was simple. 'Paolo would have wanted me to. We took an oath.'

Chapter 28

Cross-over

1.

'Rejum' (pronounced 'Ray-zhoom')

A word that I made up – somewhere between a dream, recollection and deja-vu. I don't really know what it is (or was). I was very young and the mind plays tricks. It's like a beach ball bobbing around on the ocean – try to swim towards it and the motion of your arms and legs creates a tide that carries it further and further away. Whenever the thought enters my head it is accompanied by an uncomfortable, sickening feeling of imbalance. I have no choice but to withdraw for fear of fainting. I want to remember, but for some unknown reason I cannot.

Something definitely happened. It is not true deju-vu. This, I am told, is where the same sensation arrives at the synapses twice in quick succession, giving you the impression you have been somewhere before when in fact it is merely your senses misfiring. No – I write it down every time it occurs – over eighty times so far in the course of my existence. It never gets any clearer and is always identical.

I am in a large metal box or tomb. There are two people with me – a man and a boy. The man is not you (you have already said goodbye). He is grotesque; his face covered in scars and bruising. None of us speak. We are waiting for something. They both vanish. I am alone.
Isabella, 27th August

2.

The first thing that surprised him was the title – El Hotel Provocativo ('the provocative hotel'). Carlos had known it by another name. The second thing was the presence of a roof.

'My Lord,' he gasped as he led Isabella into the circular courtyard. 'How can this be? It's amazing!'

'What is?' Isabella asked.

Carlos looked around at the swept floor, the glorious sculpture of horses rising up over the reception desk, the incessant traffic of guests, the hanging baskets, the decorum and the grace of it all.

'Everything,' he replied.

A receptionist was watching his reaction with a broad beaming smile on her face. 'Good afternoon,' she greeted him. 'You are not the first to respond in such excited fashion today.'

'And I shall not be the last!' Carlos clasped his head and shook it. 'How long have you . . . When did all this . . . what—'

'We've been here for three whole days. As you can see – business is booming!'

'Yes . . . ' Carlos was lost for words.

'You've been here before I take it?' the receptionist enquired.

'Yes, many years ago.'

'An exile returning?'

He nodded.

'Welcome home.'

'Thank you . . . sorry, my manners . . . This is Isabella . . . I am Carlos.'

'Agnetha, *mucho gusto.*'

'*Y tu tambien.*'

'Are you looking for a room?'

'No I . . . regrettably we are booked in elsewhere . . . had I known of course that . . . *extraordinary* . . . no, I'm looking for Alfonso. Is he here?'

Agnetha's smile disappeared. She straightened up and glanced at her feet. 'My father . . . is not here at this time.' She met Carlos's gaze. 'Did you know him?'

'I'm sorry,' Carlos whispered. 'No, I did not know him. I only knew *of* him . . . his dress sense and . . . er—'

'His way with the ladies?'

'Yes.'

Carlos's honesty rekindled some of Agnetha's warmth. 'What is it you wanted?'

'We're looking for someone. We thought maybe Alfonso knew them . . . a long shot really . . . I can see that now.' Carlos took a step back. 'Not to worry. Anyway, good luck with the new enterprise. I love what you've done here.'

He turned to leave but Agnetha reached over the marble counter and grasped his arm.

'I've no idea why I just did that,' she said retracting her arm.

'It's OK,' Carlos replied, 'These are exceptional times.'

'I think maybe . . . in the last three days it has been . . . *pleasant* . . . to fill people up who have been empty for such a long time. I should hate for you to leave here empty.' Agnetha got a little flustered at her sudden and unplanned speech. Carlos waited patiently with a look that said he was open to whatever she had to say. 'Perhaps you could speak with my mother . . . *Señora Ceci* . . . maybe she can help you?'

'That would be excellent,' Carlos said with a bow of appreciation. 'Very thoughtful of you. Where can we find her?'

Agnetha motioned across the courtyard. 'Over by the piano, the large lady. She's a little worse for wear, if you take my meaning.'

'A woman after my own heart,' Carlos winked, 'Thanks again.'

'Not at all.'

In the years since leaving Corderro Carlos has seen many war-torn countries. The experiences blurred into one another, variations on a theme, all equally horrific and indescribable. To Carlos, that was the worst aspect of conflict, that the acts of atrocity could not claim to be unique or even original, merely carbon copies of the previous generation, and the generation before that, and so on ad infinitum. It made the loss doubly despicable. But amidst all of the unbearable turmoil events often transpired that filled Carlos's mind with wonderment. One of the most endearing features of human endeavour was the notion that family heirlooms – paintings, furniture and jewellery – should be hidden away and survive unscathed to be defiantly paraded at the first opportunity. Carlos took great comfort from knowing that whilst one group of people were seeking to maim and kill, another group were painstakingly working to safeguard the tiniest and often most insignificant little trinkets. He considered that their quirky behaviour kept the human race anchored just shy of the precipice.

El Hotel Provocativo was a shrine to such people. Everything about its new lease of life shouted, 'You did not conquer me. I outlasted you, and look what endured with me!' Several chaises longues adorned the covered walkway that surrounded the courtyard, their intricately stitched covers ancient and unblemished. Draped over their polished mahogany arms were men and women of all shapes and sizes. The men were dressed in dinner jackets, the women in ball gowns. Their attire was beautiful, but seemed to have been assigned at random rather than to requirements. Skinny women drowned in massively oversized bustiers, while fat men's guts spilled over the top of painfully tight trousers, and vice versa. Isabella imagined that the clothes had been hidden beneath layers of dust for years, waiting without specific owners for the day when they could be thrown on in celebration.

The centrepiece of the congregation was an ebony piano. It was being played by an immensely fleshy, fantastically dressed woman, a tiny stool shaking beneath her bulk. Carlos's eyes started at the top and worked their way down through swirls of colourful contradictions – purple hair held in an elaborate style high above her head with ostrich feathers, a lime-green bower, torrents of make-up, rouge, crimson lips, false eyelashes of silver and gold, necklaces heaped one on top of the other, a lemon blouse peppered with peach-coloured hearts, a tight grey miniskirt that gave way to a mountain of monstrous thighs, thinning to spiked knee-length stilettos.

Her huge hands struck the ivory with a force that would seem aggressive were it not for the euphoric beam of joy radiating from her face. Carlos and Isabella approached as if they were returning to a lit firework. As they did so Señora Ceci and her band of fabulously dressed cohorts belted out a waltz:

Oh for the joy of my youth – I would happily imbibe all the tea in China.
Oh for a moment with you I would happily endure a thousand years of hardship and woe.

Carlos looked at his watch – 3.34 in the afternnon.

'Not just a little worse for wear,' he whispered, 'they're as drunk as lords.'

'We're going to be eaten alive,' Isabella whispered back.

'Quite possibly.'

Something caught Carlos's eye that stopped him dead in his tracks. Hidden amidst two giant yucca plants was an old, aubergine-coloured sofa. Above its right arm a bullet hole was clearly evident.

'Ah, new arrivals to our shores,' Señora Ceci bellowed upon seeing them. 'Welcome, welcome. I can always recognize exiles by their bizarre clothes and awkward demeanours.'

Her entourage laughed as one.

It was a strange opening comment, but Carlos decided that it was well intended. 'Good evening, señora. I'm glad to find you all looking so well.'

'Thank you, young man,' she replied. 'Are you here on hotel business or have you come to join the sing-song?'

'I regret to say the former. I came seeking your husband, my condolences for your loss.'

Señora Ceci nodded and gave Carlos a wily smile. 'Did you know Alfonso personally?'

'Unfortunately no.'

Her face lit up. 'Then let me tell you about him. My husband was given a puny little body, but into it God poured the testosterone of fifty men. He was insatiable. He gave me carnal pleasures that have left me tingling down through the decades . . . but alas I was not woman enough to hold his gaze . . . or perhaps he was an adulterous shit . . . or maybe both . . . yes . . . yes, I think both . . . anyway, I sired him seven children, but beyond the walls of our home he was responsible for an army of bastards. He approached women like dice, thrown to chance, seemingly at random—'

Señora Ceci interrupted herself by striking a sombre chord and warbling: '*Where are you going my love?*'

The men and women around her responded with: '*Up where the air is fragrant and pure, high in the hills of San Pedro.*'

'Anyway,' she continued, 'you roll a dice for long enough, your winning streak will come to an end, no matter how lucky you are. My husband's losing throw was called Marcela, a charming waif of a girl, eyes like a panther's, phenomenal cheekbones—'

Show me the river that leads to the valley,
The valley of all that I once held dear.

Carlos watched the drama unfold with joyous marvel. Isabella on the other hand felt ill at ease and trapped in some sort of implausible cabaret.

'She told darling Alfonso that she was in love with him and wasn't about to share him with anyone, least of all me.'

Señora Ceci rocked unsteadily on her tiny seat and belched. 'Well, monogamy was not a word Alfonso understood. Smelling the scent of obsession he broke of the liaison–' she tapped the bridge of her nose '–he still had many irons left in the fire if you take my meaning . . . *now* . . . what is that phrase you Europeans use? "Hell hath no fury like a woman scorned" . . . quite right too . . . Marcela begged my husband to take her back, but he stopped answering her calls, barred the gates to our guestless hotel, and avoided his usual places of leisure. *Well –*' her eyes surveyed the faces of the crowd who hung upon her every word '–Marcela wasn't having it. One night she climbed over the gates, shimmied up the drainpipe and clawed her way into our bedroom . . . I've no idea how she found it . . . we have over one hundred rooms . . . *oh–*' she waved her arms '–the drama is sufficient without this ridiculous build-up. Marcela had a dagger clenched between her teeth. It was facing the wrong way. When she bit down it sliced into her lip causing her to cry out. I was awoken. My husband lay soused and oblivious by my side. It was unclear who Marcela had come to harm: me, my husband, or both of us? Whichever it was, upon seeing me wide-eyed and upright she screamed and launched herself into the air . . . I put out my hands to defend myself and in the ensuing tussle I came off worse. A quick flick of the blade plucked out my left eye–' Señora Ceci tapped her iris which made a hollow 'tink' sound '–*glass* . . . I tripped and fell . . . she lunged and stumbled . . . and stabbed poor Alfonso through the heart!'

The crowd let out a perfectly synchronized 'No' and covered their mouths in horror.

'Mortified at her crime Marcela ran to the window and threw herself into the courtyard . . . *dead* . . . right where we sit today.'

'Where did you get the sofa?' Carlos interjected.

The crowd looked aggrieved that he should dare disrupt their host mid-flow, but Señora Ceci was delighted. 'You like it?'

'Yes, and I recognize it.'

'Oh, how splendid!'

'Where on earth did you find it?'

'After my Alfonso passed on it was mentioned to me in conversation . . . I don't know why it became an obsession. It just seems like the kind of prize he would've loved to own. I hunted high and low . . . eventually I found it . . . in New York of all places!'

'A lady named Magdalene?' Carlos said.

Señora Ceci was aghast. 'How could you possibly know that?'

'I stayed with her many years ago and slept on this very sofa for several weeks . . . small world. huh!'

The crowd were amazed. Carlos looked at Isabella, willing her to remember

I have just given you the biggest hint yet, mi chica bella. *It is right there in front of you. Look and see.*

Isabella was confused by the proceedings. The revelation passed her by.

'Not a small world . . .' Señora Ceci corrected '. . . a circle. It has found its way back along the rotation of a circumference to the beginning. Alfonso was a great believer in the melting pot – even in death he was a perfect illustration. *He* used to be the flamboyant drunk and *I* his scrawny, dowdy looking slave. Now look at me – enormous, larger than life, practically pickled and outrageously flamboyant. Things come around and come around—'

'You're very wise,' Carlos complimented her without a hint of irony. 'It is good to understand the nature of the universe. It allows for healing and forgiveness.'

Señora Ceci opened her arms framing an expression of rapture. 'Agnetha, get my new friends whatever they want – on the house!'

Isabella had grown impatient. The desire to find Jonathan was overbearing. 'That's very kind of you but we were hoping tha—'

'We'd be delighted,' Carlos cut in. 'Do you serve Cheva?'

'Of course.'

'Fantastic – two glasses please.'

They sat down at the outskirts of the group. Isabella was fuming.

'Stop being so presumptuous, Carlos,' she whispered through the corner of her mouth. 'You mistake rudeness for charm.'

'The rudeness is on your part, *mi chica bella*,' Carlos replied. 'It is important to possess discernment. You must be attentive to the quests of others.'

'What are you talking about?'

'I would think that this Señora Ceci has told her tale every day since her husband's death, and with every telling I imagine the pain abates a little further. Therefore be of good cheer, be patient and listen. Certainly I use bravado wherever possible, but do not confuse it with presumption. I am highly attuned to your hopes. You in turn need to be attuned to the hopes of others.'

Carlos turned back to the crowd, clearly annoyed with Isabella's tantrum.

You're right of course, she thought, *damn it.*

The afternoon mooched into evening. Señora Ceci regaled them all with stories from Corderro's history. Carlos's extensive grasp of the legacy afforded him the opportunity to embellish many of her tales, much to everyone's delight. Isabella graciously accepted several glasses of frothy beer. It was sickly sweet and instantly relaxed her. She listened to the stories and found herself feeling gratitude towards her guide for giving her the chance to learn so much of the world in which Jonathan lived.

Around about eight o'clock their host had become so inebriated that she could hardly speak. Her frequent forays into music were littered with bum notes and slurred lyrics. Her following seemed not to have noticed, languishing as they were in an equal state of ruin. It was only now that Carlos chose to pick up the conversation he had quashed hours before.

'Señora, my illustriously attractive colleague and I are looking for someone who might have had dealings with you or your husband – could you help us?'

'Ab-sol-oo-tlee,' she boomed. 'What's his name?'

'Jonathan Pemberton.'

Señora Ceci stared into the middle distance and tapped her lips with intricately painted fingernails. 'Jonathan . . . Pemberton . . . *Jonathan.*'

Isabella realized that she was leaning forward in her seat.

'No . . . I'm sorry, I don't recall ever having met someone by that name.'

The disappointment was tangible. Isabella shrank back and her whole face dropped – eyes fading, muscles sagging, mouth curling. Carlos remained upbeat.

'Any idea where else we could look?'

'Was he a good man?'

Carlos hesitated. He already knew the answer, but was unsure of the most appropriate response. 'I think so, yes.'

'Then my husband would not have known him. He only consulted with thieves, scoundrels and vagabonds, God rest his philandering soul.' Señora Ceci made a sign of the cross, as did her following. 'I take it you've tried all the reputable means of inquiry.'

Carlos beamed. 'Very astute of you, yes we have.'

'Mm.' Señora Ceci pondered momentarily. A quick tinkle of ivory.

I once knew a man named Albert Chance –lived just cross the pond in Paris, France.

Spent most of his life accumulating wealth – travelled half way round the world and found himself.

321

Isabella looked as though she could burst into tears at the absurdity of it all. Carlos squeezed her shoulder.

'There is one place you could try, down by the river in the Market quarter . . . been closed for a long time, but I hear they've opened up again . . . just like us.'

'What is it?' Carlos asked.

'Difficult to say really . . . bit of this, bit of that . . . regular band of outlaws, but with good hearts . . . it's a hostel come hospital come warehouse.'

'What's it called?'

'Oh, some fancy name or other . . . spacecraft or something—'

'*Satellite?*' Isabella cried, the word exploding from the back of her throat.

'Yes, that's it. You've already been there?'

'No,' Isabella replied. 'I've no idea where that—' She was confused.

Too much to drink.

But no.

Rejum.

I've heard that word before – Satellite.

And the sofa – it too invokes a sensation of familiarity.

Remember, damn it.

Isabella drew a blank.

'I'll have Agnetha write down the address for you . . . I'm far too drunk to hold a pen!'

'Very kind,' Carlos replied. 'We must be getting along, but thank you, it's been an absolute pleasure. Your singing is divine.'

'Oh you charmer, you . . . drop in any time . . . I'll be here, drinking Corderro dry and wearing down the keys with music. Bring your friend too . . . she's a pretty thing . . . not very talkative though.'

3.

Isabella was swept form the hotel in a haze.

'What just happened? What was all that talk of sofas and satellites?'

'You were the one mentioning satellites, *mi chica bella.*'

'Was I? Oh, it's all mixed up . . . I wish I could remember . . . I was so young.'

She was flagging. Carlos half-walked, half-carried her to The Phoenix hotel. Moving through the foyer he wrapped himself around her, forming an impenetrable barrier to Ronaldo's ever-lecherous eyes. At the bedroom Isabella became flustered at her inability to open the door.

'Allow me, señorita,' Carlos said softly. The door opened at the first attempt. He picked her up and placed her on the bed. She was already asleep. Carlos pulled up a chair, swung it around and sat beside her with his chin against the headrest.

'Isabella, Isabella,' he whispered. 'Open your eyes to what is happening here.'

Her chest rose and fell in slumber.

'I should have come clean from the outset . . . It was foolish of me not to do so . . . a romantic notion of quests and destiny . . . but now . . . I think we are too far down the road . . . I must let you discover for yourself. The thought of re-visiting Satellite fills me with dread. Tomorrow, *mi chica bella* . . . tomorrow you shall receive your answers.'

Carlos replaced the chair, covered Isabella with a blanket and left the room.

Chapter 29
Last Day

4.34 am

It was pitch black. The phone was ringing. The clock flashed an ungodly hour in unashamed red neon. Images of freak-shows and circus folk merged and faded. Isabella reached out and grabbed the receiver. 'Hello?'

'I am not an answering service,' Ronaldo bellowed into her unforgiving ear. 'I do not take kindly to be awoken at such an hour.'

'What the hell are you talking about? You phoned *me*.'

Isabella sat upright. She heard the person in the next room stir.

'There is a man downstairs wishing to see you. He will not give a name. He will not take no for an answer.'

Isabella's thoughts sprang to wild conclusions.

Jonathan – he has somehow heard of my search.

'What does he look like?'

'Do not try my patience, señorita. Come and see for yourself.'

The line went dead.

Isabella was out of bed and across the room in a flash, duvet flying up in the air, tap water flung recklessly in her face, clothes picked at random, shoes in hand, closing the door and running down the stairs.

It was Carlos.

'Good morning,' he greeted, his eyes dark and brooding. 'I am sorry to wake you at this hour, but you need to see this place before the sun rises.'

Isabella was angry. 'Carlos, it's the middle of the night.'

'It's not the middle of the night, it's early morning. There is a world of difference and the timing is deliberate.' He looked deeply unamused that she should question him.

'You kept me up till God knows when drinking. I think I'm still drunk. I am *not* impressed with your antics.'

'Oh, you and your STUPID TANTRUMS!' Carlos snapped menacingly. 'No consideration for others as long as Isabella gets what she wants! Fine . . . I shall find Jonathan myself.'

He walked away. Carlos did not look back. Within a moment he had turned the corner and was gone.

Isabella was stunned. A certainty came to rest upon her.

If you do not go after him you will never see him again. He will not return. He is as stubborn as you are.

'Carlos, wait!'

She ran to the corner. The next street was empty. Isabella sprinted down the middle of the road, unsure as to why she placed such urgency in keeping him close. She found him at the next turning, smoking a cigarette and strutting in tight circles.

'I didn't know you smoked.'

Carlos snorted. 'The wealth of things you do not know!'

'There's no need to be rude.'

'Though I hate to trouble you by inconveniencing your self-absorbed little world, some of us put others before ourselves. I myself have a far higher calling than finding one man, but I chose to put you first. Are all your words of praise to this saviour of yours mere flagellation?'

'How dare you!'

'How dare I indeed! Why don't you show your true mettle and flounce away like a spoilt little madam?'

Isabella remained rooted to the spot. There was something she was missing, some part of the puzzle that hadn't clicked into place. Carlos had the answers, she could see it in his eyes. She didn't dare leave, however wronged she felt.

'Why are you so aggrieved?'

'When we were in the field of markers we walked past the graves of my family, three in all. I told you my name – Carlos Neblina. We walked past those markers and that name flashed up time and again – Neblina, Neblina, Neblina. You read each one and yet saw nothing. You have mocked the existence of my wife, a woman to whom you quite frankly do not hold a candle, and you have presumed the people of this city exist to provide you with dutiful directions day and night. You are like a clumsy finger jabbing at a wound that is trying to heal.'

She saw it all now with great clarity. It wasn't a game. It was all entirely genuine. Carlos was right. She *had* been walking around with blinkers on, focusing solely on her own quest to the detriment of everyone around her.

'This person you seek . . . tell me his name?

'His name is unimportant.'

'What did he do?'

'I told you, he took something from me, and I from him.'

Isabella trod carefully. 'Care to elaborate?'

'No, I shouldn't have to. It should be crystal clear.'

'I'm sorry, it is . . . Carlos, help me to see it from your perspective. I *have* been ungrateful, I know that. What is it you want to show me . . . please?'

His face betrayed him. The scowl broke into a smile. 'There is hope for you yet, *mi chica bella*. Come.'

5.04 am

This time the pain was just about bearable. Slowly Kelly rose from the bed and pulled a shirt around his sling. The room had been changed around as he slept. Another bed had been wheeled in beside him. In it lay what had once been a young woman, clinging to life by her fingertips, her breathing laboured. Boxes of supplies had been stacked by the door. A cursory inspection found nothing useful.

He felt no guilt at what he was about to do.

It's a terrible thing to admit you're just the same as all the others gone before you.

You overstayed your welcome – pure and simple.

Take your beating like a man, accept the situation and get out. Get home, find your brother, seek his forgiveness, build a house, get a job, something that doesn't involve people, a park ranger or night warden.

Kelly noticed the huge oak rafters and sky protruding through the gaps in roof tiles. The room hadn't changed after all. He had been moved.

Katrina's idea of punishment no doubt – trying to disorientate you.

Trying and succeeding!

The floorboards creaked. He took his time. A greasy window told him he was in an attic overlooking the Market district. La Fantasma was retreating across the bay, ensnaring sunrise in an ominous haze as it had done for centuries, unaware of man's attempts to tame the shoreline.

The stairs were lowered by way of a pulley system. Even with his good arm Kelly felt exquisite agony as the lattice muscles in his chest pulled against the wound. He gritted his teeth and gripped the rope tighter, easing the steps gently to the floor so as to make no sound. The moment they touched down he slipped back clutching at his shoulder and exhaled a slow, controlled breath of exhaustion.

Get up!

Kelly gathered his strength and rose once again to his feet.

The corridor beneath smelled of beef stew. He vaguely remembered being spoon fed the foul broth against his will a few night's earlier. A dog lay asleep in the corner, long ears hiding its face.

Some guard you are!

Kelly could feel the doors closing behind him, the city shrinking with every step, forcing him out, contracting down to a narrow corridor.

Threadbare carpet formed islands in a sea of broken floorboards. The walls were littered with posters of vibrant colour and haphazard imagery – bowls of fruit, movie stars, musicians, landscapes – anything and everything to hide the disintegrating masonry beneath.

Kelly reached an atrium and leaned over its banister. Beneath him sunken tiles formed a mosaic of spiky flowers.

All around the upper circle doorways branched off into dormitories. Kelly wasn't sure why he chose to risk detection. His weathered hands lingered on one of the handles. It turned silently. He entered.

The room was hot and musty, the result of so many dormant bodies heaped on top of one another in three-tier bunk-beds. Kelly counted seventeen heads protruding awkwardly from beneath tattered blankets. A sea of faces that had long-since forgotten joy jerked and rippled with nervous ticks and anxious mumbling. There was a cacophony of low, uneasy breathing. They looked and sounded like people rotting and disintegrating before his eyes.

Look at yourselves – where has your cause got you?

Look at yourself – where has your cause got you?

Kelly suppressed a humourless laugh. Despite having taken polarized routes they had all ended up in the same boat.

Is there some great and glorious cosmic truth to be derived? That we are all destined for dust and damnation?

The dog-eared pages of 'Thirty-eight' hung from his back pocket.

What good are my words? Can I achieve anything with them, or are they as hollow as everything else?

Katrina was nowhere to be seen. For some strange reason her absence saddened him. He closed the door and retraced his steps.

At the foot of the stairs he found an empty rucksack hanging from a coat hook. The kitchen bore the remnants of a late-night meal – dirty plates in a stagnant sink, stewed tea in its pot, a table laid for ghosts.

Kelly searched through the cupboards depositing items in the rucksack – a first-aid kit, beans, coffee, a bottle of beer and a roll of petras. Hidden amongst the dishcloths he found 200 US dollars.

Good for a few bribes.

His keen eyes scanned the ground floor for trinkets – Several sets of car keys, a beanie hat, scarf, candles, towel, soap and a wristwatch flashing 5.13 am – all deposited in the sack.

That's it.

With each step his fluid plan began to solidify.

One of the car keys is bound to fit a lock outside. Release the handbrake, roll silently away, drive slowly, turn off the engine wherever possible, call in a few favours, transform yourself into a smuggler's commodity – disappear.

The front door was heavily reinforced around a delicate stained-glass mural of an orchard. Kelly disengaged the deadbolts to reveal a set of concrete steps leading up to street level.

'You really are *worthless!*'

Katrina was sitting at the foot of the stairs, hair pulled back in a severe ponytail that sharpened her eyebrows into spikes and made her vacant expression appear menacing.

'When did I ever try to convince you otherwise?'

'You didn't.'

It was unlike her to be so concise. Katrina's privileged upbringing had nurtured within her a confidence to say whatever she liked, but she seemed to have taken a leaf from the smuggler's book, that saying less said so much more about what you were holding back. In a strange way Kelly was impressed.

'Then you won't be surprised when I don't apologize. Take care of yourself, Esperanza.'

'Before you go I'll be having that money back. It would seem a shame to cast pearls before swine.'

'If it's all the same to you I'll keep it, thanks.'

'I'm already responsible for the death of a man. An insignificant little thief won't make any odds.'

'I'm glad to hear it. Goodbye.'

Katrina gave no further warning. She bridged the gap between them in a single stride and struck his shoulder in several short bursts. Kelly dropped to his knees clutching his chest. The rucksack was removed roughly from around his neck and the stolen money retrieved from his pockets as he lay helpless.

'I'd get that looked at if I were you. You look in a pretty bad way, Slim.'

She withdrew, placing the bounty out of reach.

Kelly was amazed by the transformation. She genuinely didn't care whether he lived or died. There was no one left to abandon him, or be abandoned by him.

He stood up. Crimson droplets began to form at his feet.

'You're making a mess of my floor. *Get out.*'

Kelly turned without further resistance and made his way up the steps into a corrugated-iron covering. His shirt felt sticky. He dreaded the thought of visiting one of Corderro's back-street surgeons, but the wound needed to be re-stitched and dressed.

How much longer?

Soon.

You're a fool.

'Mr Kelly. It truly is a pleasure.'

He looked up.

Eleanor Blake was draped over the hood of an armoured car, dark hair cascaded over bare shoulder. Behind her stood hoards of men, their rifles trained on his stomach. The scent of apricot reached him.

Eleanor smiled sumptuously and licked her lips with provocative relish.

5.16 am

For all my meticulous planning I am to be shot in the street like a rabid animal.

Eleanor seemed in no hurry to give the order. Her men stood as statues, unwilling to move a single hair on their heads without permission.

Hopeless and speechless.

Find something . . . anything.

'Likewise,' he muttered.

Eleanor's grin grew wider still. 'Somehow I doubt your sentiment, *smuggler.*'

Kelly held her hypnotic gaze, afraid to look away. 'Yours too.'

She lifted a hand and waved dismissively as if shooing him out of her sight.

She wants me to warn the others.

Kelly took a step backwards, eyes forward, arms reaching for purchase, then another step, then another, then another. Ever so slowly Eleanor disappeared from his line of vision. He pushed back against the glass. The orchard mural swung inwards on its thick-set hinges. He turned. Katrina was still sitting on the stairs.

'Have you no shame?' she shouted.

'They're here,' Kelly whispered, his gaunt and withered expression telling her all she needed to know.

Katrina turned on her heels and stormed up onto the landing screaming 'WAKE UP, WAKE UP, THE MOMENT IS UPON US!'

In a split second it seemed to Kelly as if every door in the house was flung wide open. Bodies driven abruptly from sleep thundered into corridors. Children were crying. In the kitchen, tables were overturned, gas hobs were sparked, cigarettes lit, torches ignited.

Kelly stood amongst the hive of activity and was lost.

'They're here,' he repeated. No one heard him.

A tall man with kind eyes gave him a gentle nudge and brought him back into the land of the living.

'Are you OK?'

Kelly noticed that he was wearing a dog collar.

'Did you sleep in that?' he asked pointing at the pastoral attire.

The man laughed and gave him a hearty slap. 'Sadly no, these are my spiritual armaments. I always put them on before going into battle.'

Kelly felt himself rising from delirium. Outside it was deathly quiet.

'They're at the back door,' someone shouted.

'This is it,' someone else responded.

'Hey,' Dog collar spoke softly, moving the smuggler back into the main body of the house, 'All is well. These are the times when God shines his brightest, when we have no choice but to lean on him.'

Kelly was a long way past the point of deception. 'I don't believe in God.'

Katrina reappeared. Kelly recognized the look on her face. He had seen it countless times on the features if those running from the black sedans.

Dog collar instructed several of the men to build a barricade at the front with whatever they could find. Tables were upturned and chairs piled on top of one another. He sat down on the stairs and tapped his fingertips together as if in prayer.

'You need to gather up the others and help them escape. I shall hold them here.'

Kelly was astounded. 'What it is with you people? Why are you all falling over yourselves to be sacrificed?'

'You have forgotten what it is to live for an ideal. If I die, then I will do so protecting the lives of children. Death will define me.'

'Aren't you scared?'

'*Petrified* – I have no wish to become a martyr. God willing, I'll see you again.'

'We both know that won't happen.'

'Then I must say goodbye in the absolute sense of the word.'

'What's your name?'

'What use is there in knowing my name, other than to have it haunt you after I'm gone? Get out of here and find something worth living for . . . otherwise you may as well perish here.'

It felt like an affront to turn away from such an offering but there was nothing more to be said.

'It's an insurance claim!' someone shouted. 'They're rigging the building with explosives.'

'But the people,' Katrina murmured 'they can't.'

'Has this place taught you nothing?' Kelly replied. 'They can and they *will*. Is there another way out?'

Katrina stared through him.

'*Hey!*' Kelly slapped her hard across the face, bringing her back to herself. The act caused him considerably more pain then he himself inflicted. '*Is there another way out?*'

'*No* . . . that's the only one.'

'Then we need to get to higher ground. Do you have a car?'

'Paolo's van is parked in the next street.'

'Keys?'

'In my jacket upstairs.'

'Let's go then.'

'We have to take some of them with us.'

'There's no time.'

'You help me, Kelly, or by God I'll leave you here.'

'OK, but be quick about it.'

They both looked up. At the top of the stairs a bald man stood deathly still, holding the hands of two children, a boy and a girl.

5.20 am

Tito wasn't to know that Eleanor's men had followed him to the sanctuary. Even as he attempting to distance himself from the massacres in which he was complicit the Chancellor unwittingly consigned yet another group of strangers to annihilation.

The men chasing him had radioed back to Eleanor with news of the red-headed woman who had aided his escape. Her mind leapt to the wildly accurate conclusion that it was Esperanza, the woman for whom Paolo had gone to his grave to protect.

'Follow at a safe distance but do not intercept. Well done, gentlemen. I will ensure that you are richly rewarded for your troubles.'

Even as Tito sat with his fellow exiles dunking bread in soup, Eleanor had been prowling the alleyways mere feet away. Her men were ready to storm the building, but she had pacified them with a royal wave of her claws.

'There's no rush. We'll reconvene at five for a five-thirty start. A woman needs her beauty sleep.'

Despite being broke, on the run and sentenced to death Tito slept better than had done in years.

When the shouting started he didn't know what to think. Tito had grown accustomed to observing calamity from afar. Being within the thick of mayhem left the ex-Chancellor dumbfounded.

Someone yanked the blanket from around his shoulders and dragged him to his feet. He looked down and saw that it was the servant boy, Cheech. A girl stood by his side.

'Good morning, Your Grace,' the boy said calmly. 'How the mighty have fallen.'

'What's happening?' Tito replied. 'What are you doing here?'

'Could the situation be any more ironic? We are caught up within an insurance claim and the man who started the ball rolling lies oblivious to the whole affair.'

'Insurance? But we'll be blown to kingdom come!'

'You catch on quickly, El Comedin.'

Tito frowned at the insult and raised his hand as if to strike the boy, but the expression on Cheech's face froze him to the quick. He lowered his hand.

'A wise decision, Mr Majagranzas. Come, we need to get out of here.'

They walked out onto the landing where they encountered Katrina and Kelly.

'Finally making yourself useful, El Comedin?'

Katrina's words were sarcastic but her inflection revealed an admiration for having taken the children into his care.

'Please, don't use that name,' Tito pleaded, fearful that the residents would turn on him before Eleanor's men had the chance to break in and have him decapitated.

Katrina blocked the stairwell. 'Not down, we need to go up.' She rushed into the dormitory and retrieved her coat. As she did so she remembered something her father had once said to her:

In order for gold to be purified it must come through the refiner's fire. It must be beaten out on the hot plates and suffer flames of obscene temperatures. But when it has come through the refining process it shines exquisitely, even though it is surrounded by embers and charred impurity. Only now is it ready to ascend to its true purpose in life.

How that patronizing little speech had burnt, tugged and needled at her pride as she stood clueless and penniless in a hotel reception, and yet now she could recall every single word.

5.25 am

A sultry look was all it took to cease the gunfire. Eleanor handed her megaphone to the nearest man, a sergeant with sunken eyes.

'That should get the message across. Ask them to come out. Tell them they won't be harmed. See who's daft enough to believe me.' She winked in exhilaration at her own wickedness.

The sergeant was so sickened that for a moment he considered turning the gun on his superior, but then he asked himself who would take care of his family when the other soldiers retaliated. In a heartbeat he decided that he was willing to live with a murderer's guilt if it meant seeing his wife and children again.

But then the women started to come out, their arms clasped tight around the fragile frames within their care.

The sergeant stepped back and threw up on his shoes.

'*Really*, my boy, a soldier should show more grit.'

That was when the sergeant knew – he would live and die all at once. To know Eleanor's sickened mind was to search out the cruelest path in any given situation. She would spare him a swift exit from this world, but would instead select a victim from the crowd and make him fire the first shot.

As the women drew nearer, each step a painful plea for mercy, Eleanor played with the buttons on her low-cut blouse. Slowly and terribly an arm stretched out in front of her, a hand lifted, and a dagger-shaped fingernail stabbed at the cold air.

'*That one.*'

5.27 am

The sound was like coins in a vacuum cleaner, or packing paper popping between furtive fingers. Beneath him Kelly watched in horror as the thick wooden beams shredded and splayed out jagged splinters before concertinaing in on themselves. He clutched his shoulder and drove on upwards.

At the next landing there was a window. Kelly looked down into the alleyway. The site of tiny bodies jigging up and down as if electricity were passing through them fused his eyes to the glass. Even his hardened heart jarred at what he saw.

The words 'atrocity' and 'horror' were conceived for moments such as these.

'Don't let the little ones see this,' he called back down the stairs.

The children instinctively ran to see what it was they were missing out on.

'ESPERANZA!' Kelly screamed, his eyes bulging in their sockets. She lunged forward and pulled them back from the pane, covering their faces.

'You'd do well to spare yourself the nightmares.'

Katrina found herself putting immense trust in him. She reasoned that for Kelly to have found his conscience the spectacle must be unthinkable. She summoned all of her willpower and passed by without looking.

Tito was not so fortunate. He turned, and looked, and was lost. It was like gazing upon Medusa's glare, his flesh turning to stone. He saw Eleanor hiking up her skirt on the pretext of checking her stockings, giving a tantalizing glimpse of flesh to her men, their faces consumed with bloodlust.

Eleanor looked up, as if sensing him. She grinned from ear to ear. Words formed on her lips. Tito felt as if his heart would explode in his chest.

'My, my Tito, you really are El Comedin! You've certainly put a smile on this girl's face.'

The dog was still asleep in its basket. Kelly gave it a sharp kick in the ribs as he passed. It yelped and then snarled. Kelly snarled back.

'Are you going to sleep through your own death?'

Suddenly overcome by the myriad of noises the dog started to spin around in tight circles, chasing its tail and whimpering.

Circles . . . always circles.

In the attic they found the young girl, still rasping and gargling in her bed, oblivious to the events around her.

'We have to help,' Katrina said.

'By doing *what?*' Kelly scolded, closing down the conversation and turning his back.

'Oh *mi Dios*,' Tito sobbed. 'We're trapped.'

Kelly surveyed the faces of the children. The girl was overcome, shrivelled and withered like autumn, but the boy had vibrant eyes that darted from left to right.

'Try and dislodge the tiles.'

Cheech obeyed without question. He scrambled up onto the empty bed vacated by Kelly and pulled furiously at the ceramic slabs above him. The building was ancient and the tiles came away with joyous ease, but the emerging hole was still too high to climb through, especially with Kelly's injury. As with most things the answer presented itself with brutal simplicity. He turned to Katrina.

'What's the greater good?'

'I don't understand.'

'I need you to help me do something morally questionable.'

He didn't need to explain further. She understood perfectly. 'Desperate times—'

'Exactly.'

She acted quickly, fearing the onset of a debilitating paralysis that would prevent her doing what must be done. She went to the bedside of the unconscious girl, her eyes already blinded by tears. 'I'm sorry,' she whispered, and then to Tito, 'Can you take the other side?'

Tito stepped forward and gathered up the girl's feet in the blanket so that together they lifted her off the bed in a makeshift papoose and laid her out on the floor, still growling through gravelly lungs, blissfully unaware of her abandonment.

They placed one bed on top of the other, leaving a slight overhang that served as a step. Tito went first. Katrina lifted the little girl into his arms and then followed suit. Cheech went next, and finally Kelly. As he did so thick globules of blood dropped from his shirt onto the attic floor.

Together they made their way precariously along the rooftop and onto a metal walkway that descended to the adjacent street. Paolo's dirty white van was parked directly beneath. When Katrina opened the door Kelly got a shock. Staring back at him was the sofa he had stolen from El Rey.

'We were trying to dispose of it when he was black-sedaned,' Katrina explained.

Kelly shook his head.

It has come back to me.

Circles.

Tito and the children climbed into the back and crouched on the sofa's aubergine cushions. The buildings amplified and distorted the sound of gunfire so that it appeared to come from all sides.

Katrina got behind the wheel. 'Where are we going?'

'I don't know,' Kelly replied. 'For now, just drive.'

6:30 am

The taxi dropped them by the river. Carlos walked off ahead. Isabella could clearly see a nervous pulse running the length of his body. They were drawing near to something significant, she felt certain of it, but was still none the wiser.

They passed buildings that had not been inhabited in years. Emaciated-looking cats and dogs crawled amidst the skeletal frameworks. Save for the flowing water there was no sound.

'Where are we going?' Isabella asked.

Carlos pointed up ahead to where the river forked in two. 'Just there, not far now.'

'And what will we find there?'

'In truth, I'm not sure . . . perhaps the answer.'

'*The* answer?'

'Yes.'

Carlos gave no further elaboration.

A few minutes later they reached the fork. Carlos tuned away from the water and headed over a patch of scrubland. At the far side stood what had once been a house. Its outer walls were like swish cheese, riddled with tiny pockmarks. The windows had long since rotted away and there was no visible means of entry.

'Do you recognize anything about this place?' Carlos asked. There seems to be great importance attached to the question.

'No.'

He sat down in the dirt.

'What are you doing?'

'Waiting.'

'For what?'

'For you to remember something.'

'But we've already established that I don't.'

'You will.'

Isabella trod carefully, weary of sparking another outburst. 'Carlos, I'm finding your whole approach this morning deeply unnerving.'

He turned to her and nodded as if in sympathy for her predicament. 'Hopefully the end will justify the means.'

7.11 am

The streets were more hostile than ever. Katrina tried to drive as casually as possible but her passenger was beginning to draw looks from the passer-bys.

'I've got to put something together,' Kelly soliloquized.

'For all of us?'

'Of course . . . I'm losing a lot of blood here. You're going to have to change the dressing.'

'With what?'

'I don't know – improvise.'

Katrina pulled off the road and into a car park. She tapped the dashboard.

'We're low on petrol.'

'*Fantastic!*'

'We passed a row of shops a moment ago. Maybe I can pick up some fuel and bandages.'

'OK, but be quick. We can't afford to stay too long in one place.'

'Do you think any of the others made it out?'

'No.'

'Come on.'

'You asked my opinion, that's it. They all died, every single one.'

'Where does that leave us?'

'We're going to have to get the van resprayed . . . number plates . . .

passports. I guess you're going to have to be my—' Kelly stopped shy of saying 'wife'. 'As for the kids . . . the girl looks European . . . we can probably pass her off as our daughter. The boy's too Latin-looking – it'd be too suspicious. I don't know . . . the bald guy could pose as an uncle or grandfather. Either way it needs to be quick . . . within the next twenty-four hours.'

'And then what?'

'And then *nothing*! We get across the border, we go our separate ways.'

'You can't just leave us like that?'

'Phone Daddy – get him to send his private jet.'

'That's unfair.'

'I'm sorry, force of habit.'

Katrina got out of the van and walked back to the main road. Most of the shops were derelict. Only two were open. Moving inside she found that they had been knocked through to create a single hotchpotch of unrelated items. Groceries lined one side of the room, electrical goods the other, books and clothing at the centre. The shopkeeper siphoned petrol into a can from a large metal barrel at the back. There were no bandages.

Outside all was calm. There were nineteen minutes left until the end of the curfew.

All of the people who had been her salvation over the past three months were dead.

Paolo was right. This is bigger than me. I cannot change the world by myself.

It is not cowardice to return home.

You can find a less hazardous means of fulfilment.

Her losses brought the gains into sharp focus. The fresh morning air had never tasted so good.

'Miss?'

Katrina turned. Two men were stepping from a black sedan.

You have been through the refiner's fire. You are gold.

She didn't feel afraid as others did. It wasn't that she didn't understand the ramifications of the situation. She simply could no longer fear something so pathetic. Katrina tried to see beyond their dark glasses and vacant expressions but found nothing.

You are following in Paolo's footsteps.

You are defending the lives of children.

Kelly will *rise above himself and make the right decision. I* know *it.*

The thoughts brought her immense comfort. Katrina found a poise and elegance previously absent. She rose higher on the balls of her feet, straightened her back and swept loose hair from her face.

'Yes gentlemen. What can I do for you?'

'Would you come with us, please?'

They drew nearer. Katrina noticed that one of them walked with a limp.

'I could look at that leg for you if you'd like? I have medical experience.'

'No thank you. Please come with us.'

'Do I have a choice?'

'No.'

'Then why offer me one?'

No response.

'Why take me to a dark dungeon when you can execute me nice and cleanly here and now?'

'Please do not make a scene.'

The petrol.

She remembered something Paolo's had said to her about little victories.

Kelly will come looking for you.

Ever so slowly she knelt down, placed the petrol on the ground and stood back up. 'Won't need this where I'm going, will I?'

No response.

'Oh gentlemen–' she shook her head '–you truly are lower than the dirt.'

'Miss?'

This time from behind.

She was turning.

Something heavy struck her in the face.

Katrina saw no more.

7.36 am

With great difficulty Kelly got out of the van.

For crying out loud! How long does it take to get a can of petrol?

He found it where she had left it, lying in the middle of the pavement. It could mean only one thing. As with Paolo's passing the grief mixed uncomfortably with the animosity.

In life I never said a kind word to either of you.

In another world we could have all been friends.

Kelly sat down on the curb and wept . . . for Katrina, for Paolo, for his wife and children, for everything.

8.04 am

He drove the van to El Sacramento. Alfonso sat as always behind the remnants of his disintegrating reception desk playing with a garish cravat.

'Ah Slim, good to see you.'

The acronym had never bothered him before, but now he hated it.

'What delights do you have for me today?'

'Nothing to trade. Today I need a big favour.'

'Oh?'

'I need to stow this van for a few hours.'

'This is big?

'Every black sedan in Corderro will be looking for it.'

'I see. You have finally found your infamy?'

'Something like that.'

'My condolences. Would you like the El Sacramento special?'

Kelly had called upon this service on many occasions – respray, number plates, bodywork. 'I'm afraid I don't have any money.'

'In that case, for you I will make it free of charge.'

'That's very kind of you. I appreciate it.'

'We have not been in the business of kindness or appreciation you and I.'

'No.'

'Something tells me you are going away, Slim.'

'I . . . I just don't know, Alfonso.'

The hotelier had never seen the smuggler anything other than self-assured.

'Have you been to Damascus?'

'I don't follow.'

'That look in your face – the Road to Damascus – Have you seen God?'

'No Alfonso, quite the opposite in fact.'

Standing up added little to Alfonso's overall height. He yelped orders and several men appeared. They removed padlocks and opened doors.

'Give me the keys. One of my slaves will stow the vehicle for you.'

Kelly felt reluctance at handing them over, as if he were discharging responsibility. There was always the risk that he wouldn't come back, either by choice or by bad luck. 'There's one more thing . . . before you respray . . . empty the back . . . there are people inside.'

Alfonso's face lit up, and a broad smile spread from ear to ear. 'Aha, you *have* been to Damascus! For you I think everything will be just fine.'

'I'm afraid I don't follow you're logic, but thanks anyway.'

They shook hands. The keys dropped in the hotelier's lap.

'With all the money we made together why did you never get that roof fixed?'

The hotelier shrugged. 'I just never got round to it.'

10.08 am

What are your intentions?

Café Impressario was virtually empty. Kelly wasn't sure why he had come.

You need to send Arty on his way.

That's rage talking. You need him for a passport.

Then do both.

Kelly thought of his brother.

My only aim.

Not any more – the children.

He took the pages of 'Thirty-eight' from his pocket and scrawled: *'I am sending you this manuscript so that you may, in time, come to regard me in a more favourable light.'*

Kelly looked around. A policeman had sat down at the table next to them. A burly man was at the back washing dishes.

'Café con leche,' Kelly requested. The burly man nodded his ascent.

'It has been left anonymous for three reasons. Firstly, in order to inject some much-needed suspense into the proceedings, secondly, so that by the time realization dawns you might have become sufficiently enraptured with my account so as not to torch it, but thirdly and most importantly, because I am *anonymous. I am a non-person, deconstructed and scattered. I no longer know what I was, let alone what I've become.'*

The coffee arrived.

'*Gracias.*'

341

Behind the burly man Kelly could see Ernesto cleaning tables.

'I hope these words find you both well. As for me, I have the sensation that I might be on the cusp of my defining moment. Then again I might be on the brink of extinction.'

As if to mark the insanity, the building opposite exploded.

10.28 am

Kelly drove the blue van up out of the cellar and into the courtyard of El Sacramento. Arty could still be heard in the street arguing with a taxi driver.

'Is that the informer?' Alfonso inquired.

'*Si*,' Kelly replied wearily.

'You know, I could have one of my men go out and shoot him in the back of the head?'

The smuggler smiled. 'I'd like that, but unfortunately I need him for a higher purpose.'

Alfonso shrugged. 'Pity, but I have always trusted your judgment, Slim. I will trust it now and leave him to the dogs.'

Kelly could not hide his obvious discomfort as he leaned out of the window and watched Alfonso's men running up and down stairwells and corridors trailing leads and wires in their wake.

'You are wounded,' the hotelier stated.

'I'll live.'

Alfonso's eyes narrowed. 'You should get a second opinion.'

'What are they doing?' Kelly asked changing the subject and pointing towards a large untidy pile of dynamite.

'Well, a lot has changed in the last two hours. My idea of reopening the hotel was not a good one. The inspectors came back for a surprise second visit just now. I pulled out every trick in my considerable arsenal, but they did not look convinced . . . and so I am faking my own death.'

Kelly turned off the engine. 'Go on, I have a few minutes. Enlighten me with the details.'

'Like all great ideas it is blissfully simple. I got the idea from that clown El Comedin. Apparently he is useful for something after all!'

Cramped within the confines of the van, Tito winced.

'The hotel explodes – my wife is conveniently out shopping – oh the anguish – that *poor* woman. How will she cope now that her raison d'etre has gone? But wait, an investigation points to water on the electrics, a fire and a build-up of gas. Whilst no amount of money can ever replace her husband, she can take some solace from knowing that an insurance claim will make her stinking rich – so much money – what to do with it? – "I know," she thinks, 'I shall buy a yacht and venture round the world – leave all the heartache and misery behind. She leaves port, and *behold*! A stow-away emerges from the lower decks – the end.'

'Genius!'

'I know. Stick around, we are just about ready.'

'You're joking.'

'Do I look like I'm joking? Retreat to a safe distance.'

10.57 am

Alfonso insisted on depressing the plunger himself.

'That looks like an awful lot of dynamite,' Kelly commented from across the street. 'And not too strategically placed in my humble opinion.'

'Really,' Alfonso replied, 'and what would a smuggler know about demolition?'

'Apparently nothing.'

'Exactly! So watch and learn.'

Kelly tapped the back of his seat lightly. 'There's going to be a loud bang,' he whispered. 'It's nothing to be afraid of.'

Looking out for the well-being of others was almost as painful as the wound in his chest. He didn't like investing emotions in people, especially when their futures were so precariously balanced.

11.01 am

The main force of the blast was directed upwards, out through the path of least resistance – the roofless opening – and into the late morning sky.

The flaming column and exploding glass made El Sacramento look like a fiery headdress or a chandelier refracting light. Thick plumes of smoke groped and rolled their way into the surrounding alleyways, and a rumbling aftermath could be felt underfoot.

Once the initial boom had subsided Alfonso's men could be heard whooping and hollering. As the dust settled and the smoke cleared it became evident that the hotel had survived relatively unscathed.

Their laughter stopped abruptly.

'Hey, what are the chances?' Kelly called to the distraught Alfonso.

The hotelier ignored the snipe. 'You incompetent bunch of imbeciles!'

'My condolences to the widow,' the smuggler added.

He drove away.

11.38 am

Kelly's mind drifted at the traffic lights. The world temporarily became kaleidoscopic. He looked up and saw a huge photo of Tito grimacing down at him from a bridge.

'Hey! You're famous,' Kelly slurred.

Behind him something whimpered pathetically.

12.01 pm

Ernesto met him behind the plaza as agreed. He was shocked at how rapidly Kelly's health had declined in the few hours since they'd last met.

'Have you heard?' the smuggler grunted.

'Heard what?'

Kelly's head dropped even lower. 'Eleanor hit the Satellite building this morning. They're all dead. We are all that remains.' He couldn't see the waiter's face, but imagined the effect his words were having.

'*We?*'

'Myself and a few stragglers in the back.'

'Katrina?'

'No.'

'You are taking them out of the city?'

'Yes.'

'What can I do to help?'

Kelly coughed and saw flecks of blood patter his legs. 'I need you to steal a few things for me.'

3.02 pm

'You're two hours late!' Arty screamed into the phone. Eleanor's men looked up from their coffees.

'Have you got the passport?' Kelly's tinny voice inquired.

'Does the Pope shit in the woods? Of course I have, but it was not easy, especially given your state of infamy. I am thinking that we should renegotiate.'

'Fine,' Kelly replied. 'Shall we say double?'

'How would sir like to pay?'

'In contraband as per usual. '

'Triple!'

'Deal, but this is conditional upon you coming to me.'

'Don't give me the runaround, Slim. This is not what we agreed.' There was apprehension in Arty's voice.

'Nor was tripling the price, but then life's full of small challenges, like how to meet in a coffee house when it's swarming with soldiers.'

'Come to the back door.'

'I am thinking that we should renegotiate. Meet me at five o'clock, the northern coastal road. Two miles past the last factory building there's a track into the hills. I'll be at the top in a clearing.'

'You are not in a particularly strong bargaining position, Slim. I think I will wait here'

'Get off your fat ass now.'

'I can't leave paying customers.'

'I thought you said their money was worthless.'

'These customers won't take kindly to my leaving, if you get my meaning.'

'I've done a lot for you over the years, Arty. I expect you to reciprocate.'

'Your motives were selfish. You have done well from our little arrangements.'

'Be that as it may, you *will* meet me. If I have to come to you then it will not be to negotiate.'

'Are you threatening me?'

'*Absolutely!* See you at five.'

Click.

3.04 pm

Arty put down the receiver and immediately snatched it back up again. The number was known off by heart. His fat fingers stabbed at the digits, his breathing laboured as it always was on such occasions.

Eleanor answered.

He spoke slowly and clearly, abandoning his usual flippancy, and giving as much detail as he could remember. There was a period of silence as Eleanor mulled over what had been relayed to her.

'Wait with my men. I will pick you up in one hour.'

'*Me?* I don't need to—'

The line was already dead.

4.04 pm

Exactly one hour later she glided into Arty's coffee house. The whole room changed around her. Civilians drank up and left. Her soldiers stood awkwardly to attention

'Arthur, I swear you get fatter by the day.'

She turned slowly, making sure she had the undivided attention of every man present. They laughed in formulaic unison. Arty looked down without response and played with his braces.

'Well *come on*, lead the way. The sooner we get this over with the sooner I can get back to sunbathing. There's a good three hours of rays left if we hurry.'

Arty was petrified. He knew that people suspected him of collaboration, but it had never been so publicly advertised. It didn't bode well for his future prospects. 'Yes . . . yes of course . . . my apologies. Actually I was thinking that I could give directions to one of your—'

'Don't try my patience, Arthur.'

'No . . . sorry.'

Eleanor walked catlike to the door. Her soldiers filed in behind.

The Plaza d'Armas was packed with people clearing rubble from the morning's explosion. Dozens of bodies lay hidden beneath coats. The living stopped their searching to watch Eleanor pass by. She smiled and wrapped their scorn around her like a warm glow.

Don't blame me, she thought, *blame Tito*.

Reluctantly Arty followed her into the plaza. His reaction was not so graceful and detached.

'Someone has stolen my van!' he shouted. 'I parked it right here.'

'*Really* Arthur, such insensitivity, so much death and destruction all around, and you concern yourself with an automobile. You have to be more careful in this city. There are many unscrupulous characters walking the streets.' Eleanor threw back her head and laughed, her hands cupped as if she were humbly accepting a standing ovation. 'You are an exceptional rat, Arthur. You go to extraordinary lengths to stoop your lowest. I admire that in a man, but do not presume to pull the wool over my eyes. Vehicle or no vehicle, you *are* coming with me.'

'I . . . I wasn't trying to . . . someone really has stolen my—'

'Of *course* they have. You will ride with my men. There will be no further delays.'

4.26 pm

Ernesto parked up in the clearing and switched off the engine. Kelly reached into the glove compartment and took out his revolver.

'Ever fired one of those?' the waiter asked.

'A few times.'

'I don't even want to know.'

'Then don't ask. hopefully I won't have to use it.'

'Hope? It seems you have learnt a new word, Slim.'

'Funny. Let's do this.'

4.44 pm

The convoy sped through the city streets, sirens blazing, with men hanging from the cabins barking orders at pedestrians to get out of their way. They hit the coastal road as the day was turning at its edges, beginning its slow creep into evening.

Two miles past the final factory a narrow track branched off into the hills just as Kelly said it would. Eleanor spoke into the radio so that everyone could hear her one-sided conversation.

'Arthur, the information you have provided has led to the deaths of many men. I would very much like you to see first hand the fruits of your labour.'

Her men laughed. Arty remained silent.

The road snaked around treacherous drops and beneath the roots of overhanging trees. The café owner felt sick to the stomach. Over the years he had spent many hours with the smuggler, and while it could not be said that a bond had formed between the two men, Arty had the premonition that witnessing Kelly's demise would bring an abrupt end to his cozy little world.

They roared into the clearing. A blue van was parked at its centre. It was quickly surrounded.

'Mr Kelly,' Eleanor greeted them. 'Whilst I have immensely enjoyed our little chase, it is the end of the road for you. Come out with your arms raised and I will grant you a swift death.'

There was no response from the vehicle.

'Very well, have it your way.' Eleanor gave a signal and the van was peppered with bullets. She ordered several of the men to approach with caution and retrieve the body. They opened the driver's door and exchanged bemused glances. One of them reached into the vehicle and fished out a scrap of paper from amongst the shattered glass and shredded fabric. It was handed to Eleanor. Upon reading the note she burst out laughing and handed it to Arty.

> Arty,
>   *The kids are safe – all thanks to you.*
>   *I am forever in your debt.*
>   *Slim*

'This is trickery,' he shrieked

'Come, come Arthur,' Eleanor whispered seductively, 'you led us here, the children are elsewhere. It was very noble of you.' Her voice was steeped in irony.

'He . . . he knew I'd do this . . . he set me up.'

Eleanor giggled deliciously. 'Yes he did, didn't he! And what does that make you, poor, *poor* Arthur?' She looked over his shoulder and gestured to someone behind him. Arty spun around on his considerable frame. There was no one there. He caught the words 'You're so blind you couldn't—' before a bullet shattered the back of his head.

'See the nose in front of your fat face?' Eleanor finished. 'So much for the informer! Will someone please remove this eyesore from my sight?'

They gathered around and rolled Arty's bloated body into a ditch.

5.51 pm

'*Hey!*'

Ernesto slapped him hard in the face. Kelly's eyes rolled forward. 'Sorry, I must have tuned out there for a moment.'

'Arty probably passed away as you slept.'

'My heart quite literally bleeds.'

They drove in silence for a little while. The road rose up into the hills. With every second their chances increased.

'My wife had red hair just like Katrina's . . . same style too . . . I think that's why I gave her such a hard time . . . too many memories.'

Ernesto looked across and saw that Kelly's eyes were closed. 'Hey, who are you talking to?'

'We'd been down the road before . . . winter time . . . we were coming back from the zoo . . . a car . . .' Kelly started to sob. 'A car came and . . . washed them all away.'

'Kelly?'

He opened his eyes. Everywhere he looked he saw circles – the arch of islands completing a crescent moon coast-line, the distribution of buildings, swirls of smoke.

Pupils and iris and cornea . . . circles and circles and circles.

He thought of his wife.

Of Katrina.

Of his two children.

Of the two children hidden behind him.

The vicious circle . . . repetition . . . I've lost my wife . . . twice . . . and now I am going to lose the children all over again.

There was some universal truth to be gleaned, Kelly was sure of it, but his mind flooded and fogged so that he couldn't join the dots. He desperately tried to find sobriety amidst the whirl of unsettling angst.

You can't let this happen.

It was the closest he ever came to an epiphany. There was no chorus of angelic hosts, no celestial choirs, just his own voice, spoken clearer than any thought he'd ever experienced before.

You've had your chance. Give it to someone else.

He recalled Arty's words, spoken mere hours before: 'Bit late to be searching for a sense of purpose, wouldn't you say?'

Yes, but Arty's dead. His opinion counts for nothing.

Better late than never?

Corderro watches its players closely. You cannot realistically hope to break away.

Then what is this, a resignation to fate?

Fate is bullshit. There's no grand curse. Life's what you make of it.

And what have you made of it?

'Stop the van.'

'Why?'

I don't know.

'I want to get out.'

'They'll catch us up.'

'It's precisely because they'll catch us up that I want you to stop.'

'That makes no sense whatsoever.'

'Just do it.'

Ernesto pulled over. Through a gap in the trees Kelly could see a convoy of trucks.

'They're a mile away . . . maybe less.'

'So why have I stopped?'

'I'm going to stay here.'

'What are you talking about?' Ernesto replied.

'I'm a pragmatic man. It's a simple case of mathematics.'

'What?'

'I won't be long.'

He got out before Ernesto could protest further and walked around to the back of the van. It was only as he opened the back door that the plan fully solidified in his mind.

The last time he had spoken to a child was many years ago as he lay pinned against his dead wife in the wreckage of their car. The weight of the moment should have frozen the words in his throat, but instead he found them flowing effortlessly.

'Hello beautiful. How are you?'

The girl tugged at her mousey brown hair and regarded him from sullen eyes. 'Frightened.'

'It's OK to be frightened,' Kelly replied with the quiet, assured tone of a father. 'Is this your boyfriend?' He intimated towards the other child.

'No,' the girl giggled, suddenly animated.

'I bet he is.'

'Isn't.'

'Can you be brave for me?'

'I'll try.'

'That's a good girl. What's your name?'

'Isabella.'

'Pleased to meet you Isabella, my name is . . .'

Not Kelly . . . not Slim . . . not the anonymity of Corderro.

It had been so long since he'd used his real name that it took a moment to summon it from the recesses of his mind.

'Jonathan . . . my name is Jonathan . . . Pemberton.'

'Hello Jonathan.'

'Hello back. Listen carefully, this is important. Open your hand.'

Isabella did as she was asked. Kelly took a key chain from around his neck and dropped it into her palm.

'This key opens a safe-deposit box in London, England. The name of the bank is Satchwells. The number is 4543. Can you remember that?'

Isabella stared up wide-eyed. 'Satchwells. 4543.'

'That's a good girl. Take what you find there and make something of your life. Do this and you will have redeemed me.'

He turned his attention to the boy. 'And you?'

'My nickname is Cheech,' the boy replied.

'Pleased to meet you, Cheech.'

Kelly handed him the pages of 'Thirty-eight'.

'This is my sorry story. Read it and learn from my mistakes.'

'Thank you,' Cheech replied. 'Are you coming with us?'

'I can't.'

'Is Esperanza?'

'I'm sorry, she can't either.'

Lastly he regarded the forlorn and lacerated man.

'El Comedin, if you even think of trying to rob them of their gifts, I shall have my friend here slit your throat.'

Desensitized from the endless scorn and abuse all Tito could do was smile. 'For what it's worth – thank you.'

'Don't mention it.'

There was no time for anything more poignant. He closed the door and returned to Ernesto.

'Your name's Jonathan?'

The smuggler closed his eyes and smiled. 'Yes, it is.'

'Why *Kelly*?'

'It was my wife's name. I liked to hear it spoken out loud.'

'And we all chose to call you *Slim*!'

'Yes.'

'There is an ocean of truth you and I will never learn from each other.'

'That's the way it goes. Life has been pitted squarely against me from day one. It has grown weary. For what it's worth, I think I understand what it was you were all trying to do. I would like to help in whatever capacity I have left.'

'For you to say a thing like that is no small miracle.'

'See you in the next life.'

Ernesto gave him a wry smile. 'You just might.'

'Ernesto? Strange name for a getaway driver.'

The two men shook hands.

'Is good enough for Che Guevara, is good enough for me.'

6.02 pm

The soldier had over twenty years of driving experience, but the presence of Eleanor in the passenger's seat sucked all of the confidence out of him. He stalled several times, missed a few obvious gear changes and broke so late on a particularly sharp bend that three of his colleagues fell off the back.

'I take it you've passed you test?' she inquired casually, fixing him with her bottomless eyes.

'Yes Ms Blake, my humble apologies.'

He looked straight ahead. Eleanor continued to stare. She blinked slowly, eyebrows heaped with mascara dropping and rising like a portcullis.

'That's *quite* alright. Maybe we could have a few less surprises for the remainder of the journey.'

Her words were phrased as a question. The soldier wasn't sure if he was required to answer. It was implied that he had some choice in the matter, but he knew better than to act upon his own initiative. He opted for subtly changing the subject. 'Shall I go back for them, ma'am?'

'And give up the chase? Certainly not! Let them walk back to the city if they have legs to bare them.'

The soldier glanced in the wing mirror. The men did not look capable of walking back.

Eleanor closed her eyes and concentrated on the only thought worthy of contemplation – the melting pot.

She believed that she knew its secret.

Balance.

It wasn't a vicious circle as the scare mongers and paranoid purported. It was simply a status quo. The city gave, the city took away; nothing more, nothing less. The secret was not to go too deep into the red, and to periodically appease the city's appetite with acts of servitude – penance – contrition – call them what you will.

She enjoyed a position of power, the respect and fear of her men and the joy of fulfilling her violent nature, but for that she had to bare continual and agonizing heartache, her soul mate dead at Emile 'El Rey' Verdin's hand.

Her lover thought that she was blind to this fact. No doubt a similar fate awaited her once the Emperor had finished using her up. Why then give over her body to be consumed? Why lie in naked intimacy each night with the cause of your undoing?

Balance.

No one could imagine ways of suffering like she could. In the months since her nepotistic appointment Eleanor had unleashed a barrage of her more insidious inceptions upon the inhabitants of Corderro. She had scraped and hacked, ripped and snapped her way through muscle and bone, and broken the resolve of even the strongest men and women.

Debt.

But the most exquisite and malicious of her devises she held back, cherished and reserved for Emile alone. They were written up for posterity in a diary she kept in plain site at all times. They brought her immense joy and security, even though she would never dream of using them.

Credit.

She slept with many men. None ever saw the morning to brag of their conquest.

Debt.

She was perpetually and irreconcilably heart-broken.

Credit.

El Rey was Corderro's most glittering prize. She could see that, even if no one else had fathomed it. The Emperor had dug deep into the coffers and bled them dry. Nothing had been given back in return. He was ripe for the picking and Eleanor felt the pulsing surge of expectancy. It would be soon and she knew better than to stand in destiny's way. It couldn't be hindered, but it could be helped, and so she'd held the viper to her breast and let it sink its fangs into her flesh, each venomous gulp dragging it deeper and deeper into arrears. When Eleanor gave of herself she gave everything.

My credit.

And El Rey took it all.

His debt.

It was that simple.

Her thoughts turned towards Kelly. It was a rare occurrence for someone to give her the slip. Such men were invaluable. Once again Eleanor felt the demented delights of a worthy adversary. She had instructed her men to take him alive. Together they would have tearing times in the dark beneath the palace, and then, afterwards, she would shower, walk naked to Emile's chamber and give him the best sex he'd ever had.

The vehicle jarred awkwardly. She looked up from her daze, intent on slicing the driver's jugular with her fingernails. A tall, haggard-looking man was standing in the road. Eleanor barely had time to register the weapon in his hand before the shots rang out.

6.05 pm

Kelly fired twice. The first shot passed through the woman's right eye. The second took off the driver's left ear. The truck veered into a ditch. Two more trucks pulled up behind it. Men leapt for cover. Kelly held the revolver straight and pulled the trigger until the chamber was empty. Before the soldiers returned fire he ran into the undergrowth.

Half a mile away Ernesto heard the shots. His grip tightened on the steering wheel and he screamed until his lungs were empty. Behind him Isabella clutched the key tightly to her chest. Cheech knelt facing the back window. He shuddered at what he saw.

7.01 pm

Father Medici gathered up all of his worldly belongings into a small tote bag and said goodbye to the room that had been his home for the past five years. On the far wall above a washbasin the priest regarded a cross-shaped mark where a crucifix had once hung guarding against the stains of time. It felt ominous, a vacuum left by the absence of holiness.

Something good and true died here.

He walked the short distance to El Puerto de Las Ondas Verdes, head bowed, his cassock scraping along the ground.

Since the day that Eleanor Blake had spared his life on the concourse, Father Medici had been unable to reconcile his faith in a God of unconditional love and grace with the horrors that had been witnessed. He was a humble man, not prone to arrogant or conceited thoughts. Considering the possibility that his meager intellect couldn't comprehend the logic and reason behind such senseless lunacy he prayed for wisdom, for the forgiveness of his sins, for the removal of hatred from his heart, and for the vanquishing of crushing emptiness, but in doing so he had found his prayers blocked by piercing headaches. Passages of scripture that usually brought him joy and inspiration closed themselves to understanding, locking away their revelations and providing no comfort. He went about his duties in a delusional daze, reading his sermons by rote, speaking endless 'Our Father's' with monotone delivery, placing his hands on the foreheads of children, the sick and the old alike, and whispering blessings with a detached voice, his mind wondering dark roads elsewhere.

Dear Lord, grant me a miracle.

It had been an electric thought, echoing and resounding with ever-deepening clarity as he'd approached the soldiers, sensing his own demise, his eyes on fire.

This is what it's all about. Fear no evil. Face down every hardship.

Death had seen no point in taking him.

He had begged for divine intervention but instead stood helpless as hundreds of people were needlessly buried within their own tumbling homes. There could be no rationale behind such an action and no searching for a greater good. He had tried to find one none the less.

Maybe the miracle was that I myself was saved?

What possible good could I do now? My hope is gone, my resolve broken like wood splintering beneath a hammer.

Life as a Christian had never been easy, but it had been simple. Some things were good, others were bad. Put God and your neighbour before yourself, and try and do what was right. But now even that pillar was compromised and crumbling. He had always considered the most precious of all things to be the sanctity and preservation of human life, but Eleanor had shown him that the preservation of *his* life was a punishment. Nothing made sense.

Medici could no longer wear the title of 'father', and couldn't seem to hear his saviour's voice. Each waking moment was a curse, but at the same time he feared the mortal sin of suicide. *The Vicious Circle* had ensnared him, dementedly spun him round, stripped him of his purpose, and was now spitting him out.

The boat that waited for him on the quay dwarfed every other vessel there. Its ridiculous name, '*Míreme son Masivo*' ('Look, I'm Massive'), failed to solicit a smile from the clergyman.

A van pulled up alongside him.

Medici fumbled around in the course hessian pockets of his garments for the ticket. It had broken his heart to ask for financial aid from the chaplaincy. They had so little money as it was and the funds could be deployed a thousand times better on any number of more worthy causes.

But I have to get out of here. I can't find peace in this place.

He heard something, a sound that shouldn't have been there. It broke through his self-pitying shell, revealing the world around him as if for the first time. There was the roar of engines – cars, trucks, cranes – the clatter of chains, dock workers shouting and swearing, and cutting through it all, a smaller, softer sound.

Medici looked around him – the endless lapping of water against the port walls, two guards checking rosters, one deep in conversation, the other looking down the ramp at the approaching passengers.

He became aware of the van crawling along by his side. His eyes were drawn to the driver's seat. The young man behind the wheel looked extremely nervous.

There it was again – *a sob* – and another sound – a *shhhh*.

There were people hiding in the van, *escaping*. Medici was sure of it.

One of the guards was approaching the vehicle, his suspicion clearly aroused by the wirey expression on the driver's face.

Dear Lord, grant me a miracle.

Why ask for divine intervention when God had given you the worldly power to act? After all, do evil men call upon Lucifer to grant them greater hatred in their lives? No, they simply act in isolation from God.

They succumb.

The driver turned and looked directly at the priest. Medici nodded. The driver held his stare for a moment, and then, with the look of intensity increasing, returned the gesture.

Medici finally received his revelation.

Lives to save for the lives that were lost.

I need a distraction, something with which to draw the guard's attention.

But what?

The priest stopped. Someone walked into the back of him. 'I'm sorry,' he stuttered seeing that a queue had formed behind him while he soliloquized.

Think of something.

Medici's calling had been to humble service, not inspirational leadership. He had never been a pulpit demonizer. The fire and brimstone aggression of Old Testament fury had never settled on his soul. If the meek were indeed to inherit the earth then Father Medici would certainly be at the front of the line.

His position was ludicrous!

He remembered the words of the red-headed women who had slapped him as he sat amidst the high-rise rubble: 'You are God's mouthpiece.

There is no higher office.'

'Get a move on, padre!' somebody shouted.

His mind was blank. He looked down at his feet.

There it is!

Without further thought he stepped off the curb.

'OWWWWWW!'

He hadn't meant to do himself a genuine injury, but as he put his body weight behind the stumble Father Medici heard something snap in his ankle.

That helps!

This time his screams weren't forced.

'My leg! MY LEG! Who put that there? I could sue, you know?'

Glorious gobbledegook came to him with sudden wondrous fluidity.

'I am an old man. Why are these steps so steep? OHHH . . . the pain. I may never walk again.' People were staring now. 'Will my shoes still fit me? Ohhh . . .' Some looked concerned, others were laughing. From the corner of his eye Father Medici saw one of the guards approaching the van.

'OHHH,' he called more loudly, 'A tap-dancing career in RUINS! Send my tuxedo back to the shop. I have no use for it now . . . OH MY LORD ,THE AGONY!'

The guard turned in his direction.

'As God is my witness . . . er . . . OHHH.' Fighting a sudden fit of giggles the priest rolled himself over so that he was sprawled out flat across one lane of the ramp, blocking traffic. The guard approached with his gun drawn. Medici grabbed at his legs.

'I could've been a figure skater if it wasn't for the tropical climate! OH MY WORD! THE PAIN!'

The guard was so accustomed to malice that he kicked out in reflex. His foot caught the priest on the chin.

Realizing his mistake he reached for his radio and asked for paramedics. Someone honked their horn. The queue of people and vehicles was getting longer by the second. Frustrated, the guard banged his fist down on the van's bonnet.

'Move along.'

Ernesto was waved though.

Continuing his façade of moaning and flouncing the priest leant forward ever so slightly and watched the van make its way safely into the hold. Paramedics arrived.

'Oh . . . that's better,' Medici sighed and feigned losing consciousness.

'Clumsy fool,' one of the medics commented.

'He weighs a ton,' the other remarked.

Father Medici didn't care. Inwardly he smiled. It was a small victory in the grand scheme of things, but a victory none the less. The paramedics continued to complain as they carried him through the port.

Let them do some good for once, and bare the weight of an old man.

Lying in the haze of evening he realized just how weary he had become and how badly he needed to sleep free from the feelings of constant guilt. Medici let it all go and felt himself instantly drifting. As he did so his sense of triumph was tempered by a final thought.

The city has prevented me from leaving.

10.51 pm

Carlos stirred her from sleep.

'What time is it?'

'A little before eleven.'

'We've been here for seventeen hours?'

'Yes.'

'Carlos, my patience is wearing thin.'

'I woke you because there's movement – *look*.'

Across the wasteland lights were on in the building. A four-by-four was parked outside, its engine still running.

'Who are they?' she asked.

'How should I know?' Carlos replied.

'How should *you* know? Because you've made me sit out here all day, that's how!'

Carlos ignored her and kept his attention on the four-by-four. Several people were unloading goods from its boot.

'Are you even listening to me?' Isabella demanded.

'No señorita, I am *watching*. You'd be well advised to do the same.'

The driver of the vehicle got out and shook hands with the others.

'I know that man.'

Isabella forgot about her hostility and squinted into the limited light. The man was tall and thin. Oversized clothes hung from his body. His face was gaunt and severe looking. A mass of grey hair hid his eyes.

'I think it might be Jonathan.'

Her heartbeat quickened.

'Isabella?' Carlos asked cautiously.

'Yes . . . it's him . . . *it's him!*'

'Isabella?'

She got up and started to run across the broken ground. Up ahead the man got back behind the wheel.

'Jonathan!' Isabella shouted. 'Jonathan!'

The man was out of earshot. The 4x4 pulled away, up onto the main road and away out of sight.

'No! Come back . . . come back.'

'Isabella.' Carlos caught up and wrapped her within his embrace. 'Hey, it's OK.'

'So close,' she sobbed. 'So close.'

'Let's go and ask after him. The people in that building must know something.'

Isabella dried her eyes. 'OK.'

The young woman who answered the door had Paolo's eyes. Carlos could see it. Isabella could not.

'Good evening,' she greeted them.

'Hello,' Isabella replied nervously. 'Sorry to trouble you at this hour . . . but could you tell me where Jonathan went?'

'Who?'

'Jonathan . . . the man who was here moments ago?'

'I'm afraid you're mistaken. No one of that name works here.'

'But I just saw him–' Isabella's voice rose both in pitch and urgency '–in a four-by-four outside!'

'You mean Ernesto?'

'*Ernesto?*'

Isabella felt herself being overcome with emotion. It was too much to journey so far only to endure disappointment after disappointment. She clutched her head.

'Are you OK?' the woman asked.

Carlos stepped from behind her and carried on the conversation. 'My friend is looking for someone from the past. We thought they might be here.'

'I understand. Many people passed through here at one time or another.'

'What is this place?' he inquired.

'It used to be called Satellite.'

'Yes . . . *Satellite,*' Isabella interrupted. 'I knew I recognized it. I've been here before . . . I'm sure of it . . . Jonathan was here too.'

'It has been empty for many years.'

'Where has he been all this time?'

The woman laughed at the absurdity of the question. 'I'm afraid I don't know. I only returned here a few days ago myself.'

Isabella looked distraught.

'Ernesto went out to pick up some supplies, but he'll be back later. Would you like to come in and wait for him?'

'That would be very kind of you,' Carlos replied giving Isabella a friendly push over the threshold. 'My friend is a little overwhelmed. Do you have somewhere for her to rest?'

Rather than find the request odd, the woman's face lit up. 'Absolutely, we are in the process of reopening as a hostel. There are many rooms upstairs.'

'I don't need sleep,' Isabella stamped obstinately. 'I need answers.'

'Calm down, *mi chica bella*. I will wake you the moment Ernesto arrives.'

She could not deny the fatigue that plagued her, nor the welcome thought of sleeping in a room free from Ronaldo's spy-holes.

'I am being rude. I'm sorry. Your offer is very kind. I *could* do with a lie down, maybe just for an hour or so.'

'Take whichever room you like,' the woman replied. 'There are blankets in the cupboards.'

'Thank you for your hospitality, Monica,' Carlos said.

The woman frowned. 'How do you know my name?'

'You are the spitting image of your father.'

Her frown turned to elation. 'You knew my *father!*'

Carlos grinned. 'Impressed?'

Halfway up the stairs Isabella rolled her eyes.

Chapter 30

Tito's Final Miscalculation

The man who opened the door had kind eyes and a warm smile, but the children could tell that he had been crying.

'Hello,' he said, kneeling so as to seem less imposing, 'My name is Ernesto. You are in the storage hold of a great big ship and you are safe. Do you understand?'

Both children nodded.

'I have to go back on land in a few minutes, but this man will look after you–' his glance brought Tito into the conversation '–won't you?'

Ernesto saw doubt on the man's face. Tito in return saw a flash of anger at the possibility that he could fail to step up to the mark after what had been sacrificed in getting him here.

'Yes,' he mumbled, 'of course.'

Ernesto nodded with approval and his field of vision shrunk once again to encapsulate the children alone. 'This ship is going to North America, a city called New York. It's a beautiful place, very busy, lots of bright lights.'

The children didn't look convinced. He couldn't blame them. In recent days they had been passed from pillar to post. They were orphans and their lives were being cast into the hands of chance.

'They have syrup pancakes and great big neon signs, the statue of liberty, freedom of speech—'

'Where's Jonathan?' the little girl asked, her words full of apprehension.

'He's . . . had to go somewhere else . . . but I'm sure he'll be along shortly.'

Ernesto winced. He knew better than to lie to children. They were always more wily than they let on. The girl's features eased somewhat. For the time being at least her angst was appeased.

'You'll need to hide down here for a while, but it'll be OK. This is a cargo ship. There'll be food and drink, linen, clothing, everything you need. Just be careful . . . and quiet . . . and everything will be just fine.'

The children simply stared at him wide-eyed.

'OK . . . well–' his attention turned to Tito once more '–good luck.'

'You too.'

Ernesto ruffled the boy's hair, kissed the girl on the cheek and was gone.

Tito was petrified. Running a country into the ground was one thing, but being responsible for the well-being of minors was a wholly different matter. He and Elizabeth had never discussed the possibility of parenthood, and were not likely to now that she'd fled the country with his every earthly possession having torched their house. Maria on the other hand had begged him repeatedly for offspring, but the prospect of them inheriting their mother's IQ had filled him with condescending dread.

His instinct told him that the children would be far better off without him.

However, my instinct does not have a track record to be proud of.

Far greater than his fear of responsibility was that of the Vicious Circle. Tito had studied the history of Corderro – The Melting Pot. He knew what became of people who meddled in its affairs. He'd seen first hand the callous disposal of his predecessor. It was more than bad omens – it was a curse. Tito was sure of it. Ramon Esteban Corderro had sailed into paradise and hacked its tranquility to pieces. There would be no respite from the debt owed to its shoreline, a debt it saw fit to claim against with ever more ingenious methods. Here on the brink of escape Tito saw his own actions as an affront to the city, an offence he felt certain would not go unchallenged.

'What are we going to do?' the little girl asked. Tito had no idea.

Seeing the man's indecision Cheech suggested, 'We should probably try and find some blankets before it gets too dark.'

'Yes, good idea. You two stay here . . . I'll have a look around.'

The van was parked at the edge of a ramp that dropped down into a sea of crates and boxes. Behind him dozens of other vehicles stood locked in place with imposing-looking chains and clamps. Floodlights stretched up to a ceiling several stories above. Tito wondered how long it would be before the lights were extinguished for a very long time.

I will fall victim to a vicious circle. I am certain.

Get a hold of yourself. There are others to consider.

He made his way down the ramp, his eyes searching for anything that might serve as bedding for the night. The first batch of pallets he passed were labeled 'white goods', the second 'ironing boards', the third and fourth were in English, the fifth in Russian.

He could hear water lapping against the hull, muffled voices shouting commands, the clunk and echo of metal on metal.

They're raising anchor. Not much time.

Tito looked back. Already he was starting to lose his way. The ramp was obscured by a fork lift truck. He couldn't see the van.

Don't worry about that, one thing at a time.

Strangely the task felt soothing. As Chancellor of the Exchequer his goal had been virtually unattainable, and his methods both ridiculous and fanatical. But here and now the objective was clear and simple – find food, find shelter, look after children. He could do that, unlike anything else that had been asked of him in recent months, he could do that.

Tito came to a second ramp that dropped to a further chamber filled with large steel containers the size of buses, reaching back as far as the eye could see. A cursory inspection of the front row told him that they were sealed shut with immovable bolts.

'There must be something,' he told himself with uncharacteristic optimism.

There was just enough space between the containers to squeeze through. Behind them Tito found the second row, also locked. Defiant, he tried the next row, and then the next; each time being disappointed. Within minutes he was at the far side of the ship.

To his right, just within view, one of the containers was open.

Tito ran to it, his mind filled with wondrous possibility. He wasn't disappointed.

Though the full contents of the crate was hidden in darkness, the words 'caviar' and 'vintage' were clearly visible from the entrance.

Outstanding! Now all we need is some brandy and cigars.

What about the children?

Tito's enthusiasm waned. It wasn't easy thinking of others. He'd had no practice.

He rooted around in his pocket and found a lighter. The giant flame illustrated a treasure trove of goodies – baked beans, beer, biscuits, bottled water, breakfast cereals, canned vegetables, chocolate, cordial, crisps, dried fruit, honey, hotdog chipolatas in brine, jam, mixed herbs, olives, pasta shells, powdered milk, red wine, salted pork, soup, tea bags, tomato pasta and tuna – anything and everything that could last the lengthy crossing.

Tito stepped inside the crate and moved down its aisles growing more and more excited. They weren't just going to survive, they were going to live in style. He was going to be able to go back to the children with his head held high.

You were placed within my care and look how magnificently I have discharged my responsibility. We shall eat like kings.

Just then the ships engine roared into life and the vessel lurched forwards causing the container's door to slam shut. Tito span around in shock; the lighter flickering momentarily to darkness. He struck the flint and the resultant flame illuminated a perfectly sealed chamber.

A coffin.

Don't . . .

He pushed against the door. It held steadfast.

. . . give up just yet.

The vicious circle! It was too good to be true.

The seal looked airtight. He guessed there could be no more than a few hours of oxygen in the container, less if he continued to use the lighter.

The children?

He had told them to stay put. They were at the farthest end of the ship, out of earshot. Even if they *could* hear and *could* find him Tito doubted whether either of them would be able to force the door.

It was an end befitting El Comedin, dying of starvation in a room full of food.

Tito laughed and took an extra deep gulp of air.

Let it come.

The inner walls were filthy. In the dirt Tito wrote: 'Life has been a joke, and I its clown.'

He held his thumb down on the flint until the fuel was expended and the flame flickered and expired.

By the time light touched his body again he had been dead for over three weeks. After his demise Tito's hair miraculously rejuvenated. It sprouted back in thick black clumps that merged with straggly sideburns, ran into a bushy grey beard and knitted with an immense mat of chest hair. He was carrying no forms of identification and was unrecognizable from his old self. No one ever discovered who he truly was.

Chapter 31

The View from the Hill

I'm forty-two years old and no one ever really knew anything about me.

Why this thought chose to voice itself above all the others he didn't know. Lightning-hot lead peppered the ground around his ankles sending up chunks of sodden earth. Kelly ran for all he was worth.

He had seen Eleanor's head rip back from her shoulders. The velocity and weight of his actions could not be grasped. He wasn't in control of his mind. He was barely in control of his legs. The weapon was lost to the undergrowth. The road was abandoned. There was angry shouting all around.

'STOP! We will be merciful.'

How much longer?

Soon.

I should have gone home years ago.

He would have forgiven me. I'm sure of it.

All that money, given away on a whim to a child you met mere hours ago.

Strangely it was the one decision that sat at ease within his compromised conscience.

He glanced behind. Soldiers at least twenty years his junior were flanking him on both sides.

The ground was rising. Kelly dug deep, bursting from the treeline. He was at the foot of a hill. Salty air filled his lungs. There was blood running down his neck, the shoulder injury opening wide.

I'm heading back towards the ocean.

Travelling in a circle.

A circle.

Damn this place and everything in it.

The grass was wet. His feet slipped back as they searched for purchase and his hands grasped at roots. Progress was painfully slow. The voices grew ever louder all around. His mind threw up an image of his wife, the two of them walking the streets of Lichfield.

Now there's a fine memory, one of the few.

More shots.

Katrina.

Was she my salvation or my downfall?

Do I hate her or think the world of her?

There was no denying the animosity he'd felt ever since meeting her – that sanctimonious belief in a quest to save mankind from itself.

Esperanza – that ridiculous notion of hope.

But he believed it all now, every last word. Facing what he faced, Kelly accepted that a man was not an island; that he needed to reach out beyond his own boundaries.

Too late for revelations.

He had not thanked her. Of all the regrets this one burnt the brightest.

The view from the hill was lovely – the slow-burning sun, the crests on the ocean glowing with bronze and golden light, La Fantasma rolling in like a ghost and a small white van carrying a precious cargo out of harm's way. And if he could have only seen it, and realized just how much he had achieved in one day alone, Kelly would have smiled.

But he didn't see it. A hail of bullets cut him down long before he reached the top, and as life left his body his final thoughts were:

Not enough time.

I chose badly.

I never amounted to anything.

Chapter 32
Corderro's Legacy (2)

1.

Fifty years after its original publication an undisclosed investor purchased the rights to *Corderro's Legacy* and commissioned a limited print run. Two thousand copies arrived secretly in the capital one stormy November evening, smuggled within crates of coffee. A single soul crept catlike through the streets distributing them evenly throughout the districts. By the morning they had created chaos.

The book was presented in its original heavily subjective format, but with one key addition – a new final chapter. In devastatingly precise verse the writer set out El Rey's rise to dictatorship with lists of the known atrocities committed during his half-century reign. The reader was then presented with a blank page and invited to add his or her own personal tragedies, to be collated at a later date. But the real sting came in the final few pages, something truly magical. Written in the past tense the writer spoke of a people's uprising that had stripped the Emperor of his throne and forced him from power. The date of the uprising was in the future – 1 January – six short weeks away.

The events and strategies were laid out in wonderfully graphic detail – the crumbling of the regime, the disintegration and decimation of its command, the solid, united, relentless determination of its people, the defences being overrun, the foe fleeing.

On the back page of each and every copy was a handwritten note:

Dear Citizen,

No man has a birthright to Corderro. Down through the centuries the city has shown generation after generation that it will not be owned, will not be tamed or harnessed, neither domineered in war nor given over to man's inept notions of peace.

El Rey's fate will be no different from that of his ancestors, his folly just as great.

I give you my word.

I can see your past – you have endured much bitterness, distress, sorrow and loss – more than anyone ever should have to bear.

But I can also see your future!

You are like a diamond – you were deemed worthless as rock, but the constant unabating pressure has turned you into something priceless. You are on the brink of becoming your most beautiful.

I will prove it to you.

On New Year's Day your dictator will wither like wheat beneath the scythe, he will fold like paper, topple like dominoes, shrivel like burning leaves, wilt like season's end, evaporate like vapour in the sunlight, dissolve like sand castles in the tide and fade like a whisper in a storm.

His rule is an illusion based on your fear. Shed that fear and he has nothing.

For a long time I have been barred from joining you, but I have watched from afar, waiting to seize the moment.

Here it is!

I don't call you to anger and violence. I call you to crippling defiance, clever, deviously saintly acts of sabotage. Do not look for heroes to lead you. Each man and woman must lead themselves. Treat your enemies with compassion, remember your blood-soaked heritage and eschew it with effortless ease.

Yours in peace and hope.

El Ambiente

The revelation was like electricity, purging people of their doubt and reviving long-forgotten beliefs. El Ambiente had been silent for over a decade, presumed dead, but there was no mistaking the writing style and enigmatic message. Each person lucky enough to receive a copy felt as if they had been written to personally.

A great change came over the city that morning. People raised their heads and greeted one another. They looked at rooftops rather than shuffling feet, found a hidden swagger, dared to stand out from the crowd, breathed a little deeper than normal and spoke with words that tapered and oscillated in nervous excitement.

El Rey's men were clearly anxious. Their flickering fingers hovered over triggers, fidgety and uncomfortable. In contrast the men and women of Corderro seemed to loosen up. Shoulder knots untied themselves and hands became playful and creative by their sides. They smiled at their adversaries, granting them the courtesy that El Ambiente had spoken of. The soldier's faces betrayed them. They were in the midst of something bigger than themselves, unleashed and out of control. They were living on borrowed time.

2.

El Rey was in the winter years of his life. In the time since the theft of his memoirs, *The Plague of Lethargy*, he had failed to recapture the thoughts and visions first expressed in its pages. The onset of old age was a constant reminder that he had fallen short of his own aspirations, and failed in his quest for immortality.

For a long time he had been unable to stomach reading the book that he'd passed off as his own. What had once seemed a glorious insight into the dark descent of mankind now existed merely to mock him for his fallibility.

He still kept a journal, but in recent weeks and months the entries had become introspective and unstructured, filled more with questions than statements. On the morning that he discovered he'd been written into the legacy he wrote: 'Have I now become a caricature, the archetypal monster?'

There was no longer any purpose. Every self-effacing comment began with:

When I die . . .

. . . the people will dance and sing.

. . . They will hang my body from the palace walls.

. . . I will be forgotten.

With a barter culture having long since replaced the petra it had become increasingly difficult to buy the support of his armed forces. The resultant paranoia drove the Emperor to forge what he called 'The Succession Plan'.

Every six months he would invite the brightest, most ambitious and morally questionable of his soldiers to a banquet at the palace. There he would mingle with the rank and file disguised as a waiter. The staff were contracted in for the occasion so that no one would be suspicious of his presence. Hidden amongst his minions he would treat the art of servitude as a novelty, bowing a little deeper than the other waiters and addressing even the lowest-ranking officials as 'Your Grace'.

The conversations were always the same – field tactics, conspiracy theories on the identity of El Ambiente, speculation that the Emperor had been dead for some time and his place taken by some shadowy mastermind.

Each year the rumours became evermore far-fetched. Concealed within plain sight the Emperor lapped them up, considering each new story a fresh layer for his legend.

However, the main reason for his deception was not the gossip, but to scan the faces of his men and women, and watch the positioning for dominance, the body language and hawkish glares of contempt. It took an extreme type of callousness to fulfill the role he had in mind.

El Rey was very good at searching out the darkest qualities of the soul.

One week later the chosen person would be summoned to a personal audience. Dressed in his imperial robes and devoid of the wig and false moustache El Rey was unrecognizable from his cowering, subservient alter ego. For all their guile and cunning the candidates never suspected a thing.

The pitch was always the same: 'You have been chosen for an accelerated talent program. I hereby promote you to the rank of General.'

The candidate would then be presented with their badge of rank and a glass of champagne.

'It has been brought to my attention that a plot is under way to deprive me of my life and seize control of the throne. It is of the utmost importance that this plot be halted and the conspirators eradicated. Do I have your full support?'

No matter how hard-faced the individual they would always glaze over with starry-eyed entrapment, drunk with the sudden potent intimacy.

Their responses were variations on a theme. Some would splutter 'Yes, Your Highness', others simply nodded. One had even knelt and kissed his hand.

'It is very distressing for me to discuss this next issue,' El Rey would continue; further enticing them into his confidence, 'but I have learnt that the conspiracy goes right to the heart of this organization, to my most trusted emissaries.'

The Emperor would then discover whether or not he had made the right selection. With consummate control he would drop his voice to a whisper and utter the name of the current General.

The implication was clear: 'You must kill this man.'

The reaction he was searching for: absolutely nothing – cold unflinching acceptance of the task in hand.

He had never been disappointed yet. Invariably the candidate would drain his or her glass, thank the Emperor for this wondrous opportunity and leave the room.

Within days the predecessor would be dead and the candidate would assume their mantle. Six months later El Rey would hold another banquet and the whole process would begin again in earnest. In this way the emperor had disposed of nineteen such hopefuls over the last decade – eighteen men and one woman (not a patch on Eleanor). The frequency of change was explained away by retirements, resignations, secondments and foreign assignments. On initial reflection the method was an unmitigated success. The pitfalls took several years to fully manifest themselves.

With no continuity to the people around him El Rey was always starting again, always having to reassess the motives of those around him. Trust was a concept long since abandoned, and he was forced to withdraw further and further back from the city he purported to own.

News of El Ambiente's resurgence was everywhere. The Emperor heard it whispered on the lips of guards, in the final breathes of tortured prisoners, even in his sleep. His journal became bloated with disjointed scrawl:

Who are you? Who are you – you night-crawling, vindictive, parasitic, shit, rat, crusading thorn, hijo de puto? WHO? WHO?

He took his pen to the palace walls in letters four foot high:

WHO ARE YOU? – YOU VERMIN – YOU EVASIVE, SABOTAGING, GODAWFUL IDEALIST? WHO? WHO? WHOOOO?'

He released an announcement to 'his subjects' offering to 'pay handsomely' those who handed in copies of the offending literature. None were forthcoming. Random searches revealed nothing. For all the Emperor knew the book may not even exist. El Ambiente's propaganda swirled relentlessly around him.

In the days and nights that followed unflattering images and effigies of Corderro's ruler began to appear in parks and plazas. With no clear idea of what El Rey looked like the features varied dramatically from piece to piece, but all captured a vacant look of stupidity, pomposity and bloodlust. El Ambiente's tag was sprayed on benches, windows, doors, pavements, roads, trees, cars, railings and rooftops. It saturated the landscape and painted a picture of rebellion.

There were visibly more people on the streets, venturing out of their prison-homes in greater and greater numbers, growing in confidence and forming distinct groups.

A week after El Ambiente's message a men stepped into the road blocking the path of an oncoming black sedan.

'Would you come with me, please?' he spoke calmly, his whole body vibrating in exhilaration.

'Would you come with me, please?' he repeated. It was more a statement than a question. He was joined by a second man.

'Get out of the car!'

A third thumped the bonnet with his fist. 'GET OUT OF THE CAR NOW!'

The black sedan reversed and made a swift retreat.

3.

On the last evening of the year there were ships on the horizon. Word had spread that the sanctions would be lifted the following day. Pressure mounted. Surely the possibility of sweet unconditional freedom was too good to be true? There was collective inhalation. No one dared breathe out for fear of shattering the dream. Lungs threatened to burst at the seams, and then came the night.

The darkness was absolute. Power cuts that had become an accepted way of life extinguished the street lighting and the stars were hidden behind unseen clouds. Without warning the ground began to shake. People cowered in their beds. The sound of roaring engines filled the blackness. Window panes shuddered and vibrating ornaments fell from shelves.

Mothers clung to rosary beads draped around their children's necks. Fathers crept from slumber and stood behind doors brandishing whatever makeshift weapons they could assemble in the blindness, poised to make a last stand in defence of their families. They considered themselves foolish for their pitiful insurrection. Surely now El Rey would take them all down into the dust with him, obliterating the city in a final act of desperation?

Outside there were no voices, only the incessant rumbling of tyre treads over broken road.

4.

At first light they began to emerge sheepishly from their homes. There were no troops, no cars. The factories were all closed, as was the port. No one had delivered the morning papers, and the TV and radio were both walls of static.

Something beyond comprehension was happening. The residents of Corderro stared through sleep-deprived eyes at one another, sharing the simultaneous sensations of having awoken from hibernation into disorientating amnesia. No one knew how to feel. They had not expressed themselves in so long that it was as if their limbs had forgotten how to rejoice.

The implications of silence were too wondrous to behold.

'HELLO?' an old woman bellowed at the top of her lungs. The previous day her raised voice would have been met with severe recriminations. Now however it was met with nothing.

'ECHO!' shouted someone else 'CHO-CHO-HO-O-o-o.'

Streams of dazed euphoric people trickled through the streets forming rivers. With unspoken, unintentional cohesion they converged on the huge, wide-open, iron gates that protected the driveway to El Rey's palace.

The site of empty guard huts reignited revolutionary fervour. Footsteps quickly became strides as the mob marched unchallenged into the palace grounds.

They poured through the archway and along the corridors of power, up the elaborate stairwells and onto the terrace roof. They slid down banisters, jumping up and down on the ginormous beds, fed each other grapes, drew moustaches on the wall paintings and systematically stripped the rooms of their trinkets.

Away from the festivities a smaller group found a side entrance that led down into the interrogation chambers. There they found a furnace full of cold ash and bodies piled high in their cells.

No one had been left alive to speak of the evils that had taken place.

The group stood in silence. They could hear the distant sound of cheering.

'It's too much to take in,' one of the men said, 'to gain the world and lose it all within a single day.'

A comforting hand came to rest on his shoulder. 'What is your name?'

'Piedro.'

'Be at peace Piedro.'

'Thank you, and your name?'

Piedro turned. The other had vanished.

5.

A carnival atmosphere enveloped the city. Piedro was amongst those who returned from the palace with news of its abandonment. His words were met with revelry he felt incapable of sharing in. He wandered through the crowds in a daze, down into central Corderro and to the Plaza d'Armas.

It was one hundred and five years since Marie had branded McCafferty a thief on the steps of the town hall. Though severely weather-beaten her graffiti was still visible across the mighty stone plinth, but now it was joined by a second, more vibrantly coloured sentence etched beneath. In the night someone had written the words:

Piedro – You have gained the world, not lost it – Celebrate

'This message is aimed at me!' Piedro shouted joyously. 'I stood next to El Ambiente!'

He was immediately swamped with people wanting to know: 'What does he look like? What is his voice like? What colour are his eyes?'

'I . . . I didn't see his face' he stammered. 'He touched my shoulder . . . he asked me my name . . . he . . . he asked me to be at peace . . . we must celebrate!'

Every bar in the city was systematically drunk dry. When the beer barrels were empty they hit the spirits, bringing in sugar and limes by the truck load in order to keep the Santos's flowing. When the last bottle had been drained they moved on to more immediate measures. The favourite approach was to bring a bathtub into the main room and fill it with yeast, water and sugar. The bath would then be covered with a tarpaulin, sealed and left for one week in order to ferment. The concoction that emerged was gloopy and foul-smelling, but it did the trick. Each afternoon the residents of Corderro would emerge from slumber, their heads lost in a thick fug of bemusement. Demand quickly outstripped supply. At first they took to increasing the number of vessels – sinks, buckets, paddling pools, wheelbarrows – but still the people guzzled their way down to dregs. Finally they took to shortening the fermentation period, a bit at a time until eventually it dropped from one week to three days. What had started off as disgusting was now virtually undrinkable. The brew was labelled 'Mano a la Boca' ('hand to mouth').

374

Twenty-seven days after celebrations began the tap water started to taste funny. At first it was a mild metallic tinge, but it quickly rose repellently through ammonia, egg and effluence. On the same day the city's electricity tripped out and didn't come back. In looted and abandoned supermarkets the remaining food was rotting on shelves.

In response a call went out for candidates and an interim government was hastily assembled. Most citizens were reluctant to put their names forward, acutely aware of the legacy they could well be joining. Eventually, however, enough roles were recruited to constitute a quorum, people started returning to work and flimsy bonds formed with the outside world. Foreign trade was banned in order to prevent what little remained of the nation's wealth flooding out through the city's port.

The last position in the government to be announced was Chancellor of the Exchequer. It was finally filled when a nineteen-year-old economist named Federico stepped up to the mantle. No one had officially occupied this post since Tito's disappearance fifteen years previously. Like most things in Corderro it was considered cursed.

The teenager had been in play school last time the balance sheets had been perused with any real gusto, but his keen eyes saw in moments what Tito had failed to grasp in months – a pattern of movements, laundering huge sums in complicated multiple transactions that eventually left the country, deposited in ten numbered accounts. Under investigation the accounts were found to belong to Dimitri, Tito's predecessor.

The young Chancellor imposed a confidence budget centred round a new currency called El Comienzo ('The Start'). He set a minimum wage and converted petras at a rate that restored them to the exact relative worth of the day before El Rey came to power. Federico explained in a public address that there would be no 'money miracle', that people would have to work hard, but that he had a clear, simple plan for rejuvenating the financial system. He presented his methods with such enthusiasm that there were calls for him to be elevated to party leader.

Federico thanked the crowds and answered, 'I am just a man, as I imagine El Rey himself was once. Like him I am not cut out for the temptations and trappings of power, therefore I must graciously decline.'

His response, while semi-chastizing in nature, made him and the government even more popular.

With stability very much in sight attention turned to dismantling El Rey's empire. Over half a century the Emperor had amassed fortunes that filled several underground warehouses – golden statues, jewelry, paintings, chandeliers, wooden caskets of coins, ornaments and antique furniture. It was astounding to think the hoard had remained all this time while above ground his people starved.

The new government was wary of any and all forms of corruption. After much deliberation it was decided to sell everything to international buyers and use the money to rebuild the city from the ground upwards. The space where Tito's house had once stood was purchased by an insurance company.

Whilst investigating the palace grounds a group of the newly elected officials unearthed a hidden garage containing twenty-seven black sedans. Somebody made the comment that it was like finding the ferryman's boat, tied up at the edge of the River Styx – the vessel by which so many hapless souls had been born away to their garish ends. Gazing upon the plush leather seats and leaning into an executive environment it was hard to grasp what the vehicles represented and what they had helped to accomplish.

A new magazine was produced entitled *Los Tiempos Emocionantes* ('The Exciting Times'). In it the government ran an advert that read: 'To our esteemed resident El Ambiente. Reveal yourself and receive the long overdue praise of a grateful nation.'

Corderro waiting anxiously for its saviour to appear. When finally he presented himself he was not at all how they had expected.

Nathaniel Arturo stood just shy of 5 feet, his buck-tooth grin hidden amidst a nest of matted black hair. Balloon shaped and bow-legged he came down from the mountains announcing himself as the face behind their elusive benefactor.

News of his arrival spread like wildfire. Throngs of men and women flooded out of the city, up onto a plateau overlooking the ocean. Nathaniel spoke with an extremely high-pitched voice, his face burning red with embarrassment.

'No need to thank me. It was my pleasure.'

As the crowds rejoiced and rewarded their hero with raucous applause and booming foot stomps it was discovered that across the city several other men had also come forward claiming to be El Ambiente.

Unaware of one another they were swept up the mountainside against their will by the jostling hands of their followers, to an uncomfortable meeting at its summit. The men, eleven in all, found themselves at the centre of an immense circle.

'Which one of you is the real El Ambiente?' the people shouted.

They were not a hostile crowd. There was no malice in there voices, only the feverish excitement to uncover the truth. Reacting to probing one of the men announced that he was the real El Ambiente.

'Liar,' another shouted, 'I am El Ambiente.'

'You both seek to deceive,' said a third, 'Any rational person can see that it is I who am the true prophet.'

It was marvellous theatre. The crowd loved it. They organized themselves into a primitive court room and took it in turns to impersonate barristers and judges, shouting 'order, order' and banging make-believe gavels onto equally non-apparent tables.

Finally it was revealed after many hours of cross-examination that none of the men were El Ambiente. Rather than being scorned the men were applauded. The spectacle had brought much-needed humour and goodwill to the capital. There was no need to question why they had felt it necessary to deceive. The answer was obvious to all. El Rey had systematically stripped them of their dreams. To avoid standing out in the crowd a person must bury all notions of creativity deep within themselves. But now, after decades of repression they were being given the opportunity to shine in all their glory. If was only human to want to be someone.

'Remember your blood-soaked heritage and eschew it with effortless ease,' someone shouted. The sentence was instantly recognizable as the final line in El Ambiente's letter. The crowds parted but it was unclear who had spoken.

'Damn, he's good,' someone else replied and they all began to laugh.

As light-hearted as the event turned out to be, it was also tinged with a sombre note. Against a backdrop of ambition and cynicism it was unlikely that the real El Ambiente would now come forward. But then perhaps it was better that way. No man could ever live up to the expectations of a legend. If the past had shown the people anything then it was that their benefactor had never asked for thanks or recognition. It was not in his nature to take credit.

But one thing was certain. After many years in exile El Ambiente *had* returned and walked amongst them once more.

A short while later the foreign sanctions were officially lifted and a young woman arrived searching for a man named Jonathan.

Chapter 33

That which is Unseen

1.

Epilogue.

And so in conclusion, Jonathan, I can barely contain my excitement at the prospect of meeting you. Life started out as something so terrible, and became something so wonderful, all thanks to you. For all of my garbled ramblings I have only just begun to scrape the surface. We shall need at least a month of conversations into the early hours. I want to tell you everything and know everything about you.

Here are a few more silly little ditties before I stop.

- *A man once stopped my stepfather in the street claiming to be the Prince of Tunisia and offered four million pounds for my hand in marriage. My stepfather asked for five!*
- *One of the girls who works for me at Café Justamente has recently asked me to be godmother to their little boy James – a massive honour and responsibility.*
- *Last Saturday I was a bridesmaid for an old school friend. As a man you may not share in the joy of dressing up in a posh frock and having your hair done, but I can assure you it's what we women live for!*

But I don't want to finish this account talking about myself. It's all about you, Jonathan. You have made all things possible and it is you who deserves all of the praise. Because of this unassailable fact I strive to do all things to the best of my ability, and when I achieve even the smallest of accomplishments it reflects back your immeasurable success.

Thank you.

Isabella, 11th August

2.

Isabella was disturbed from slumber by the rising sun. Carlos had not woken her as he'd promised. She crept down the stairs and found him sitting cross-legged on the floor, a candle burnt down to a stub, her journal resting in his lap.

'What are you doing?' she asked, suddenly furious. 'I expressly forbade you fro—'

Carlos was crying.

'What is it?'

He wiped his eyes and beckoned for her to sit down. 'I have something to tell you.'

Isabella felt the strength leave her legs, the premonition of foreboding. Carlos closed her journal and laid it down carefully by his side. His face portrayed an inner turmoil. Several times he opened his mouth to speak but then thought better of it, shivering and shaking his head in self-disapproval. Finally it came – without introduction or explanation.

'Jonathan Pemberton is dead.'

'How can you know this?'

'Because I saw him die.'

'When?'

'Fifteen years ago. I was lying next to you in a van being smuggled out of the city.'

It was like seeing him for the first time.

'*Cheech?*'

Carlos bowed reverently. 'The very same.'

'My God, how did you find me?'

'It was pure chance. Like you I got the first boat in once they lifted the sanctions.'

'How did you recognize me?'

Carlos pointed to her necklace. '*The key without a door.* I remember him giving it to you.'

After the initial shock and surprise, anger once again welled up within her. 'And yet you choose to withhold it till now, taking me round on a wild goose chase and watching me make a fool of myself. *Why?*'

'Because the journey is more important than the arrival.'

Isabella slapped him across the face. 'Even now you're toying with me.'

'No, not at all, *mi chica bella*. Do you think that I haven't struggled with the decision since I first set eyes on you, hoping that I had chosen the right course of action and praying that you would understand once you discovered the truth?'

Isabella did not look convinced.

'You have been taking lessons from my wife,' Carlos added, rubbing his chin. 'She hits like you!'

Against her better judgement Isabella smiled. 'Hits you a lot, does she?'

'Oh God, all the time, and I deserve each and every one. I'm not blind to my own nature. I would try the patience of any woman.'

'You had no right to manipulate me in such a fashion.'

'I know and I'm sorry, but you *have* seen something of Jonathan's world as a result. It was not my intention to embarrass, but to enlighten.'

Isabella sat down next to him. 'He's been dead all this time. I have been living a lie.'

'No,' Carlos turned so that they were directly facing one another, 'that's not true. This man whom you hold in so high regard – *he* lived a lie, but *you* redeemed *him*.'

Isabella clutched her head. 'I don't understand. What are you saying?'

'Jonathan gave you the key. Do you remember that he also gave me something?'

Carlos reached into his bag and retrieved a dog-eared manuscript. Written across its front cover was the number thirty-eight.

'This is Jonathan's testimony. I'd like you to have it.'

Isabella extended her hand with a mixture of excitement and dread.

'But it comes with a warning.'

'Which is?'

'You *should* read this, but although it will irretrievably alter your image of the man, I think that this is a good thing.'

She held the flimsy pages as if they were Pandora's Box. 'How do I know this isn't simply more trickery? How can I trust you?'

Carlos sat up straight and placed his hands on his diaphragm. He looked like he was about to deliver an oration. 'Because my name is Charles "Carlos Cheech" Neblina. I was smuggled out of Corderro fifteen years ago within an aubergine-coloured sofa. The sofa was sold to an elderly American woman. I spent six months hiding in an attic in central Manhattan. Later I was adopted by an eccentric millionaire. He sent me to a prestigious boys' school where I was subsequently expelled for girl-smuggling. I can speak seven languages. I taught percussion and jazz bass at a school in Paris for two years. I have a Spanish wife, Clarina, and two kids Paolo and Siedah. Like you I have drawn immense joy from sorrow and like you I owe it all to Jonathan Pemberton.'

For all his bravado Isabella could tell that he was being sincere.

The vicious circle has swept around and deprived me of purpose.

Carlos saw the shadow pass across her face. He leaned in closer. 'Can

I make a suggestion? You have a real gift with words, Isabella. It would seem a shame to waste it. Why don't you write a narrative around your journal, add in Jonathan's testimony, get it published, show the world what these people did for us?'

'I don't know . . . I feel . . . deflated.'

'It'll pass . . . think it over.'

'OK . . . I will . . . what now?'

'There is one more thing I must do and then I shall place this whole sorry chapter somewhere deep in the recesses of my mind, out of reach.'

'Ah yes, your mysterious quest! You never did tell me the man's name.'

'No I didn't.'

'Would you like to keep in touch?

Carlos took a long time to answer. 'No . . . I don't think so. Don't get me wrong, meeting you again and rediscovering the city, the whole thing has been awe-inspiring, but it has also been bittersweet. My family met their untimely ends on these streets. Anything that reminds me of it must now be put away for ever.'

Isabella put her arms around him. 'Wow, that really is a no!'

Carlos nodded slowly. 'Yes it is.'

3.

They parted company with a handshake. As she walked back to the hotel Isabella reminded herself that she had only known the man a few days. The loss felt much greater than that, like the passing of a lifelong friend. She packed her small suitcase, settled up and left.

El Puerto de Las Ondas Verdes was still heaving under the influx of returning exiles. Isabella saw herself in each and every face.

'I hope you find what you are looking for,' she whispered.

Did you?

I don't know. I thought I hadn't, but then I wasn't so sure. Now I don't even know what it was I sought.

She saw a Union Jack billowing from one of the ship's masts. Its captain stood by an immense gangplank smoking an equally immense cigar.

'You are going to Europe?' Isabella asked.

'Yes señorita,' the captain replied.

'How much?'

381

The captain laughed and guided her up the gangplank.

'Thank you, señor.'

'*De nada*' ('It's nothing').

Once below deck a steward led her down a long corridor and allocated her the next available room. Isabella steadied her nerves with a drink from a fully stocked mini-bar, lay down on the bed and began to read 'Thirty-eight'.

With each turn of a page the foundations on which Isabelle had built her life were systematically knocked away. The glossy heroic vision of her saviour was assaulted by the words of a man who had lost his family, his faith in others, and his desire for moral direction – a man who seemed to have only grasped at a purpose in the dying moments of his life.

He talked of others – Katrina, Paolo, Raoul – names she couldn't place – people who had given everything without her knowledge.

'Thirty-eight' was the work of a man in a moment of transition, riddled with spelling mistakes and grammatical errors. Isabella imagined Jonathan feverishly writing through the night, spewing out his true self before it was too late, acutely aware of the walls closing in around him, a new-found hope in its final pages, a chance for brotherly redemption, a sliver of possibility.

Carlos had scribbled a note to her in the back which read: '*Mi Chica Bella* – what you have achieved in life – *you* have achieved – no one else.'

Her first reaction was anger, anger that Carlos should so pointedly pull the rug out from under her. Wasn't it enough to have walked the streets of Corderro and have had them repaint a picture of childhood in so bleak and desperate colours? Why then knowingly destroy what little semblance of happiness was left?

Because it was all a lie.

With Carlos idealism and pragmatism sat uncomfortably side by side. He had decided that for her the greater good resided in cold harsh truth, and yet he had still led her down deceptive paths in order to lessen the pain.

The resentment receded. He was right.

Why go another day believing in fiction?

Isabella decided there and then to take him up on his suggestion and write a book. Jonathan had spoken of there being no beginning, middle and end, but he'd been unable to see the wider context. His entire life had been the beginning, the last fifteen years the middle, and this moment o revelation the end.

She was seized with a new excitement. To bring Jonathan's story to the world, albeit posthumously, would show him for the success that he really was. Despite his selfish intentions, when it came to the test he had chosen the futures of two children's over his own. She could think of no greater thing.

A story needs a title.

What adequately sums up what happened here?

'Making sense of it'?

'The Road to Redemption'?

'Jonathan's Journey'?

No, all too schmaltzy. It needs to be something a bit more graceful . . . and metaphorical.

Isabelle put down the manuscript and went up on deck. She was surprised to find that the ship had already set sail. Corderro was now several miles behind, shrinking and blending with the horizon. Seeing the city in its entirety, it was strange to think that such a small principality could have held so menacing a legacy, down through the ages of bloodshed, betrayal and tyranny. Regarded from a distance it simply looked like the innocent little fishing community of its birth.

I have done what few people can claim. I have escaped twice.

On the hillside she could see El Rey's deserted palace. She imagined herself at its gates looking out to sea at a ship sailing away, out of reach.

That's it.

Isabella ran back down to her cabin, picked up a pen and wrote on a fresh sheet of paper: 'The view from the hill.'

The phrase perfectly encapsulated the notion of seeing events in a wider context. It was the point from which all further inspiration would flow. She turned the page and began chapter one.

Dear Jonathan . . .

Chapter 34
The Cabin in the Woods (2)

The old man awoke from an unpleasant dream and surveyed his frugal surroundings – four walls without decoration, a lamp without a shade, a chest without drawers.

He no longer remembered why it was he continued to rise each day.

The stairs creaked as he descended. He had relied on slaves and servants his entire life and subsequently did not know how to fix them. In the hallway he had a choice of two rooms – left into the main room, or right into the kitchen. He chose right.

The cabin had no electricity. Wiping sleep from his eyes the man reached under a makeshift hob and turned on a gas cylinder. He lifted a book of matches from a nearby shelf, lit the stove and wondered how much longer the gas would last – just over a month so far. Getting a replacement was not an option.

In fact, very few options were available nowadays. The irony was not lost on him, neither was it relished. He filled a pan with cold water and placed it on the stove. It was then that he turned and saw it.

Lying on the surface of his warped and rickety table was a purple, velvet-bound journal. Carved next to it in deeply etched grooves was a large 'A' with a circle around it.

The old man let out a gasp and then stood perfectly still. There was no sound.

He knew the history, knew that leaders were always caught off guard – Corderro murdered by his son in the same way he himself had murdered, Ramon dying at the hands of an avenging stepfather, Santos stabbed in the marketplace as he begged for a new way of life, McCafferty branded a thief as he lay screaming in the snow by Marie.

Sweet Marie.

And now me.

He took a revolver from the cutlery drawer, one of many planted around the cabin, and made his way back through the hallway and into the main room.

The only piece of furniture was a moth-eaten sofa. On it sat a young man reading a book. He seemed engrossed and took a few moments to notice the older man's arrival. The weapon was noted with a nod and then dismissed.

'Good morning, Emile.'

The old man eyed him suspiciously. 'You are not old enough to be El Ambiente.'

Carlos smiled in deep satisfaction. '*That* is why you never caught me.'

'How old are you?'

'Twenty-seven.'

'Your face is familiar.'

'Yes, I worked in your palace for five years.'

'Of course . . . *Cheech?*'

'A nickname . . . call me Carlos.'

'Car-los,' Emile repeated, rolling the two syllables over his tongue and nodding, 'I shall not forget that name in a hurry.'

Carlos looked away to the window as if disinterested. 'Do with it what you will. Do you remember the first time we met?'

'No.'

'Good. That was the idea. *I* remember. You were dressed like Julius Caesar – toga, sandals, laurel leaf – a girl was fanning you with peacock feathers. I imagine she's dead now?'

Emile chose not to reply.

'I served you breakfast each morning, made your bed, washed your underwear. I was right there under your nose. How that must tingle with embarrassment?'

Emile raised the gun so that it moved from Carlos's stomach to his head. 'How did you find me?'

'Your memoirs – all that talk of a secret hiding place. You hinted at its location from so many different angles that it was no longer a secret – *Go into the woods after dark and El Rey will get you* – I managed to piece together a general idea, and then I came looking. I read your book as a twelve year old, and in doing so realized that my adversary was a fool. Life is for living, not worrying about how you will be remembered. By then it's too late, as it is indeed for you.'

Carlos stood and took a step towards Emile.

'In all probability you will be forgotten within a matter of months,' he continued, 'but if you *are* remembered for anything then it will be as the king who was outwitted by a child. It will sit alongside the Emperor's new clothes, only this tale will be true. Incidentally, *The Plague of Lethargy* is a terrible title for a book. It spectacularly fails to adequately surmise its content. A more apt name would be *The Blight of Ambition*!'

Emile pressed the gun barrel against Carlos's temple. 'You are deliberately trying to provoke me, even though you know that I will kill you without hesitation.'

'And yet you don't! You are asking yourself – why would El Ambiente come to me, alone, when he must know this would happen? I shall enlighten you. When you came to power you said in your inaugural speech that it was like a clock chiming midnight; a new day. If that was the case, then it has come full circle and is chiming once again. It could now be the age of the great El Ambiente! I could reveal myself to the nation and bask in its unending praise and worship. But pride comes before the fall. In seeking recognition for my actions I, like you, would become just another rotation in the city's history. In time I would start to believe my own hype, ascend to glory and ultimately plummet from grace. This is the true nature of Corderro. For all your intellectual ramblings you have never grasped it. *I* am happy to leave my true identity hidden from the world. It is enough for me that *you* know.'

'None of which saves you from being put out of my misery.'

'Bear with me, Your Highness. It will all become blissfully clear to you in a moment. I would like you to imagine that there are four more people in the room with us. They are lined up on either side of me, facing you. Their names are Paolo, Raoul, Katrina and Jonathan. Whilst imaginary, they were once real people, and each in turn gave their life in order that I might escape Corderro. Look closely upon their features, Emile. They are your downfall.'

Carlos paused. He could see his adversary's eyes moving from left to right, scanning the non-existent faces.

'I once promised Paolo that this would happen; that I would stand before you and speak his name. If he and his colleagues were alive today they would join me in pointing behind you and whispering, 'Emile, look out of the window.'

With the intensity of their exchange the world had shrunk to encapsulate the space between the two men, but now it exploded outwards again as Emile realized that an unpleasant surprise awaited him beyond the sanctuary of his cabin. He took a step back. The barrel came away from Carlos's skin leaving a small red imprint. He reached behind him, pulled back the curtain and glanced over his shoulder.

The cabin was surrounded by black sedans.

In his mind the Emperor envisaged journalists and historians down through the ages documenting his grand humiliation with ever-increasing mockery. Capture was not an eventuality he had ever considered. His grip on the gun faltered and he steadied himself with the other hand.

'So I am trapped, washed up, *spent*. Well done. But you have miscalculated, Carlos. I must have racked up a thousand lifetimes in prison. What's another murder to me but a drop in the ocean? What bargaining chip do you hold?'

Carlos's eyes narrowed and his body stiffened. 'I told them that I would reveal your whereabouts on the proviso that they let me speak to you first. If they hear a shot they will storm the building and kill you. They were concerned for my safety and extremely reluctant to let me go in. I pacified them be telling them what I knew of your nature. I said that for all your pontificating about remembrance after death, the one thing you craved more than wealth and power was life itself. You would do anything to protect your own existence, and if harming me threatened that you would not lift a finger. That is the bargaining chip I hold, Emile – *your life*. Do not gaze at me with those greedy little hate-filled eyes. You took away my family. You took away so much, and you made nothing of your life. I cannot even summon pity for you.'

Carlos moved past Emile towards the door.

'I would put down that weapon if I was you. If they see you holding it they are likely to shoot you on sight.'

As he slid open the bolt he was conscious that he might have misjudged Emile terribly. Fifteen years was a long time to remain constant. As unlikely as it seemed his adversary might chose death over incarceration. The door swung open. Carlos turned and saw that the Emperor had placed the gun at his feet.

They came in, filling the room to bursting point. Emile was only one old man, but his legacy went before him. They had expected to be confronted by a monster. Each person in turn was disappointed by what they saw and yet still they felt the need to restrain him. With the utmost caution they placed shackles around his ankles and ropes around his wrists.

Emile stood dumbfounded. The last person to chastise him openly had been his father almost fifty years beforehand. He simply didn't know how to think or feel.

'What now?' he asked.

Carlos shrugged. 'Now you will be placed in a room and forgotten about.'

'I have the right to a fair trial.'

'Yes you do . . . even after everything you've done . . . and you shall have it, but it will be a closed session. No one will even know you have been captured.'

Emile smiled. 'Then I will have my infamy after all.'

Carlos shook his head. 'When a fresh breeze blows people forget the stench. So it will be with you.'

The smile slipped. They led the Emperor out into the open.

'There is one other thing,' Carlos added. Emile turned and the two men faced one another for the last time. 'In not killing you for your actions I believe that *we* have just broken the vicious circle – congratulations, Your Highness!'